Sweet Cheeks

K. BROMBERG

This book is a work of fiction. Names, characters, places, and incidents are the product of the author's imagination or are used fictitiously. Any resemblance to actual events, locales, or persons, living or dead, is coincidental.

Cover art created by: Perfect Pear Creative Covers
Photo Credit: WANDER AGUIAR PHOTOGRAPHY

Formatting by: Champagne Formats

ISBN#: 978-1-942832-14-0

Except for the original material written by the author, all songs, song titles, and lyrics mentioned in the novel *Sweet Cheeks* are the property of the respective songwriters and copyright holders.

Other Works by K. Bromberg

Love doesn't need to be perfect,
it just needs to be true.
-Anonymous

Prologue

Saylor

THIS HAS TO BE A JOKE.

It's my only thought as I stare at the square invitation in my hands and take in the uncanny similarities.

Champagne-style font. ✓

A scroll pattern embellishment. ✓

Cream-colored linen cardstock. ✓

The words, the physical layout of them on the paper, and every other detail I can discern. ✓✓ Double ✓✓

How is it possible that the invitation in my hand looks exactly like the one I'd spent hours obsessing over when deciding the particulars for my own wedding invitations?

I rub the expensive paper between my fingers as if I need to make sure it's real. Finally convinced it is, I scrutinize the details all over again.

It looks like my wedding invitation all right. Same groom—Mitch Layton. Same ceremony time. Same destination: the tropical paradise of Turks and Caicos.

Everything is identical except the bride's name and the date.

Because this invitation says *Sarah Taylor*.

And that's not me.

In fact, the only place it says Saylor Rodgers is on the outside of the envelope where it sits discarded on my desk. I double-check the address one more time. Yep, it was definitely sent to me. On purpose.

I'm an *invited guest*? *Seriously*?

Surely the man I left high and dry the week before *our* wedding wouldn't invite me to his wedding—*to someone else*—a mere six months after I called ours off.

But there it is. My name. My address.

Sweet Cheeks CupCakery
Attn: Ms. Saylor Rodgers
1313 State Street
Santa Barbara, CA 93101

Definitely not a mistake because that's me, and this is where he knows to find me.

The irony. It's been six months, and not once has Mitch sought me out to ask for a more detailed explanation other than "because I just can't do this anymore" as to why I left.

And his first attempt at communication is like this? Inviting me to his wedding in what I can only assume is an obvious attempt to show me how easily I could be replaced? To try to make me feel inadequate while boosting that bruised ego of his?

Such a classic Mitch Layton move; passive-aggression at its finest.

My temper fires but I don't understand why I'm angry. This doesn't matter. *He doesn't matter.* But if I don't care about him in the least, why does the sight of this invitation make my stomach churn?

And even more importantly, why am I setting down the RSVP card, picking up a pen, and opting for the filet mignon rather than the macadamia nut encrusted halibut as my entrée selection when I have no intention of going?

None.

Whatsoever.

Making a selection is just my crazy talking.

So even stranger, why am I placing an X next to the "plus-one" for a guest when there is no plus-one in my life?

I stare at where I wrote my name on the RSVP card, think about everything I've been through over the past six months, and know the answer: *because it makes me feel good to do it.* To know that Mitch can't affect me anymore. He wanted to upset me with the invitation, and hell yes, for a minute I was just that, angry and hurt. Wouldn't anyone be when they find out their ex-fiancé has moved on so quickly? But when all is said and done, he accomplished nothing more than making me grateful I'm not the one marrying him. I chalk it up to Mitch being Mitch. Egotistical, arrogant, and childish.

Screw him.

So I stuff the RSVP card inside the little self-addressed stamped return envelope.

All the while imagining the look on Mitch's face when he opens it and finds my name written on the card inside.

I run my tongue over the adhesive on the flap.

Envision his surprise when he sees I'm bringing a date. You're not the only one who has found someone to make them happy, Mitch.

Close the flap and press it so it sticks. *Picture the look on Rebound Sarah's face when he hands it to her and tells her to add two more to her headcount. Does she sneer? Does it cause a fight? Or do they snicker over it until they sit back and wonder if I'm really going to show up.*

And then worry that I am.

Even if I'm the only one who'll ever know it, there's an oddly therapeutic sense of satisfaction holding the sealed envelope in my hand. In knowing his plan has backfired.

God, I'm being ridiculous.

I roll my eyes and toss the sealed envelope on my desk with no intention of ever thinking about it again. I shouldn't have wasted my time filling it out in the first place because *I don't care.* Not one bit. Not about him or what the future Mrs. Layton looks like or his childish need to get the last word in about our relationship by sending me this.

In fact, leaving him was the best thing I've ever done.

I'm happier now.
Without a doubt.
Definitely happier.
I think.

One

Saylor

"**S**AYLOR."

My brother grumbles my name for what feels like the tenth time in as many minutes. I ignore him and keep my focus on the elaborate design I'm perfecting on the cupcake in front of me instead.

It's so much easier to keep my head in the sand than listen to the lecture I know is coming. The comments about how the payables are more than the receivables. The *do you know that even with this small business loan you acquired you're still going to drown in debt unless you figure out how to acquire more business?* The *you need to come up with a marketing plan different than everyone else so you'll attract more customers.*

And then he'll start his spiel. How I need to be more active on social media. How Internet orders are huge these days and where the bakery can find longevity and success. Get enough online orders, up the demand for my product in surrounding cities, sell franchise opportunities to service those demands, then sit back and reap the rewards.

Doesn't he see I'm doing everything I can? That I've poured my blood, sweat, and tears into my dream since breaking up with Mitch? Not only to prove to myself that it was the right decision, but probably more so to prove to everyone else that it was. That I can make it on my own. Without him or his family name or their bank accounts full of money. That none of that defines *me*.

And so I keep my head down, add the pearl lacing around the edge of the cupcake I'm decorating (for a wedding no less) while intermittently glancing to the foot traffic outside, hoping they'll stop in and buy a cupcake.

Or several dozen.

Because his groan is only going to get louder the deeper he gets into the mess I've made of the spreadsheet his number-crunching brain deems easy. His columns, rows, and formulas with symbols that make no sense to me. I've got more important things to do than stress over adding numbers into the sheet.

Like running all aspects of the business he's currently—and deservedly—bitching about.

"Saylor?"

The change in his tone has me lifting my head to look through the open doorway where he stands watching me. The look in his aqua-blue eyes is full of confusion and what I think is anger. There's something in his hand I can't quite see.

Crap. *What did I do now*?

"Did that asshole seriously have the audacity to invite you to his wedding?"

I slowly set the piping tube down and brace my hands on the butcher block in front of me in preparation for Ryder's protective older-brother gene to kick in. For the anger to come out on my behalf when he should be the one pissed off after what Mitch's family did to him because of me. And due to my own stupidity for not tearing up the invitation in the first place.

I'd completely forgotten about it.

Or at least that's what I tell myself as I look at the champagne cardstock in his hand and remember the RSVP card I filled out in haste last month. More as an act of "screw you" than of real intent. Regardless, the dread I felt was more than real when my assistant, DeeDee, told me she mailed out the envelope I'd left on my desk. The one I'd meant to throw out but had become distracted by a customer and had forgotten all about.

My smile is tight as I pretend to be perfectly fine with having been invited. Because it's easier to pretend than to let the tears of guilt burn bright over the fallout that has affected him as well. My sweet, gruff, overprotective brother who loaned me the money to start this business and then found out his largest account—Layton Industries—withdrew their business, his top source of dependable income over the past eight years.

I see the stress in the lines on his face. Know he's trying to help me as much as he can and at the same time chase new clients to keep his consulting business afloat. Be the mom, dad, and big brother to me all in one fell swoop. But I know he hates when I thank him for it, so I focus on answering his question instead. I recognized the *did that fucker Mitch really invite you*? in his tone despite the polite way he phrased it.

"It appears so," I murmur and worry my bottom lip between my teeth, attempting to divert the topic at hand. "How bad did I mess up the spreadsheet?"

"Screw the spreadsheet, Say. Does that prick really think that—?"

"I left him, Ryder." My voice is quiet when I speak. A mixture of uncertainty tingeing its edges. "Not the other way around."

"And for good reason." He grimaces when he realizes his tone is harsher than he'd intended, his own anger at Mitch shining through. "Look. I know it's been hard for you. You basically had to start all over. A new place to live, your friends all siding with him and treating you like you never existed, working endless hours in the bakery, being lonely . . . all of it. But you're doing it. You're starting a new life. Have a business up and running and—"

"Barely," I mutter as I scrub away the frustration on my face with my hands and in the process smear icing all over my cheeks.

"It's a lot more than most people would be doing seven months after a long-term breakup."

I inhale deeply and nod my head as I pull up my proverbial bootstraps. This was my doing. *My choice.* Walking away when I could have stayed. Realizing that even though Mitch and I had been together for six years, the spark had died long before. Sure there is more to a relationship than just the *want to throw him up against the wall the minute he gets home and have wild reckless sex with him*, but then again, that spark was never there to begin with.

Growing up with parents who had loved so fiercely, yet constantly referred to the numerous goals, dreams, and wants they gave up because Ryder and I took precedence, gave me pause to what I'd be giving up by marrying into Mitch's family. Because the compromise would have been solely on my part. Not his.

Regardless of my reasons, no one on the outside can fathom why I chose to walk away. I mean, he was Mitch Layton, perfect in every way imaginable—polite, successful, Ralph Lauren-handsome—and even with all that perfection, I can still recall looking in the mirror in the weeks before our wedding and thinking while all that was *nice*, I didn't want to live a life always wondering if *nice was enough.*

I pull my mind from the thoughts and look back at my brother, to the intricate and colorful ink on his forearms. Study the images that are typically hidden beneath the crisply starched dress shirts he wears for work as he lifts the invitation to read it again. "I'm sorry this affected you, too. That my breaking up with him—"

"I told you not to bring it up again. This was not your doing."

"Spoken like a true friend." I chuckle and pick up the piping tube again. More like my only one—and sadly it's because he's my brother so he has to be—given the circle of friends Mitch and I had over the years seemed to side with him after the breakup. The weekly lunch dates suddenly were rescheduled by text saying, "I'll call you when I get free time," and the monthly girls-only dinners for some reason stopped happening. Even my manicurist, who did Mitch's mom's nails, suddenly had no openings for my long-standing appointments.

"Does he actually think you'll show up?"

"He invited me, didn't he? Or maybe it was the bride-to-be who did? Who knows? Who cares?"

"Do you know her?"

"Never heard of her before."

"Whoever it was probably just wanted to rub your nose in it. He's arrogant enough. Thinks he's such a prize. So why not make you worry and wonder if you made a huge mistake leaving him since someone else would snatch him up so quickly? What a fucking joke."

I love that he immediately came to the same conclusion that I did about Mitch's intention behind sending me an invitation. At the same time, I silently loathe that since I've received it, I've been going over my reasons for calling off our wedding more than I should be.

I refuse to acknowledge it has anything to do with Mitch or the invitation.

It's perfectly normal to have doubts. Like *middle of the night stare at the ceiling when I can't sleep wondering if the grass is greener on the other side* doubts. You don't make major changes in your life without having them.

And walking away from the man you've loved and been with for most of your adult life qualifies as a major change, so it's justifiable to have some level of uncertainty.

"Agreed," I muse as I lace another row of beads on the next cupcake. "But wouldn't you feel the same way if someone did that to you?" My brother just stares at me, the snarl on his face betraying the calm in his eyes. "I get why you're pissed at him—and I am too for what he did to you—but when it comes to me, Ryder, he has a right to be mad. I was the one who called it off without warning."

"Oh, I remember, all right," he says over his shoulder as he heads back to the desk. And I know he does. How could he forget holding me while I sobbed when I realized I couldn't go through with the wedding? Or how he was the voice of reason through all of my hysterics, talking me down from the ledge and urging me to listen to my heart? And then later, holding my hand while I picked up the phone and told Mitch I needed to talk to him. "You want to really know what pissed me off more than anything? You broke off an almost seven-year relationship with him and not once did he get angry or rage or sit on your doorstep and beg you to reconsider. He didn't fight for you, and you're worth fighting for. Instead, he acted like the passive-aggressive asshole he is by sending you an invitation to his new wedding."

I shrug, loving that he thinks I'm worth fighting for, and at the same time understand the fact that Mitch not fighting for me, was an answer in itself. "If you were in his shoes, how would you have handled it?"

"Me?" He laughs with a sheepish grin that suggests what he's about to tell me may or may not have happened in the past. "After the girl refused to talk to me, I would have gotten shitfaced. It wouldn't have been pretty. Then I probably would've pounded on her door all night long until she was so sick of it, she'd have to face me. And if she wouldn't and I had to gather some sort of self-respect, I would've probably gone out, drank some more, slept with the first willing candidate because . . . well because, if I ask someone to marry me, I mean it. And now I've just wasted six years of my life, am pissed as hell, and would want some way to feel better about myself. So yeah . . . not classy but that's what I would have done."

I snort. "Sounds about right, and yet for the life of me I can't see Mitch acting like that—the going out and screwing the first thing he laid eyes on part."

His sarcastic laugh rings around the empty bakery. "Hate to break it to you, sis, but obviously he did or else he wouldn't be getting married this quickly."

And I can't hide the fact that the notion stings. But at least it solidifies one of two things: he either felt the same way about our relationship as I did, or he fell in love with *Rebound Sarah* because I bruised his ego and she made him feel good again.

"Maybe he wants to prove he's over me despite the comments I've overheard that she's a carbon copy of me." Out of the corner of my eye, I watch as those words stop his trek back into the office. The notion that Mitch is marrying another tall, aqua-eyed, blonde-haired woman with olive skin hits him.

He laughs, sarcasm ringing in it as I hear the shuffle of papers on my messy desk in the back room. "Where's the RSVP card? I'll send it back and let him know just what I think about how smart you were to dump his ass. Pretentious prick."

Luckily Ryder can't see me from where he stands because I'm certain my scrunched up nose and the falter in my icing would give away what I did.

"Saylor?"

"Hmm?" Indifference.

And there must be something in how I respond that catches the tiny inflection in my tone.

"Please tell me you're not actually considering going."

"No. Of course not." Eyes on the next cupcake. My fingers squeezing another row of pearls around the edge. My feet shifting to abate the weight of his scrutinizing stare.

"Where's the card then?"

"I must have lost it. Or thrown it out." Dodge. Avoid. Ignore. "Oh. Maybe it fell on the floor and is under the desk—"

"You've always been a horrible liar." I can hear the confused disbelief in his tone as he takes a few steps toward me. I immediately let go of my hair wound around my finger. *My tell.* "The question is, what exactly are you lying about?"

"Nothing. Drop it."

"Did you return the RSVP, Saylor?"

"Yes. No. It's not what you think . . ." I blow out an exasperated sigh while he stares, waiting for me to continue. I hate that I feel like a child about to get scolded for doing something stupid. "I marked the card out of spite. I had no intention of going at all . . . but then DeeDee picked it up and mailed it in by accident and . . . well, now they think I'm coming. With a date no less."

"That's classic." He laughs but the sound fades as he narrows his eyes and his thoughts connect. "Hold up. So you marked the card out of spite. I can buy that. But if you had no intention of ever going, then why did you put it in the envelope? That kind of tells me the thought *somewhat* crossed your mind."

"I don't know." I shrug, trying to figure out where he's going with this. "I just did. There was no hidden meaning behind it, Ryder." He's starting to piss me off. I know he's reading into this, thinking more of it than he should, and I just want him to go away so I can decorate in peace.

But he doesn't. He just stands there and continues to stare like I've done something wrong.

"You do realize Mitch sent you the invitation as a joke, right? That neither of them actually want you at their wedding."

I roll my eyes and huff. "I'm not a child. Or an idiot. I know they don't want me there and I assure you, I don't want to be there."

"You sure about that?"

My head snaps up to meet the questioning in his eyes. "Am I sure about what?" There's a bite of anger in my voice. A tinge of *why are you questioning me*?

"I'm just trying to figure out if you're having second thoughts."

I snort. "If I did it's a bit late since it seems he's getting married."

"Mm-hmm." There's something condescending in the way he says it, and it makes me grit my teeth.

"And mm-hmm means what?" My hands are on my hips now, my temper starting to flare.

"I find it interesting that you haven't said shit to me about getting the invitation. So that tells me it has gotten to you more than you're letting on. If it didn't bug you or if you weren't having second thoughts, then you would have said something."

"I didn't tell you because it isn't a big deal."

"Mm-hmm."

There's that response again.

"Just say whatever it is you're not saying, Ryd. I'm not in the mood for whatever reverse psychology game you're playing here."

"It would be totally normal for you to have doubts you know."

"Agreed, but what do doubts have to do with this?" I point to the invitation on the table between us.

"I'm just making sure you're not planning on doing anything stupid you'll regret, that's all."

"Excuse me?"

"Like you showing up to the wedding type of stupid." He lifts his eyebrows as he says the words and snaps the last thread holding my temper at bay.

"Why do you keep harping on about this? Get off my back, will you? Do you think I have a secret plan to sneak off to the wedding? Cash in the travel voucher the resort gave me as a credit for my own cancelled wedding and just show up because all of a sudden I'm worried that I've made a huge mistake? What do you think I'm going to do, spy through the hedges during the ceremony so I can satisfy my morbid curiosity over what the future Mrs. Layton looks like all the while silently thanking God that it isn't me walking down the aisle to him?"

"Say, that's not what I meant by—"

"Better yet. I think I should go." My temper is lit and I couldn't stop the words from rushing out if I tried. "In fact, I'll hire some totally hot stud from an escort service to take me. I mean, I put *plus-one*, after all. So when we walk into the reception, it'll be obvious he's so madly in love with me that those assholes—the people I thought were my friends, yet were nowhere to be found when I needed them the most—can see us. Why not, right? If I showed up head over heels in love with some hot guy, then God willing, they'd all see that I'm not at home in the corner licking my wounds because I realized I made a mistake like they all think I am." I finally stop, chest heaving, hands fisted, and anger over being questioned weighing heavy in the space between us. Ryder's eyes remain locked on mine yet he doesn't say a word. "So if that's what you mean by doing something stupid, then no worries Ryder, I've got stupid covered. Thanks for the vote of confidence, though."

I slam the piping bag down for emphasis. A huge blob of the teal-colored frosting shoots out from the force and squirts across the distance onto the butcher block. I stare at it for a moment, wanting to laugh and cry at the same time over the situation. At Ryder thinking I actually want to get back together with Mitch and at myself for going off on him and letting my temper get the best of me.

It's not his fault. *It's mine.* It's the overload of emotion that I've held in since my breakup with Mitch. It's the knowing that everything

I just pretended to make up—wanting to see what Rebound Sarah looks like, wanting to see Mitch and feel relief that I had walked away, wanting to prove to our old friends that I'm better off now—are thoughts I've actually had over the past few weeks. Validations I don't need but have crept into my mind nonetheless.

"Say." There's nothing but empathy in his voice, and yet I can't look at him. Can't lose it when I've been trying so hard to keep everything—my life, my emotions, my sanity—together to prove to everyone, including him, that I made the best decision.

Needing a minute to collect myself, I hang my head, draw in a deep breath, and tell myself it's okay to feel a bit unhinged. That leaving the life I once had and essentially starting over again would leave most people feeling crazy.

"No. I'm okay." I clear my throat and focus on scrubbing the colored icing from the countertop so he can't see the tears welling in my eyes. All the while, I wait for him to say more. Know he wants to. And yet when only silence weighs down the air around us, I'm forced to look up.

Ryder's head is angled to the side as he stares at me with nothing but compassion in his eyes.

"That's not what I meant, Say. I just meant that doubts and curiosity are a normal thing to have. That there's nothing wrong if you do and I didn't want you to feel you had to hide them from me."

I chuckle nervously, not wanting to discuss this. "Thanks, I'm sorry. I guess I went off the deep end there."

"It was entertaining picturing you peeking through the bushes with leaves in your hair."

I glare at him. "Funny."

His expression softens but the intensity in his eyes remains. "For the record, you didn't make a mistake leaving Mitch. Not one that I can see, anyway." I appreciate the show of solidarity. His support of my decision.

The tears I've held back, threaten once again. "Thank you. I appreciate hearing that more than you know. Can we just forget about it? I don't plan on going to his wedding. I never did. It was just a mishap the RSVP got mailed."

"Okay, deal. But I have to admit, I kind of like knowing he's worried that you're actually going to show up. Serves him right for sending it to you."

"What I really need to do is get back to work. The clock is ticking, and these cupcakes need to be frosted." I pick up the piping tube without looking at him, survey the hundred cupcakes left to ice, and appreciate the need to focus on getting them done and delivered rather than Mitch and his copycat wedding.

My wedding.

Thankfully Ryder leaves me be and returns to the little alcove off the kitchen. A heavy sigh of discord still comes every couple minutes when he finds something else I must have done wrong on the little spreadsheet he made me. But there is definitely a reason he's the numbers guy between the two of us and I bake for a living.

I decorate to the beat of the music. A little Maroon 5 to lighten my mood as I add designs to cupcake after cupcake, stopping after every ten or so to flex my hands and stretch my fingers when they cramp. My mind veers to Mitch. I can't help it. It's almost as if it would be easier for people to understand if there was some huge smoking gun that ended our relationship, but there wasn't.

He was perfect in every way. Polite. Successful. Kind. You name every characteristic of who you'd want to marry, and his country club mug shot would be posted right beside it.

But too much perfection is sometimes a bad thing. Especially when I'm far from perfect myself. How did I ever think I could marry him and live up to his and his family's ridiculous societal standards and ideals of what is expected of a wife?

We were the classic case of *it's not you, it's me*. And I wear the big, shiny crown taking the blame on that like there is no tomorrow.

But as perfect as he was, there had been a lack of passion. And not just the kind that happens when you've been with someone for years, but rather the kind that never was there to begin with. The kind I overlooked from day one because if a guy treats you as well as Mitch treated me, and is as good a catch as our friends with wide-eyes full of jealousy kept telling me he was, then you're supposed to overlook that, right?

But there was more than that. He never understood why I'd prefer to be up to my elbows in a vat of cake batter with pink frosting smeared in my hair, rather than with the Junior League celebrating the coming of spring at some kind of social event that was more of an excuse to buy a fancy new dress and red-soled shoes. Or how tea with his mother—where she talked endlessly about superficial topics—was enough to bore me to sleep, but to me spending a few hours volunteering at the local ASPCA, cleaning dog kennels and giving extra attention to the lonely fur-babies, was an afternoon well spent.

Because God forbid we had a dog of our own. To Mitch, dogs meant fur, and fur meant mess, and I was already messy enough with my frosting and sprinkles for him.

It wasn't the difference in our upbringings, because opposites often attract, but rather it was so much more of the day-to-day wants and needs.

His want for me to stay at home rather than work, versus my need to go out and create something for my own self-satisfaction. Our weekly bout of scheduled sex got the job done but never fulfilled that need within me to have the earth-shattering orgasm some of my girlfriends had bragged about. That want within me to smile automatically when I received a midday text from him rather than cringe wondering what I had done wrong this time.

I shake my head and recall the day the realization hit me out of nowhere. I was spending so much time obsessing about every single detail of our wedding, trying to make everything perfect, because if the wedding was perfect then the marriage was going to be too, right?

However, I wasn't blind to my own bullshit. I had been so focused on selecting vows and table centerpieces and favor choices that when I had a day to sit and do nothing while Mitch was off on one of his boys' country club weekends, it hit me like a ton of bricks.

"A part of me—one I'm really hating right now—thinks you're *brilliant.*"

Ryder's words pull me from the thoughts that have run a

marathon in my head over the past six months. When I look toward him, my smile comes easily for the first time in the past hour. "It took you, what? Almost twenty-eight years to figure out what I've known all along—that I'm the smarter one?"

"Dream on." He rolls his eyes.

"Then what are you talking about?"

"For the record, I still think your idea is horrible, but you might be onto something."

"My idea? What are you talking about?"

"You've had the business for what? Ten months now?"

"Since it's officially been up and running here at the store, more like eight. Why? What am I missing?" I set the piping bag down and lean back against the counter behind me.

"During that time, has it ever crossed your mind that the machine that is the Layton family may be influencing your sales?" I chortle out a laugh, immediately discrediting him. "No. I'm serious, Say. I know this is a big town and it's just one family, but they are well known around here. Mitch's uncle is a congressman and his father owns half the town. I think it makes more sense than not that they—"

"I doubt the Laytons are making a point in their busy lives to sabotage Sweet Cheeks. They've got small countries to run or something."

"That's not what I'm implying."

"Get to the point then." Patience. Gone.

"All I'm saying is, when there's a breakup, people back away from the person they think is to blame, right? They typically side with the one they feel has been wronged."

I eye him suspiciously. "Should I assume you're referring to me as being the one to blame?" Crossing my arms, I hate that his comment miffs me.

"Yes. And no." He takes a step closer and dips a finger in one of my empty frosting tubs and licks the dab. "Mitch's friends have already proven to be shallow and judgmental. Proof being the way they basically cut you out of their lives after you broke it off. So . . . what if we turn the tide?"

"Dude. I love you. I'm sure you have a point to make. But,

seriously? I'm not following your reasoning and have what feels like a million cupcakes left to frost, so can you please get to whatever you're getting to so I can finish them?"

"It's all about perception."

I snort and roll my eyes at him. "And how is whatever brilliant thing I said going to make my business suddenly successful by changing the perception of my ex-friends? After how they've treated me, I would never really want to be friends with them again anyway."

"Your little rant gave me an idea."

What? "I was joking, Ryder." Unease tickles the back of my neck.

"Just hear me out." He holds his hands up in front of him. His *chill out, Saylor* look is on his face. "Let's say you do show up at the wedding with someone who is better looking, more influential, *more something* in their eyes than their precious friend Mitch. There's no doubt in my mind that they'd look at you in a different light."

"That's ridiculous." I sputter the words out and immediately chastise myself for automatically defending the very people who hurt me.

"To us it is, yes. We were taught not to pledge allegiance to the friend with the biggest bank account but after how they've acted, it seems they do."

"Fine. Sure. If that's the case, then it's a good thing I no longer associate with them." I turn my attention back to the cupcakes, not wanting to waste another thought on them or wherever he's going with this.

"You're completely missing what I'm saying."

"Then just say it."

"I think you should go to the wedding. Do exactly what you joked about." He smacks his hands on the butcher block for emphasis. "Walk in there with your head held high and act like leaving Mitch was the best damn decision you've ever made, even if seeing him feels like you've been punched in the gut. The fact that you've traveled thousands of miles and have enough balls to be there should make a huge statement in itself without you ever having to say a word."

He's lost it. Like totally lost it. "You forgot one thing. I don't have balls." I try to lighten the mood. Derail the topic.

"Hardy har har. C'mon, I'm being serious, here."

"I am too." How did he go from listening to me rant to thinking this is a good idea? I sigh. "So, what? You think that by me showing them I'm more confident, they're going to somehow support the business? It's not like baking cupcakes is solving the world hunger crisis or anything. That's a huge stretch."

"Maybe. Maybe not. But if you left the golden boy and are no worse for wear and actually have the guts to show up at the wedding, you sure as hell know they're all going to wonder what you know that they don't."

"For the record I still think you're crazy, Ryd, but thank God I'm not looking at the world through their snob-colored glasses, either."

He flashes me the same cocky grin he has since childhood. "Just think of it this way: if they see you with this newfound confidence, they'll think the bakery is rolling in the dough. Pun intended," he says with a lift of his eyebrows as I roll my eyes. "Being the shallow assholes they are, they'll sniff the proverbial money in the air and think they need to try out your new shop to see what has changed *in you.*"

We stare at each other across the table. His eyes search to see if I agree with what he's saying. And I do see some merit in it. I remember the many times I sat at lunch with all of my then-friends and listened to them talk about so and so and how they must be doing well. The discussion would turn to maybe we should go see for ourselves.

I can't even believe I'm entertaining the thought or that this crazy set of mishaps has led to this discussion in the first place. It's one thing to envision Mitch panicking. It's another to find out the RSVP was actually mailed. And now this? Ryder thinking I need to show up to save the bakery?

I can't believe I'm finding an ounce of merit in what he's saying.

"Possibly," I finally murmur, breaking his gaze and starting the next identical line of piping. I'm mad at him for making sense and annoyed with myself for even entertaining this conversation. And then it hits me how to stop this conversation, once and for all. "You forgot one more thing though, Ryder. I'd have to have a hot guy who's madly in love with me. Isn't that what *my friends* need to see in order for me to even remotely think I can pull this off? You've seen my dating life of late. Netflix and Nutella are about as exciting as I get. And hiring some paid-for escort to take me to a foreign country is not going to happen. So sorry."

When I look up, I can't read the intention in his hint of a smile, but something about it has me straightening up. Our eyes hold, his head nodding ever so subtly as he rubs his hands over his jaw line.

"I can think of a few options."

"Drop it," I huff. "You're crazy. Discussion is over." I bend back over, effectively dismissing the topic at hand.

But he doesn't move. Just stands there and watches me. And I hate every second of it. But I don't look up, don't say a word.

Discussion is over.

Two

Hayes

"**D**O YOU KNOW HOW MUCH I WANT YOU?" MY HANDS ARE braced on either side of her. Her nipples are hard and pressed to my chest. The cool silk of the sheets slide over my ass as I grind between the heat of her thighs.

"Show me." Tessa's eyes flutter closed as her lips meet mine. My dick hardens. It's impossible to ignore the memories of last night—her kiss, her moans, her nails—when *this* was real between us. Skin to skin. Without the merkin or the glycerin spray for sweat. Void of the heat of the set lights or eyes of the crew watching us. Or rather, watching *her*, because she's definitely a visual orgasm.

It's Saylor. She needs your help.

My next line falters on my lips. The words I know by heart escaping me as the text I received earlier distracts me once again. Tessa's body stiffens beneath mine, her face twists in annoyance, and I know there's no way we can smooth over my missed line.

"*Shit*. Sorry." I sit back on my haunches and go to scrub my hands over my face but stop myself before smearing the makeup artist's hour-long job creating my two-day-old black eye and stitched-up cut on my cheek. Instead, I scrunch up my nose as I look down at Tessa. Beautiful, sexy Tessa who is sneering at me from behind her dark lashes and thick stage makeup. Pissed because I can't get my shit straight today, my concentration continually hijacked.

But it's not like I don't know my lines. I'm sure the director thinks I was out late partying and not studying the script for today's fifteen-plus-hour marathon shoot. Just what I need—him to get pissy and do a million retakes until it's perfected, which will result in one of Tessa's well-publicized starlet tantrums.

The criticism I deserve. The tantrum I don't.

The irony is Tessa knows exactly where I was. On top of her. Beneath her. *In her.* All night long.

And if she throws a tantrum then what happened between us last night will come out somehow. She runs at the mouth when angry and that won't bode well since I'm trying to keep a low public profile. Because even though this is a closed set, someone will talk. Talk leads to tabloids. Tabloids lead to snooping. And in my current situation, snooping leads to disaster.

And as much as I'm taking the fall for all of the other shit going on—the tabloid accusations of cheating—I'd rather keep them to just that: accusations, instead of verified facts.

Besides I fucked up. The thing with Tessa wasn't on the agenda. We were running our lines for today. This sex scene . . . and one thing led to another.

Not that I'm complaining because Tessa Gravestone equals spank-bank material for most men.

But when I look down at her where she lies on the bed, perfect tits uncovered and on display—because her theory is if she bought them, then people should see them—I just sigh and shake my head. Another apology on my lips.

And as much as I'd like to convince myself it was the great sex with her last night and wanting to do it again right now that has me forgetting my lines like a first year SAG card holder, *it's not.*

It's not the stress of keeping what happened with her under wraps or what's going on in the tabloids with Jenna or anything else.

It's fucking Ryder. I don't talk to the guy for over eight months and then all of a sudden we talk twice in one week. But it wasn't plans we made to meet up when I finally head home for the first time in forever that have me screwing up my lines. It was his damn text.

His simple request. The mention of the one person we both had an unspoken agreement never to bring up: *Saylor*.

And fuck if I'll admit that just seeing her name is the reason my concentration has been shot to hell.

"Hayes?" It's the director's voice.

"Yeah?" I look up, my mind pulled immediately from long, tanned legs dangling from the dock, warm summer nights making out in the tree house we'd long since outgrown, and seeing my name on the back of my letterman jacket as she walked up the sidewalk to her front door.

Every person on the set is staring at me. Time is money. And I'm sitting here wasting it, thinking about way back when. Another life I escaped from but suddenly feel like I'm being sucked back into.

All because of a simple damn name.

"Sorry. I got distracted."

Tessa puffs her chest out—pink nipples on display—thinking she's the cause of my distraction. I fight the roll of my eyes. Bite back telling her she's not that great if for nothing more than to knock down that ego of hers that grows bigger every day.

"Are you *un*distracted now?" the director asks. Chuckles filter through the room as the grips and cameramen assume it's my dick distracting me. *Understandably*. I bet a few of theirs are flying half-mast too at the sight of Tessa.

She smiles smugly as I shift off her and back to my original blocking for the start of the scene. "Yeah. Let's take it from the last mark. I'll nail it this time."

At least I earn some chuckles with that one.

The hours roll together. Take after take. Line after line. All on repeat until deemed perfect by the acclaimed director, Andy Westin. The main reason I begged, borrowed, and stole just to get the role. So I could get the monumental chance to work with him. Learn from him.

I throw everything into my character. Tell myself to block the noise out. *Ignore all thoughts of Saylor.* And get through the first part of the day and its expedited filming schedule sped up for my own benefit.

When we break for lunch at four in the afternoon, I grab a quick bite at craft services and head back to my trailer for some downtime.

My cell on the dinette greets me as I enter. *The* text on it still lingering on my mind. The woman it pertains to even more so.

Wanting to catch a quick snooze during the ninety-minute break till next call, I lie down on the couch, feet on one armrest and my head on the other. I run the next scene through my head. The lines I know like the back of my hand. The ones I definitely can't fuck up next go-round.

. . . Saylor . . .

The emotion and intonation I need to inflect in each word of the script.

. . . the seventeen-year-old girl I left behind . . .

The facial expressions I'll need to emulate to convey my character's inner turmoil.

. . . sweet smiles, soft lips, my teenage world . . .

The physical actions required to show a man in conflict as he makes love to the woman he suspects had a hand in murdering his father and yet he can't help but love.

. . . the only regret I've ever had . . .

"Goddammit." I scrub my hands over my face in frustration. I need to focus. To concentrate. And not on Saylor. The girl I never said goodbye to. The promises left empty. The door I slammed shut so I didn't feel like the selfish prick I was for chasing my dreams without a single thought to hers.

Shit. It's amazing how the bright lights in this big city have pushed all that away. Faded the memories. Reinforced my decision with the success it has brought me.

And all it takes to bring me right back is one text from my oldest friend who never asks for anything.

Cashing in that IOU. It's Saylor. She needs your help. Call when you can.

Fuck, man. Trying to forget her is like trying to remember someone I've never met. *It's impossible.* And no matter how hard I try to push Ryder's text out of my mind, she's still there.

Clear as day.

Because nothing improves the memory like trying to forget.

Three

Saylor

"T HAT'S A GOOD COLOR ON YOU."

I glance up from the cupcakes before me and glare at DeeDee. "Funny."

"Let me guess, it was you versus the frosting and the frosting won?"

"Is it that bad?" I reach up to pat down my hair but stop the natural reaction since my hands are covered in frosting too.

DeeDee's smile widens as she takes in the fallout from trying to do too many things at once. Like use the hand mixer and reach for the phone at the same time so the beaters lift from the bowl and spray blue icing all over the place.

More specifically, all over me. If my apron is any indication, I can only imagine the million blue flecks in my hair as if someone threw confetti at me.

"Nah. It's *just you.*"

I laugh and know this is exactly one of the things that irked Mitch so much. My ability to get so lost in my work that I don't give a second thought to being covered in ingredients. How some days I'd slide into his car and get something—batter, frosting, or God forbid, *sprinkles*—on the custom leather seats of his precious Mercedes. "Guess that explains why my dating life is so jam-packed these days, huh?"

"You and me both," she says as she looks up from the computer with a lift of her eyebrows. "Checking social media for you."

"Per Ryder's request, I'm sure."

She laughs for good measure, giving me an answer without saying a word. "Bride's mom from last weekend tweeted last night saying she loved the cupcakes and wanted to thank you. I private messaged her and asked if she'd be a reference for us. She agreed and asked if it would be okay if she recommended Sweet Cheeks to the catering manager she works with at the convention center."

"Really?" The thought of getting on their coveted vendor list has me smiling despite the nine hours I've already put in today.

"Yes. Fingers crossed she follows through. See? The power of social media." *Someone's been talking to Ryder too much.* I shake my head at the thought as she stands and walks toward the table where I'm working.

"Wow. These look great. Is this the order for the Rosemont family that came in yesterday?" She steps forward to look closer at the ten dozen cupcakes I'm putting the finishing touches on. All of them are decorated like a Marine's dress blue uniform, complete with accurate bars and accolades.

I angle my head to the side, scrutinize my own work and nod, pleased with how they turned out. "Yes. They're for a celebration of life event. He was a retired Marine."

"Highly decorated by the looks of it."

"Seems so."

"Do you want me to deliver them for you?"

"No need to. They're getting picked up after five." I glance at the clock on the wall and cringe. I have forty minutes left to get them finished.

The bell on the door to the bakery jingles, announcing a customer, and DeeDee smiles.

"The game must be over. I'll man the counter," she says as she heads out front to greet them. And thank God for the game, or rather the series of basketball games in a state cup tournament, being held right down the street at the high school. A lot of new faces have been stopping in this week with the *buy three get one free* flyer we papered the school with, resulting in some boosted sales.

I'll take any little victory I can get right now.

The intermittent jingle of the door lightens my mood as I finish up the final dozen uniform-themed cupcakes, package them up, and place them in the display case for completed orders behind the counter. I know Ryder will be happy with this week's receipts and that, more than anything, gives me an ounce of hope I'll be able to figure something out to keep my dream afloat.

The colors in the sky begin to fade as I clean up the back room and take a few phone orders. What I really want to do is run upstairs to my apartment atop the bakery and grab a quick shower. But I figure if I wait until we close, then I can reward myself with a glass or two of wine while soaking in a hot bath.

The bell jingles again and I hear a man say, "Good afternoon." Something about the sound of his voice gives me pause, and I stop long enough to notice that after a few seconds, DeeDee hasn't responded.

"Dee?" I call out as I move through the doorway to the retail front. She comes into view first—eyes wide, mouth agape—staring straight ahead. I immediately open my mouth to apologize to the customer for her rudeness, but the words—just like my heart—stop abruptly when the customer comes into sight.

I feel like every part of me staggers backward, and yet my feet stay completely still, as a pair of chocolate-brown eyes meet mine. A cocky yet cautious smile slowly curls up the corner of his mouth.

That mouth. The one that whispered sweet nothings. *Lies.* Told me he'd stay forever. *And left without ever saying a word.*

It's like the air has been vacuumed from the room. I struggle to draw in a steady breath, and time seems to stand still as we stare at each other.

Because it's him.

Hayes Whitley.

An older version of the boy who walked away all those years ago. Washed his hands of me and what we had without a word. The one who broke my heart in every way imaginable and stole more than just my innocence when he drove off.

Seconds pass. They feel like those first weeks after he left—long, confusing, and painful. And the hurt I thought I'd let go of years ago, slams into me like a battering ram.

But hell if I'm going to let him know it.

"Ships Ahoy." His voice . . . silk over gravel. How can it still cause goosebumps to race over my skin despite everything? How can that stupid nickname I haven't heard in almost ten years still ruffle my feathers and make me remember things I thought I'd purged from my memory? How can it make me say the one name I swore I'd never say again?

"Hayes." My voice is calm. Even. Expertly disguising my racing pulse and the sudden surge of every imaginable emotion overwhelming me.

"It's been a long time, Saylor." No smile now, just a set jaw with intense eyes fixed on mine, and a flex of his hands at his side.

"A lifetime." I break his stare and look around at my fledgling cupcake shop and suddenly feel completely inadequate. My cozy, little bakery compared to his larger-than-life public career. I wipe my damp palms on my apron, smear some frosting in the process, but am too overwhelmed seeing him again to care. I take a few steps forward, nerves suddenly jittering within, and have never been more thankful for the counter in between us as I am right now. A barrier. Some distance. *Anything* to break the pull those eyes of his have always had on me.

I glance over to DeeDee. I don't have the wherewithal to try and figure out if the shock blanketing her face is because the famous heartthrob, Hollywood A-Lister Hayes Whitley is standing in Sweet Cheeks or because he obviously knows me somehow.

Her eyes flicker back and forth between us in an uncomfortable silence, amplified with years of unanswered questions before she nods as if she knows we need a moment to ourselves. She glances back to

Hayes for a second and then leaves us alone.

I turn to physically watch her retreat into the kitchen area and use the few seconds to try and get over the shock of seeing him again. But when she disappears, I have no choice but to turn and face him. Unsure of what to say, I address everything but the elephant in the room. "Congratulations on all of your success."

"Thank you." His voice is soft—almost apologetic—and it pulls my attention to look closer to see the unspoken questions flitting through his eyes. He begins to speak and then stops. Hesitates. Looks down at the cupcakes in the case beside me then back up to me. "You look great, Saylor."

His unexpected words surprise me. The simple compliment flusters me. And while a small part of me preens that he notices how I look, I also know he's lying. Being splattered in a ticker-tape parade of blue frosting doesn't look good on anyone.

But I need this reminder of just how smooth Hayes Whitley can be so I can rein in the strange mix of emotions I'm feeling. The familiarity from seeing an old friend and the bitterness of being left behind by my first love.

I'd prefer to hold tight to the bitterness and anger than acknowledge that fledgling flutter of hope my teenage self must have held on to somewhere deep down. *Someday Hayes might come back for me.*

Don't even think it, Saylor. That's not why he's here. Besides, he's ten years too late.

"Thanks. You too." I clear my throat. Dart my eyes. Try to focus on getting through the next few moments without blurting out the questions I've held on to for years over why he left me. Tell myself to let it go. After all, I did try. I'd messaged and called, time and again without a response after he first left. If he'd wanted me to know the answers, he would have responded.

But he didn't.

End of story.

When the silence stretches, my eyes are drawn back to him.

Everything about him.

How kind the years have been to him. The dark shirt and designer jeans that look worn but probably cost more than the new display case I'd love to buy. He's still as ruggedly handsome as before, still has that mysterious edge to him that drew me in as a teenager, but there's more character to his face now. More lines and angles—a maturity to his features—that make me wonder what those eyes have seen. His body is bigger, broader, more filled out compared to the teenager I once knew, and yet it's his eyes that hold me rapt. They're the same warm brown, same dark lashes, but the intensity in them is new. The way he looks at me—unrelenting and thoroughly—leaves any words I was hoping to speak faltering on my tongue.

"I talked to Ryder last week. He told me about the bakery, so I figured I'd come in and check it out when I got into town."

I stare at him, my mind spinning as to why my brother would tell Hayes anything about me. Years ago, we'd had a fight after I'd learned he and Hayes talked occasionally. I was livid and felt betrayed by both of them. Hayes couldn't pick up a phone and talk to me, but he could do just that and talk to Ryder? And Ryder was okay being friends with Hayes after how he hurt me? The only solution we could agree on was a type of *don't ask, don't tell* policy. I didn't ask if Ryder talked to Hayes, and he didn't tell me if he did. That and the promise I'd never be a topic in one of their discussions.

So either Ryder's been lying to me all this time or something has changed to make him break the latter part of our agreement.

I can think of a few options.

Ryder's words come back to me. Cause that flutter of panic to trigger deep down inside me as pieces fall into place. The knowing look he gave me when he said that. The sudden appearance of the one man we both know is decidedly more successful than Mitch or any of the Laytons. And publicly so.

Holy. Shit.

My brother didn't let the discussion, or his ridiculous thoughts about why I should go to Mitch's wedding drop like I thought he had. Weeks have passed. *Weeks!* And suddenly Hayes Whitley appears out of the blue?

All it takes is a split second of time to conclude why Hayes is here. What Ryder has gone and done. And I die a slow death of indignity, my pride thoroughly obliterated.

Fury fires within: at Ryder for calling him; at Hayes for coming here, which could potentially twist my insides and bring back feelings, emotions, and memories when I don't want to be reminded. I want to be angry at him—for leaving me, for never speaking to me again, for showing up here with that disarming smile and knowing look like he's going to win me over in the blink of an eye.

Well, he won't.

"I don't need your help." My pride wars on every level with the comment. My acknowledgement of why he's here. My not needing him to think I look good or bad or anywhere in between. "Or your compliments." I bite back the emotion swimming in my voice. The bitterness inflamed over time.

"Did I miss something here?" He draws the question out while I just stare at him, hands on my hips, the chip lodged firmly on my shoulder.

"I'm going to kill him," I mutter under my breath choosing to focus my brewing anger at my brother because it's easier than acknowledging the confusion I'm feeling.

His chuckle rings around the empty bakery. It scrapes over my soul and opens those wounds I thought had healed. "Well, good thing you said *him* so I can assume you're talking about someone else."

"You're not far behind Ryder on the hit list."

"You always were quick with that temper of yours." A flash of a grin. A shake of his head. His unrelenting stare.

And I hate that he seems amused. I feel like I'm being mocked. Played. And every part of it grates against my sensibilities. My body's visceral reaction to him—the undeniable attraction still simmering beneath the layers of resentment—battles against my mind's staunch refusal to acknowledge him.

"You lost the right to know anything about me ten years ago."

"Agreed." He purses his lips and nods, hands shoved deep in his pockets, shoulders shrugged up like he understands my position. And I don't want him to be understanding. I want him to be the cocky asshole because I refuse to fall under that boy-next-door charm, I know from experience he can turn on like the flick of a switch.

Talk about mortifying. Having your brother call the one man who crushed you and asking him to be your date to your ex-fiancé's wedding. It couldn't get any more daytime talk show topic if I tried.

"I should have known better," I mutter to myself, thinking how I thought I was in the clear on this. That Ryder hadn't brought up the RSVP or Mitch's wedding since the day he found the invitation and therefore the topic had been forgotten.

I'm going to kill him.

Repeating it in my head makes me feel better. Well, not really but it's easier to focus on that than anything about the man standing before me.

My hands fist. My jaw clenches.

Hayes chuckles and yet all I hear is condescension. Mockery. "Do you mind explaining to me why you're—?"

"Whatever Ryder told you I needed help with, I no longer need it . . . I'm a big girl. A grown woman who can handle her own life, so thanks, but no thanks. I'd like to say it's great to see you, Hayes, but it's not. While I appreciate the gesture, because I'm not that much of a bitch, it's actually just uncomfortable knowing why you're here. This has to be amusing to you to come back, after being asked by my brother no less, to play the part of escort to try and help the girl you dumped." I stop for a second to catch my breath, the purge of words almost cathartic. His eyes narrow, forehead creases, and his head shakes as he looks at me like he doesn't understand what I'm saying. So I continue while my courage is winning out over the hurt and embarrassment. Hostility owns my voice. "Look, it's been a long time and yet nothing's changed. You're still Mr. Perfect and I'm far from it, and the last thing I need is you here thinking you're making it better when in the end it will just be worse. So I appreciate it, Hayes . . . I really do. It's a nice gesture but it's been a long day, I'm tired, and so I'm going to close up shop a little early tonight and forgo any more embarrassment for the day. Okay?"

I blow a breath out and just stare at him, impatience emanating off me with my stance—hands across my chest and teeth clenched tight—while he digests what I've said. I'm sure the look of shock on his face stems from the fact that no one probably says no to him now that he's one of People's Most Beautiful. Yet right now I can't find the wherewithal to even care.

Until he speaks.

"Guess I underestimated your ability to hold a grudge, Saylor. But I get why you're angry. I had my reasons back then, but the boy I was then is not the man I am now. I know what I did was chickenshit." I hate the glimpse of emotion I see in his eyes but can't read. It's been too long, and I don't know anything about the man he's become to even try to assume what it is. All I know is the regret in his voice hits me and weaves through my anger but doesn't penetrate the mortification I feel, knowing my brother recruited Hayes. *How can he* not *think I'm desperate?*

"Hayes." I say his name. A request for him to stop. A plea for him to turn around and walk out the door without another word. A warning to just leave it be and forget everything Ryder told him. Anything so the teenager in me still clinging to her first love remains buried beneath the strong woman I've become. An apology is just a word and when it's coming from an actor, I can't trust its sincerity any more than I can trust myself not to believe it.

"No need. I understand," he says as he holds his hands up in surrender. "I'll just pick up my order and leave."

"*Order*?" My voice breaks. The singular word has me standing straighter as dread begins to bleed into the edges of my temper.

I wrack my mind for an order I may have missed under the name Whitley. No order for his mother. No order for anyone I know associated with his family.

"Yes. It's under Rosemont."

Oh. My. God.

"That's my mom's maiden name."

The blood drains from my face.

"I'm in town for my great-uncle's funeral."

He's not here because of Ryder. *Or me.* Or some convoluted plan to be my date so I could seek redemption.

Shit. Shit. Double shit.

"I offered to pick up the order so I could . . . I don't know." He shrugs, voice tight. "I'd heard this was your place and wanted to see how you were doing."

Do something. Say something. And yet I do neither as I stare at Hayes like a deer in the headlights. My mortification reaching new heights but for a different reason.

"Your great-uncle?" My voice squeaks and he nods his head, eyes never leaving mine. "Oh my God, Hayes. I'm so sorry. For what I said. I had no idea these were for your great-uncle. Or that he died. I–uh– I'm such an idiot." I can't stop stuttering out apologies as I move to the refrigerated case and busy my hands as if getting him the cupcakes faster will right the wrong I just made in unleashing my temper. I move each of the five boxes to the counter as quickly as possible in the hopes that my preoccupation and lack of eye contact during the time will allow me to recover some of my dignity.

"So there you are," I say as I set the last box down. "One hundred twenty cupcakes, paid in full. I hope you . . . your great-uncle's family thinks they are reflective of his service." I keep my eyes trained on the boxes, my voice full of forced cheer as if I didn't just make a complete ass out of myself.

Hayes's hands come into my view as they lift the pink and white striped lid of the uppermost box. I focus on them. I always had a thing for his hands. My mind flashes back. *Lying on the Pendleton blanket in the bed of his truck. The trees swaying above us. The heat of him beside me. My fingers tracing over the lines on his palm. Our talk turning to our futures. Our hopes. Our dreams.*

"Saylor?"

His voice calling my name feels like déjà vu, but it's enough to pull me from thoughts I shouldn't be having. My eyes flash up to his and I'm immediately brought back to reality. To the nerves suddenly vibrating through me. To that quick pang the memory caused.

"Yeah?"

"These are incredible. Thank you. My mom will love them."

31

My smile is natural when I think of his mom. "Please give her my condolences. I didn't realize the connection or else I would have called her. Sent her a card. Something." I sigh, the awkwardness never ending. The curiosity in his eyes over what my rant was about never manifests itself into words, and I don't volunteer the answers. I glance down to my fidgeting fingers and then back up to him. "Can you just forget everything I've said? I thought . . . I misunderstood something and I . . . can we just pretend like it never happened?"

Pretty please? My eyes beg him while my posture remains rigid.

"Sure." That's all he says. His expression is guarded and gives me no indication whether he thinks I'm crazy. If I were him, I'd be pissed if someone treated me like I did—made the assumptions I made—and he has every right to want to walk out of here and never want to see me again. "I'll give my mom your condolences."

He picks up the first three stacked boxes of cupcakes and I scramble around the counter. "Here, let me help you."

"No. Please don't," he says as he heads toward the door. "I don't need your help, either."

I stop in my tracks as he pushes open the door with his hip and disappears outside. Pride has me needing to save face. The unknown I feel inside has me wanting to make things right so the lasting impression he has of me is not this schizophrenic woman.

Grabbing the remaining two boxes of his order, I make my way out of the shop to where he's placing them in the trunk of a ridiculously sexy, sleek sports car. When he stands up and meets my eyes, a lock of hair has fallen over his forehead, and I'm reminded of who we used to be together. He takes the boxes from me without a word, sets them inside, and shuts the trunk. His eyes are on the keys in his hands as he walks slowly to the driver's side of the car.

So many things I need to say to him, about what happened minutes ago and over ten years ago, and yet I think I've already said enough.

He rests his forearms on the top of his car, his eyes still focused on where his fingers toy with his keys. "You always were quick with that temper, Say. Used to cause a lot of problems for you. Seems it still does." He lifts his face to meet mine but his sunglasses hide his eyes. "Thanks for the cupcakes. I'll see you around."

Without another word, Hayes lowers himself into the car. The engine purrs to life, rumbles in my chest, and he pulls out of the parking lot while I stand there watching him leave.

The difference is this time I know he's leaving.

And at least I know why.

Was it my fault he left last time too? My impatience? My assumptions? Had I not read him then as I couldn't read him today? I hate the unanswered questions that drift through my mind and despise the doubts that weigh them down. Because regardless of how many times I've discredited them in the past, they still linger.

Still haunt.

I don't know how long I stand there and stare but I'm well aware that DeeDee is waiting to pounce on me for information the minute I go inside. When I push open the door, the sight of her standing there—arms crossed, foot tapping, grin so big her cheeks might crack—confirms my suspicion.

"No. Fricking. Way." DeeDee's eyes bug out of her head as I walk into Sweet Cheeks. "That was . . . he was . . . oh my God, you know Hayes Whitley. Like know-know him."

I hear what she says, her prattling, yet I walk past her and into the back kitchen area without a word. I just need a few minutes to wrap my head around exactly what happened. My assumptions. My temper.

Why, when Hayes drove off, so did a small part of my nostalgic hope that he'd come back for me. And that in itself irritates me.

Ten years have passed. I'm no longer that young girl he once knew. I've lived and grown and learned from my mistakes. Most notably the ones I made in loving him.

"Saylor."

"Not now, Dee." I hold up my hand to her, my heart racing and head reeling.

"No. You don't get to ignore me on this one, Saylor. How did I not know that you know him? I mean I knew he grew up around here but, holy crap, I just made a complete ass out of myself in front of him."

I snort. "You and me both." I head straight into the back room and unlock the door that leads up to my apartment. "Give me a few."

When I shut the door behind me, DeeDee is still talking. Still telling me she's not going to stop asking questions until I answer. And all I can think as I enter my apartment is that the answers don't matter. Hayes Whitley was a part of my past. *Is* a part of my past. And if seeing him has churned up all of these unacknowledged emotions that I swore I'd dealt with a long time ago, then he needs to stay right where he is.

In the past.

Because by never looking back, he let me know he didn't want anything to do with my future.

Four

Saylor

"**Y**OU UP THERE, SHIPS AHOY?"

I cross my arms over my chest, roll my eyes. Sigh. Will he ever stop calling me that stupid nickname?

The sound of his feet clomping up the stairs of the old tree house greets my frustration and I know like always, he's not going to leave me alone. He's so annoying. And such a guy. Ugh.

Keeping my eyes fixed on the hole in the roof of my most favorite place in the world, I stare at the stars above in the night sky—visually trace the constellations—rather than look over to where the makeshift door has creaked open announcing his presence.

"Hey, kiddo."

I grit my teeth. Hate the feeling as my stomach flip-flops at the sound of his voice. At the stupid nickname that makes me feel like he thinks of me as a little kid when I'm not. He's only two years older than me.

Boys are so frustrating. And stupid. And gross.

But he's Hayes Whitley. All swoony and tall with his light brown hair and dark brown eyes. He's funny and flirty and supposedly knows how to kiss better than any of the other guys in school. At least that's what the older girls claim when they're giggling on the other side of the locker room before gym class.

Because I've never kissed a boy before.

But I don't believe them. He's just Hayes Whitley. My brother's best friend. The one who, during my last slumber party, helped Ryder squirt drops of mustard on all of my sleeping friends' faces before slowly tickling their cheeks with a feather so they'd smear it all over. The boy who takes a cookie out of my hand after school without so much as a thanks *before heading to my brother's room and slamming the door shut to do who knows what before they head out to whatever practice they have for the day. The same guy who, every time Ryder has a party when my parents go out of town to wherever they go, makes sure to climb up the ladder to my tree house to make sure I don't want to come down and do whatever all the cool kids are doing down below.*

I like it and hate it and don't understand why I feel that way.

"I'm not a kid anymore so don't call me kiddo. Go away."

And of course being the stubborn teenager I know him to be, he doesn't leave. Rather his footsteps clomping around the small area tell me he's invading my space. My reprieve from the annoying giggles of the popular senior girls downstairs, trying to impress the jocks.

The floorboards flex beneath me from his weight. The subtle scent of his shampoo and beer fill the space around us. The sound of his body shifting—shoes scraping, jeans sliding over wood, the grunt as he lies down beside me. The heat of his upper arm pressing against mine as he scoots next to me.

"What are you looking at? Ah man, there's tons up there tonight," *he says as he sees the bright stars spread across the darkened sky above us.*

"Mm-hmm." *For some reason I can't say anything else. Nerves rattle around inside me when it's just Hayes.*

Irritating.

Frustrating.

The boy who's like a third child in our house most days. A second, annoying, brother.

And yet despite all of that, the nerves I don't understand are there.

I concentrate on the sky above. Try to draw lines from star to star and make them any shape I want them to be. It's so much easier to focus on that than the funny way my blood rushes in my ears. Or the chills that suddenly blanket my bare skin despite the warm night.

"Have you?"

His question pulls me from my thoughts. Makes me realize he asked something. I wipe my sweaty palms on my shorts. Swallow over the words tying up my throat. "Have I what?" It's barely a whisper and I wonder if he even heard me with the party's music and laughter carrying up here.

I turn my head and startle when I find his face turned toward mine, our noses inches apart. The heat of his breath hits my lips. My heart feels like it somersaults in my chest and lands somewhere in the pit of my belly. I meet the dark brown of his eyes and avert my gaze immediately, way too uncomfortable and at the same time wanting to look right back at them.

He waits. It feels like forever in the tiny space of the tree house, but I know it's only seconds. Seconds where I neglect to breathe. Forget to think. And it's only when I bring my eyes back to his, suddenly leery that I might have boogers in my nose or leaves in my hair, that he answers my question.

"Have you seen any shooting stars?"

My breath hitches as he moves his arm and the back of his hand brushes against mine.

Is this how a boy tries to hold your hand?

I don't want him to.

I do want him to.

This is Hayes. Just Hayes. Don't be stupid. He's not going to hold your hand.

The question. Answer the question.

I clear my throat, trying to make my tongue, that feels like three times its normal size, work. "Yeah."

I can't see his mouth but know he smiles because the corners of his eyes bunch up as his hair, wet from swimming, falls onto his forehead.

"What did you wish for?"

You to kiss me.

My eyes fling open, and the familiar shadows on my bedroom ceiling do nothing to slow the rapid beat of my heart in my chest. The dream, reliving the memory, feels like just yesterday and so very long ago at the same time.

That first longing to be kissed by a boy. The smell of summer around us, and those first moments in my teenage life where Hayes Whitley became so much more than my big brother's best friend.

He became my first crush.

Then later my first love.

And later again my first heartbreak.

I sigh, snuggle back down into the covers of my big, empty bed, and hate how seeing Hayes yesterday caused forgotten memories to resurface. Like those first flutters of how I felt that night in the tree house when something shifted between us. Such a contrast to the regret that's been eating at me since I jumped to conclusions. *My temper.* The twist of my gut as he drove away without allowing me to explain my actions, even though I couldn't really explain them anyway without feeling more pathetic.

Damn you, Hayes Whitley.

Damn him for always popping back into my life somehow: his movie trailer on constant repeat during television commercials, running into his mom in the grocery store, sitting at a Starbucks in town and seeing him from afar on the very few occasions he's bothered to venture back home. They've all caused those feelings of rejection and hurt to rile back up when all I had wanted was for them to be dead and buried.

Even when I was engaged to Mitch. That spark, the one that had been missing, it was Hayes Whitley's fault it wasn't there in the first place. Why can't I be free of him? It has been ten years. I was going to marry another man, for God's sake. *Shit.* I don't want this. Don't have time for this churned-up memory. Don't want this unsettled feeling.

But it's not like Hayes even cares. He most likely chalked up what we had to teenage love with his best friend's little sister. A blip on the radar before he was swallowed whole by the flashes of the cameras that constantly follow him around to document his every move. So why would I assume he'd even think twice about me, a ghost of a memory from his past?

It's not like I thought of him much either. Once I met Mitch, he was the patient one earning my trust. The trust I never gave anyone after the job Hayes did on it. Because yes, while I can admit that what Hayes and I had was most likely puppy love, it was also the first time my heart was broken, and you don't forget either of those occurrences very easily.

But if it was puppy love, why did seeing him yesterday affect me so strongly?

It's ironic. I'm lying in bed thinking about Hayes all these years later and not questioning why it's not Mitch I'm thinking of.

It's only been eight months. Not ten years. And yet, Hayes's pull on me dominates without question.

Mitch was gentle and patient and the man I was going to marry. Hayes was brash and assertive and left me with a battered and bruised heart.

Maybe it's just because Hayes is the one I couldn't have. Maybe it's an inherent thing to feel that way even though I was young without a clue about life or love. Regardless, it doesn't matter.

There will be no seeing Hayes again other than on his larger-than-life billboard ads. Or on one of the bazillion magazine covers that adorn the checkout stands, accusing him of cheating on Jenna Dixon: his girlfriend or ex-girlfriend or who knows what she is to him because they *are* tabloids after all. Or if I don't flip the channel quick enough when he makes a promotional appearance on Ellen or Jimmy Fallon. Because I screwed up. I assumed Hayes had shown up because Ryder called him. And maybe he felt bad about what had happened a long time ago, thought I was pathetic and pitied my situation with Mitch so he came to save the day. Or laugh at me. Both would have made me feel the same way.

But he hadn't.

Not even close. He didn't even have a clue what I was talking about, but my temper was unleashed, my mouth in motion without thinking. All Hayes wanted to do was pick up an order for his great-uncle's memorial. Mitch used to joke that he needed to carry duct tape for my mouth in case I lost my cool, so I wouldn't make a scene and tarnish the pristine Layton reputation. *Now I can see why.*

Talk about being an idiot with a capital I.

Even worse is that, despite all of this as I lie here in bed, every part of me wants to find some way to apologize to Hayes. I need to explain but know that would only result in me feeling like more of an idiot when I tell him I was a runaway bride. That the wedding bells I thought I heard were actually alarm bells warning me to save myself and run the opposite way. How do I save face and make him see I'm not crazy when I tell him any of that? That I was in a perfectly solid relationship for six years but when it came down to brass tacks, I couldn't do it.

I'll just have to lie low. Keep to myself and away from any of the places I know he frequents when he's here. Avoidance is probably best at this point.

With that decided and feeling a bit more settled, I slowly sink into the edge of sleep.

My mind drifting to that first kiss.

To our last kiss.

To how my heart jumped in my throat and every female part of me reacted to the sight of him in the bakery.

To the man I shouldn't be thinking about but can't seem to shake from my mind.

Five

Saylor

I SHOULD BE WORKING.

I should be listening to the promises I made to myself.

I should be doing a lot of things and the one I shouldn't, I'm about to do.

The bar was loud when I entered. The deep pulse of bass bumped through the speakers, and it took a second for my eyes to adjust to the darkness inside the Blue Devil.

It's all Ryder's fault. Him and his *you need to get out and have some fun.* His *a bunch of us are going out tonight to just have a few drinks and relax after a long week.* His *you're gonna burn yourself out because you're working too hard. You've been through a lot and it's not going to kill you if you're not there one night.*

Maybe I feel like I owe it to him to show up after turning him down week after week when he's just trying to be a good brother by looking out for me. Then again, maybe I showed up tonight because I feel guilty for immediately assuming he had contacted Hayes and my threatening to kill him. *Not that he knew, of course.*

Regardless, I'm here and now suddenly feel totally out of place

41

in this huge club packed full of bulging biceps and pushed-up boobs. I take in the short skirts riding up the thighs of women around me and the tight shirts putting the rest of their assets on display, and feel completely inadequate in my black slacks and light pink top.

It's not like I'm a slouch in the looks department—at least I'm lacking the blue frosting that decorated my hair yesterday—but this place is so very different than the places Mitch and I used to frequent. It's more my age than the country club scene, and yet I hate that I feel so uncomfortable when, at age twenty-seven, I should fit right in.

I think back to how I let Mitch's influence slowly change the wild and reckless in me to sophisticated and reserved. From vibrant colors to muted beiges. How even though I understand the complexity of the concept now—that less can also be more—a part of me vows from here forward to throw a few splashes of color back in there to regain the spirit of the girl I used to be.

The one Hayes liked.

The one that made Mitch grimace.

I glance up at Ryder when he places another cocktail in front of me and shake my head—glad for the drink and the derailment of my thoughts. "Are you trying to get me drunk?" A giggle escapes my lips and it sounds strange because I don't giggle. Ever.

"It's not my fault you're a lightweight." He smirks and leans down closer to my ear so I can hear what he says. "You deserve a night off. I appreciate how hard you're working so we don't lose our asses, but you're going to burn out if you don't take a break. Besides, you're young. You haven't been out once since you've been single. Live a little, sis. *Be everything Mitch wouldn't let you be.* I'll make sure you don't get into too much trouble."

He winks at me as he steps back, a boyish grin on his face that transforms as a pretty brunette walks up to him. He slides his hand onto her lower back, his laugh becomes a little louder, his free attention taken. I watch mesmerized, wondering when the last time was I felt like he looks: carefree, young, confident. I also wonder when I last felt like a woman who holds a man's attention. Attractive.

Alluring. Someone to claim. *Was I ever that girl?*

Be everything Mitch wouldn't let you be.

Ryder's words strike a chord within me. One I'm not sure I'm ready to face yet, but can't stop thinking about as I sit and watch the other patrons in the club from our coveted position in the rear corner. The couples who came together and are having a night out with friends after a long workweek. The pack of women standing in the opposite corner, acting as if they don't care to be approached by any men but whose eyes are constantly roaming over the bachelors in the club and then suddenly acting coy when they finally approach. The men on the prowl: cocky in swagger and with a drink in hand, trying to find someone to hook up with. I watch them all as I sip my drink and chat idly with my brother's friends and acquaintances. Enjoying myself but still feeling out of place in this scene I stopped being a part of six years ago.

The funny thing is most people would want to sow their wild oats. And maybe in time I will, but for now, I'm still trying to settle the ever-shifting world beneath my feet.

Time passes. The music becomes louder. The alcohol flows. The laughter in the club becomes louder as inhibitions are left with one more sip, one more drink, one more smile from the guy across the club.

I laugh at one of Ryder's friends, Frankie, as he attempts to perform a popular dance to a song. Attempt being the operative word. My head's thrown back, eyes closed, and my hand is pressed to my stomach. It hurts from laughing so hard. But when I open my eyes to find Hayes sitting directly across from me, his gaze a mixture of curious and intense as he stares at me through the dimly lit club, the sound dies on my lips.

The music plays on and yet, despite the brim of his baseball hat resting low on his forehead, my eyes are riveted to his. Words, apologies, excuses for how I acted the other day ghost through my mind and yet none form the proper words to express what I need to say.

Then again, why do I care? It's Hayes. The man I know from experience will breeze into town and then back out again without a single word.

Yet I do. And I despise that I do.

"Hayes! You made it, brother. Just like you to sneak in without telling a soul and make an appearance." Our connection breaks. One last narrowing of his brow before the etched lines of his face turn softer, smile spreading, eyes crinkling up, hand reaching out to shake my brother's. I watch the transformation in his body language as they fall back into a rhythm only they know. I'm left to wonder how he can seem so relaxed when the simple look from him has left my entire body a mess of frenzied adrenaline and unspecified emotions.

I push away the feelings I don't understand—chalk it up to the drinks I've had and the alcohol making me read into things that don't exist—and deal with the all-consuming presence of Hayes the only way I know how to: by ordering another drink. Hopefully the alcohol will help take the edge off my thoughts. The ones that are struggling over wanting to know what he thinks of me and not wanting to know what he thinks of me all at the same time.

And I hate that I'm sitting here wasting time wondering if he even thinks of me *at all. It shouldn't matter. He has moved so far beyond my orbit.* Yet every time I look up from whomever I'm speaking with my gaze finds its way to him.

I loathe it.

And even more confusing, why, when I look his way, is his focus on me?

I love it.

He seems completely unfazed that I've caught him staring. It unnerves me. Makes me self-conscious. And after a few times, awakens the defiance in me that has been dormant for what feels like forever. I meet him stare for stare. A lift of my eyebrows. A shrug of my shoulders. A *you have no idea who I am anymore or what I've been through, so don't you dare judge me.*

I hate that it makes me wonder if what the tabloids have said are actually true. Their countless reports over the past few months accusing him of cheating on his match-made-in-Hollywood girlfriend, Jenna Dixon. And in the typical Hayes you-push-me-too-hard-one-way-I'll-ignore-you fashion I grew up with, he has not once addressed the comments. No confirming. No denying. Not even a *no comment*. Nothing whatsoever.

I despise that I know this. That I've followed just enough about him that I know the gossip. Even worse, when I look up and meet his eyes again, is that I don't want it to be true. Because if it's true, then Hayes Whitley isn't the Hayes I used to know—Hollywood has changed him—and something about that makes my stomach churn.

My attempts to keep my distance from him fail. Word has gotten out to those in the club that the hometown star, Hayes Whitley, is here. Lucky for him, the club's bouncers have cordoned off our area to keep the onslaught of admirers from bombarding him and causing a riot in the club. The darkness and our exclusive spot in the VIP corner near a private entrance affording him some privacy from the ever-ready camera phones. Unlucky for me, it means I can't turn around without noticing him.

I just want to get out of here now.

But I don't make any effort to leave. For some reason my feet refuse to walk toward the exit. So I decide to ignore him. But after a short time I realize ignoring him is impossible because every little thing about him catches my attention. The strain of his shirt cuffs over his biceps as he lifts his bottle of beer to his lips. The distinct sound of his laugh hitting my ears. How, when he leans over to talk to Ryder who is sitting on a sofa, his pants hug the very nice curve of his ass. The clean scent of his shampoo that hasn't changed after all this time. His eyes constantly watching me in silent judgment.

He's everywhere when I want him to be nowhere.

Yet isn't that why I came tonight? I can tell myself till I'm blue in the face that I agreed to hang with Ryder and his friends because I feel guilty for blowing them off in the past, but I'd be lying to myself. And not a very good lie either.

As I meet Hayes's gaze yet again from across the small space, I know *he* is the reason I'm here tonight. The off-chance he would show up to see Ryder, his oldest friend, had me putting more effort into my appearance than I have in a while. Like going through my closet to find something that was non-bakery attire to wear, washing the frosting from my hair, and actually putting on more than my usual, lip gloss and mascara.

The fact that he has me questioning myself infuriates me. And the notion that I've spent so much of the past hour and a half thinking more about what Hayes sees when he looks at me than actually having a good time is the last straw.

Screw him. Screw his opinions and his thoughts and his judgmental eyes that are looking my way once again. He's the one who walked away. He's the one who gave up a good thing without a fight, and if he's going to keep staring at me, I'm going to show him just what he's missed out on.

I take another sip, well aware that my courage is in the form of liquid, but I don't care.

Pride is still pride.

My laugh becomes a tad louder. My hips sway to the beat a bit more. When I look his way the next time, his jaw pulses and his focus is more intense. My only acknowledgement is a smirk in return.

Another sip. A playful twirl out from another of Ryder's friends that leaves me pressed flat against his chest when I spin back into him. I'm breathless from the exertion and extremely buzzed so it might take me a bit longer to step away as our chests heave against one another's. Or I might just be well aware that Hayes has his very fine ass resting against the back of a stool a few feet to our right and his eyes haven't left me.

The night plays on. My concern over what Hayes thinks or doesn't think about me slowly fades with each drink I have, each person I chat up, and every laugh that falls from my lips.

Ryder senses something is going on. Notices this unspoken dance between Hayes and me and the invisible barrier of our shared history vibrating between us. My brother catches my eye a few times, asks if I'm okay, and I smile in return.

He told me I had to find my confidence again. Little did he know I'm choosing tonight to do just that.

I'm laughing at something trivial, attention focused on some antic of one of the guys when I feel a hand on the bare nape of my neck. I still, somehow knowing who the hand belongs to.

Heat. It's all I can feel. All my mind focuses on. From his skin touching mine. From the unexpected presence of his body behind me, his lips to my ear, his breath hitting my skin. From the sudden ache in the V of my thighs.

"I love the laughter much more than the temper." Hayes's comment is barely a murmur, and yet I can hear every single word despite the constant boom of the music.

I force a swallow down my throat and nod my head, needing to hold tight to my confidence, and hoping to keep solid ground beneath my feet, because being near him is making it off-kilter for some reason.

"Then maybe you shouldn't piss me off." I turn my head toward him, eyebrows raised, proud of myself for my comeback, until I realize he's so close we're breathing the same breath. I startle back—uncomfortable at his proximity and confused over the sudden awareness of everything about him. His cologne. His fingers still resting on my neck. The scent of mint and beer on his breath.

It has to be the alcohol. That has to be the explanation for my visceral and very carnal reaction to this man I shouldn't want to like. Ten years should have curbed this desire.

And yet it didn't.

His smile is quick and disarming. "Seems like pissing you off is something I know how to do all too well."

I snort. Can't think of anything else to do because between the brush of his body against mine and the alcohol swimming in my head, words fail me. All I want to do is hate him—validate the hurt I've harbored over the years—while at the same time sag back against him and just remember the feelings I once felt. Feelings he doesn't deserve.

Stupid alcohol. Stupid feelings.

My defiance remains, but it's much harder to stand by it when those chocolate-colored eyes are staring at me up close, and I know from memory that those little flecks in them are almost gold in color.

But I will resist you. Because you missed out, Hayes. You didn't want me.

Or how his lips, now slightly parted and only inches from mine, could kiss me senseless. And that was when he was a teenager. He's had years of practice now. I'm sure he's gotten even better at it with age.

I don't like you. You or your swoony eyes and perfect kisses.

Or what his body looks like. I'm tired. My feet hurt. I bet if I leaned against him his body would feel as muscular as it looks. Because I've never watched his movies. Ever. Never seen the sex scenes he acts in or the one where he walks bare-assed to the shower. Never rewound them to watch them again. Nope. Well, at least that's what I'd tell him.

I giggle as his eyes narrow at me. A slight smirk on those lips again when I don't want to think about them anymore.

He glances over to my brother and nods at something. I roll my eyes. Here we go again. They see each other for the first time in forever and without missing a beat, fall right back into their silent way of talking without words. Frustrating me because I know whatever they said is about me.

Just like they used to when we were kids.

But this time it can't be about me because I made Ryder swear to never talk to Hayes about me again. Not even mention my name. Because he's the reason I met Hayes. And Hayes is the one who hurt me. And so whatever Ryder just agreed to definitely has nothing to do with me.

"It's closing time, Ships."

"But they can't close because I'm not even drunk yet."

His laugh is loud and distinct, and I hate that it makes me smile.

"You're plenty drunk. C'mon. I'll drive you home."

"No." *I'm not going anywhere with you.*

And then his arm is around my shoulders. His biceps firm. His cologne sexy. Everything about him so much more potent than my drinks tonight.

I'm sure I just said no. Or did I just think it and not say it?

"Yes."

"I have a temper. Remember?"

That laugh again. "God, yes, I remember. It never scared me away before. I assure you it's not going to scare me now."

Six

Hayes

"ARE YOU SERIOUS?" SAYLOR LOOKS ME OVER WITH THOSE eyes of hers, wide with surprise, as the giggle falls from her mouth. At least this got a smile out of her, considering she's been pouting like a damn five-year-old the whole time in the car—hating me one minute, liking me the next. A continuous battle between glaring at me in silence and then laughing with me like old times. "What are we doing here?"

"I wanted to see if it was still here."

"Of course it is," she says as she walks on the dirt path with unsteady feet. The certainty in her voice makes me smile. She glances back at me, cheeks flushed from the alcohol and the brisk night air, and for a moment, I glimpse the girl I used to know. And it's funny that even though she's trying to be a hard ass, hold a grudge (which I deserve), the real Saylor still peeks through. "Did you think my parents tore it down just because we grew up?"

Her voice breaks on the last words, and I feel like such a callous asshole. Bringing her here on a whim. Not being considerate.

"I wasn't sure what happened to it," I murmur quietly, suddenly

50

uncomfortable with what to say as we reach the bottom of the tree house just at the edge of her parents' property. I look toward their old house up the hill and to the left of us.

All the lights are off.

"I'm sorry, Saylor. I wasn't thinking. I shouldn't have brought you here."

She looks to me, her smile bittersweet. "It's a good place. Good memories. Ryder lives here now so it doesn't make me sad anymore." She stares up to the house for a moment. Nods her head as if she's trying to accept her own words.

"I wanted to call you when I found out, to come to the service, but I was on location in Indonesia . . ." My words fade off. The excuse sounds lame. *She had just lost both parents—her whole damn world—and I couldn't make the time to be there?*

". . . And I didn't know what to say to you." *Just like I don't now.*

"It's okay. Really." She sniffles softly and reaches out to squeeze my forearm as if I'm the one who needs comforting. "There's not much you could have said anyway."

"I could have been there for you."

The look she gives me—ice mixed in a sea of pain—stops me from saying anything more. Because she's right. I had no right to offer comfort to her, and yet a part of me hates knowing I never tried.

"I haven't been up there in years," she says as she breaks our stare and looks up at the tree house above and then back to me. I can tell she's desperately trying to change the topic. Can see her push the sadness from her eyes and replace it with the mischief I used to love seeing there, giving me a glimpse of the strong girl I know is hiding somewhere beneath.

I ask myself again what in the hell I'm doing here. With her. In the middle of the night. Wonder what possessed me to stop by here on a trip down memory lane when I'm supposed to be driving her home. Dropping her off. Then giving Tessa a call back.

"C'mon," she part whispers, part giggles and while it sounds forced, it's much better than the look in her eyes, so I let the topic go. Use the moment to allow her to shift her mental arrow on the do-I-like-Hayes scale from hate over to like. And before I can stop her, her high-heeled feet are making their way up the slat-board steps. She looks back at me and gives me a full-fledged smile—heavy topic overshadowed by nostalgia—and fuck if it doesn't make me think thoughts about that wild child of a girl, who owned my heart.

I'm not gonna lie and say I don't enjoy the view of her ass as she climbs her way up. Shit, she's been shaking it all night for everyone except me, and I have a feeling even to spite me. It's about damn time I get a chance to admire it without others watching my every move. And without others watching *her* every move.

So I stare for no other reason than because Saylor always did have a mighty fine ass. Way back when and most definitely now. It'd be a shame not to appreciate it. In tight black pants that cling perfectly to her curves as she makes her way, rung by rung, in shoes that have no business climbing up a tree, but fuck does it not add to the appeal.

I work my way up the rungs behind her, telling myself I'm just following her because she's a tad drunk and it's my obligation to make sure after all this time the old structure is safe. It has nothing to do with the fact that when I'm near her, especially in this backyard where we spent hours upon hours together, that I would follow her anywhere.

So now I'm climbing up a rickety ladder to chase memories down at two o'clock in the morning with my first love. I *should* be steering clear of everything I feel when I look at her: complicated, nostalgic, curious, turned-on, amused.

There's the familiar creak of the door opening and then Saylor disappears into the darkness. When I boost myself up into the area a few seconds later, she's on that very fine ass of hers with her back leaning against the trunk of the tree that serves as the center of the structure.

And I swear, when I see her sitting there looking around at the faded paint on the walls with a goofy grin—like she's so proud she made it up the ladder with her shoes on—I feel like I've been transported back to our youth. To those stolen kisses and innocent hopes. To sneaking out on summer nights and having sex down by the lake in the bed of my truck.

And I wonder for the second time, what in the hell I'm doing here. How is Saylor sitting across from me with her wild eyes and a few leaves stuck in her hair that she doesn't care are there and a flush on her cheeks? How this girl—definitely now a woman—who used to be my world, is making me question everything in my current life: the people, their sincerity, the chaos.

The answer's simple: I owed Ryder big time.

But hell if I expected to show up to help Saylor, only to get that knocked in the gut feeling the minute I saw her in her bakery. Thinking your old flame will still look the same with her straight lines and tomboy demeanor, then seeing her . . . Curves, filled out, and sexy as sin was something I definitely didn't expect.

"What's your problem?" And her eyes are back on me, grin replaced by a sneer, as her question pulls me from thoughts I shouldn't even be thinking. Brings me back to the present. To the lines I should be memorizing back in the hotel, and the shit I've got to do to help my mom tomorrow. To the life I have to get back to. But when I look at Saylor, all I think about is the here and now. *And her.*

"Who said I had a problem?"

She narrows her eyes, glaring at me through the moonlit space, and I wonder how long it's going to take to make her not angry with me. She started off spitting fire at the bakery the other day to being completely apologetic and then to tonight . . . to I don't know what she was trying to do. But the one thing I do know is Saylor doesn't do something unless it has a purpose.

Question is, what exactly was that purpose? Regardless, it's going to make repaying this favor to Ryder ten times harder if I can't win her over sooner than later.

"If you're curious about something, just ask, Hayes. Sitting and staring at someone is not polite. Or cool."

Ah. There's a glimpse of that fire and brimstone temper.

"I wasn't staring at you."

"Liar." She snorts. "You kept staring at me in the club and you're staring at me now. Most people would find it rather creepy."

I laugh. Can't resist as she rolls her eyes and crosses her arms across her chest. A chest that now is pushed up by the motion, and luckily it's dark enough that my wandering gaze of her cleavage isn't noticed. "Creepy. I'll remember that."

"You should. You do creepy well. Maybe it will help you get a part someday."

"Perhaps. And I'll owe it all to you. I'll even give you credit in my Academy acceptance speech."

"I'll be watching for it. But, uh, if you weren't staring, then what were you doing?"

Our eyes hold across the space while I debate the answer to give. I know I can bullshit her, which is probably expected, but for some reason, I don't want to. Maybe it's guilt over the past; maybe it's the sense that I owe her some honesty. "I was trying to see how much of the girl I once knew is still there."

Her head shakes subtly as if she's uncertain she likes my honesty. It takes her a second to respond. Both of us treading carefully through the unresolved issues between us. "None of her."

"I disagree. I see a lot of her." *And then some.*

She purses her lips. Hugs her arms tighter around herself. That temper I know all too well starting to fire. Good. The teenager I was feared that hellcat side of her. The grown man I am kind of likes it. Knowing she can handle her own is definitely a plus.

"Why do you care?" Her question throws me. The defensive tone even more so.

"Not sure. Maybe being with you makes me feel like my old self. Reminds me of who I used to be before I . . ." I shrug as my words trail off with the realization that I just stepped on a land mine of sorts: acknowledging my life before means having to acknowledge how I left and never looked back. It was when my life was so much simpler without the constant pressure of the paparazzi and fans. When I could get a pizza without cameras flashing or date a woman I knew really liked me for me. When there were no rumors about cheating I had to ignore because I was being the good guy and taking the fall to protect my future.

"Before you walked out and left me confused and heartbroken

without saying a word? *You mean that before?*" Her voice rises in pitch with each word. Hurt flashes in her gaze, clear as day through the moonlit night.

I did that to her.

And I fucking hate the sight of it. Maybe that's because I was too much of a pussy to face it. Then again maybe it was because I took that once-in-a-lifetime shot I was given and ran with it, made a killer life for myself, and if I came back, one look at her might have sucked me back in.

I was right. There's no denying the tug on my heart seeing her again. The reemergence of feelings I thought had died.

Shit. I was young and inexperienced back then. Let the allure of Hollywood rule my thoughts and own my heart.

It still owns my heart. The thing is, I'm not young or inexperienced anymore. Could the man I am now handle both her and Hollywood?

Jesus Christ, Whitley. What are you even thinking? Do you not see the hurt in her eyes? The defense in her posture? You're the one who put it there.

Guilt returns with a vengeance. The least I can do is give her an honest answer. "*Exactly.* That before." My tone is even; my gaze unwavering.

"Huh."

"Huh?" *How am I supposed to take that response?*

"Yeah. *Huh.*"

"Do you care to elaborate?" My chuckle is strained as I try to figure what she means with the sound. Hell, more like as I try to figure her out.

"Nah. Just trying to gauge how big your ego is to think I'd want to see you ever again."

"It's obviously not too big, since I fit in the door to the tree house." She fights a smile but fails so she looks back to the stars in the sky rather than show me I've gotten to her. Cracked that tough-girl façade with the help of her ability to suck down the drinks tonight.

"You're an asshole, you know that?"

"See. It's that right there. That's why you being the old you is what I need. You're not afraid to call me out. Everyone else just wants to kiss my ass."

"I've got a bunch more names I can call you if you want me to keep going."

"You always were creative." Her eyes flicker to mine and then down to where her fingers are peeling some paint on the floor beside her.

"A treasure trove of names, in fact."

She completely ignores my comment so I adjust my tactics. "Lay them on me, drunk girl."

"I am not drunk." Her eyes meet mine, lips pouting, with a crease in her forehead. "Can't a girl go out and have a good time without getting shit for it?"

She snorts again and it's fucking adorable. I bite my lip to keep from smiling because right now, I don't think she wants to be anything close to adorable. She wants to stand her ground and prove to me she doesn't want anything to do with me. But it's damn hard not to react when she follows the snort by rubbing the back of her hand over her nose.

Because right now she looks like the pesky Saylor—Ryder's little sister who used to annoy us when we were playing video games. The whiny voice and skinned knees. The roll of her eyes when I called her Ships Ahoy to annoy her. All that's missing is the row of freckles across the bridge of her nose.

I stare at her. The memories clear as day. Ryder and I running and her chasing. The two of us tricking her and then sometimes letting her hang with us. Because sometimes she was cool. *For a girl.*

"You're looking at me like that again," she warns.

"You haven't changed, have you? Still bossy." I'm baiting her. Figure if I get that temper going, she'll yell at me, and I can figure out what the hell she was trying to do tonight in the club. The extra swing to her hips and the added taunt in her smile wasn't for nothing.

"Neither have you. Still causing trouble everywhere you go. I figured Hollywood would've tamed that side of you, and yet the National

Enquirer seems to love you these days."

I take her dig for what it is. Understand she's trying to hurt me any little way she can. Shit, she has every right to. My ego likes knowing she's followed me. My pride hates that she's noticed the bad press that's always blown way the fuck out of proportion.

I bite the rebuke on my tongue. Fight the want for her to know I'm not that guy and confess the truth behind the bullshit rumors. And yet, I can't. I may be having a good time, trying to help her out, and yet she's a part of my past, and the rumors are trying to protect my present.

"Don't always believe what you read about me."

"No worries. I don't ever read anything about you." A hint of hurt. A trace of spite.

"I deserve that." *She's lying.* The finger twirling in the hair at her neck tells me so. I fight a smile at seeing the simple tell she still has.

"No, you don't deserve shit from me." *And here comes the temper.*

"Good thing I don't want anything from you then." Why does it feel like I'm the one telling a lie now?

"Then why are you here, Hayes? Why? Not the 'in town for the funeral' part but rather I'm talking about tonight. Why come to the club and more so, why are we here right now? If you want nothing from me, then why'd you bring me to the tree house?"

What the fuck am I supposed to say to that when I don't know the answer myself?

"I was at the club because Ryder invited me, and I wanted to catch up. I didn't expect you to be there. Thought you'd be out with your fiancé. What's his name? Mitch something-or-other?" *Layton.* I know the last name all right. Remember him to be a pompous prick when I played baseball against him in high school.

But let's see if she takes the bait. Finishes the question. Gives me an in to open the door and start the conversation we need to have.

"Mmm." That's all she says in response.

I study her reaction. Notice the purse of her lips. The hair wrapped around her finger again. The sudden shifting of her legs as she fidgets.

I could press her right now. Push those buttons of hers. But there's something beneath the surface I can't quite peg. So instead, I opt to finish answering her question. Try to gain her trust so she stops hating me.

"And we're here . . . we're here because it's kind of fitting. After the other day at the bakery and then tonight at the club, I don't know . . . I needed to apologize to you. Explain why I . . ." I blow out a sigh and run my fingers through my hair unsure myself what I'm going to say. "This was where we always came when we needed to talk."

"It's in the past," she whispers, eyes angled back up to the sky but the contempt in her voice has been replaced by guarded hurt.

It's not in the past. Not for her. And that's the bitch of it, isn't it? Knowing someone so well for so long, even though time's passed, you still know them. Can read their body language and infer from their tone so you can't escape the fallout of your actions.

"You don't owe me anything. No apology. No anything. It wouldn't matter if you gave me one anyway," she replies as she lowers her face from the sky so she can meet my eyes. The defiance I see in them wars against my guilty conscience. "It's a whole lot too late."

I nod my head in understanding. The split-second decision I had to make back then seemed so simple, but now owns my thoughts as I look at Saylor in the moonlight across this old tree house.

"Saylor." Her name is part sigh, part apology on my part.

"Just don't. Save it." She shifts abruptly, effectively ending the topic by scooting to the floor and lying on her back.

Anything to avoid meeting my eyes.

She's not going to make this easy on me, is she?

I stare at her. Hair fanned on the floor and eyes toward the sky, irritated as fuck with me, and I'm reminded of that night when things first started between us.

What did I expect when I brought her here? That the memories were going to soften her and *not* affect me?

I should just take her home. Pick up the phone and call Ryder to apologize that I can't return the favor this time around. Lie that the studio has called, needs me back to reshoot a few scenes before moving to the next location. Get the fuck out of here before shit gets complicated. Because looking at her, being reminded of *before*, is stirring up way more than I expected. Shit I don't need in my already complicated life. Something I definitely can't start without walking away and repeating history with her I don't want to repeat. Can't repeat.

I'm not that much of an asshole.

Goddamn memories, man. They're fucking with my head.

So I sigh and do the only thing I can do—try to make this right. I shift onto my knees, cross the space between us, and unfold my legs until I'm lying beside her, just like I did that night. Her body stills and her breath hitches as our arms touch, but she doesn't pull away.

We lie there for some time staring at the stars that light up the night sky despite the full moon. Crickets chirp around us but there's not a word spoken between us.

Seconds turn to minutes. Her perfume hits my nose. Our history owns my thoughts. My mind veers to shit I shouldn't be thinking. *Hands off, Whitley.* Much easier said than done when I'm lying in the dark with a gorgeous woman.

And she is just that, *gorgeous*. And all woman. Yet, despite the years that have passed, this feels normal. The being here with her. The feeling that she still knows me better than anyone else when that can't be possible.

She did back then though. She could finish my sentences. Had loved me unconditionally. Had encouraged me to chase my dreams despite my doubts.

Until I allowed my dreams to consume me. Rip us apart. Leave her.

Leave us.

"Look!" She saves me from my thoughts when she points to a shooting star as it streaks across the sky.

"Make a wish," we both say in unison and laugh. A throwback to another night, another time, and I feel her body tense the minute she says it. As if she realizes she accidentally let her guard down, but the small moment is enough to break up the tension filling the space around us. Giving me an in.

"I made mine," she whispers after a few seconds and has me immediately wondering what her wish was. Ten years ago I would have known the answer without question. But not now. Not with the grown woman, so very different but all the same, beside me.

"Me too," I finally say but know my dreams have already come true—I'm a lucky son of a bitch—so I throw my extra wish her way. Use the lapse in her guard to my advantage. "See that constellation? The one right there?" I point to the sky, to a trio of stars that I make my own pattern out of.

"Like you really know astronomy," she scoffs, remembering how much it bored me when we were in school.

"No seriously. I do. I had to learn it for a role I played."

"Is that so?" The exasperated tone is back in her voice and I'm glad to hear it. Annoyed I can deal with much better than sadness. "If that's the case, then what is that one right there?" I follow her finger as she points to what looks like someone shook a salt shaker filled with glitter to the sky . . . little flecks of bright lights everywhere.

I smile wide knowing exactly what I need to do. I lift my finger and point. "That right there is the constellation named 'I'm Sorry.'"

Her sigh fills the tree house. "Oh, please."

"No. Wait. I get the one named 'I Was a Dick' confused with the one 'I'm Sorry' so give me a minute. Nope. I'm right. That's definitely, 'I'm Sorry.'"

"That's very convenient."

"First rule of acting is learning how to improvise." Her laugh fills the night and I might have gotten my foot in the door.

"Seems you've got that down pat."

"I mean it, Saylor. I'm sorry." The explanations I had worked out in my head die on my lips because they'd just sound like bullshit excuses. I can see that now, so I leave it at that. I hope she hears the apology and knows how much I mean it.

But she doesn't say anything for a while. Just stares quietly at the stars while I try and figure out what to do next. In reality, I'm perfectly comfortable on this hard wooden floor with my legs folded like a pretzel so I can fit in this small space beside her.

"Mitch's last name is Layton." Saylor's sudden comment surprises me.

"I think I remember him." *How could I not?* The popped collar, egotistical, trust fund baby. Even in high school he thought he was better than everyone else. I can't imagine how he is now. I tread carefully. "How's he doing?" Feign interest. Pretend I care.

She laughs but the sound isn't lighthearted. "He's getting married." I hesitate in response because I haven't thought this through far enough ahead, and I'm not sure if I should play that I know this yet or act like I don't. "*And not to me.*"

"Oh." My response is as much shock that she's just confessed, as it is an act. And I decide to keep quiet. To let her take this conversation where she wants to ease my guilt over lying to her once again.

"Yep." Her laugh holds no humor at all. "I just couldn't do it. Couldn't marry him. Over six years, Hayes. Six years down the fricking drain and all because I looked at him and . . . I don't know."

"You looked at him and what?" I can't help it. I have to ask. Have to pry. Have to find out why it sounds like she still loves the prick when she's the one who broke things off.

That much I do know from Ryder. He had sounded proud as hell of Say when he told me she dumped the sorry ass.

She turns her head to face me, the heat of her breath hitting the side of my cheek as I keep my eyes trained on the sky, because fuck if I trust myself right now to not take advantage of a situation I shouldn't even be in.

"I looked at him and realized he didn't make me feel how yo . . . Nothing. Never mind. It just wasn't right." She laughs again. Nerves tinge the edges. "Can you believe he had the audacity to invite me to the wedding? To *my* wedding?"

"Your wedding?" She can't be that drunk she's mixing things up, can she?

"*Yep.* My wedding. All my planning. All the stupid hours I spent perfecting every detail. All he did was change the date and the bride. *Who does that?*"

"Wait a minute. They're copying your plans?"

"Yep. From what I can tell it seems so. Same paradise location. Same ceremony time. Even the damn invitations. What kind of woman gets married to a man and keeps all of the ex's wedding plans? Well, good thing she has the same initial in her first name so they could save all the monogrammed crap his mom bought."

I laugh. Can't help it. Ryder never told me this part of the story. "Maybe his mother talked her into it."

She snorts again. "*Uptight Ursula.*"

I laugh. She sounds like the freckled face girl from before. "That's her name?"

"No. But that's what I call her. And you're probably right about her talking the new girlfriend into it. She was such a controlling bitch. And to think she was going to be my mother-in-law."

I feel her shiver beside me in mock disgust. Maybe she doesn't still love him.

"Do they actually think you're going to hop on a plane and show up?" *Shit.* Let's hope she's had enough to drink that she doesn't realize I knew she'd have to fly to get there.

"That's the thing—Whoa!" she says as she sits up quickly and then puts her hand down on my upper thigh to steady herself.

"You okay?" I ask as she giggles.

"I haven't gone out drinking like this in quite a while, wow . . . this feels funny." She sounds embarrassed.

I clear my throat. Try to concentrate on the conversation instead of her hand on my thigh where her fingers are dangerously close to my dick. Focus on anything but that.

"You okay?"

She looks down at me: lips parted, eyes wide, and fuck if the look on her face—innocent, complicated, pure Saylor—doesn't make me think of the pressure of her fingers again. "Yeah." She swallows and nods. "I'm fine. Just caught me off guard."

"Okay." I shift up. Figure that's the best way to get her hand off my thigh. Try to be the good guy here. And the minute I move, she immediately jerks her hand back as if she didn't realize it was there. Good thing her hand's not on my thigh now. Bad thing? Bad thing is her lips are inches from mine.

I smell her perfume. See the moonlight in her hair. Hear her draw in a breath. And hell if I don't need a distraction from stepping over a line I can't cross.

The sway of her ass tonight at the club.

The sound of her laugh as she climbed the steps up here.

The way she went from fiery to cute in a goddamn second.

Step back, Whitley. Way the fuck back.

"You were saying something about being invited, Saylor?" *Distraction.* Get the conversation back on track. And my thoughts off of her lips.

"Uh. Yeah." She shakes her head as if to clear the moment we just had and reaches forward to pick up nothing in particular to have a reason to shift away from me. "Ryder's lost his mind."

"And that's something new?"

I get the smile I was working for but this time it's more shy than confident. She plucks at the legs of her pants with her fingers. I wait.

"We both agree that Mitch sent the invitation as a kind of fuck you to me, but Ryder thinks I should play him at his own game. That I should accept the invitation and show up at the wedding. He believes the Laytons are badmouthing the bakery and that's why it's not doing too well. That they have enough pull with the people in this town, so now I'm like a pariah or something. I don't know." She shrugs and chews the inside of her cheek as she pauses for a moment. I can tell she's hurt by the possibility that her brother's assumption is true. The girl without a mean bone in her body. "He thinks if I were to stride into the wedding I walked away from and exude absolute confidence, like I knew for a fact that I had made the best decision ever by not marrying Mitch, it wouldn't go unnoticed. In fact, he thinks that since it's likely most of the guests have been told horrible things about me, seeing me so unaffected would make them curious. They'd wonder what I know about Mitch that they don't, and curiosity might lead them to check out the bakery and—"

"And curious people will come to the store and possibly generate business."

She looks at me, surprised I've come to the same conclusion as Ryder, and I cringe inwardly in case I've revealed too much.

"So you think he's right?"

"I think there's some merit to it," I muse.

"Why?"

I think of Jenna. Of the burden I'm bearing to play a similar game all for image's sake. And know if I am doing it for her, and how it could affect my career, I sure as shit will help Saylor if she asks. Now I just need to convince her of that.

"Because I see it every day. Take an actress who breaks up with an A-Lister. There are rumors as to why but no one knows the truth and neither of them comment publicly about their split. All of a sudden, the press wants nothing to do with her. She's overlooked for parts. Not invited to any parties. She might even be snubbed by their friends if they run in the same circles because it sucks, but people don't want to piss off the one who has the most power in the relationship."

"Because that's fair. Sheesh."

"Yeah, but she gets the last laugh. She somehow gets her foot in the door somewhere. Shows up looking ten times better than she did before with some star or director or mogul more powerful than her ex on her arm, and it's amazing how suddenly the people who wanted nothing to do with her are now knocking down her door to be her best friend."

"Shallow assholes," she mutters, and I'm pretty sure she's ticking off names in her head of who that criticism matches.

"Very. But that's life."

"In your Hollywood bubble, maybe. Not mine," she grumbles as if she's seeing this through different eyes for the first time and is begrudgingly accepting it.

"Not my bubble at all." I laugh with a shake of my head, needing her to know I'm not like that in the least. She glares at me and I'm not sure why. Is she putting two and two together?

"So what? I'm just supposed to fly there and show up at the wedding? Twiddle my thumbs while acting confidently, and then that's all it will take? The tide will turn?"

"No."

"No? Ah yes, I forgot. In order to appear self-assured, I apparently need to have a big, powerful, strapping man at my side because that's the only way a woman can be confident, right?" Bitterness.

Can't say I blame her.

"Not in my eyes, but in theirs? Possibly." My comment settles between us. She rolls her shoulders. Her only physical tell of how pissed she is over this.

"So what? I'm just supposed to say, 'Hey Hayes, wanna ditch your filming schedule and glamorous life and go on a ridiculous trip with me to my wedding that's no longer my wedding?'" I hate the part of me that loves I'm the one she thinks of when she needs a man to accompany her. "Like you'd really fly to some island with me, so we can show my ex-fiancé and his family and uptight friends that I'm better off without him, because I'm "fake" dating you instead. A man who is so much bigger and better and more successful and handsome than he is? Like that's going to happen."

"Why wouldn't it?" That stops her rant. Knocks the sarcasm from her last sentence.

Her head whips up and her eyes meet mine. Hand stops halfway to her hair as a disbelieving laugh falls from her mouth. "You'd actually go?"

I shrug. "Yeah. Why not? I could use a little R&R with someone I know and who doesn't expect anything from me." Something flashes in her eyes that I can't read. "Besides, now that I remember him, Mitch always was an asshole in high school, I'd get some sick satisfaction from showing that fucker what he was missing out on by not being with you."

"The irony," she whispers and the two words hit me in the gut. The pang of regret not far behind it.

"Saylor—"

"No. Never mind. That was a cheap shot." She says the words but the truth of them linger in her eyes. She reaches out and puts her hand on top of mine. "Thank you. The offer is sweet. The intent behind it even more so. But even if I wanted to, I'd never be able to pull it off."

"Did you forget what I do for a living?" My laugh rings louder than it should. The Oscar on my shelf at home flashes in my mind as my need to convince her suddenly grows stronger than when Ryder first called. Greater than when I saw her earlier tonight. "I assure you we could pull it off."

"We should leave." She shifts to her knees suddenly and moves toward the door. I hate the hurt in her tone. Hate knowing that the fucker Mitch isn't the only one who put it there.

I did, too.

"Saylor."

"No. I'm tired. I need to get home."

"Okay. Let me go down first in case you need help."

She levels me with a glare for implying she can't do it herself but I move past her, bodies brushing against one another, and take the lead anyway.

My feet are through the doorway when I look back at her. "For what it's worth, Say, I think you should go. And I'd drop whatever to be there for you. It's the least I could do."

She doesn't say a word to me, just nods as I lower myself out of her sight and down the rungs.

I'm on the ground in a few seconds, a very quiet Saylor not far behind me as I wait at the bottom. When she's on the second step from the ground, her heel slips. Just as I step forward and reach out to her hips to help her, she spins around.

Our bodies are pressed against each other with her hands flat against my chest. Her expression is startled, but her eyes remain on mine. Her breath an audible hitch.

And fuck if standing like this with her doesn't make me want to lean in and kiss her. It all comes back: her taste, that little sound she used to make in the back of her throat, the scar on the back of her head from falling off the brick wall that I'd feel when grabbing the back of it to direct the angle of our kiss. All of it.

And it's a temptation like I haven't felt in forever.

"Hayes."

"Yeah?" My gaze flickers from hers down to her lips and then back up. I want to know what her eyes are telling me.

"Nothing. Never mind." She shakes her head and steps back.

I clench my jaw. Fist my hands. Tell myself to let her walk away. To not notice the freckles on her nose are still there. The ones I used to tease her about as a kid, then later, loved staring at when she fell asleep in the bed of my truck at the drive-in when we were teenagers.

The thought triggers so many more things I used to love about her. Reminds me how close we were. How many parts of our lives were woven so tightly it was like we were one.

My God. I know we were young. Know that I did the right thing in chasing my dreams since she was only seventeen and I was nineteen. But how selfish was I to leave without an explanation or a goodbye?

Ass. Hole. *Yep. You sure as hell were one, Whitley.*

And for that I deserve her understandable caution, every bit of her wrath, and every ounce of her hatred.

I start behind her down the worn path toward the car. Use the sight of her hips swaying to distract me from the memories rushing back.

My mind still runs but turns instead to how this was supposed to be easy. How I was going to come back, convince her to go to the wedding, and do my part to help her show up Mitch. Debt repaid just in time to walk away. *Again.*

And yet one look at Saylor the other day and I knew it was going to be far from easy. That combination of the fresh-faced girl-next-door I left mixed with the hurt and feistiness I see now, and I can't help but wonder *what if.* What if I hadn't left? And how did my leaving change her life's path somehow?

Fuck that, Whitley. You did what you had to do. Took advantage of a once-in-a-lifetime opportunity that definitely panned out.

But watching her ahead of me with the hurt in her eyes fresh in my mind, I know this is going to be harder than I expected.

Good thing she rejected the offer.

I have a plan. I have my world. My perfect, chaotic, surreal, fucking awesome world and there's no room for error. She fits nowhere in it. That's what I told myself when I left. That's what I'm standing by now.

I'm just here to repay a debt to Ryder.

Just here to ease the guilt over what I did to her.

So why am I already thinking about the next time I can see her again?

Seven

Saylor

I WANTED HIM TO KISS ME.

That's my first thought when I wake up. How standing beneath the tree house with his hands on my hips and the moonlight in his hair in the field we used to play in as kids, I wanted him to kiss me. Lean in and take over. Wash away any of the doubt about why I walked away from Mitch. Rationalize why seeing him again makes me want in ways I shouldn't want.

And then I move. My head pounds. My mouth's dry. My hair is matted. And I'm still in last night's clothes.

I want to die. Like *throw my head in the toilet, and puke my brains out to make this roiling in my stomach, spinning of my head, and hot flash over my skin* type of sick go away.

But I can't. I think my body wants to punish me for being such an idiot last night. For thinking if I swung my hips enough or flirted with Ryder's friends more, that it would make Hayes realize what he lost.

A foolish, amateur bullshit move. Like he hasn't seen that one before from one of the million women who would do just about anything to be a notch on his belt.

And the joke's on me as I lie in bed while the rest of the night—or what I remember of it—replays through my mind. How right now I probably couldn't even dry heave if I tried so I can feel better, and yet last night I was able to word vomit every little detail about Mitch to Hayes. How I walked away from a perfectly good relationship and every little girl's dream wedding. How Mitch invited me to watch him marry his *successful*, no doubt *more-suited* match. How I blamed Ryder for taking my RSVP response, twisting it every which way, and then planting the notion that I should attend because my presence might help the shop. All of it, right down to when he asked why I left.

I looked at Mitch and realized he didn't make me feel how you had, Hayes.

The thought ghosts through my mind and I bolt up in bed. And then I hate myself when the room spins. But even worse is I can't remember if I finished the thought aloud last night or if I had enough wherewithal to stop myself.

Shit. Shit. Double shit.

The refrain is constant until I remember that I didn't finish the sentence. That I caught myself before making the monster of all mistakes.

Because that's not why I didn't marry Mitch. There was no comparison to Hayes then. Or Hayes now.

And yet as I lie back down to try and combat the drum beating against my temples, I can't help but recall my first thought this morning: *I wanted him to kiss me.*

Was that why I walked away from Mitch? Did I subconsciously compare the way both of them made me feel and after seeing Hayes last night—after being reminded of that pulse-pounding, lower-belly ache that he made me feel with just a look my way—is that how I knew?

It's nonsense. Utter bullshit. There's no part of Hayes that belongs in my life.

Not his brown eyes or thick lashes.

It had to be the alcohol that made me think that.

Not his Hollywood life and glamorous parties.

It was the tree house. A step back in time to when the only things we knew about life was that it was simple and our lives revolved around each other.

Not his offer to help me now when he walked away before.

It was nostalgia. Déjà vu. Just a moment in time. A stupid thought that I'm better off forgetting.

Not the way he looked at me as he walked me to the door, made sure I got inside safely, before just staring at me. Eyes so damn intense with that muscle pulsing in his jaw that made me want to reach up and run my hand over it.

Stop it, Saylor. He was just being nice. Just offering to help you out because you ran your mouth about being invited to the wedding. He probably felt bad so he said he'd go with you.

Like *travel to an exotic island just to help you out because he's a nice guy* type of feel bad.

But there's no way in hell I'm going to Mitch's wedding. I'm not desperate. I have nothing to prove and if I did, the last people I'd need to prove it to would be the Laytons and all their insipid, shallow guests.

Nope. I'm perfectly fine with my decision to walk away. And to tell Hayes thank you, but no thank you. Decision made.

Besides, it's not like I'm ever going to see him again anyway.

"Thank you. Have a great day." I watch sweet Mrs. McMann make her way out the door of the shop.

"The edges of this batch are a bit burned but definitely better since the repair," DeeDee says as she walks out from the back, wiping her hands on her apron.

I sigh and silently thank the universe for letting the oven make it one more day, and not ruin another batch of cupcakes. "Thank God. Fingers crossed this repair holds us over because having to buy a new oven isn't an option." I cringe with the knowledge of how much a new one costs.

"For now, it's holding its own—" The bells on the bakery door interrupt DeeDee, and her face transforms into a wide, goofy grin. I know immediately who is going to be there when I look over my shoulder.

And I won't lie that my stomach flips at the simple thought.

So I turn around. A straight punch of lust mixed with surprise registers in a flash of a second when I take in the dark brown eyes, lazy smile, board shorts, and tank top showing off biceps that I have to drag my eyes away from.

And just like the other two times I've seen him in the last week, my body's visceral reaction to him wars against my innate ability to make a complete fool of myself in front of him. How did this man, who used to know every single thing about me, who was part of almost every childhood memory I have, now cause me to feel tongue-tied and out of sorts?

Because I'm a dork. That's my only thought when his eyes light up the minute they meet mine. *Thud.* My heart shouldn't feel like it was jump-started and yet it does.

"Hey. I didn't expect to see you here." I try to appear indifferent, and I'm proud I don't sound like the high-pitched hyena I'm sure most women sound like around him.

"Yeah, well, I would have stopped by sooner but I was busy helping my mom sort through some of my great-uncle's things."

He hooks his sunglasses into the front of his shirt while I tuck both my hands in the back pockets of my jeans and rock on my heels. I fumble with words and how to string them together because the way he's staring at me makes it hard to do anything other than stand there.

Did he always stare at me like this or is it just now?

"I, uh, wanted to thank you for making sure I got home okay the other night. I was in rare form." I shrug. Heat warms my cheeks. "And I apologize for anything stupid I might possibly have said."

He chuckles as he steps up to the counter between us. "Stupid, no. Cute, yes."

I take a deep breath and glance down before looking back up to him. "I wasn't so cute when I woke up the next morning with my head pounding."

"I bet not, but sometimes you've just got to tie a few on to relax. No shame in that."

"So what can I do for you?" Curiosity owns me.

"I'm hitting the road. Gotta get back since the production schedule rolls on. It's the last two weeks of shooting." I hate that a little part of me deflates at his words. Dislike the fact that, as much as he unnerves me in every way imaginable when I don't want him to, I want him to stay one more day. I want to see him one more time.

Because I know when he walks out the door, I most likely won't see him for another ten years.

"*Oh.*"

"But I wanted to pick up some cupcakes to take back to my assistant. She has quite the sweet tooth and deserves something for putting up with my crap." He shrugs, his smile sheepish, and I'm immediately irritated at her. "And I wanted to talk to you again."

My irritation wanes as my smile widens. "About what?" His eyes flicker over to where DeeDee is making herself busy in the refrigerated case behind me. I know he's going to bring up Mitch, the wedding, and his offer to take me. Besides the fact that it's a complete non-issue, it's just more information I don't want DeeDee to know.

There's enough gossip about me in this town as it is.

"It's okay," I say, trying to deflect. "It's not even worth talking about."

"You're frustrating." He steps forward, smile tight, and eyes glancing over my shoulder to DeeDee again. "What's the big deal? If you don't go, you'll always wonder what if, and if you do go, you'll know the answer."

"I don't need to know the answer. Things are fine just how they are."

He raises his eyebrows and gives me a look that tells me he's been talking with Ryder and knows how much I'm struggling to make the business work. "C'mon, Say, I've already looked at my schedule and I can swing the free time."

My eyes narrow. "How did you know the date?"

"I asked Ryder." He shrugs but his eyes hold no apology.

"You're arrogant to assume I'd say yes. I don't care what people think about me. Never have. Never will."

"If there's one thing I do remember, it's definitely that." His smile turns soft. Eyes unrelenting. "I always loved that about you."

His comment strikes a very unwelcome chord. *Loved. Loved about me. Past tense, Saylor. Past tense.* Regardless, memories flash through my mind. The times I'd run wild and carefree and he'd just sit back and shake his head with that little smirk and let me do whatever it was I was doing without saying a word. No roll of his eyes. No flush of embarrassment. Just complete acceptance.

Be everything Mitch wouldn't let you be.

Funny thing is, Hayes let me be me.

"Yeah, well . . . some things never change." I shrug, a bit uncomfortable with the praise and needing to change the course of the conversation. "What kind of cupcakes can I get you?"

He doesn't speak for a minute, lips pursed, eyes questioning me without uttering a word, but I get the sense he wants to say more but is holding back. His gaze flickers to the case and then back to mine. "Just a dozen of whatever is your favorite."

"I'll get them," DeeDee says as she steps up to the display case with a pink and white striped box in her hand.

"Okay. Thanks." I'm a bit startled because I wanted something to do to busy my hands and now I'm stuck looking at Hayes.

He smiles. "One of these days, Saylor, you and I are going to sit down and have a proper conversation where I can explain what happened. Why I left. And then you can decide whether you want to accept my apology or not. It will make life so much easier on you to have a reason, because this *one minute you're pissed at me, the next minute you're smiling* dance you keep doing has to be exhausting."

And just like that he's flipped the switch to my anger. "Like I said, you're an arrogant ass."

"Perhaps. But even so, I'd rather you know the why behind—"

"It's been ten years, Hayes. Explanations don't really matter anymore." My fingers twist together. My feet shift again. The topic in general unnerves me.

"Reasons always matter. *Always*," he says as he reaches into his back pocket and pulls out his wallet. We stand in heated silence because as much as I don't want to admit he's right, he is: about my constantly warring attitude toward him in the three times I've seen him since he's been home, and about the fact that knowing why might help add closure to something I thought I'd gotten over but obviously haven't.

"Here you go," DeeDee says breaking the moment between us, placing the box on the counter beside me.

"Thank you, DeeDee. I appreciate it." Hayes looks at her nametag and then back up to her, offering up his megawatt smile. DeeDee stands speechless, grin so wide her cheeks probably hurt. "How much do I owe?"

"It's on the house," I say.

"Don't be ridiculous. I don't want your charit—"

"I'll walk you out, Hayes." I move from behind the counter, effectively ending the argument I feel like purposely picking with him over calling me out on my schizophrenic behavior.

"Whatever the lady wants, she gets," he grumbles to DeeDee but I can hear his amusement, know he's probably flashing her a smile as he gathers his box of cupcakes.

I wait outside, surprised at the chill despite the sunny sky, and cross my arms over my chest to ward it off. The bell on the door sounds, telling me Hayes is behind me.

"You know, you're still cute when you're pissed off at me."

"You are so frustrating," I mutter and at the same time dislike that parts of me melt inside at the fact that he still notices. Still remembers.

"Saylor, I've been gone a long time. I don't blame you for holding a grudge . . . but at some point, I'd like to think we can be friends again."

"Friends? Is that what you want from me?" I tighten my arms across my chest, not to ward off the chill this time, but rather to protect my heart because there's something about Hayes Whitley that just gets to me. To the parts I want to guard and yet know he can weasel his way into without really trying.

And that's why I need to keep my temper front and center. Use my anger as a shield against this charming man, who is that perfect mix of rugged and pretty-boy handsome. The man who knows from experience exactly what buttons to push.

Because he screams trouble from a mile away in every sense of the word, especially to my heart, because he'll never stay. Because he's Hayes.

"Remember that night on Todd Schilling's property?"

His change of topic gives me whiplash. I'm about to say *which time*, since there were so many nights we all hung out on his family's stretch of land. Endless hours lost to the lot of us, acting like misspent youth when in reality we did nothing out of the ordinary. But I don't need to ask which time he's referring to because even with the many memories, I know.

How could I not?

"Yes." My voice is quiet. Eyes inquisitive.

"Do you remember what I said after?"

I nod.

I protect those I love.

The emotions of that night are so powerful, the feeling of security he provided me with, even more so.

And I hate that with that single memory, that off-the-cuff phrase, he's softened me. Made me remember those words and that promise while trying to push him away.

"I meant what I said then, and I mean it now. I did some shitty things to you and don't deserve your forgiveness even though I've asked for it, but in the end, Saylor, you're part of my family. Ryder's part of my family. I can't think of a memory before my twenties that the two of you weren't a part of in some way or another. The Laytons have done more than their fair share of crap to you whether intentional or not. And I'd like nothing more than to help you out if you need it. Okay?"

The combustive fuel to my temper just burned out from the unrelenting look in his eyes and the honesty in his words. My pride wars against the emotions of my past. Against wanting to forgive and needing to move on.

On not wanting to still have feelings for this man—to hold on to the hurt he caused when he left, and remind me why I shouldn't feel anything now. But how can I when he says something like that?

"Thank you. I appreciate it. It's not necessary though. It's probably best to leave Mitch in my past and try to make a new and different future."

Like what I did after you.

Hayes makes the connection between my words and what my eyes are saying. He knows he doesn't fit in this world of common people and State Street anymore.

"The next time I see you, Saylor, I'm going to earn back the chance to be your friend." The muscle in his jaw pulses. His tongue darts out to lick his bottom lip.

But friends can break your heart too.

"Goodbye, Hayes. It was really good to see you again."

I battle against every single part of me that wants to wait and see what he says next, to believe his declaration, but at the end of the day, all I have left is my pride. The only thing I can do is trudge forward. And with that in mind, I offer a slight smile and turn my back on the man I used to think held my future.

Because I need to return to my reality.

The sweet smell of the bakery and the comforting ring of the bell greet me when I pull the door open. DeeDee meets me with a wide grin and eyes still trained over my shoulder where Hayes is probably getting into his car. And I don't want her million questions. Don't want to feel like I just broke up with Hayes again when we never really broke up in the first place.

He left.

And I need to remember that. Need to not be blinded by the feelings he stirred up when I'm feeling vulnerable about Mitch's wedding. I'm still recreating my life, and to some extent . . . *me.*

"So, uh, why do I sense that Hayes Whitley was more than just a childhood friend like you told me before?" DeeDee asks at my back as I wash my hands in the sink, attempting to refocus. However, the pounding of my heart tells me it's going to take a few minutes.

I shrug in response and grab a towel to dry my hands on. "We dated for a while. Then he left for Los Angeles and I never heard from him again." Why is that so hard to admit? When I turn around her eyes are wide, mouth opening and closing like she wants to ask so much more but isn't sure how much she should pry into her boss's past. *Wise girl.*

"That explains why there was so much sexual tension between you two. It was so thick you could cut it with a knife."

"Oh Dee." I laugh. Harder than is probably warranted but I don't know where she gets these things from. "That's funny. He's definitely not suffering in the sex appeal department, but I think you need to step back from your romance novel addiction. Life is not like your books. Sexual tension can't be cut. People don't meet lifelong soul mates in grade school. And I assure you, the heroine doesn't have an orgasm every single time she has sex with the hero. Okay?"

"But the hero sometimes pays for his cupcakes even though he's told they're on the house and then leaves a mysterious plane ticket on the counter before telling the assistant to wait and give this to her boss after he drives away."

I narrow my eyes, trying to figure out what she's talking about until she slowly pulls a dark blue envelope from behind her back and holds it out to me.

"I think he still likes you, Saylor."

"No. He doesn't." *I protect those I love.* Why do his words choose *that* moment to return to my mind? "I think you are both off your rockers." I sigh as I turn the envelope over in my hand, disbelief owning my thoughts and the feeling of being handled fueling my temper.

I take a deep breath, prepare to be irritated, and open the envelope. Inside is a first-class ticket on American Airlines to Turks and Caicos. A paid-in-full reservation for the Seven Stars Resort and Spa under my name.

My pulse thunders in my ears. My hands shake. Tears sting the back of my throat. So many emotions—disbelief, anger, gratitude, irritation, everything—reverberate within me at the sight of these reservations and the amount Hayes must have paid in upgrades.

I move aside the hotel confirmation to find a yellow Post-It note in penmanship I know all too well.

> *Just in case you want to escape to paradise with me for a few days. It's not to prove a point to them, but to prove one to you. You're better than them, Ships. I'd love to help you believe it.*
>
> *- Hayes*

I stare at the note for a few moments and try to identify how I feel. I am so very grateful that Hayes is willing to take time out from his demanding schedule, if I wanted him to, and feel flattered he thinks so highly of me *even* after the past few days.

And I wonder if he remembers anything about me. In particular, how I hate to have my hand forced at anything. And if it is forced, how I'll do the exact opposite to prove the point that I won't be persuaded.

Kind of like how I'm feeling right now.

I look to the ticket in my hands. Know I'm not going to go. Can't. The past is better left in the past. The bakery will survive somehow without it. So I try to figure out how to get his money refunded. How to thank him but at the same time pass on his offer.

And yet I can't deny the feelings these little pieces of paper have filled me with: warmth that he'd even think to do this for me, disbelief that he has so much faith in me after how I've treated him this week, and peace by giving me the opportunity to make a choice over what to do.

I lift my eyes to see DeeDee waiting patiently and watching my reaction. Her smile tentative, her hope that I opt for the romantic happily ever after her novels provide visible in her eyes.

But we all know books are fiction.

The romance in novels is a crock of shit.

Sometimes the hero still leaves in the end.

And the heroine is once again left to pick up the pieces.

Eight

Saylor

HANDS.

His hands are everywhere when I don't want them to be. Over my mouth. On my chest.

The bite of gravel in my back. The press of his knees between my thighs. His excited laugh as I try to jerk my head free. So I can yell. So I can bite.

The taste of fear. It fills my mouth. Owns my senses.

The sound of crickets. They seem so loud. Screaming at him to stop since I can't.

The wisp of grass against my legs. Cold. Bitter. Deceptive. Hiding the jagged rocks beneath it that are biting into my skin.

Just like him.

The scent of beer. On his breath. Seeping into the ground beside me from where I knocked it over in my struggle.

The distinct sound of the strap on my new sundress tearing. I saved up for weeks to buy it. And now it's broken.

I'm not sure why I focus on that. On the rip of fabric.

Because it's easier than thinking of what comes next.

Oh. God.

The strength in his hands. Holding me down. Preventing my escape.

I struggle. I kick. I fight. But a few things seem so vivid in my mind. The one that's closing down. That doesn't want to process what might happen next. Can't.

"Saylor? Saylor?" The shouts of my name. Hayes. It's Hayes.

I'm over here. Please. Please find me.

The sensation of warmth as my tears leak out and slide from the corners of my eyes down to my earlobes.

Cool night air on my belly from where he's pulled up my dress.

A roar of sound. I think. I don't know. I can't process anything. But I hear it again and then his weight is gone. Missing.

I'm empty. Hollow.

I scramble up. Crawl—rocks scraping against my bare knees—to escape as quick as I can.

There's a crunch.

A lot of shouting.

The oomph *of an exhale as a fist hits a stomach.*

An "I'm going to kill you" through gritted teeth.

The smack of knuckles on flesh.

"Go get help, Ryder. GO now."

Another crunch of bone against bone.

My ears ring. My body is cold. I can't stop shaking. Or crying. Or rocking back and forth with my hands holding my knees against my chest.

So I can disappear. From here. In my mind.

So I can pretend. Forget.

"Saylor. Saylor."

I flinch as hands touch me. Try to fight against them.

"It's me."

I push him away.

"It's me."

My struggle ceases.

Safe hands run over my arms and back and cheeks. Direct my face up to meet his eyes looking right at me. Blood on his knuckles. A red mark on his cheek. A rivulet of sweat running down his temple.

Concern. Fear. Fury. Uncertainty. Disbelief. They're all in his eyes, telling me he's just as freaked out as I am.

But his voice is calm and comforting.

"I'm here, Say. Right here."

His hands urge me to move. Lift me off the ground and position me to sit on his lap. Arms slide around me. Pull me into his chest. Against him.

My nose into his neck. His scent breaks through the fear. It smells like safety.

His warmth on my skin. My insides still cold.

"It's okay. I've got you. I've got you. You're okay. I promise you're okay."

He holds me in the dark. One hand smoothing my hair down. The other running up and down my spine. The heat of his breath on my head. The vibration in his chest as he speaks. The tremble of his hand as he continues to soothe.

With words. And by touch.

Sirens in the distance.

I'm safe now. In Hayes's arms.

"You're safe, Saylor. Always. I've got you. I protect those I love."

Nine

Saylor

I STIFLE WHAT FEELS LIKE MY HUNDREDTH YAWN OF THE DAY. MY head hurts. My body is exhausted. My emotions are frayed. The dream from last night still heavy on my mind.

The sip of coffee scalds my tongue as I look around Starbucks. I turn from where I sit, my back to most of the tables so I can watch the ebb and flow of people approaching the counter. Followed by their trip to the station to doctor their java and then the frantic search to find a seat in the always-packed café.

Regardless of how much I focus on people watching, my mind still veers back to the nightmare I haven't had in forever. It had to be Hayes's words last week. His reiteration of the promise he'd made then, and the reminder in his note that he'd still keep it now.

Why does he think I need to be protected? Does he think I'm going to need it?

Typical man. Riding in to save the day when the damsel is not in distress. Or his to save.

It doesn't help that I had a fight with Ryder over how Hayes came upon the knowledge of Mitch's wedding details. How Ryder had come into the shop early one morning when I was out picking up some supplies and pulled up the details about the rain check reservations from *my* wedding on the computer. How he then gave Hayes the travel voucher information so he could call and arrange the travel. *Our travel.*

Or most likely his personal assistant did. The one he took the cupcakes to.

So needless to say he's on my shit list. And conversely, I'm most likely on Hayes's list since I had to ask Ryder for his phone number, then call him to politely refuse the tickets. His response of "The offer still stands," not exactly the response I wanted.

That means the offer's still open.

Even though I don't want it to be.

Too much turmoil. Too many memories dredged up in such a short amount of time. *No wonder* my head hurts.

I take a sip. Jot down a few ideas for the store: new flavors, new promotions, a change up in packaging. Anything to try and increase the sales. When I glance up, my smile is automatic when I see a lady at the only other table past mine, opening the distinct pink and white box—with the Sweet Cheeks logo displayed prominently on the front—and pulling one of my Chocolate Goodness cupcakes out.

A silly thrill goes through me at the notion that someone is choosing to eat my cupcake versus one of the items in the Starbucks pastry case. Realizing I'm staring, waiting to see her facial expression when she bites into it to see if she enjoys it or not, I force myself to focus back on the notes in front of me. Just as I'm poised to write my next item I hear a comment behind me that gives me pause.

"Yes. Those are the cupcakes from *her* shop."

"Pfft. She better enjoy them now because that place will never make it. Never."

I freeze at the last comment. The one from the nasally voiced girl at my back. I blink several times, almost as if I'm trying to see if I believe what they're saying is true when you can't see words to begin with.

"How can it with a name like Sweet Cheeks?"

"Sweet Cheeks. Ugh. What a tacky name. Makes me think of . . . of unsavory things." Disgust laces her nasal drawl and I sit in disbelief. In anger. In *I don't know what* because a part of me wants to shove my chair back, turn around so they can see my face, see who I am, and let them know exactly what I think of *them*.

But the other part of me slinks lower in my chair. I *want* to hear more about what is being said behind my back, yet *don't* want to hear any of it at all. The whole situation seems contrived. Like there's a hidden camera somewhere filming my reaction and the joke is on me.

"Well, she seems to like it," the higher-pitched, squeaky-voiced one says. I assume she means the lady across from me currently taking a huge bite of chocolate heaven.

Nasal *tsks*. "At the monthly luncheon the other day, Mrs. Layton told the ladies that her cupcakes were dry and crumbly and . . . and unoriginal. She explained she'd tasted them before the whole . . . *situation*." She lowers her voice on the last word as if she's talking about some huge scandal. "You know . . . *poor Mitch*. That *Saylor* put him through so much."

Dumbfounded, I subtly shake my head and try to wrap my mind around the coincidence of this happening—me sitting where I am to hear this conversation.

This has to be a joke. A trick by Ryder to get me to go to the wedding because I feel like these two women have taken a page right out of his playbook.

Is that why I'm sitting here cowering in disbelief instead of standing up and telling them to go to hell?

I hate that I don't know the answer.

"He's definitely better off without her." Squeaky sighs out loud and I swear I can hear her eyes rolling with the sound.

"*Right*? They never fit together in the first place. The funny thing is people like her would kill to live the life Mitch could have provided."

People like her? My blood boils and body vibrates at the insult that I wear proudly like a badge. I don't want to be anything like them if this is the kind of person they expected me to be.

"So stupid on her part. Something has to be wrong with her. I mean, she'll never get a chance again at a catch like him."

"That's the truth. Could you imagine how embarrassing that was for Mitch? And for his family to be rejected by *trash*? Good riddance." Nasal draws the last word out.

My fist clenches on the pen in my hand. Cupcake girl across the aisle is oblivious of the decimation of my character and criticism of the crumbs she's licking from the tips of her fingers.

"Not to mention the amount of money in deposits his family probably lost on the vendors because, you know, she didn't care. She was originally from *the valley* so you know her family wasn't paying for it."

A snort that doesn't fit their upper crust, snooty tones. "Most definitely not."

"Good thing karma's kicking her in the ass for it."

And I've got to give it to Nasal because she just gave me whiplash with that comment.

"Wait! What do you mean by karma? Are you holding out on me, Tish?" Squeaky asks, now giving Nasal a name that is familiar but that I can't quite put a face to.

"Not really. Just chatter I heard from the ladies at The Club. I guess Saylor started her bakery with the understanding that Mrs. Layton was going to encourage her friends to hire her to cater the desserts at their never-ending events." I can all but see their lips forming into smug smiles.

Seriously? That's the bullshit Uptight Ursula is telling people?

"Yeah, but since she left him and called off the wedding—"

"Thank goodness," Squeaky interrupts.

"Totally. Think of the bullet he dodged with that one. Marrying someone that's not one of us? What was he thinking? But back to my story. I guess since the breakup, rumor from one of her suppliers whose dad knows one of Mrs. Layton's house staff, is that business has slowed down considerably. Like making-no-profit slow."

"Oh, poor thing." Her laugh is pompous as I blink rapidly trying to figure out where the hell they're getting this shit. *I am the supplier.* Me and my weekly runs to Costco. "Go back to how the other half lives, sweetheart."

"God, yes. Leave the upper class alone, little girl."

"No matter, I'm sure once Momma Layton is done badmouthing her, she'll have to shut her doors."

"Good riddance."

"Agreed. You ready?"

"Of course. Saks Fifth Avenue is calling my name."

Their voices fade off as they leave and I sit where I am. Stunned. Deflated. Furious.

That conversation was not a plant. Ryder would never go that far. I'd rather be wrong. Rather think that vapid, shortsighted people like them don't exist in the world.

But it wasn't.

They were real and they exist.

My hands tremble. Heated tears burn in my eyes because I'm pissed at myself for not telling them both to go to hell. For not standing up for myself and making a huge scene to make them feel like the shallow assholes they are. The problem is I'm so upset—so flustered—that even if I had turned around and said something, I know it would have come out a jumbled mess and made me look like the fool they were saying I am. Disgrace burns bright and it's aimed one hundred percent at me for failing to find a backbone.

Their insipid comments repeat in my head. *Their* suppositions. *Their* judgments. *Their* everything.

So I do the only thing I can–my temper on fire, my mind dazed by its smoke. I dig in my purse until I find my phone. My fingers hit the wrong button several times as I fumble for the number. The one I recently entered in my contacts but swore I'd never use.

The phone rings. My body vibrates with a shame I shouldn't feel, with an anger I own wholeheartedly, and with the notion that I was the naïve one thinking Ryder's assumptions were wrong.

"Ships Ahoy?" He sounds as surprised to be receiving my phone call as I am in making it.

"I need your help, Hayes. Offer accepted."

Ten

Saylor

WHAT AM I DOING?

Dread over my decision filled me on the plane. The memory of Hayes's words about my temper and the situations it gets me in taunted me. So I forced myself to sleep. To remember the catty words of the women at Starbucks. To hold on to the notion that I'm going to save my business. My passion. *My dignity.*

The one Ryder helped me fund.

Is this really worth it?

Doubt increased with each step through the airport on the way to the baggage claim. Horrible scenarios played out in my mind. Ones with me losing the nerve to attend the outdoor ceremony, turning to flee in the moments before Rebound Sarah walks down the aisle, and running smack dab into Mitch. Like literally body against body so we both fall backward, me landing on top of him, my dress over my head, Spanx-covered ass in plain view for all the guests to see. Or of me walking into the reception, tripping and falling head first into the cake. All the guests turning to see me stand up, face covered in icing.

The irony, that I'd be covered in frosting—Mitch's worst

nightmare. But at least I'd be unrecognizable.

What if Hayes doesn't show?

That's my thought as the tropical air hits my face, and I take in everything around me.

The island is absolutely beautiful. The beaches are picturesque. Its main street colorful and full of sleepy island life as we drive through it.

I repeat the promises I made to myself when I stepped foot onto the plane at the crack of dawn this morning: I'm here to save my business and in the process put to rest the two men I've loved in my life.

Because saving my business is first and foremost. Proving to the Laytons and their friends that I'm confident and happy when I'm certain they assume the exact opposite.

And that leads me to my next promise to myself. To use the time here to rid myself of any lingering doubts I may have in regards to Mitch. To reaffirm that I made the right decision walking away and feel nothing for him other than complete indifference.

That and the need to prove to his shallow, smug guests that I don't need them or their lifestyle and am doing perfectly fine on my own.

Of course that leads me to my last resolution: Hayes Whitley. And every single damn thing about him. I told myself I needed to let go of what happened ten years ago. Forgive him, although I'm not sure what to do with the hurt I've harbored within. And while it might be trickier than forgiveness, I also need to realize that I don't need answers as to why he left. What's more important is to focus on the fact that he's taking a huge chunk of time out of his personal schedule to be here for me. To help me prove a point and redeem a few of the things I lost when I left Mitch—most notably a chance for my business to succeed.

I have a feeling there are a few other things Hayes is going to show me too. He always did have that knack. To bring things out of me that I never knew I had in me: to look at the world from a different light, to challenge me in one way or another, to make me see a situation differently. Even as a teenager I recognized that.

Hand in hand with that is the notion that I'm heading into this weekend knowing I'm not going to walk away unscathed when it comes to Hayes. It's impossible not to.

The question is what exactly the damage will be. Will it be to my heart, to the memory I had of us, or to my ego?

I have a feeling it might be all three.

It'll be pretty hard to protect myself when it's him doing the damage. Again.

So I focus on the scenery. On the little boys with dirt-smeared faces playing soccer in the alley. On the lady selling her handmade bracelets on the corner. On the cobblestone streets lined with wandering tourists eating shaved ice, or the couples walking hand in hand sharing a kiss.

The scenery changes. The trees still lush, the views amazingly spectacular, but the coast with its hypnotizing water comes back into view and stretches endlessly. We turn onto a drive with its lavishly landscaped grounds. Palm trees and vibrant flowers rustle in the ocean breeze.

The cab slows when it pulls up in front of the hotel's entrance, and for one quiet second, I forget why I'm here. A small thrill of excitement tickles the base of my spine as I exit the car. My head swivels from side to side when I take in the grandeur of the hotel and smile at the sound of accented voices while the bellhop takes my luggage from the trunk.

So this is how the other half lives, huh? Well, this girl from the valley is going to soak up every ounce of it while I'm here.

I can almost picture myself relaxing—a drink in my hand, my feet in the sand, the sun on my skin—as I walk into the lobby. It's even prettier than the brochures and online pictures portrayed. But when the cool rush of air-conditioned air hits my face, it also brings me back to reality. Either the air or the huge sign on an easel with elaborate calligraphy that says, *Welcome Layton and Taylor wedding guests.* Because the sight of *that* sign hits me full force as to what I'm about to do.

My stomach churns instantly. I'm here to attend Mitch's new wedding. Not mine. In the place I'd dreamed of getting married.

My bravado wanes on my walk toward the registration counter. To calm my sudden bout of nerves, I take in the marble floors beneath me and lush plants around me. I keep my eyes straight ahead, focused on the nice lady with the gentle smile welcoming me to the hotel, because I just realized that it's quite possible I could run into Mitch, his parents, or any of my supposed friends with each corner I turn in this hotel.

The funny thing is, I was prepared for that. Told myself it was going to be easy to do. But words are often easy to speak until reality slaps you in the face.

And oh how they are hitting me, now.

"I hope you're enjoying your stay at the Seven Stars Resort, Miss Taylor. I look forward to making your wedding a memorable one. What can—?"

"I'm sorry, you must have me confused with someone else." One Rebound Sarah Taylor to be exact. "I'm not getting married. Just a wedding guest here to check in."

Her eyes widen. "I'm so sorry. I thought . . . You look like—oh, my apologies. The wedding coordinator showed me a picture of Miss Taylor earlier, so I could greet her if she came to the front desk. And you look so similar. You could be sisters. I'm so sorry, I—"

"It's okay." I force a smile at the irony of the entire situation. More importantly, I was right in my assumption that just like everything else, Sarah looks like me too. I shouldn't be surprised. But still . . . "Saylor Rodgers checking in, please."

"Yes, ma'am. I do apologize for my error. I'd like to welcome you to the Seven Stars Resort and thank you for choosing to stay with us, Ms. Rodgers. Let's see . . . we have you . . . Oh, we have you in the Copa Villa. Such a beautiful place." Her fingers click over the keyboard as my brow furrows at why the name of the villa sounds so familiar. "And it seems your travel companion, a Mr.—oh—Hayes Whitley," she says, eyes widening when she recognizes the name, "has already checked in so I'll have Rico show you the way to your villa."

The news that Hayes is here surprises me, considering his last text to me had said he'd arrive tomorrow, due to a scheduled meeting.

I had welcomed the idea of having a day to myself to build up the courage to actually go through with this.

Little too late to back out now.

With a bit more resolve, I hold my head high and follow Rico through the lobby to outside. I'm in awe of the grounds as we walk. The brochures I'd poured over when planning come to life before me in a bittersweet yet surreal way. The sun is high in the sky as we meander down a path bordering the white sand of the beach toward the far end of the resort's property. When the path ends, we are at a rather large bungalow, trellised with greenery and positioned for privacy.

Oh my God. *The Copa Villa.* The most private and expensive of all of the villas in the resort. I remember it now. Mrs. Layton's insistence that this was where Mitch and I should spend our first night together as a married couple. How when I looked at the ridiculous room rate, I laughed out loud. And when the humor subsided, I'd been too embarrassed to tell her there was no way I could afford it. How I lied about booking an Internet deal for the vacation package to justify why I said that no upgrades were allowed. And of course she'd seen right through the lie. Knew I couldn't afford anything else on my already maxed-out credit card and then insisted she personally foot the bill.

I shake my head thinking of that argument. How it should have been a warning sign to me how controlling she could be. But I didn't back down. No. I stood my ground and held firm to my dignity. It was so very important to pay for some part of my wedding instead of letting the Laytons happily foot every cost.

It was the only time in my years with Mitch that I saw her back down.

And so much irony now with the fact this is where I'm staying with Hayes.

Hayes.

I'm so furious at him. How dare he pay such a ridiculous amount to stay here this weekend? He's already doing enough as it is.

Maybe it's a security thing. He needs to be away from other guests for his safety? Perhaps. I try to talk myself into the notion so that when I walk into the villa and see him, I'm not grumpy right off the bat over this.

Then the thought creeps in my mind and I don't even bother biting back the chuckle that falls from my mouth. Rico looks back at me, and I just shake my head that I'm okay. I wonder what Squeaky, Nasal, and Mrs. Layton will think if they find out where I'm staying.

And then I wonder if there is nothing but the best for her son, where exactly are Mitch and Sarah staying on their wedding night if we're staying in the villa?

Guess this girl from the valley gets the last laugh after all.

Rico slows and hands me the keycard with a promise my luggage will be delivered shortly, smiles, wishes me a good day, and then leaves me alone with a whole new set of nerves for a completely different reason.

I feel like an imposter the minute I step inside the luxurious villa. It has clean lines and warm colors. A cool breeze filters down the hall and teases the hair that's fallen from my ponytail so it tickles my cheeks. I move through the foyer and down the hallway to a decadent great room. *Wow. What a view.* My feet falter as the back of the house and its wall of glass come into sight. Its pocket doors are open wide so the ocean breeze flows in and swirls the curtains on the bay windows to the side of me. The aqua water and white sand of the beach is just a few feet from the covered veranda beyond the sliding doors.

The kitchen is to my right: spacious granite countertops, huge island with brown rattan stools, and stainless steel appliances with white cabinets. When I turn to my left to take in the sitting room— luxurious leather couches and soft pillows—I stop midstride.

Lying sound asleep on one of the couches is Hayes. One arm bent and resting above his head, the other falling slightly off the couch, legs crossed and propped up on the armrest. His shirt is off, and his board shorts hang dangerously low on his hips.

My feet move in reflex, my eyes fixated on him—on *everything* about him—as I take the few steps down into the living room toward him. He's so damn handsome, my breath catches.

Removing both the gilded lights of Hollywood and my veil of

contempt, it's impossible to deny how striking Hayes is. In so many ways. And seeing him like this—completely relaxed—I'm in awe over how the boy I used to love has become this man.

Because he *definitely* is a man.

All six foot plus of him is filled out now, firm and muscular. My eyes roam over defined pecs, sculpted abs, and toned legs prompting a memory of the skinny boy with two missing front teeth who used to knock on the front door and ask if Ryder could come out and play.

The smile is automatic as I see the scar on the right side of his abdomen, a jagged, white line barely noticeable unless you know to look for it. I think back to the brace-faced teenager who would just walk in my house without knocking.

"Double dare you, Whitley!"

I can still hear my brother at twelve years old. Still hear Hayes boast how easy it would be to clear the fence from a dead standstill. Can remember the shout of triumph as he cleared it, but then the cry of pain when he immediately lost his balance, and fell onto the jagged rock on the other side. Then the concern on my mom's face as she drove him to the doctor's office to get the stitches that made the scar.

I study his face: the day's growth on his jaw, the fan of his dark lashes against his cheeks, his perfect lips.

I remember those lips. *Everything* about them. The way they felt against mine. The way his eyes seemed to smile when they curved up. The promises he made me with them. The love he professed with them. *The words he didn't say with them.*

I shake my head. Sigh. Pull myself from the memories that seem to come in a constant flood when I'm around him.

Maybe I'm just having trouble processing the teenage boy I once knew with this man in front of me. How can I still feel the sting of his rejection—after all this time—and yet have that sweet ache stir deep in the pit of my belly from just staring at him?

He shifts and I startle. Sleep-drugged eyes flutter open and look up at me. A lazy grin follows. A glimpse of the little boy shines through causing my heart to jump in my chest.

"Hey, you made it." There's gravel to his voice. Sincerity too.

"Just got here," I murmur as he scrubs his hands over his face. I force myself to step back and create some distance. I turn and look out the window to the beautiful scenery beyond and listen to him shifting on the leather behind me.

"Your flight okay?"

"Yes. Thank you. It was my first time." I blush even though he can't see it and hate that I just invited him to follow up on my comment.

"First time flying?"

"No. First class." I keep my feet moving. A way to abate the restlessness I feel from the possibility of running into Mitch, or old friends beyond the villa's walls, and from being in such a small space inside it with Hayes.

"What? You mean Mitch never—?"

"No. We never really traveled. And if we did—"

"Wait a minute. You were with the guy for six years. A guy who constantly brags about how much money he has." I turn and level him a look, curiosity in my eyes over how he'd know that. He rolls his eyes as he rises from the couch. "Yes, Saylor. I checked out his social media accounts. All the prick posts about is his privileged life with pictures to show what a high roller he is . . . So sorry, I'm a little surprised that he can spend a bazillion dollars on boys' weekends to the Hamptons and San Francisco, and yet he can't fly his fiancée first class. Call me judgmental. Call me a jerk. But that kind of bugs me. You should be more important than *his boys*."

Hayes's words throw me for a loop. His assessment of Mitch's character from Facebook posts alone is dead on. An assessment I've only been able to see with the passage of time and distance from our relationship.

I feel a sudden sense of validation over opinions I've had. Odd that Hayes of all people provided that.

"Thank you." My voice is quiet, eyes still on his so I see the moment they soften. I chuckle at a memory of something that bugged me but I never felt I had the right to be angry at because it was his money he was spending. "I used to call him Golf Boy. Tease him that he'd rather go on trips with his buddies to hit par than be home with

95

me. He hated that nickname."

"And I hate golf so no worries. There will be no golfing at all on this trip. Deal?" The grumpiness I felt over him booking this villa disappears entirely as his lopsided smile warms me from the inside out.

"Deal."

"Sorry. I know I overstepped." He shoves his hand through his hair and his shorts slip down a bit with the movement. "But the more I think about this whole situation, the more pissed I get."

"Thank you, but . . . it's not worth it. He's not worth it." I chew the inside of my lip as we stare at each other for a moment.

"Why?" His eyes ask the rest of the loaded question: *why did I put up with Mitch's behavior?*

The sad truth is, I hadn't even realized I had. And I'm embarrassed to admit how insignificant I felt on a daily basis. So I keep quiet in this awkward silence between us and hope he'll let it go for now. Pretend that he doesn't see what I assume is humiliation in my eyes over allowing myself to be constantly devalued.

We both startle when the doorbell rings announcing what I assume is the arrival of my luggage. Grateful for the interruption, I move to the door without a word but know he's going to want an answer at some point.

And hopefully I'll have enough courage to tell him what I now know to be the truth.

Because he wasn't you.

Eleven

Hayes

"DON'T CALL ME AGAIN, JENNA. I'VE ALREADY DONE MY part. Do yours."

"But Hayes . . . I'm . . . I'm struggling and really need you here right now," she pleads.

So says the actress. The queen of melodramatics. The attention whore.

I grit my teeth and don't buy into the lie this time. "No. You don't. You're perfectly fine without me."

"But Hayes—"

"No, *but Hayes*, Jenna. You've texted me at least thirty times in the last few hours. I'm on vacation. This is my time. Not yours. Not the studio's. Any problems you're having, you've created yourself. So deal with them. I've gotta go. My cell will be off the rest of the trip."

I hang up my phone and clench my fists. I hate this nightmare I'm in but am so very thankful for the reprieve. For Saylor and a chance at temporary normalcy instead of the crazy of my life.

Why the hell did I ever agree to go along with Jenna's shit?

I have no intention of turning my phone off but when a new text alerts—yet another from Jenna—I put it on Do Not Disturb. Shoving it in my pocket, I figure it's time to get out of here for a while and explore. But when I come to the doorway of Saylor's room, I stop. Just stop and watch her unpack her things. Efficient in her movements, she never breaks from folding her clothes to look out the window where the breeze blows in to admire the crystal clear water. She's all business.

Everything about her trip here is. And yet I know from Ryder she's been working nonstop to make the bakery a success. Starting her life from scratch after being with *the prick* for six years took courage. And then to realize her friends found the Layton's clout and money more alluring than her friendship? That had to have been brutal.

And lonely.

How could they just drop her like that? Cut her out of their lives and forgo her friendship?

Fuck. *Pot? Meet kettle.*

The parallels between Saylor and me, and the fallout between her and Mitch, are getting a bit ridiculous now. Nothing like making me feel like I'm more of an asshole with each and every similarity that comes to light.

But that's why I'm here. To redeem myself. To heal old wounds.

And it's all of these revelations that confirm how hard it must have been for her to call me—the guy who hurt her just as badly—and take me up on my offer to help.

She tucks some hair behind her ear and then tightens the sash on her robe. Those legs-for-days beg me to take a long look at them. *And damn.* They're definitely worth a second look.

It's like I know her but don't. It's a fucked-up feeling for a man not used to caring at all. Not needing to.

She continues her methodical movements. Unpack. Unfold. Refold. Place in the drawer.

What happened to the spitfire personality? The screw-you attitude? The girl who didn't care who was watching or what they thought? Is it because of that fucker? Did Layton steal that from her? Is that what her silence was telling me earlier when she told me he wasn't worth it? Why would he tame the fearless side that made her who she was?

Time to make her cut loose, and get the girl back I used to know with the wicked smile and wild eyes.

Her phone rings. It startles both of us but her back's still to me. "Dee, what's up?" She pauses refolding a T-shirt. "Again? Seriously? Christ. Call the same place we used before. See if he can get the temperature to steady so you can manage until I get back. Then I'll figure something out . . . Yeah. Thanks. I appreciate you taking care of it for me."

She tosses her phone on the bed and sighs out loud.

"Five-minute warning."

She yelps and spins around. Her hand goes immediately to the opening of her robe on her chest, while her eyes—blue and wide—lower momentarily. Every woman loves the V. Thank fuck working out is part of my job for most roles because mine's definitely defined.

And she sure as shit just noticed.

"Five-minute warning?"

"Yep." *Eyes up here, Ships. Then again, feel free to look away.* "That's how much time you have to get ready before we leave."

Her lips shock into an O. My mind fills with images I shouldn't have. Of what can slip between them. And it doesn't help when I glance down to see her nipples tight against the thin material of the robe.

"What do you mean?"

Eyes up, Whitley.

I hold my hand out to her. "First, I'm taking your phone away. And then we're going exploring."

"You want my phone?"

Among other things. If a robe is having this effect on me, causing me to want things I can't have, then . . .

"Yep. Mine's gone off what feels like a hundred times already and is driving me up a wall, and by the sound of your call, yours is stressing you out, too. So I think we need to turn our phones off and unplug this weekend."

"Unplug? You're serious, aren't you?"

A flash of her legs as she shifts her feet and her robe parts.

"As a heart attack." I look down to my outstretched hand and then back up to her eyes. "We're in paradise, Ships." One side of her lips curls up and I know I'm winning her over. "Send a text to Ryder or whoever that was and let them know your cell is off so no one worries that you've been abducted by Uptight Ursula. Then turn it off and hand it over. I'll do mine at the same time."

She eyes me again. "Okay. Deal."

I nod and we both pick up our phones, fire off texts, and then she hands hers to me when it's shut down.

"Are you happy?" She lifts her eyebrows like she's annoyed but I can tell she likes this idea.

"*Very*. Now that that's out of the way, it's time to explore. Go check out the island and then have some fun here." Her eyes look panicked from the suggestion. *Fuck.*

"I figured you'd want to avoid attention. Hang out here so you'd have some peace and quiet and enjoy your anonymity."

Nice try, Ships, but that won't fly this weekend.

"I learned years ago that attention is something I can't control. We're on a tropical island, Saylor. In the middle of the ocean. There's sand, sea, and fun to be had. Besides, getting out and about is the best way to make it known we've arrived. I assure you on this little island, word travels fast."

She bites her bottom lip and sits down on the bed. She really did think we were just going to sit here. And even though that's what I had every intention of doing tonight, there's no way we're doing that now. Plans change. And I'm determined to get Saylor back. *My old Saylor back.*

It's time to go have some fun and find her.

Right when she's about to speak, to disagree, to reject, I look at my watch and then back up to those aqua blues of hers.

"You're wasting time. The clock's ticking."

Twelve

Saylor

"I SN'T YOUR NEW FLAME GOING TO BE PISSED AT YOU FOR taking off to a tropical island and leaving her at home?" I avoid glancing over to Hayes although every part of me wants to see his reaction to my question.

I've seen the tabloids. The field day they've had with him over the past few months. Know his high-profile relationship with Jenna Dixon is over. That supposedly he cheated on her and she's since gone into hiding to cope. Their fairy-tale relationship ended.

The press has played it all out. The rumors have been printed and reprinted each time with a new spin to them. Speculations over who he cheated with cover the gamut of anyone he comes in contact with. And yet he's remained silent the whole time.

Does that mean they'll target me, too?

I shake away the thought. We're just friends. Friends on a tiny island in the Atlantic Ocean at an all-inclusive resort. There's no way anyone would even care about me anyway. I'm nobody in the Hollywood circle of need-to-know.

I don't even remotely resemble the women he's been associated with, past and present, who have been floated about as possibilities. Besides, the most recent rumors state he's dating Tessa Gravestone—his gorgeous and completely temperamental (if I believe the tabloids) costar. I'm curious if it's true, and if so, what does she think about him being here?

He chuckles and yet the sound is lacking any amusement.

"Obviously you haven't been reading tabloids lately or else you'd know I don't have a girlfriend, Saylor." Tone steadfast. Voice without hesitation.

I risk a look to where he sits beside me, back against the seawall, bare feet in the sand, and am met with a lift of his eyebrows. A nonverbal, just ask what you want to ask, expression on his face.

I snort at his response. He flashes a quick grin for some reason, and I just shake my head. "Aren't you dating, *whatshername* though?"

"Considering you don't know what her name is, then no, I'm not dating her."

"That's a cop-out answer if I've ever heard one." And I do know her name . . . just don't want to let him know that I follow his life in skewed tabloid ink.

He shifts to turn and look at me. Eyes intense, head angled to the side, irritation obviously awakened. "Really?" he says dryly. "Considering the coals I've been raked over lately regarding Jenna and the accusations made about my character, I'd think saying I don't have a girlfriend is a logical answer." His expression is severe, lips tight as he waits for me to respond. There must be something in my countenance that questions him because he shifts and purses his lips. Starts to talk. Then stops. Starts again. "Go ahead and ask the question, Saylor. Ask me or believe *them*. Your choice."

And as much as I want to know if he cheated on his girlfriend, as important as it is for me to know he didn't, I don't say a word. There's something about the look in his eyes, the irritation over the fact I might believe the rumors, that stops me from continuing. Because asking means I might be convinced it's true and therefore don't trust him.

"Don't believe everything you see, Saylor." His tone is wry. A warning. "Even salt looks like sugar at first glance."

His comment makes me rethink my assumptions and puts me in my place. "No questions, Hayes." I lick my lips and glance down to my fidgeting hands before looking back up at him. I wonder what is the truth and what is a front in a town that thrives on earning a living out of playing make-believe. "And honestly, I was talking about Tessa. Not Jenna." I need to make myself clear. Let him know I was fishing but not about Jenna.

"Oh," he says, shy grin sliding over his lips. "Sorry. I get a little touchy on the Jenna thing."

I nod. Understand. I want to ask more but don't because obviously there's more to the story than meets the eye. He's allowed to be upset over their breakup, considering how long they dated.

"Well, in that case . . ." He laughs, his tone is teasing, and the mood suddenly eases again. His smile returns and there is mischief in his eyes.

"Ah, Tessa." It's all I say. My own smile spreading despite the pang of jealousy that hits a little harder than I'd like to admit.

"We're working together."

I roll my eyes. "So you're sleeping together."

"On screen, yes." His voice is unapologetic and yet a small part of me feels like he is toying with me. Gauging my reaction.

"And off screen." I chuckle but question why I care. *Jesus, Saylor, stop asking.*

"Is there a reason you care?" He steals the thought from my head and doesn't stop staring, so I shift my gaze to the ocean ahead, wondering the same thing.

The difference is I know why. I care because of that fluttery feeling I get when he smiles at me, the warmth that flushed through me when he put his arm around me on the way out of the little restaurant where we grabbed a quick bite to eat. I just don't want to admit it.

"No. Not at all." Uncomfortable under the weight of his stare, I let the silence fall between us. A steel drum is heard somewhere in the distance. The intermittent buzz of tourists' laughter or shuffling of footsteps meandering through this sleepy Caribbean town can be heard behind us. I watch some local children play in the water, some in suits, some not, as their parents watch from the ocean's edge.

"It's nothing serious," he says unexpectedly. "In fact I haven't seen her in a few weeks."

"Huh." I let the comment settle between us, enjoying the fact that he didn't have some huge farewell session with some beautiful starlet before coming to hang out with me.

"You're awfully quiet, Ships."

I can't help my smile. The nickname not so bothersome now. "Yeah. I'm just trying really hard to enjoy tonight. To not think about the next few days. To—"

"Enjoy the company of the handsome man beside you."

I laugh out loud and love that he can do that to me. Just like he did earlier as we sat in the local recommended favorite, Fresh Catch, while we ate our appetizers and sipped our cocktails. When we talked about our childhood escapades and arguments, steering clear of everything that happened after there was an *us,* and the aftermath I still don't understand. I *had* promised myself I wouldn't bring it up again while here.

It's the least I can do considering he's here, doing who knows what for me in this atypical situation.

I look over to him—wind-ruffled hair and dimples deepening— and think he's so much more than handsome. He's comfort and my past, mysterious yet familiar, funny and yet aloof.

"Yes. That too."

"Why are you nervous?"

"I'm not nervous." My too quick response says I'm anything but. His chuckle tells me he doesn't buy it. "You know me, I'm not good with the unpredictable. With putting myself out there when I know everyone in the room will be looking at me."

There's an intensity in his eyes that unnerves me. Like he's searching for an answer I can't give him. "The girl I used to know didn't care who was looking." His voice is quiet, and I hate the urge to immediately refute him. To be defensive. Especially when I've wondered the same thing as of late. Distance from Mitch has only proven how much the time spent with him had changed me. Toned down my personality.

I shrug. Almost in an apology to him when it should really be to myself. "Maybe it just depends on who's looking, I guess."

He licks his lips and nods his head as if he understands, but the shift of his eyes and set of his shoulders say differently. Hayes lifts his face to look at me again. "Well, I guess I should warn you, you're with me so don't worry, when people are staring, it's at me." I think he's dead serious at first, but when he cracks a smile, I can see he's trying to put me at ease.

"Ah, I see. The famous Hollywood actor," I tease but know he's right. The glances at dinner. The interruptions on the boardwalk for a quick picture. I truly appreciate his attempt to lessen my anxiety.

He blows on his knuckles and pretends to polish them on his chest and winks at me. "So remember every time you think they're looking at you—"

"They're really looking at you," I finish for him.

"Exactly." He nods for emphasis. "And for your information, I have a very detailed schedule of how the next few days are going to go if that will help you with your need for predictability."

I jerk my head in reaction. "There's a schedule?"

"Yes. There was a schedule for the wedding handed to me when I checked in. It's all mapped out for us. Golf for the guys and salon day for the ladies tomorrow." He rolls his eyes. "No worries, I promised you no golf, and I mean it. We're not going. We'll make 'em sweat. Give them a chance to gossip about the rumor we're here. Did you bring the invitation like I asked?"

"Yeah. Why?" I narrow my eyes.

"Because I bet you they never told Uptight Ursula they invited you. They did it to mock you, never expecting you to show. I want to make sure you have it on you in case she attempts to kick you out—"

"Hayes?" I have to get something off my chest.

"Yeah." Eyes looking. Expression perplexed.

"I've thought a lot about this, and I just want to make sure you understand that I'm not here to ruin their wedding. That's not the type of person I am. Every little girl dreams about their wedding day and who am I to say that Mitch isn't Sarah's Prince Charming? Just because he wasn't mine, doesn't mean he's not hers." I twist my lips, look down at where my fingers are drawing aimless designs in the sand before looking back up to him. "The only reason I'm here is to prove I'm okay with it. To show that leaving Mitch was a good decision for both of us. *He's happy and marrying someone else.* Only someone who is ashamed runs and hides, and I am not that. I want my business to thrive and if there's a chance that coming here—to be smiling and supportive and giddily confident—will prove them otherwise, then I have to take it. If I hadn't come and Sweet Cheeks failed, then I'd always wonder . . . and I'm sick of wondering things."

My words trail off, my voice breaking on the last few words. I hate that I brought the conversation back to where I swore to myself it wouldn't go—to where everything seems to lead these days—to thoughts of us back then and the what-ifs I've lived with.

We consider each other in the dimming light, each passing second feeling like it's erasing the years since we've seen each other. Brown eyes to blue. His silence to my comments.

"I knew you were still the same girl I used to know." His voice is a murmur. I look down to catch a dart of his tongue to lick those lips of his, and then meet his gaze again. "I know what your intent is, Saylor. You're too kind to want anything less. You're selfless. Forgiving."

"I thought you said I hold grudges."

"Only with me." He smirks. "You always did. Let's hope I'm on my best behavior this weekend so you don't hold any with me by the time this is over."

"Good plan." I laugh again and realize it seems like forever since I laughed this much over absolutely nothing. It's a good feeling.

"Getting back to plans—"

"Ah yes . . . tomorrow, we're ditching the salon and golf because your nails are already done and golf is boring as fuck. So we'll do our own thing. I have to run some lines for a part I'm screen-testing for when I return and then we have the rehearsal dinner that they've invited their guests to. The wedding the following day. The reception. Then—"

"No more." I cover my ears and laugh. "Thank you. Really. I'm relieved to know you have all the particulars of our schedule worked out. Seems like the normal wedding events. *And those I know all too well.* I can rest easier now."

He chuckles and all of a sudden my back straightens. "That's their schedule, Ships. *Ours is a secret.*" He abruptly stands and grabs my hand to pull me up. My body jolts at the connection that sitting side by side with him all this time has had buzzing just beneath the surface. As if knowing he was close enough to touch but not really touching was an awareness all in itself. I know he can feel it too. That I'm not alone. Because the words on his lips falter momentarily before he recovers. And a part of me wants to stay like this a bit longer but know it's just that missed connection we lost so long ago that's causing the sensations to simmer to the surface. Nostalgia. Muscle memory of the heart. "C'mon. Let's go."

"*Go?*"

"Yes. Go. It'll be easier if you think of this whole trip as an adventure rather than *their* wedding."

"And what? You're my tour guide?"

"If that's what you want to call me. I prefer cruise director though, considering we're kind of stuck with the nautical theme, *Ships.*" He winks and holds his hand out.

"Oh, please." I roll my eyes.

"Or *captain.*"

"You're certifiable, you know that?" I shake my head and he pulls on my hand to help me stand.

"Quite possibly, but all that matters is I'm in charge of this schedule, and we need to get a move on it. Your adventure awaits."

"And, oh captain, my captain, that adventure is what?" I drag my feet like a child, curious what he's talking about but smiling nonetheless.

"Do you actually think I'm going to tell you?" He dazzles me with that smile I can't resist. "Didn't you know? Spontaneity is the best kind of adventure."

Oh. Shit.

Thirteen

Saylor

"**N**O WAY. UH-UH." I TRY TO STEP AWAY BUT MY BACK HITS the unyielding wall of Hayes's front. We're pressed body to body and panic flickers through me.

"Remember what I said." His voice is warm against my ear.

Spontaneity is the best kind of adventure, my ass. I tried to do this once before. On a double-dog dare at the age of sixteen. From him.

I turn around, a blatant rejection of Hayes's idea of *spontaneous fun.* Of the stage before me, the people sitting in chairs around it, and the microphone and screen that will hold lyrics.

And yet when I do turn, I run smack dab into every long, lean, firm inch of him. My body reacts immediately to the feel of his. Hair stands up on the base of my neck. My nipples press against the smooth fabric of my bra and are more than aware of the warmth of his chest. My muscles tense everywhere.

All I can do is suck in my breath when his eyes hold mine. They're full of the same mischief that paints his smile. "Remember that time at Wild Irish?"

"How could I forget?" Sneaking in the back door of the local bar a few towns over, feeling like we were so cool. The anxiety of being caught in a bar underage making the night that much more exhilarating. Hayes's dare to go put my name in, take the stage, and perform a song of his choosing.

"Remember how much you had to psych yourself up to do it?" he murmurs. I can smell the hint of Red Stripe on his breath.

These are treacherous waters.

But it's The Captain leading me into them.

I laugh. My body hums with awareness. *He hasn't stepped away.* Hasn't broken the connection between our bodies. And yet it's probably because it's crowded and he wants me to hear him. Regardless, every jostle of someone bumping into one of us, makes the awareness that much more.

"I remember. I spent all night freaked about it and just as I was walking up to the stage—"

"Principal Hellman walked up right before you."

We both laugh at the memory. At how I scurried back to the table in the far, darkened corner of the club before leaving shortly thereafter.

"My God, I was so freaked out we were going to get detention or worse if Hell's Bells saw us there."

Our laughter fades. Somewhere in the moment we've stepped apart when the crowd has given us room to. "So what do you say, Ships?"

"To what?" I feign nonchalance but worry my bottom lip between my teeth.

"You never finished the dare." He shrugs. Taunts me with a smile and a glance of his gaze to the stage and then back to me.

"Seriously?"

"You were never one to chicken out before." Words to match his smile.

"We're not teenagers anymore, Hayes," I huff but know he's starting to win me over. That sheepish grin and impish gleam in his eye reminding me of the fearless, carefree girl I used to be. The one who never backed down from one of his or Ryder's dares.

He leans in, mouth to my ear. "I double-dog dare you, Saylor."

My smile is instant. My reaction is half-hearted. "You know I can't sing for shit," I shout above the music that just started playing again. His hands are on my shoulders, directing me toward the stage, the melodic tone of his laugh in my ear.

"Perfect. There's nothing better than an off-key karaoke singer to catch everyone's attention."

I want to strangle him, and yet I find myself laughing instead. I grab his hand, and his falter in motion tells me I've caught him off guard. "If I'm going to make an ass out of myself, you are too."

I'm surprised when he stumbles along behind me. "Did you forget I like when everyone's looking at me?"

"I don't care. No one is going to convince me otherwise," I say, in an attempt to sound serious despite the smile that hasn't left my lips since we started our dominating karaoke run on the mic.

His laugh echoes off the concrete as we weave through the outdoor corridors of the hotel. "You need help."

"Says the man who demanded he be called *The Captain* every time the announcer summoned us to the stage despite everyone knowing you were Hayes Whitley." I giggle as he hangs an arm over my shoulders and pulls me against him for support. Or maybe it's the other way around. I don't know and I don't care because I'm having more fun in what feels like forever and it's all because of him.

"Says the woman who sang, 'Might as well face it you're a dick with a glove.'" His laugh rings out again.

"And what is wrong with that? Look it up. I bet you . . . I don't know what I bet you." I slur my words a little bit. "But I assure you those are the correct lyrics that Robert Palmer sings."

"No. It's *addicted to love*, Ships. Addicted to love," he enunciates while fighting back the laugh. "Not *a dick with a glove*."

"Hmpf." I try to pout but it's just no use. His words are sluggish too and his body so warm against mine. I feel lighthearted after so much weight lately that all I can do is smile and laugh and not want the sidewalk to end at our door where I can see it does a few yards ahead.

"Are you going to pout?"

"No."

"Yes, you are, and I've got the perfect cure for that." In a completely unexpected move, he takes my arm and twirls me out and then pulls me back in. Paradise spins around me. It keeps moving even when I land solidly against him.

Our laughter fades and our smiles slide into parted lips. His hand still holds mine against my lower back and his chest moves against mine. My face lifts up as his tilts down and our eyes fasten on each other's. There's an earnestness I haven't seen in his before. There's also amusement. Such an odd combination, almost as if he can see things I don't want him to see just yet.

Kiss me.

Oh my God. What am I thinking? He can't kiss me. It's a horrible idea. Too many reasons to list why he shouldn't.

And yet I want him to kiss me. *Just once.*

So we can get it out of our systems, put the past to rest, and move on. But then again, would I be able to move on?

Even at the age of seventeen, Hayes could kiss in a way that made me feel like I'd just laid every part of my soul on the line when his lips left mine. And I'm not sure I can handle feeling that right now. Every part of this situation already makes me feel so vulnerable and exposed as it is. Add in being confused over how the kiss would make me feel and that's not something I need to add to the mix.

Yet as the silence stretches, neither of us move. And when his eyes flicker down to my lips and then back up to my eyes again, I don't think I ever want to.

My desire wars against my better judgment.

His body is warm and firm against mine. A tangible temptation that's hard to resist.

Just kiss me.

I wait for him to. I want him to.

And then I realize what an idiot I'm being. How he's probably thinking how pathetic I look standing here waiting to be kissed in the moonlight like some pathetic sap. Embarrassed and flustered, I step back needing to create some distance from him.

"I'm sorry." I turn and walk to the front door.

"Saylor." Hayes calls out to me and I tell myself to keep walking. That there is a famous starlet named Tessa who he isn't dating but most likely sleeps with. That there is a world of difference between our two lives—glitz, red carpets, and glamour versus frosting-spattered hair, Nutella, and NetFlix—and even if we share a kiss, nothing will lessen that chasm.

I'm such a wreck. I'm over here turning a playful twirl in the moonlight into a kiss I don't want to want, to fantasizing how it would lead to my happily ever after.

He calls my name again as his footsteps sound on the pavement behind me. I don't want to face him right now and yet as I reach the door, I realize he's holding the key to unlock it. *Fucking perfect.* A self-deprecating laugh falls from my mouth. There's a tinge of hysteria to it. A bit of disbelief fringing its edges from my out-of-control imagination.

My sudden irrationality has to be a combination of everything jading my thoughts: the alcohol, the fun evening, the comfort of being with someone who used to know everything about me, the indescribable paradise surrounding us. It all contributes to the *Saylor was almost going to make an ass out of herself* moment I just had. I guarantee *that* won't be happening again anytime soon.

He's right behind me now. I can feel him before I hear him.

"Say? *What is it?*"

I hang my head. Hate that so many of my thoughts are on the tip of my tongue, and yet I say none of them because they are absolutely ridiculous.

His hand is on my shoulder, prompting me to turn to face him. But I resist. I don't want him to see the embarrassment stinging my eyes or read the errant thoughts that have no business being there.

"I'm fine, Hayes. Just tired is all."

"Hmm." He gives a non-committal sound that makes me scrunch my nose because I know he's trying to figure out what's going through my mind.

"Can you open the door, please?"

"What is your biggest fear about this weekend?"

What? The question comes out of nowhere and I hate that my immediate thought is that he means in regards to us. But that's the crazy talking and once I rein it in, I know he's referring to Mitch and Sweet Cheeks.

"I told you earlier at the beach. It's not so much a fear but more my need to prove to them all that I made the right decision. Because if the women in Starbucks were speaking truthfully and if Ryder's and your hunches are correct, this is what I have to do in order to give my business the chance it deserves to succeed."

"Do you still love him?"

His question is unexpected and shocks me enough that I whip my head up to meet his eyes. I immediately wish I hadn't. The porch light is bright and there's no way I can hide the truth in my eyes from him.

"No."

"Hmm."

I don't know if he believes me. The furrow of his brow and his unrelenting stare tell me otherwise.

"Six years is a long time to be with someone, love them, and then turn the love off like a switch."

How do I explain to him that while I no longer love Mitch, I can love some of the memories we had together? That there will always be those shared experiences that I'll look at fondly, but do I still love Mitch? No. I don't think so.

"I just want my life back to normal," I whisper, hoping he might be able to understand that. *Needing him to be satisfied and leave me be.*

His brown eyes hold an empathy I'm not sure I deserve, considering I'm the one who caused all of these changes. "What do you mean by normal?"

"I don't know anymore." I shake my head, thankful for the change in topic, and try to explain. "Since Mitch and I split, my life's been in chaos. The moving out and starting over. The endless hours I spend in the bakery to try and make it work. It's exhausting and yet I love every single minute of it so I'm not sure how to answer that." *It's lonely.* Not the everyday part because I'm so very happy with my choices, but rather the loneliness associated with not having someone to cuddle with at the end of the night and share stories about my day. I leave that part out.

"Would you change any part of it?"

He asks the question that I know I can answer without hesitation. "No."

His smile is slight, but there. A nod of his head. A rub of his hand up and down my spine in encouragement.

"Then maybe you're finding that new normal."

Fourteen

Saylor

THERE'S NOTHING LIKE WAKING UP TO THE SUN SHINING AND the crash of waves on the beach outside my window. I let myself be lazy. I doodle in my notebook over new potential varieties of cupcakes.

At some point I hear Hayes on the phone somewhere in the house. I'm immediately irritated that he turned *his* cell on when we'd agreed to unplug. But when I set down my notebook to go say something, I notice the red light blinking on the Villa's phone. The line is being used. So technically he's not breaking the rules since he's on the landline.

I glare at it for a minute. So typical of Hayes to skirt the rules but not break them. He hasn't changed a bit and why does knowing that bring a stupid smile to my lips?

I figure I'll let it slide. He's probably negotiating a bazillion-dollar contract or something so who am I to interfere? Business being done in paradise. I pick up my pad again and start to write just as his voice gets louder. He sounds irritated. Frustrated. Adamant. Snippets of his conversation float down the hall. I overhear him talk about how his public image is taking a hit and then carry on about not giving a shit about the ironclad non-disclosure agreement. How he refuses to play the game anymore.

I'm intrigued at first. Hayes has never been one to rile easily so I'm curious what has him so heated. But then again, my knowledge comes from the teenager I used to know; maybe the fuse of his temper has shortened with age.

Feeling guilty for eavesdropping, I busy myself with a shower and then change the polish on my toes to a brighter color. I enjoy my quiet peace, private space, and the breeze blowing in the window. I even contemplate taking a jog on the beach . . . but since my toenails are still tacky I don't want to ruin the polish. Besides, I'm on vacation, and exercise is work.

Then I'm brought back to reality and that this isn't really a vacation. I'm here for a reason. I'm also most likely hiding out in my room to avoid Hayes since I made a fool out of myself last night. And while he may never have known my thoughts, I sure as heck did, and that in itself warrants feeling embarrassed.

But isn't he just as much to blame as I was? Holding me close? Looking at me with that unrelenting intensity in his eyes? *Yes.* It was definitely all his fault. Ha. At least that's what I'll keep telling myself to justify my overreaction and wistful longing last night.

Hell, I have three more days of sharing the same space with Hayes. Of being around him and trying not to feel confused every time he looks at me. Or smiles at me. Or calls me Ships Ahoy.

Hayes Whitley twists me up like a Rubik's cube. He did way back when and still does now. He's changed me. Turned that naïve, solid-color blocked puzzle I once was and left me scattered all over the place. I'm a mix of emotions when it comes to him. And no matter how hard I've tried to get back to that solid state I was before him, I know I never will.

He's left his fingerprint on me, marking me with invisible ink.

And being here is like stepping under a black light. Every single one of those scars becomes visible, brought to light so I can't ignore them anymore.

Forcing me to face them once and for all.

I take my time getting ready. Fight the endless flyaway hairs from the humidity until I give up and just pull my hair back into a clip. After adding some mascara and lip gloss, I lather on the sunblock, unsure what adventure *The Captain* has for me today.

Just like that, he brings a silly smile to my face, even when he's not in front of me. It's like old times. When I'd wake up on summer break and he'd be at the front door, telling Ryder and me what adventures we were going on for the day.

And as if on cue, I hear him shout through the closed door. I can't make out any words, but hear more than just a growl of frustration. Finally, my curiosity prevails and I leave my room to go satisfy it.

I hear his voice immediately and can see him out on the patio from where I stand in the hallway. He's turned sideways, body obscured by the pillar, face angled as he talks to someone.

"Did you really think I'd give in so easily? Walk away without a fight?" He shakes his head and laughs but there's no amusement in it.

Keeping against the wall, I take a step closer, craning my neck to see who he's speaking to, but I can't see or hear whoever it is.

"You don't get it, do you? I begged, borrowed, and lied to get this chance again. To stand here in front of you one more time. To right my wrongs. To make you see why I am, can't—SHIT!" There's a bang as he hits his fist against the side of the pillar. His sigh is loud, his frustration evident in the sound alone. He steps back, and I can see him fully now. Board shorts, no shirt, a baseball cap slung low over his forehead with dark hair curling out at the back, and blue sheets of paper in his hand.

"Hayes?" I step out from my spot in the hallway and into the great room. His head snaps up at the sound of my voice through the opened pocket doors. He blushes immediately and it gives me pause because I don't think I've ever seen Hayes Whitley blush.

Be still my heart. Because Confident Hayes is one thing, but Shy Hayes? That's a whole other stratosphere of attraction. Like *I'm-screwed* type of attraction.

But then I remember him being embarrassed means I've caught

him with someone or doing something and now I feel like an idiot. Serves me right for being nosy.

"Hey." He sets the papers in his hand down and leans against the pillar behind him. His smile soothes away my unease.

"Sorry. I didn't mean to interrupt you and . . ." My voice fades off as I step out onto the patio and am surprised to find no one else out there.

He laughs at the perplexed look on my face. "Sorry. I was running lines and got frustrated trying to figure out how to play this scene."

"Oh. I'm sorry. I didn't know. I thought . . . never mind." When I look back up from where he just hung his thumbs into his board shorts—my mind temporarily dazed by the abs and happy trail and the V—our eyes meet and hold.

Something about the fact that he actually has to practice at his craft kind of throws me. He's always been perfect at everything he tries first time around and the notion that he is practicing, rehearsing, tells me he truly does care about what he does. That he takes it seriously. It's such a change from the fly-by-the-seat-of-the-pants mentality he used to have.

Practice before baseball try-outs? Of course not. And then he made starting lineup. Study before his final exams? Why would he? He aced them anyway.

So I just stare at him as the realization hits home: he's the same boy I once knew and yet so very different. He's matured. Changed. But in a good way.

Luckily he speaks and interrupts my overthinking. "I usually run them with my PA. She's an aspiring actress." He rolls his eyes as if everyone is in his life. "Rehearsing is hard when it's one-sided."

"Can I help?" His face reflects the same shock that I feel in asking.

He stifles a laugh but lets the lopsided smile spread across his lips and studies me. "You want to help?"

"Don't sound so shocked, Whitley. I know I can't act worth a shit, but I'll help if you need me to. What's the movie about?" I step closer, the breeze hitting my face and the view catching my breath momentarily as if I'd forgotten the paradise outside.

His lopsided grin turns sly. "It's a romantic suspense project. This scene . . . is about the main characters. They've fought their attraction for what feels like a lifetime."

"Why would you fight it?" The question is off my lips before I can pull it back, and it earns me a quirk of his eyebrow.

"Good question." He shrugs, his gaze never wavering. "The way I see it, sometimes things happen in life and love's put on hold. But if someone's your soul mate, nothing is going to stop you from being together in the end."

His words throw me. This introspective opinion so unexpected. The notion that I know him, and yet don't know him, becomes more and more clear. It makes me want to talk to him that much more. Understand who he's grown into. See the depth in his thoughts. The maturity in his opinions. *Sure I loved him before.* Loved the teenager he was—playful, loyal, sincere, funny—but I've changed and matured too. The things I look for in a man have evolved with that. Insight. Compassion. Security. Character. Integrity. All of those things in a man are important to me.

And as I look at him standing before me, I realize the more I discover about the almost thirty-year-old version of him, the more I realize he embodies all of those traits.

His comment repeats through my mind. *If someone's your soul mate, nothing is going to stop you from being together in the end.*

"Is that you speaking or the character?"

"There's a little bit of me in every character I play."

"Nice deflection." I laugh, thankful for it too. "I'll make sure to remember when I need you to lift something that you have the superhero strength of that Marvel character you played last year."

He just laughs and hands me the script. "Cute, Ships. You want to help, or not?"

"Ah, it's all fun and games until someone makes fun of the tights you had to wear," I tease, knowing his superhero costume received quite a lot of buzz over the Spandex pants and definitive bulge they showed.

"Hey, whatever pays the bills." His smile tells me he's heard it all before and it doesn't bug him. And it shouldn't, considering the rumors regarding the paycheck he earned for wearing those tights. *As should any man having to walk around in very tight Spandex.* "You ready?"

Shit. I guess I better focus. And not on him. Or his bare chest. Or his biceps. Or the thought of his bulge in Spandex.

"Is it ridiculous that I'm suddenly nervous?" I ask with a skittish chuckle to boot.

"Not at all. I know something—a role, an award, an anything—is worth the trouble it causes if it makes me nervous."

"Good to know." I take a deep breath and glance down at the script in front of me. Ignoring the staging I don't understand, I make a quick study of the exchange between the two characters, Gabby and Noah. "Okay, I think I've got it."

I can't read the smile he gives me. It's almost as if he knows something I don't. I shake the thought and just play it off as he finds me helping him humorous. And he most definitely will laugh at my attempt to act, but I don't care. How many people get the chance to say they rehearsed lines with an Oscar winning actor?

"Let's take it from right here," Hayes says as he leans over and points to a line. "And why don't you sit on the edge of the chair for me. It will help me with blocking."

"Okay." Nerves suddenly flutter to life. Stupid really, but they do. I take a seat, my eyes skimming the lines over and over. Trying to figure out the context of the scene when I haven't read the entire story proves rather difficult, but I'll just go with it.

"That's bullshit, Gabby, and you know it." The expression on Hayes's face transforms instantly and catches me completely off guard. He's angry, frustrated, and tormented. His voice and posture reflect all three.

I stumble for my line as I look back down, knowing there is no way I can even match how seamlessly he slipped into his character. "I don't know anything anymore." My voice seems flat compared to his, but I keep going. "All I know is after tonight . . . after watching . . . never mind. It's probably best if you just go now."

"Huh." He shakes his head. Disappointment is reflected on his face as he takes two steps toward me. "You'd like that, wouldn't you?"

"You lost the right to know what I'd like and not like when you walked out." My voice breaks. Life imitating art in a way I never expected when I told him I'd run lines with him. I swallow over the lump in my throat, because *I* know that pain. I start to talk and stop. "I didn't make you leave, Noah. I didn't start the fire. I didn't hurt anyone. I wasn't the reason shit went south. And more than anything, I didn't make you erase me from your life."

"I never erased you!" he shouts with shoulders squared and eyes alive. We stare at each other for a beat before his defensive posture slips away. His shoulders slump, head drops, and voice lowers so I can barely hear him. "I could never erase you, Gabby."

"Don't do this to me. Don't waltz back into town like you own this place with that chip on your shoulder. I've moved on, Noah. I've made my own life. One that has no place for you in it."

He lifts his head, strides across the patio with determination, and slams his hands onto both sides of my chair. I jolt at the sound, at the force that moves my seat, at the unmistakable virility of both Noah and Hayes combined in the eyes of the man looking at me. "Anywhere you are is my place, Gabriella."

I snort. Know Gabby would do just the same and catch the flicker of surprise in Hayes's reaction. "No. It's not." I can barely speak the words. Hate the pang I feel in saying them. *Shit. Shit. Double shit. Do I feel the same way about him in real life?*

"Tell me you don't love me." His hands are on my chin directing my face up. His eyes are so honest, so true, that I almost forget I have a script in my hand. Silence stretches between us and I convince myself I need to look down at the lines. Yet I can't find it within me to break the hold he has on me, let alone breathe.

Script, Saylor. The script.

I force myself to look down to the papers. To the words I need to say. I exhale unsteadily when I read them and then look up to meet Hayes's eyes. "I don't love you, Noah. I've met someone else. Another man who I know won't leave." I avert my gaze. Push down the emotions rioting through me. How funny. I thought I was going to feel so silly doing this and yet *everything I am* is in the tone of my voice right now. "Like I said before, *it's over*. It's best that you leave."

"You're lying," he grits out between clenched teeth as he pounds a fist on the arm of the chair again. "*Lying*! Did you really think I'd give in so easily? Walk away without a fight?"

I'm mesmerized. Can't take my eyes off him. "You did before." My voice is a whisper of sound. My emotions raw in a scene that has nothing to do with me.

This is Noah and Gabby. Noah. And. Gabby.

Not *Hayes and Saylor.*

"You don't get it, do you?" He's exasperated. Frustrated. Pleading. He reaches out and tilts my face back up to his again. I hold my breath as he leans forward ever so slowly and puts his lips right to my ear. I smell the signature Hayes Whitley clean scent of soap and shampoo. Feel the heat of his breath. Warm under the touch of his hand. "*It's you. It's only ever been you.* I begged, borrowed, and lied to get this chance. To stand here in front of you again. To right my wrongs. To make you see why I am . . . why I can't just walk away this time without knowing, Gabby."

"Without knowing what?" I'm glad I remember the line because if I lean forward to look, I'll come face first with his chest and that's not something I need right now. The situation, the lines we're rehearsing, the man before me—all three are powerful enough, and I don't need the physical aspect of him to intoxicate me even more.

Hayes leans back so that our lips are inches apart. "Knowing what my forever tastes like."

Neither of us move. Or breathe. And when he finally takes a step back, his mouth slides into a satisfied grin.

"You're good, Say. Gotta hand it to you." He ruffles a hand through his hair. "I've been running that line all morning and hadn't figured it out. I was going in too hard, too angry. Having you to bounce it off made it easier. Let me see I needed to be softer with the delivery. Thank you."

I remain motionless in the chair, completely affected and unsure how he can go from the exchange we just had to, well, to him being him. And I'm reminded of his cryptic smile when I offered to run the lines. Wonder if he thought I would find this scene ironic, considering the history between us. And ironic is definitely one way to describe it.

Hitting too close to home is another way.

"I'm glad I could help," I say when I find my voice again.

"Do you mind if we run through it a few more times so I can tweak a few more things?"

Oh, hell.

And so we do. Each time through, my own emotion becomes more transparent. More vulnerable.

My body more turned on.

The constant repeat of the scene, in the intimacy of the words between two characters longing for each other is almost like foreplay in its own right. The emotion in his voice and reflected in his posture feels so real. So tangible. That with each take I forget he is acting.

But he is acting, Saylor. There is no hidden message he is trying to convey about how he feels about you. *And soon he will be running through this scene with another actor. Another woman. Not you.* It's just a role to him. Watch how easily he bounces back when the scene's over and he steps out of character.

And so when *he* finally feels satisfied with the delivery of his lines, *I* need a break from his presence. From the thoughts this entire scene has evoked. From the sexual tension that coats my skin so thick I almost feel it. From the pressure in my chest making it painful to draw in air despite being out in the open.

I opt to go for a walk on the beach to gain some physical distance from him and to quiet the unexpected emotions of the morning.

Funnily enough, the entire time I'm on my walk, I'm thinking of him.

Fifteen

Saylor

"THIS PLACE IS EVERYTHING I'D IMAGINED IT WOULD BE," I murmur more to myself than to Hayes.

"When you planned your wedding?"

I bristle, but deserve the straightforward question considering we are in the very hotel I had spent hours ruminating over for my wedding plans. I glance over to where he sits beside me at the hotel's outdoor bar. The drinks are stiff and the food is westernized but it feels good to be out and about in the hotel. Especially because I can enjoy the resort without feeling like I'm being watched since the entire wedding party is supposedly playing golf or at the salon. At least they're supposed to be according to the handy itinerary on the villa's kitchen counter.

"Yeah, but there was more to my decision to come here than just wanting a destination wedding. This was one of my mom's dream vacations. It was always their 'next trip' but it never happened. Money got tight. They had Ryder and me. Then came saving for college for us. They just kept putting it off and said they'd go after they retired. . ." My voice fades off, the memories so poignant and real all these years later.

"But they never made it to retirement." Hayes's voice is quiet, empathetic as he finishes the phrase for me. He places a hand on top of mine and squeezes it in support. "They were the best. Always fair. So full of love but also strict when they needed to be. Everything I wanted my parents to be like but weren't. I think of them often."

"They loved you, too, you know." It's important he knows that.

He nods his head as my heart hurts at the thought of them. I miss them every day but something about being here with Hayes—in the place they always wanted to visit—makes it a bit more poignant. And I think of how pleased they'd probably be, knowing I came here with Hayes. Especially since my mom used to always tell me one day I was going to marry *that boy*. Even after he left when she was nursing my broken heart, she was his biggest cheerleader telling me he was just off growing up but that he'd come back for me someday.

The smile is bittersweet. The memory even more so. The void in my heart from their absence a permanent fixture but feeling a little less empty when I look at Hayes.

I clear the emotion from my throat. "There were so many things they put off doing, waited for, or said they never had the chance to do once they had kids and I . . . shit, I don't know, Hayes . . . I don't want to be that way or feel like they did, and never fulfill the things I dream of doing. I don't want to be in the car on the way to dinner and get hit by a drunk driver and as I die, realize I never knew what those things I wanted to do felt like."

"I can understand that. Hell, anyone can, Saylor."

It feels like emotion after emotion is being churned up today and my parents' death is just the next thing to add to it. The memories hit me like photographs on a reel: the policemen at the door; my screams when I fought Ryder's arms as he tried to comfort me, when really, he had no comfort to give; the two caskets side by side lowered slowly into the ground. *Ashes to ashes. Dust to dust.* The constant cloud of inconsolable grief.

And then, meeting Mitch at a mutual friend's party seven months later. He was kind, paid attention to me, and took me places I'd never been before. Places that held no memories of my parents when everywhere else I went was flooded with them. Those things combined with the positive feelings he evoked in me slowly overshadowed the grief that had owned me.

Is that why I stayed with Mitch for so long? Because he took the pain away—more like put it on a backburner—and helped me slowly crawl out of the haze of grief? Did a part of me—the non-rational part of me—fear if there was no Mitch, that the pain might return?

Had he ever really known the real me? Was it once I felt more like myself—less meek and agreeable—that things started going downhill?

The thought is ludicrous, and yet it strikes me to the core. Love and obligation are two different things, Saylor. Not one and the same.

"Did I lose you?" Hayes's voice breaks through the fog of my thoughts.

I shake my head, clear my mind. "I'm sorry. Just thinking about them. What were you saying?"

His smile is cautiously sympathetic while his eyes search mine to make sure I'm okay. "All I said was I can understand your need to actively chase your dreams."

"No, I don't think you can. It's maddening." It's an unfair statement to make to him and yet I appreciate the fact he doesn't argue it. "They were so young and had so much life left to live, and yet I feel like they partly gave up on their dreams and hopes when they married, and I don't want to do that. *Be* that. Regret the chances I never took." I recall my mom's repeated comments about what she could have done—her dream career as a dancer on Broadway and how marriage and kids derailed that. A good derailment but a jump off the tracks nonetheless. I think of my dad and the baseball draft he missed out on because he thought the best thing to do for his family would be to be home and work a steady nine-to-five.

Missed opportunities. Dreams put on hold. Completely honorable decisions on their part. Ones that I benefitted from. A life still great by any standards lived in their perfect marriage but the theme of what-if always a constant undertone.

"Saylor?"

"What?" When I look up from where I'm playing with the

umbrella garnish from my fruity rum punch, I meet his eyes and realize he's asked me yet another question. I was too engrossed in thoughts of my parents—of the guilt I continually feel over loving them to death but wanting to be nothing like them—to have heard him.

It strikes me how weird this is to be talking about this now. It's been nearly seven years and yet it feels good to talk to someone who knew them like I did.

"I asked if your parents' unrealized plans had anything to do with you not marrying Mitch."

I stare at him long and hard, my gaze impenetrable, my thoughts a whirlwind, and chew the inside of my cheek. But I don't need to think at all because I know the answer. It's clear as day now that I've had this time away from him.

"Yes." My voice is quiet, eyes fixated on my drink and the condensation slowly sliding down the side of the glass. I question myself, hate that I almost feel like I'm cheating on Mitch by talking about him to Hayes, but then realize how absolutely absurd that is considering the situation. And I have to hand it to Hayes; he is patient. He sits and waits for me to find the words to express the conflicted emotions I'm certain blanket my face. "Mitch treated me well. I just think that his idea of what a wife should be and mine are two completely different things."

"I can assume here," he says as he lifts the bottle of Red Stripe to his lips, "but I'd prefer if you'd explain."

"Well, for one thing, he hated the bakery. Even before I rented the actual space and applied for my business license, I was running it as a side business out of our house. It drove him crazy. And not just the mess of it, but more the mess on me. He disliked that I was so lost in it that I didn't care if I had frosting in my hair or if my clothes were smeared with piping. And it wasn't that I didn't care but rather I was just so absorbed in whatever I was creating that I didn't notice the mess. God, he loathed the days I forgot to put on makeup because I had a harebrained idea for a new flavor and had to go do it right then before I forgot it."

"You always were that way. Spontaneous. Needing to see for yourself. I used to love and admire that about you."

I preen under his simple praise. Feel stupid that I do but can't help it considering I'm so used to the opposite opinion.

"Yeah well, not everyone does." I laugh. "I guess I wasn't proper wife material."

"That's the biggest bunch of bullshit, and if you believe it for a single second, I'm going to kick Ryder's ass for letting you." His eyebrows are lifted, lips pursed, expression unforgiving. And I've seen them throw punches at each other so I have no doubt he would.

This time around, Hayes definitely has the advantage.

My laugh floats out and draws the attention of the bartender who flashes a smile my way—eyes roaming over Hayes momentarily—before turning back to her customer. "When it came down to it, our marriage would have worked. I would have made it work," I say with more conviction than I feel. Resentment I never realized I harbored comes out of nowhere.

Hayes snorts and I'm not sure how to read the sound since his eyes are focused on people on the golf course beyond.

"You would have made it work so long as you sacrificed yourself. That sounds like a stellar marriage. One made to last."

I stare at him, his sarcasm loud and clear, wanting him to meet my eyes and not meet them all at the same time. I need to show him I'm not that woman. *Was I back then?* Maybe that's another reason I stayed with Mitch for so long.

"It doesn't matter now, really. That or any of the other reasons because we're not together."

"Hmpf."

"*Hmpf?* What does that mean?" I straighten my spine, suddenly defensive over the feeling that I'm being judged. And who is he to judge when he wasn't the one here for me after my parents died?

"It could mean a lot of things," he murmurs as he tips the bottle up to his lips and signals for another one. We're interrupted momentarily when another guest comes up and asks for his autograph. He handles the woman's nervous chattering like a pro before turning back to me. His eyes are unrelenting as they stare into mine, gauging how candid he wants his next comment to be. He starts to say something and then shakes his head and closes his mouth before turning back to the view beyond.

"Just say it, Hayes. It's not like you hold back."

"The way I see it from the outside is that he was the problem in your relationship, Saylor, not you, as you seem to continually assume. Having a passion like your baking is something that just happens. It's not controllable. It's a huge part of you that makes you happy. Calms you. Any person who tells you to suppress it for their own benefit is trying to stifle you. Mold you. Make you someone different than you are. *Never let someone steal your passion*. If you do, then you'll resent them. And resentment is the death of any relationship."

For the umpteenth time since he's walked back into my life, I just sit and stare at Hayes. Wonder how he's in my head and knows exactly how I'm feeling. First he connects the dots with my parents. How I don't want to miss chances like they did. And now this. Understanding the numerous nights I'd sit stewing at home because Mitch made a big fuss about me spending too much time at the bakery. How I'd be miserable, sitting idly by while he perused the Wall Street Journal or New York Times. It's like he wanted me to want to be with him more for his own ego's sake, to know I chose him over my work, and not because he actually wanted to spend time with me.

Hearing Hayes say it only reinforces that it was right to end things with Mitch.

"Thank you." My voice is soft, relieved that someone understands why I felt how I felt.

"There's no need to thank me." He shrugs as he sets his bottle down and stands up from his barstool. "Truth is truth, and I'm sorry you had to experience that particular truth. C'mon, I need to do something."

I look down to the hand he holds out to me and then back up to the brown of his eyes. "Keep this up, Whitley, and I just might start to like you again."

"You never stopped liking me." The smile he flashes—one full of arrogance, amusement, and adoration—causes the parts that he's awakened in me, the ones that wanted to be kissed, to roar back to life.

It's just the fresh air and different perspective, Saylor. Get a grip.

And so I do just that—get a grip—but this time it's by taking the hand he offers and following him without asking where we're going. We walk through the lush grounds and laugh at silly memories I can't even believe he remembers from our youth. We talk about Ryder and why he hasn't settled down yet. About the project we rehearsed this morning. About my favorite flavor of cupcakes.

And in all our wandering, I become distracted by both the scenery and by him with his board short-clad hips and his tanned, chiseled chest. Why would I want to pay attention to anything else? So I let him walk in front of me for a while as I happily meander behind, not having a clue where he's leading me.

I think about my parents. About their love. About how they only wanted the best for me. *They would have loved my bakery.* And I know deep down that despite the heartache I had walking away from Mitch, my mother may have turned over in her grave if I had married him here at her dream destination.

Because she would have known—*always did*—what was best for me even when I couldn't see it myself. Youthfulness often has a way of blinding you to truths.

And Mitch wasn't what was best for me.

But Hayes on the other hand . . . *she always did have a soft spot for him.* I think she'd be smiling, knowing I'm presently enjoying her idea of paradise with him. That we're burying the past so we can be friends. And that despite the heartbreak he caused me, she was right: he is the good guy she thought he was because he's here trying to help me save face.

I'm distracted from my thoughts when a resort employee walks out of a fork in the path in front of us. She momentarily meets Hayes's gaze, nods her head at him before smiling at me, and then makes her way down the path beyond us.

"So I have a confession," he says solemnly, causing my feet to falter and my eyes to wander to anywhere but on him.

"Nothing good ever comes from those opening words." I'm not sure why I'm already nervous about this. Why the single phrase has my pulse accelerating.

He chuckles but doesn't respond before walking a few feet, looking back to me, and then disappearing the same way the resort worker had just come from. I follow him into this little alcove carved out of the thick, tropical foliage. Its fronds shade us from the sun overhead and partially obscure us from any other guests exploring like we were. "Sit."

I narrow my eyes but oblige him after he sits down first. And I'm so fixated on the discord humming within me that I don't notice the box on the bench until he picks it up. And when I do, my eyes immediately home in on the pink pastry packaging.

"Hayes?"

He doesn't respond but rather opens the box so I can see a dozen lavishly decorated cupcakes inside. I'm so confused. What do cupcakes have to do with his confession?

"Just humor me, okay?" His dimples deepen with his smile.

"Sure." I rub my hands on my thighs and wait.

"When I arrived the other day before you, I thought I'd be nice and go buy some cupcakes, have them in the villa as a little treat for when you arrived. Looking back, the idea was stupid since you are usually up to your elbows in cupcake batter and frosting, so why would you want more? But my God, Ships, they tasted like shit. Nothing like yours whatsoever."

My laugh rings out. He likes my cupcakes. My ego has definitely been boosted. "So that's your confession? That the cupcakes are horrible?"

"In a sense." He nods his head and looks back down to the box's contents. "But you see, I know how long your anger can last, and I don't want you to be angry with me anymore. You can hold a mean grudge, Saylor Rodgers, and so I bought you these."

He holds the box out to me and now I'm even more confused. My chuckle reflects my mix of emotions. "Let me get this straight. You don't want me to hold a grudge against you, so you bought me a box of cupcakes you think taste like crap?"

"Yep." His smile broadens and body shifts so his knee is on the bench and shoulders face me.

"Okay." I laugh the word out, befuddled but amused. "But I'm not holding a grudge against you. I told myself I was going to come here and wash the slate clean. The past is the past, and it's over and done with."

He mulls the words over, the look on his face says he's skeptical whether he really believes me or not, then picks up a cupcake and hands it to me. What in the hell is going on here? "Hayes?"

"Just hold it because while I think they may taste like shit, I do think they'll be perfect grudge-busters."

"Grudge-busters? What? I'm so confused right now. What the hell is a grudge-buster?"

"It's this." I bite out a yelp as he picks a cupcake up and smacks his hands together with a dramatic flair. Bits of cupcake and frosting fly everywhere, like a confectionary explosion. There are crumbs stuck to his chest, all over his board shorts, in his hair, on his lips that are open and laughing, and understandably, smashed all over his hands.

Probably exactly what I look like at the end of a long day.

"Are you crazy?" I shriek but the words come out in a vomit of laughter. To see a man, who always looks so perfect no matter what time of day, look like the mischievous little boy from my childhood makes my heart swell.

"Your turn." Despite his tongue darting out to lick some frosting off his smiling lips, his tone is dead serious. And of course I hesitate, unsure if he's losing it but then again with that smile on his lips . . . I know he's not.

"Why? Can you just tell me why you want me to smash a cupcake in my hand—shitty tasting or not?" My eyes are wide, but my hands are itching to try it. Lips fighting the smile I can't seem to help when I'm around him.

"Because spontaneity is the best kind of adventure," he repeats the mantra from the other night. "And because it's a grudge-buster."

He shrugs as if he's making perfect sense and hopefully to himself, he is.

I stare at him long and hard, realizing he set this all this up with the resort employee delivering them to the spot for us and then leaving when she saw us. And if he's gone through this much trouble, I decide to go for it.

Within seconds, my hands are a mass of frosting and cake. The fallout from the force of my smash has resulted in an equal number of crumbs landing on Hayes as they have me. And while I may not be sure why I've just smashed a cupcake between my hands, I'm not going to lie when I say that it did feel pretty damn good. Cathartic.

"Should we do another one?" Hayes asks, as he looks down to where he's trying to remove a large chunk of chocolate frosting from his chest and only manages to smear it further.

I could help you get that.

With my lips.

And my tongue.

Holy hell, the thoughts have me shifting to abate the sudden ache of want in my core.

When his hand stills mid motion, I glance up from where I'm staring at it on his chest to find he's caught me watching. There's a flash of something darker in his eyes mixed with a glimpse of desire. The words on my tongue suddenly feel like molasses.

I blink my eyes and try to refocus on what he asked me. *Do I want to smash another one?* Yes, for obvious reasons. And no, because he's trying to distract me for some reason.

"No. I'm good."

"You sure?"

"Why would I hold a grudge against you, Hayes?" My wits have been restored. So long as I keep my eyes on his. Off his body. And *not* on his lips.

"I lied to you, Ships."

Now there's a definitive way to distract me from thinking about his body.

"Okay." I stretch the word out as I wrack my brain for what he's referring to.

"When I walked into Sweet Cheeks that first day, yes, I was picking up the order for my mom, but I lied about that being the only reason."

"Hayes." His name is a warning I don't want to have to give.

"Hear me out." His chocolate-smeared palms are up in the defensive position. I glare. "I came in with every intention of telling you I had talked to Ryder and knew what had happened. But when I saw you . . . shit, Say, I fumbled. It'd been years since I'd seen you. And when I did, everything about what used to be us—*our friendship, our love, our connection*—rushed right back like it was yesterday. Then you assumed. And I saw how hurt you were. How much your pride had been fucked with by Mitch and the jerks you thought were your friends. I heard it in your voice. It killed me, Say. Made me think of how bad I'd hurt you before and knew I couldn't hurt you again. And then after I heard you talk about Mitch, about why you walked away, I realized what you needed more than anything was honesty. It seems you've already faced enough on your own, and the least I could do was be honest too. So, yeah, I chickened out that first day I saw you. Thought if you told me on your own terms then I'd feel better about it, and only then would I do this if you asked."

His words fade off and I'm not sure what to feel. I want to be mad at him. Want to feel embarrassed that he's known all this time, and yet I can't be. How lucky am I to have a friend willing to see how much I was hurting and not want to add to it?

"Sorry." He speaks the word with such weight that I know the apology is for so much more than just not telling me.

"Thank you." The two words are a whisper while the new cupcake in my hand taunts loudly to be smashed. On Hayes.

Hayes nods his head, our eyes still locked, but my thoughts are completely consumed with the idea.

"Hey," I say, voice soft, lips curved in mischief. "No grudges." He lifts his eyebrows as if he's shocked I've forgiven him so easily, and then he gasps when I land the first confectionary blow. One beautifully decorated chocolate ganache cupcake is smashed on the exact location I'd thought about licking only moments before.

He's silent as he looks down to where my hand is still pressed against him, chocolate frosting the only barrier between us. I grind it in, slowly slide it down his abs, and then lift my hand to bring a coated finger to my mouth. His eyes lift from the aftermath of my assault to watch me wrap my lips around my finger and suck the frosting off it.

A myriad of things flicker through his darkening irises. What I assume is hunger and desire. Need and want. The same feelings that are rioting through me. I slide my finger from my mouth and run my tongue over the chocolate still on my bottom lip. His jaw pulses. His eyes hold fast. Sexual tension sparks when it just can't.

I remind myself of all the reasons this is a bad idea. How in two days he's going to leave and go back to his life in Hollywood, and I'll return to my mixer and ovens and passion. *Alone.*

So I try to bring us back to the playful part of us. The neutral zone.

"You're right," I murmur, a taunting smile on my lips, and a scrunch of my nose. "Not enough cream."

I more than notice Hayes's expression: mischief to match mine, challenge, disbelief.

And it's only a fraction of a moment, a split second of time where we let spontaneity take over, and the kids we used to be emerge. In a frenzy of activity, we both scramble up from the bench and grab the remaining cupcakes from the box. Our laughter floats around us like the rustle of the palm leaves in the breeze. We're armed and ready for a cupcake war.

He strikes next. A pink frosted one that glances off of my shoulder. My yelp rings out above the waves on the beach. His footsteps behind me tell me he's given chase down the pathway. I turn a bend where he can't see me and dart in between a break in the hedge. Just as he passes me, I jump out and smash a vanilla frosted cupcake square against his back.

"Still a little shit all these years later, Ships." He laughs out the insult as we circle each other like dogs with smiles on our faces, lungs out of breath, and intention in our movements.

"Hmm, you forget how fast I am, Whitley?" I lunge toward him, ready to strike, and he jumps back. We continue this dance until I take one step too many and he grabs my arm and twists me against him, my back to his front.

"I think you forget how strong I am."

I don't even have a second to prepare before he lands a cupcake to my collarbone. And with his body behind me and his hand against me, I definitely feel his strength. Using his leverage, he takes his hand and purposely smears the cupcake against my skin and bathing suit.

"You asshole!" I shriek in jest as I escape the confines of his arms and chase after him down the footpath.

He taunts me from ahead. *You're such a wimp. You can't catch me. How do you like them apples, huh, Say?*

"You're dead meat," I call after him as we weave in and out of paths. I chuck a cupcake at him from behind, and it bounces off the back of his neck.

"Close but no cigar," he heckles as I scoop up the dropped cupcake for a reloadable weapon and continue down the path to where he disappeared.

"Come out, come out, wherever you are," I call when I can't find him. With a cupcake in one hand, my sarong gathered up in my other hand, and an enthusiastic smile on my lips, I search through breaks in the foliage to find his hiding spot.

I yelp when hands grab my waist from behind and spin me around. "Olly olly oxen free," he whispers as he cocks his arm back and aims the cupcake at my face.

"No!" The sound is part laughter, part warning. "You wouldn't."

"I would."

We playfully struggle our way into a clearing. There's laughter around us. I'm sure we are quite the sight—two grown adults covered in various colors of frosting having an epic battle—yet I don't think once to care. My only focus is the cupcake in Hayes's hand.

I hear my name. I think I do anyway, and it distracts me enough momentarily that Hayes is able to grab and pull me tighter into him, the cupcake now inches from my face.

We stare at each other in a silent standoff, hearts racing and eyes daring. His gaze flickers over my shoulder and then back to mine as I prepare myself for *the smash*.

But it doesn't come.

Instead he eases up and only dabs the frosting against the tip of my nose.

I sigh in relief.

Then gasp out in shock.

Because Hayes's lips are on mine.

And not just a friendly peck. Not hardly. The hand that held the cupcake is now empty. Chocolate fallen by the wayside for a kiss. His fingers, sticky with frosting, are on my cheeks directing my face. But there's no thought of the frosting he'll get on my face or how funny it's going to look when we walk back to our villa because all I can think about is Hayes.

I could tell myself I part my lips—grant him access—because I'm winded and need to breathe, *but that would be a lie.* Because the minute his tongue dances against mine, all I want to do is drown in his kiss. In the familiarity of it. In the difference of it. The unexpectedness of it. The comfort of it. *In everything about him.*

Hayes Whitley is kissing me. Again.

Finally.

His fingers are possessive—on the underside of my jaw and the small of my back—and the soft groan he emits communicates everything his lips are expressing and more.

His taste consumes me. The chocolate on his tongue. The spark of desire. The lick of lust. The sense of calm riled up by an overload of emotion.

My hands slide up the plane of his back over skin heated by the sun and slick with frosting. His muscles bunch beneath my palms as he shifts the angle of the kiss.

His tongue tantalizes and torments. Begs me to want more with its tender caresses and then switches gear and demands me to keep pace. To allow him to possess and claim.

I feel in droves. Want. *Need.* Lust. *More.* Too much. *Not enough.*

Don't ever stop. *What am I doing?*

And as much as I should be panicked, as much as I should be thinking about what all this means and how I already know I'm going to get hurt somehow, I don't. Instead I lose myself in the kiss. Surrender myself to him. The guests and the staff I heard moments ago no longer exist.

It's just me.

And Hayes.

And the singular sensation of rightness he is making me feel. A sensation I don't think I had ever realized was missing since he'd left, but now know I'll never be able to live without.

Sixteen

Hayes

JESUS FUCKING CHRIST.

Soft lips. Skilled tongue. That little moan.

Did I really walk away from this? From her? *Why?*

Goddamn it, Saylor.

I kissed her because I saw them looking.

I kissed her because I wanted there to be no doubt who she was with, and the status of our *nonexistent* relationship.

I kissed her because it's been too damn tempting not to, and so why not when it was the perfect opportunity?

And fuck, now I don't want to come up for air. I just want to stand right here with this woman who owns every sensation within me. The one coated in frosting who left the pain behind and is currently pressed against me. The one whose laughter I can hear still in that sweet goddamn moan she made and whose taste I don't think I ever forgot.

How could I?

Her fingers press into my back. Little scrapes of her nails to let me know this is real. Not some movie set. Not ten years ago in the tree

139

house with my letterman jacket on the floor beneath her. But here in paradise with the smell of suntan lotion on her skin and the tickle of the breeze blowing her hair onto my cheeks.

I'm in two minds. Two sets of thoughts struggling to be heard through the roar of want that's firing in my blood. One begs me to drag her off to the villa and see what else is the same and different about her all this time later. Dip between her thighs and have a taste. Feel her pussy grip around my cock and hear my name pant on her lips when she comes.

I deepen the kiss. Grip her jaw tighter and take what I want from her because, fuck if taking her right now on the putting green isn't a possibility.

My sensibility fights back. Tells me this can't happen. Saylor is Saylor with her little cupcake shop and her own dreams, and I'm just the asshole who lives in Hollywood with a life so different than hers that it would never work. I'd only hurt her again in the end. And she's had enough hurt lately.

I want to tell my mind to shut the fuck down. To let my dick do the talking. The one that's currently pressed against the warmth of her bare belly.

I have to end the kiss for my own fucking sanity. And because I'm pretty sure there are laws against having sex in public. I fight the urge to dive back in and deepen the kiss. To give in to my need and take what I want.

But I don't. Can't. This isn't about me.

This is about Ships and making things right.

So I take one last draw on her lips. One last nip of the forbidden fucking fruit I want more than I thought I would but now realize I shouldn't have. And end the kiss.

But I don't let her go just yet. I know how hard quitting Saylor cold turkey can be. Recall the burn in my gut that lasted for almost a year. *Gut? More like heart.* And then I realize that it probably took even longer since every one of those feelings just came back with a vengeance after a single damn kiss.

So I hold onto her and steal one more moment. Take one more

draw of the same breath. Let my mind stumble through memories of the past we shared and be thankful our paths have crossed again.

"Now I know why I've always compared every woman I've ever kissed to you." The words are out before I can stop them. A confession I never should have made but now can't seem to purge from my mind.

Her breath hitches. Fingers flex against my skin. And then the murmurs of those around us provide the reason I need to take a step back. Break the hold she has on me. Play the part I came here to play.

And when I do break our connection, she still holds me captive. I take in her full lips, the frosting smudged on her cheeks, and read the confusion in her eyes. The perfect goddamn combination of sexy, sweet and uniquely Saylor standing before me slaps me in the face and begs to know how I could have been so stupid to walk away from her.

Shut it down, Whitley. Keep your distance. End the scene.

I remind myself to breathe and force a smirk instead of stepping back into her. To get my wits about me and refocus on if the twenty or so members of the wedding party across the green are still watching. The ones I caught sight of while Saylor and I were having our cupcake war.

And they are definitely watching.

"C'mon. Let's go." I grab her hand and steer her from where curious eyes continue to stare. To wonder. To judge. And I want them to question how the woman they knew her to be, the one Ryder explained to me as being so proper and reserved over the past six years, has enough of a wild streak in her to chase a man through a posh resort and have a food fight with him.

Not just any man, though. *Me.*

But my desire to head back to the villa has a helluva lot more to do with me than with her right now. I need to work. Because work has always allowed me to forget about Saylor, and God, how I need to forget about her right now. Because with her within arm's length, with her taste on my lips, with the warmth of her body still heating my skin, I'm not sure I'm going to be able to keep the one promise I made to myself when I agreed to come here: leave her better off than how I found her.

"Hayes?" Her voice is confused, the amusement it was rich with now gone. It takes me a second to realize she had no idea we were being watched. And I'm so goddamn self-absorbed, so mad at myself for wanting to do the right thing, that I forgot to tell her.

"Sorry. We had company." I stop on the path and turn to look at her to make sure she heard me.

"What? Wh—oh." Realization hits her eyes, a healthy dose of hurt too, as I let her assume the sole reason I kissed her was because there was an audience and not because I wanted to. She clears her throat and lifts her chin in a show of false bravado. "Yes. I know. I saw them."

She's lying. She wanted the kiss just as much as I did. The twirl of her finger around her hair and the stiffening of her body prove she did, but for some reason I don't elaborate or correct her line of thinking.

Instead I stand there like an asshole as she forces a smile to save herself the embarrassment over thinking what happened was out of mutual desire. And that she threw herself into the kiss—*and fuck me, how she threw herself into the kiss*—for no other reason than to help sell our fake relationship to the wedding party.

That in itself is comical because we both wanted it. There's no denying that. And yet I don't correct her. I don't confess how sleeping in the villa last night with her in the bedroom directly across from mine was the sweetest kind of torture. Or explain how rehearsing the scene this morning didn't make me wonder about and want her in every way imaginable. And I definitely don't tell her how badly I want to drag her up against me right now and kiss her all over again.

But I don't say a word because the next time I touch her, I don't think I'm going to be able to stop with just a kiss. And I'm not sure it's smart to open up that door until I can figure out what in the hell I'm going to do about keeping that damn promise I made myself.

"C'mon," I murmur, turning around before I can see that wounded pride in her eyes again. The one I put there. "I've got stuff I need to do before . . . I booked you a private massage in the spa room down from our villa." I glance at my watch to emphasize she's going to be late. Hate myself for pawning her off so *I* can have a minute—or sixty—to get my head straight.

"I don't wa . . ." Blue eyes full of unanswered questions meet mine and the words die on her lips.

"It's that way." I point. "See you in a bit."

I walk off down the path, like the asshole I am. I tell myself not to stop and turn back. Not to grab her hand or open the door of the villa, lick that frosting off her chest, and slide down the slippery slope that would follow.

And it would surely follow. No doubt in my mind there.

But it's not meant to be. Can't happen. I'm here to make sure she's okay and pulling her into any part of my crazy life would lead to anything but *okay*. So why do my hands falter as I slide the key card in the door? Because ten years have passed. Because I'm a different man now than I was then, and she is without doubt a different woman. She's stronger. Independent. She's Saylor.

So why couldn't something work now?

Fuck. That's the shit I can't be thinking. The one thing I came here telling myself wasn't going to happen. Because what was supposed to happen was that we were going to live in the same villa for a few days and remember old times. I was hoping to help her restore her confidence, prove a point to the Layton groupies, and then walk away when the time was up as *friends*—something few and far between for me these days.

How's that working for you, Whitley?

Kind of hard to remain impartial when everywhere we go, assholes from the wedding have stared at her. She may not have noticed them—so busy with her eyes wide at the tropical scenery around us—but I sure as shit did. I saw the packed tables in the back corner of the karaoke bar—eyes glued, tongues wagging, noses turned up. But they did take notice of who she was with. Then the halt of conversation and turning of heads as we walked by the pool earlier today—the floppy hats being lifted so they could stare a little longer from behind their sunglasses and grimace over *that girl from the other side of town* as I heard one of them mutter. And of course then again, in the bar a while ago. The pairs of eyes looking over the edge of menus, ready to whisper the minute I turned my attention from them and back to her.

But the joke's on them. I'm not fucking stupid and have played this game perfectly in her defense. Made sure I'm loud so it's noticed that I'm here at the resort. Looked like an egotistical fucker throwing my name around, when typically, I use an alias to go incognito so I can enjoy my time off rather than be constantly wary of the sly pictures taken on cell phones or time interrupted when asked for autographs.

But this weekend is for Saylor. Not me. My way of easing my guilt from all those years ago. My need to make sure she's okay because as tough as she is, I can still see the hurt she's hiding behind her gutsy façade. It seems that fucker, Mitch, has put her through the wringer.

So yeah. I'll throw my name around. Take my time eating our meals in the wide-open bar. Sit beside her poolside and sip some cocktails. Go to the hottest spots in town when I know the whole wedding party will be there just to make sure there is no mistaking we're a couple.

If I'm famous, I might as well put it to good use in her favor.

Besides, I've got my publicist on the ready. She's already issued statements to the press stating I'm taking a little R&R after wrapping the last film to hang out with an old childhood friend. I certainly haven't felt the normal hairs on the back of my neck when I sense an intrusive lens aimed in my direction, which has been incredibly freeing.

Kissing Saylor in public was a stupid mistake on my part, but hell if I expected any of this—*the feelings, the connection, wanting to kiss her senseless*—to happen when I offered to bring her here in the first place. *But she was far too tempting not to taste.*

I shake the thought from my head, certain that this little bubble around us in this all-inclusive resort will remain intact. And just as I know it will, I also know that our simple kiss won't change the wedding party's thoughts of her.

They'll still judge her and thumb their snooty noses at her. And since she's going to be judged, I'll make sure they see the real her. The laughing, funny, spontaneous girl I used to know. The one whose friendship they're missing due to their arrogance and exclusivity.

The irony? I'm realizing how much I missed out on it too.

Thank fuck I'm an actor, can play the part like nobody's business, because I've just fooled both the audience watching across the green and, by the hurt in her eyes, Saylor herself. And maybe even myself.

They think I want her.

She thinks I don't.

I know I want her.

I know I can't.

Seventeen

Saylor

N ow I know why I've always compared every woman I've ever kissed to you.

I cream the butter and sugar together. Do it by hand and forgo the perfectly capable mixer sitting on the counter behind me because I need the physicality of it. The therapy it provides.

The comment repeats in my mind. Confounds me. If the kiss was for show, why did he make that comment? I'm so confused. And right alongside my confusion sits my sexual frustration.

The massage Hayes booked for me was meant to be relaxing. Meant to make me forget everything that was to come tonight with the rehearsal dinner. Kind of hard to do when each time the masseuse slid his hands over my skin, all I could think about was how I wanted Hayes's hands on me instead.

Add an egg. Beat the mixture. *Is he as worked up over this as I am?* Crack another with one hand while I keep stirring with the other. Add that one in. Stir. A dash of vanilla. Stir.

Because since our kiss earlier, the only thing stronger than the desire owning my body, is the confusion ruling my heart.

The constant reminder to myself that the kiss was all for show.

For Mitch.

For his family.

For his friends.

Whatever combination of the three standing on the golf course while Hayes pulled me against him and kissed me. *Senseless.* Thoroughly. Handily.

It was all for show.

I repeat the phrase. Tell myself I can't be hurt by it because I knew it was going to happen at some point. A simple kiss to convince the wedding party that Hayes and my relationship was legitimate.

At least we got it out of our systems. But it's definitely not out of my system—not by a long shot—because that kiss was anything but simple. It was a no-holds-barred, steal-your-breath, make-you-want-without-regret kiss.

Hence the reason I'm still so damn emotional over it a few hours later.

Sift the flour with the baking powder. Check the oven to see if it's at temperature yet. *Is he questioning himself now like I am? Wanting more yet not acting on it because he realizes it's an all around bad idea?* Add a pinch of salt. *Or is this all a scene to act out in a comedic script to him?* Lift my eyes and stare at the view beyond but not really see it because I'm lost in thought. Lost over everything really when it comes to Hayes.

I kept thinking that if we kissed under the guise of it being for onlookers, it was going to help rid the ghost of us from my memory. But I was so very wrong. Now I feel like it's awakened them rather than bury them for good.

Stir.

He's an actor, Saylor. This is what he does for a living. Plays to the crowd.

Stir.

He was just playing the part. It was a kiss. A moment. And then he turned it off like a light switch the second you were out of sight of everyone else. *Just like he did when we ran lines.*

Stir.

You're reading too much into it, Saylor. But if it was all an act, why did Hayes murmur those words against my lips? Why did he hesitate pulling away?

A part of me thinks it was more than show. Hopes it was. Doesn't hope it was. *Jesus, I'm a mess.* And yet I was there. I sensed his hunger behind the kiss, felt the intent in his touch, and saw the desire in his eyes.

Pick up the rubber spatula. Scrape the batter down the sides of the bowl.

> **Ships,**
> **Just in case you need to busy your hands in batter.**
> **- Hayes**

The note he'd left me on the counter catches my eye again over the edge of the bowl. The one I had found on top of a stack of ingredients, bowls, and utensils when I walked into the kitchen from my post-massage shower.

If he didn't care, he wouldn't have done this. He wouldn't have known that when I'm confused I use baking as my therapy. Use the comfort it brings to help me work through my thoughts.

No. If he didn't care, he would have acted more like Mitch: focus on him. On his needs. His wants. Without a thought to my need for a mental recess.

But he does care. The note. The ingredients. The cooking instruments. Ensuring the villa had cupcake trays and liners. Understanding I'm confused and need this to help me work through it. All of those things say he does.

Don't they?

Check to see if the oven has hit temperature. Hands falter mid-stir.

I had to have misread him and his intentions. Had to have thought there was more to his touch than there really was, because afterward, he dismissed me without a second look. In fact he almost seemed irritated with me, like I did something wrong.

Ready to spoon the batter, I pick up the metal cupcake tray from the counter behind me and slam it down onto the granite top a little harder than necessary. The sound reverberates through the house but does nothing to abate my frustration. *This is so screwed.*

Place the cupcake liners in the tray. Count the rows. Placate my obsessive thoughts.

What if I'm wrong? What if Hayes wanted to kiss me? What if he shared in my curiosity and wanted to know if there was anything lingering between us so he took advantage of the moment?

And damn, what a moment it was.

But now I'm drowning in perplexity. In bewilderment. In the fear and desire of wanting him to kiss me again despite knowing that wanting more is only going to lead to getting hurt again. And in the confusion over how a single kiss from Hayes can wind me up tighter than a spring when not once in the six years with Mitch did he ever make me feel this way.

But Hayes pulled back. He erased the emotion from his face and walked away—*again*—as if I irritated him.

I spoon batter into the cups. A little more forcefully than I should. With each scoop my anger builds. My emotions wrenched open like a can opener.

Scoop.

What? I'm not good enough for him anymore? Not posh enough? Not pretty enough on the Hollywood starlet scale of beauty?

Scoop.

Well, screw you, Hayes Whitley. Screw you and your Academy Award and your walking shoes that you still seem to wear.

Scoop.

Tears blur my vision. Rejection burns brighter than logic. Hurt resurfaces when I force myself to admit that I knew exactly what I was getting into when I arrived here.

Scoop.

I should be mad at myself for not keeping a leash on my emotions. For not remembering how devastating Hayes can be on my heart. For letting the ladies in Starbucks and their catty comments fuel my temper so I screwed over my own sensibility and accepted Hayes's offer to come here.

Scoop.

Just call it off, Saylor. Tell Hayes we already made our point today in the clearing—that I'm deliriously happy with a much more successful man than Mitch—and then hop on a plane. Leave all of this tumult behind and keep what's left of your heart *and dignity* intact.

Scoop.

Get a grip, Say. You're letting one kiss make you lose your ever-loving mind and jump to conclusions that are all supposition.

I blame it all on him. From taking the trip down memory lane with the old Hayes I used to love and then switching gears and having new experiences with the mature Hayes who brought me here. The one who makes unexpected observations, makes me laugh until my stomach hurts, and who doesn't care if he's covered in cupcake splatter so long as I'm not mad at him.

The one who came here to try and help me gain some kind of redemption and hopefully save my store.

I brace my hands on the edge of the counter, hang my head, and remind myself why I'm here in the first place. To save the bakery and to restore my reputation.

Not for the more than enjoyable distraction of Hayes Whitley.

When I lift my head, the distraction himself is standing on the other side of the kitchen. Shirt off. Chest heaving. Running shorts on. Hair damp with sweat. Jaw muscle pulsing. Eyes locked on mine.

My breath catches. At the sheer beauty of him. At the force in his expression. At the raw emotions rioting through me just from the sight of him. At how every single part of me stands at attention when his hands fist at his sides and his muscles tense.

Hello, distraction.

I hate him and love him, want him and don't want him.

He takes a step forward. Stops.

I remind myself to breathe. To say something to break the hold he has over me. To ignore the sudden ache in my lower belly and that slow burn of arousal that coats my skin in goosebumps.

"I went for a run." His words are strained. Hoarse. And yet I'm not exactly sure why he's telling me the obvious.

"I'm making cupcakes."

He nods his head as if this is a normal, everyday conversation. But it's far from it if the way my body is reacting to every single thing about him can be used as a barometer.

My nipples harden and my mouth waters. My body aches in places I've never felt before as I take him in. The way he runs his tongue over his bottom lip. The fine mist of sweat on his chest. The flex of one of his pecs causes me to realize I'm staring. I look up and notice the barely there arrogant smile on his lips before meeting his eyes again.

"I keep telling myself that we can't do this, Saylor."

His words cut through the tension settling around us. Throw water on the sexual fire sparking between us.

And even though his words say no, every single thing about his body says yes. The predatory posture. The gleam in his eyes. The tautness of his muscles. Visible restraint that a part of me wants to test. I wonder how hard I'll have to push before it snaps.

I know without a doubt that snap will sting, but for some reason I have a feeling when it comes to Hayes Whitley, the sting might just be worth it.

Another step.

Predator toward prey.

"Can't do what?" My voice is barely a whisper. The tight buds of my nipples press against my thin bikini top and communicate what the rasp of my voice can't. *I want you. Kiss me. I only want to think about here. And now. And the way you make me feel.*

His chuckle is soft. Low. Strained. He's closer now. Within touching distance. He reaches out to the bowl beside us on the counter, runs a finger around the edge of it, and brings it to his lips. He waits to make sure I'm watching him as he sucks the batter from it. And damn it to hell if the groan he makes when he pulls his finger from his mouth doesn't pluck on the strings of desire running throughout me.

"What can't we do, Hayes?" I ask again. Have to. I need an answer to know if what I think he's saying and what I want him to be saying are the same damn thing.

Another step.

He withdraws his finger from his mouth as he angles his head and holds my gaze. Waiting. Gauging. Anticipating. I can feel the heat of his body. Hear his steady inhale of breath. And I'm more than ready for his touch when he reaches out and places his hand on the side of my neck.

"Everything." He licks his lips, glances down to my mouth, and then back up to my eyes as his thumb rubs ever so slightly over my collarbone. "And nothing."

"Oh." My mind spins. My body aches. Every part of me wants.

"This is a bad idea."

He leans in and brushes his lips against mine. It's just a simple taste of a kiss but with that singular action my reasons disappear, *my heart tumbles*, and my body aches for him.

"A terrible idea," I murmur and this time I take the initiative and kiss him back. A soft part of the lips. A barely there brush of tongues.

"Horrible," he whispers before matching the depth of my kiss and adding to it. His other hand comes up to frame the side of my face, his thumb resting just beneath the line of my jaw so he can control the angle of the kiss.

"Awful." Our bodies mesh the same time our tongues do. His body still hot from his run. Still firm. Still slick with sweat.

"Stupid," he whispers. A slight smile forming on his lips before he dives back in to taste and take. Taunt and tantalize. Demand and offer.

I moan. Can't help that I do because there's a dominating tenderness to his kiss. A forgiving relentlessness. A desperate calmness. There's no rush to it. No hurry to get to the next part.

Thoughts escape me with each dance of our tongues. With each tug on my bottom lip by his. With each soft directive of his lips moving against mine.

My hands skim up the sides of his torso, loving the feel of the bunching of his muscles beneath my palms. He fists a hand in my hair and changes the angle of the kiss. Choreographs the next step in our slow dance of desire.

"Saylor." My name on his lips in that gravelly tone scrapes over me. Drags me from the haze his kisses have pulled me under. He leans back so our eyes can meet.

Seconds pass. Questions, wants, needs, flicker through his eyes. *Should we? Can we? How is this happening again?*

His jaw pulses. His dick is hard against my hip. His waning control reflected in the tightening of his fingers in my hair.

My lips part. *Yes. Yes.*

Because it's us.

But I can't give the answers because I'm silenced by the moment and by the bright burn of arousal coursing through my body. By the need to want and the want to need this connection with him.

By acknowledging that I love him. *Probably always have.*

"I've never been able to resist you. Not then. Not now."

Not ever.

Our past and present collide in one sweeping moment of time. Our mouths meet again in a savage union of lips and tongue and want and desire and greed and hunger. Our hands slide and grab and feel and possess each other's flesh.

We're a frenzy of movements. Of not being able to touch each other quickly enough, and yet wanting to slow down and take our time with this reunion that has been years in the making.

His mouth is on the underside of my neck. His hands are pulling down the straps of my swimsuit, then palming my breasts. Thumbs run over the tips of my nipples sending a tsunami of sensation through my body.

His lips lace hungry kisses against the sensitive skin to my ear. I fumble with his shorts while he pushes down my bikini bottoms. My cool hands slide beneath the waistband to find him hot and hard and ready. My mouth falls open from his teeth scraping over my nipple while his hands are everywhere and not enough places all at the same time. The evidence of what I do to him stiff in my hand.

His hands are on my waist. My feet leave the floor, and the hard granite of the countertop is cold beneath my ass. There's a clatter of utensils. A thud of something falling over. A plume of flour in the air.

But Hayes doesn't miss a beat. He steps between my thighs and pulls my ass to the edge so I'm perched there, needing his body to ensure I don't fall. And then he claims my mouth again in a kiss that promises possession and surrender.

My hands are on his shoulders. His fingers feather over the entrance of my sex, part it, then slide up and back through my arousal. My head falls back. My thighs spread wider, my body instantly giving him access to every single part of me without a word.

I moan when he slips his fingers into me. A teasing inch at first. A suggestion of what's to come. And then his mouth is on mine, pulling me under once again. And just when I'm drugged enough, he slips his fingers all the way in, circles them to ignite the nerves within, and rubs his thumb with a hint of touch over my clit.

My hips buck at the onslaught of sensation. Tongue. Fingers. Thumb. His groan. My plea for more. Then it starts all over again. A slow build up. A soft seduction of my nerves. A murmur of praise. An assault of pleasure.

The orgasm surprises me. It sounds stupid but it feels so very different from what I'm used to. A slow surge of warmth. A tensing of muscles. Hayes's name on my lips as the wave rises and pulls me in its unexpected undertow. Drowns me in the surge of pleasure and a wash of desire. My muscles pulse around his fingers as his thumb continues to circle over my clit. My fingernails dig into his biceps and hips twist in pleasurable pain.

I'm still lost in the orgasmic fog, still on the high from it when he withdraws his fingers from me and brings them to my parted lips. His eyes are on mine—locked and intense—when he coats my lips with my own arousal. I draw in a shaky breath as he slowly leans forward and runs his tongue over the path his fingers left. The moan he emits is sex personified.

It's unexpectedly arousing.

It's entirely consuming.

It's intoxicatingly erotic.

His lips follow. A brush against mine. When I lick my tongue against my lips to ask for more, his chuckle rumbles through the room.

"My pace, Saylor. Not yours. I'm in control now. You may own pieces of me you never even knew, but right now, I'm going to own you. Every single part of you."

My blood fires at the words. Libido ignites, and yet I'm stunned into silence. Shocked by his confession. Body rocked by his touch.

"Hayes." One word. A plea. A question. A sigh.

He kisses me again, but this time with more demand. More greed. He's tongue and lips and little nips of teeth, all the while my body is still vibrating from the remnants of the orgasm.

His hand is on my neck, holding my head still as he seduces my lips and relights the fire that he left smoldering. My hands reach down and circle his length to stroke the hardness of him. I feel the drop of pre-cum on his head. Smear it around with my thumb before deliberately leaning back and sucking on my thumb.

I close my eyes and taste him on my skin. Moan softly. When I open them back up, his eyes are ablaze with a hunger that's new to me.

"I want you, Say." His voice is guttural. Desperate. Empowering.

I slide my hands to my breasts and rub my nipples between my thumbs and forefingers. The flour he knocked over coats my hands. Adds a difference of sensation. My lips part in a soft gasp.

He swallows visibly and darts his tongue to his lips. "Right here. Right now." He steps into me. Slides a hand up my torso, over my hands on my breasts, and replaces my fingers with his own. The sensation is heavenly. My back arches and my head falls back but not enough to lose eye contact with him.

And just when I want to close my eyes he dips forward and circles my nipple with his tongue. Then sucks. It's like an electric current has been sent straight to every nerve in my body. Shocking them aware. Making them feel every singular sensation: the heat of his tongue, the scrape of his stubble, and the vibration of his groan against my skin.

"No one's watching now." He looks up to me from beneath lids heavy with desire. "It's just you. And me."

His words are like an aphrodisiac. A stimulant. An eraser to the errant thoughts I had before he walked in.

I was wrong. He did want to kiss me.

"And fuck how much I want you right now."

Wanting to test the control he claims to want, I bring a hand to the back of his neck and pull him to me. My mouth is against his. A taunt of a kiss. A nip to his lip. His name a moan. I show him I want *him* just as fiercely. Running my tongue over the coarseness of his jaw to his ear, I say, "I've always wanted you."

The words are out before I can stop them. The transparency of the moment taking over and speaking truths I can't take back. A confession I don't think I even wanted to admit to myself.

There's a falter in motion. A second where our eyes meet and our emotional guard is lowered. And then the moment takes over.

A growl deep in his throat as he slides his hand back up my midline between my breasts before pushing me to lie back onto the flour-coated granite slab behind me. His hands hook around my thighs and pull me toward him.

A moment of separation. A curse as his feet pad from the room before coming back. The telltale rip of foil.

Anticipation builds. His fingers part me and cool air touches my heated skin. The thick curve of his head as he presses it against my wet center. I widen my thighs. Close my eyes. And revel in that soft, sweet, all-consuming burn as he slowly pushes his way into me.

Good. God. Yes.

My back arches. My hands press flat against the cool counter. My breath catches. The ache builds, inch by agonizingly slow inch until he's sheathed root to tip.

His soft groan of, "Jesus Fucking Christ, Saylor," is enough of a response to tell me he feels the same way I do.

His fingers tighten on my hips and desire is reflected in the touch. My muscles tremble. My eyes are closed, mind lost to the thought of how, after all this time, only one person has ever made me feel like this: full, complete, wanted, desired, loved.

And then he moves. Dragging my mind from thoughts that will just complicate matters and flooding me with the slow and steady rhythm he pulls us into. I'm swamped with pleasure immediately. The warmth is so intense. The manipulation of every part of me over-whelming. *It's been so long.*

He pushes all the way into me and grinds his hips so the base of his shaft adds a touch of friction against my clit. On his withdrawal, the crest of his cock rubs against the pleasure point of nerves inside. Then he eases almost all the way out, teases me with just the tip and then begins the slow slide back in.

I'm drugged by his adept skill. His insatiable finesse.

My eyes flutter open to take in the sight of him before me. Muscles tense, teeth biting into his bottom lip, head angled down to watch where we're joined.

He looks up and meets my eyes. A dare and a warning flash in his expression. His nonverbal advice to hold on as he begins to pick up the pace.

The unmistakable sound of our bodies connecting, uniting, sep-arating, and then starting the process all over again fill the kitchen. My body glides on the flour beneath me. Backward with each push in, then toward him, as his hands on my hips pull my ass over the edge of the counter again. He uses the unbalanced weight of my hips off the edge to push into me until he bottoms out.

His guttural sounds. The unrelenting pace. My name groaned on his lips. The grip of his hands on my flesh. The harshness of the gran-ite beneath me, and his hardness within me.

Our words are as frenzied as our movements. Like we can't get them out fast enough and at the same time want to draw this out as long as possible.

Right there.

More.

Oh God.

So tight.

Deeper.

So good.

Oh God.

Saylor.

My body chills and heats. An ache like I've never experienced before tears through me making my want turn desperate. Makes my moans become demands. And without warning, I tumble over the edge into that delirious free fall of ecstasy. My mind shuts down. My body takes over. An explosion of heat. A desperate gulp of air. A cry of his name. My muscles contracting around him so that even the slightest movement from him brings me such intense pleasure that I want him to stop and not stop simultaneously.

I'm swamped in the bliss of the orgasm. Lost to its euphoric haze.

And then Hayes can't hold back anymore. He starts to move again. To pump and thrust. To worship and take. To own and possess. Then it's my name on his lips followed by a ragged cry of release. A few more pumps of his hips before the room falls silent save for the ragged draw of his breath.

Without a word, he slips out and leans forward to press his forehead against my chest, lips against my belly, and just stills there for a moment.

I thread my fingers through his hair and revel in the warmth of the moment. In the difference of making love to the man now versus the teenagers fumbling in the dark that we used to be.

And the line we rehearsed earlier today comes back to my mind: *It's only ever been you.*

Eighteen

Hayes

I WAKE WITH A START. THE ROOM IS DARKENED. MY ARM IS NUMB from where Saylor's head rests on it.

Saylor.

The goddamn drug I forgot about. The yardstick I've measured *all* against. The one woman I've always wondered *what-if* about.

Well, now you know, Whitley. Ten times better than you remembered. Richter-scale sex. But how does knowing help the situation?

Fuck if I know, but holy shit was that incredible sex.

And then it hits me. Is she the real reason I stayed away from Tessa in the weeks before coming here? We weren't dating. I'd even told Say that. But spending that small amount of time with Saylor, our one hour of fun in our old stomping ground—the tree house—was clearly enough.

I hadn't ever been interested in Tessa. A good lay? Sure. Available? Yes. Emotionally connected? Not a chance in hell.

Tessa could never hold a candle to everything Saylor Rodgers is.

I shift on the chaise and turn so I can see her face and watch her sleep. Take in the soft lips and long lashes. The freckles I used to tease her about, and that stubborn chin she's lifted more times to me during our lifetime than I can count.

And I know my hunch is right. Tessa—perhaps any woman—pales in comparison to Saylor.

How in the hell did this happen? And why the fuck do I want to lean forward, taste those lips, and do it all over again?

Because it's Saylor.

My afternoon run was supposed to cure this want. The exertion should have staunched the unexpected need and calmed the ache in my gut I've had since we walked down the path together last night. And yet it did the complete opposite. Each step of my jog was a pounding reminder how much I wanted her and an affirmation that the ball-tightening kiss we'd had was more than just for show.

I kissed her because I wanted to. Had to. Couldn't resist not knowing if she still kissed the same. Tasted the same. Made that same little sound that used to get me hard in a split second (but in all fairness, for a teenage boy, a cool breeze could do that).

And selfishly my ego wanted the fucker, Mitch, to see she was with me. Call it a dickish move, tell me it doesn't matter because he's getting married and didn't fight hard enough to keep her, but I know it does. I'll make him wonder what I have that he doesn't. A bigger dick? A larger bank account? A better personality?

Yes, to all three.

So fuck, the kiss might have been a combination of all the above, but the sex? That was all me. All want. All greed. Everything I need. And fuck yes, it was against my better judgment. But sure as shit, my better judgment is not communicating with my dick.

And now I'm screwed. *Because all I want is more.*

I scrub my free hand over my face to try and figure out how that's possible, and I'm greeted with the scent of her pussy on my fingers. I'm hard instantly. I want to take her like this with flour smeared on her cheek and some still peppered in her hair. With a pan of cupcake batter on the counter still not baked. A mess all over the floor. And the bastard she was supposed to be marrying having his rehearsal dinner somewhere nearby.

I need to mark her in some way. Own her the same damn way she's owned me in one way or another since that first day I knocked on her screen door, told her I was the new kid on the street, and asked if her brother could come out and play.

She was all sweet and soft, and straight lines and innocent in every way imaginable. That's how I remembered her. And since I walked in the cupcake shop I've found out she's still sweet but also a helluva lot of feisty. Her innocence is matched with unwavering confidence and those straight lines of hers have turned into gorgeous curves.

Curves currently warm against my body and calling me to run my hands over them. I fight the urge. Need to wrap my head around the words she said during sex—*I've always wanted you*—and how they made me feel. *Still make me feel.* Possessive. Alive. Scared. Relieved. Protective.

You're never supposed to believe the words someone says during sex. You know they're jaded by the act. And yet, deep in my gut, I know she meant them.

She moves in her sleep. Brings her knee up to rest against my dick and fists her hand over my heart.

There's an ache in my chest. A feeling I choose to ignore. The longer I stare at her, watching her chest rise and fall, I realize the ache is more of a twinge and the twinge is jealousy. Of Mitch. Because he's had a million moments like this that I never did. He wasted them. Took them for granted.

And anger. Because he didn't think enough of her to fight for her. She's worth the goddamn fight. Especially when her temper's raging, and her stubbornness reigns.

And relief. That she knew better and walked away from him. That Ryder called me to cash in the IOU and that when I walked in the villa tonight she looked at me with those wild eyes of hers that told me so much more than her lips ever would.

The irony's not lost on me. How can I be pissed at Mitch when I should direct it all at myself since I'm the asshole who walked away from her and left the door wide open?

But it's easier to blame him. To despise him. Because if I do then

I don't have to look too closely at myself and wonder what this all means. How this will play out. How the weekend's going to end when we return to our respective worlds.

Then what?

Walk back into the lives we lead knowing *this* is still here between us? Resolved and unresolved?

Shut the fuck up. Live in the moment. Enjoy the killer sex and having her around. Sex doesn't mean commitment. Doesn't mean love.

Love?

Where the fuck did that thought come from?

She murmurs something I can't make out. Pulls my attention when it's never left her. Then moves again. I can't help but smile when she brings her hand up to her earlobe and rubs it between her thumb and forefinger.

And fuck if a feeling doesn't surge through me—warms me when it shouldn't—at seeing her do that. At knowing she still does it. That ache is back in my chest but this time it's not from jealousy.

Not hardly.

She murmurs again. Snuggles closer against me.

Haven't I always loved her in some way, shape, or form?

It's just the shared history. The reconnection with someone who has known me since way back when. A person who can still finish my sentences even after all this time.

Keep telling yourself that, dude. Maybe you'll believe it hasn't always been her.

She mumbles something. A soft laugh follows. And that fucking tinge is back with a vengeance when she mumbles again, but this time, the word is clear as day. *Mitch.*

Nineteen

Saylor

I WAKE SLOWLY. I'M NESTLED IN THE SATISFACTION OF SEX AND the unmistakable warmth of Hayes's strong body against mine. Groggy but content, my eyes flutter open to find him staring intently at me. His bicep flexes beneath my neck.

The lazy smile on my lips is as automatic as the post-sex stiffness I feel in my muscles when I stretch my legs out. "You're not plotting a way to put mustard on my cheek and tickle me to smear it, are you?"

The solemn lines of his face transform instantly with the laugh that falls from his lips. His eyes warm, and his hand moves to the side of my face where he rubs his thumb back and forth over my bottom lip. The action makes every single part of me sag in contentment.

"You wouldn't have a spare feather lying around, would you?" His voice is raspy, sleep drugged, and so damn sexy.

I laugh and snuggle closer to him. And I'm not sure that's even possible, considering I'm already halfway on top of him on the chaise longue we made our way to in that awkward-post-sex moment we should have had, but didn't.

And why was that? Why are we so comfortable with each other, when in reality we don't really know each other anymore? We've had different life experiences. Reached different milestones. He lives in glamour and glitz, and I live in cupcakes and frosting.

Because it's only ever been him.

I shove the thought away. Clear my head of the crap I was over-thinking before he walked in here and sexed me up so good I sat down on the chaise with him and fell asleep like a guy would. Because how wrong were my thoughts? How off-base was I?

I absorb the moment. The feel of his hard body next to me. How his hand absently plays with my hair. That carnal grin and look in his eyes that tells me he wants to do me all over again. And I definitely wouldn't say no because holy shit, the man has perfected some serious skills during the years we were apart.

"No. No feathers. No mustard," I say with a nod of my head.

"Just flour and sugar," he deadpans. He laughs and it rumbles through his chest and into mine. How could I forget the plume of flour and the granules of sugar beneath my back?

"Is it that bad?"

"Let's just say you've given a whole new meaning to the term sweet cheeks."

His hand slaps my ass in a playful manner but doesn't leave. Rather he digs his fingers into my flesh there and uses the leverage to pull my body up at the same time he leans down. Our mouths meet somewhere in between.

The kiss is soft and tender with an underlying edge of hunger. Or is it desperation? I'm not sure, but I let him take the lead. Allow him to choose the direction of what happens next because I honestly wasn't sure how the *what happens next* was going to play out between us.

But this? This I can handle. The soft caress of his hand. The slow lick of his tongue. The warm heat of his breath. The feeling of sinking into him rather than running away. The comfort instead of the panic.

Or maybe he's just distracting us from voicing the questions we should probably be asking.

"Mmm," he murmurs as he ends the kiss. "Definitely sweet."

I roll my eyes and laugh but can't deny the little charge to the ache within me that he seems to constantly keep stoked.

He continues with that lazy draw of his finger up and down my biceps. I'm so content, so fulfilled, that it takes more than a few minutes for it to hit me. The darkened sky. The time of day.

"Oh my God. We missed the rehearsal dinner." Hayes's arms hold me still as I try to sit up.

"Mm-hmm," he murmurs, the heat of his breath hitting the crown of my head. "I rethought our strategy."

"You what?" I lift my head to meet his, shift so I place my hands on his bare chest and rest my chin on top of them. The action is natural, and something about it also feels so incredibly intimate.

"I rethought our strategy," he repeats with a resounding nod of his head. "They saw us today. Laughing. Kissing. Not caring who was watching. So I kind of think that by not showing up, we'll let them assume whatever they want to assume we're doing."

"Like swimming with turtles." I love the surprised look on his face at my benign suggestion.

"I was thinking something a bit more satisfying." His fingertips trace up my spine. Goosebumps follow their path, but my body warms beneath his touch.

"More satisfying, huh?" I decide to play along. "Like karaoke?"

His laugh rumbles again. The bite of his teeth into his bottom lip holds my attention. "What was that lyric again?"

"Addicted to love, I think."

"Nice try. Funny how you change your tune now." He shakes his head.

"Whatever, *Captain*." I fight my smirk but lose the battle when he shifts me so I'm lying more on top of him than not. The unmistakable feel of his hardening dick presses against me and wakens my sex-drugged senses.

"Watch it, Ships. You're trying to distract me from explaining my new game plan."

And oh, how I want to distract him.

"Right. Sorry. Where were we, again?"

"Thinking of something more satisfying to do than attend a stuffy wedding rehearsal dinner because neither of us are in the wedding and therefore have nothing to rehearse."

"Correct," I say, following the logic I've always thought but never voiced out loud when Mrs. Layton insisted that *all* guests attend the rehearsal dinner. *They'll have traveled a long way to see you, Saylor, the least we can do is feed them twice.* Ugh. Her voice has no place in my head right now. Not with Hayes beneath me, and his lips so damn close to mine.

"And so you were telling me what might be way more pleasurable than sitting in a formal dining room trying to decide which damn fork to eat your salad with when all you really wanted was a pepperoni pizza with jalapenos on half of it."

I laugh. And then melt at the fact that he still remembers my favorite pizza toppings. "Right. Yes." I straighten my shoulders and narrow my eyes to pretend like I'm thinking of an answer. "Something pleasurable. Hmm. Oh, I know. We could make cupcakes. I always find that *extremely satisfying*." I purr the last words out. Taunt him. Test him. Wonder how he's going to finish this game we're playing.

He hums in his throat and the sound winds through my body. "While I know your batter is addictively sweet . . ." he darts his tongue out and licks his lip, his inference loud and clear, ". . . like *I can't wait to dip my fingers in it and taste it again* sweet. But no, I think there is something more pleasurable we should do to make missing the dinner worthwhile."

My breath is ragged and my lips fall lax as the memory of look in his eyes as I licked my arousal off his fingers replays in my mind.

"Like what?" My question is a hushed whisper. Lust thick in my voice.

He runs a hand ever so slowly along my spine and down my hip then back up to the curve of my knee. He hitches it up higher so my knee angles up next to his torso.

Our eyes hold in the short distance between us. I swear I can feel his heartbeat speed up. Or maybe it's mine. I'm not sure because they are beating against each other, but the sensation is overshadowed by the feel and sound of his hand sliding back down my thigh to cup the roundness of my ass.

"Hmm, I can think of a few pressing matters." The deep timbre of his voice is oral foreplay alongside the stretch of the fingers cupping my butt so that the tips of them brush ever so softly over the seam of my sex. A hint of touch. A whisper of want.

And now he's the one trying to distract me.

"And they are . . .?"

He lifts his head forward and brushes his lips tenderly against mine. "First I'm going to fuck you, Saylor. Right here. On this chair." *Another kiss.* The heat of his breath on my lips. The deliberate slide of his fingers over my sensitized flesh just soft enough to make the muscles clench and beg for more. "I'm going to pull you astride me. Make your pussy stretch around my cock and then watch you as I make you come."

My lips shock open and cheeks flush with heat. *Hello, dirty talk. Hello, to an all grown up Hayes Whitley.* My libido burns bright at his explicit promise.

"Oh, don't you act all shy on me now, Saylor. Not when you sat in that kitchen and played a goddamn siren. Teased me with your lips. Tested my restraint." He leans forward and kisses me again, but this time with a little bit of tongue and a lot more demand. He fists a hand in my hair and pulls my head back so I'm forced to look in his eyes when I suddenly want to avert them in shyness.

"This is me, Say. You might remember the teenage boy I used to be who didn't have a clue what he was doing besides the basics. But I assure you, the man I grew into knows exactly how to pleasure a woman. *I know how to pleasure you.*"

I swallow over the desire suddenly tight in my throat. "I thought you just did." Once again, my voice is barely a whisper. The hunger in his eyes burns darker.

"That was nothing, Ships. Not in the least. There's toys and tongue and touch and ties, and I'm sure I can find a few more T's to tease you with."

"Oh." It's the only coherent sound I can form as his dick hardens and pulses against me.

"Save your *ohs* because you'll be moaning them a whole lot more in a minute."

And before I can respond, his mouth claims mine once again. I welcome it. Revel in the change of pace. In the unknown. In the dirty-talking dominance I didn't expect from Hayes but now can't wait to explore more of.

A thrill streaks through me as his hands guide me astride him as promised. And sighs turn to moans.

"If we're going to miss that dinner," Hayes murmurs against my lips, "I promise you, I'm going to make the reason more than worth it."

Twenty

Saylor

"ARE YOU GOING TO TELL ME WHAT WE'RE DOING HERE?" I try to act annoyed, pretend I'd rather be at the salon getting a manicure, but the wedding party is probably in there getting their hair done or something, and so no, thank you. And honestly, why do I need my nails done? The only person I'd be trying to impress is Hayes, and considering he's the one leading me by the hand down a stretch of sand that's as pristine as it is beautiful, I don't think I need to.

He stops and turns to face me. I can't deny the thud of my heart when he flashes me a huge grin. I love the warmth in his expression, and as much as I'm curious over where we're headed, I also can't deny the desire to pull him into me and kiss him senseless.

And the thought seems so odd to me. Mitch abhorred public displays of affection other than the polite peck on the lips or an arm around the shoulder. I'd grown used to it. Was compliant. But standing here with Hayes, I suddenly realize how much I missed it. How very important affection is between two people. *How important it is to me.*

So while we aren't in a relationship and regardless of how hard I've shoved any and all ideas of what happens to us tomorrow when this weekend ends out of my head, I decide to act on the spontaneous thought. Without preamble, I walk up to him, slide my arms around his neck, and meet his lips.

The kiss is packed with the emotion I feel but am not sure how to process. It's sweet and soft but so damn seductive. I think he's surprised at first but within seconds his hands are sliding up the bare skin of my back, pulling me in tighter against him, and giving in to the demand of my lips.

When I end the kiss, I love seeing the shy smile sliding across his lips. "What was that for?"

"Just figured I need to make sure we keep doing things that are satisfying in order to not feel guilty for missing dinner last night."

His laugh is quick and loud. "After last night . . . and this morning, Ships, I think there's no need to feel guilty, considering I'm a whole helluva lot of satisfied."

He pulls me against him and presses a chaste kiss onto the crown of my head before releasing me, grabbing my hand, and starting on our trek through the sand again. And I follow willingly, my mind still lost to the turn of events. The mind-blowing sex on the counter. Followed by the slow and sweet sex on the chaise where he let me have the control and used that dirty mouth of his to wind me up so tight that by the time we climaxed every part of me—mind and body—was worked into a frenzy. To the playful double-dog dare he knew I wouldn't refuse to skinny dip in the ocean. How when he joined me it was so nice to lounge in the warmth of the water beneath the light of the moon and just be with him. No pressures. No words needed. And then of course, waking up this morning to his adept fingers kneading my shoulders, then my lower back, and on down until his fingers found their way between my thighs. How we made love lazily with no hurry. No rush. Just him and me and ten years' worth of moments like that to make up for.

I shake the thought from my head. Tell myself to focus on the heated sand beneath my bare feet, the breeze on my face, and the sun on my skin. To forget ideas of making up time or the notion that we're catching up so we can move forward.

Because neither of us have addressed that. We haven't had time to because we've been too busy enjoying each other instead. And that makes me smile thinking of his comment before: *Ships, I'm a whole helluva lot of satisfied.* Is it wrong to feel just a little smug at that?

"Are you going to tell me . . .?" My voice fades as I see a local man on the beach about twenty feet in front of us wave to Hayes. There's a blanket beside him where snorkeling gear is all laid out. A catamaran moored out in the water beyond.

Hayes turns to look at me, grin huge. "You said you wanted to swim with turtles, and so . . ." he shrugs, "we're swimming with turtles."

"Are you kidding me?" Excitement pulses through my veins. Surprise and appreciation do too, but those are directed squarely to Hayes.

"Nope."

"How did you . . . how is it even possible?" I ask, trying to think if there was any time whatsoever this morning where we were apart and he could set this up.

"What can I say?" He mock bows. "I am *The Captain.*"

"Lord help us." I laugh but love it all the same. My arms wrap around his neck and when my lips meet his again, I murmur, "Thank you, *Captain.*"

The lull of the boat rocking is more than enough to put me to sleep. Add to it the sun on my skin, the two hours of snorkeling in the beautiful waters of Smith's reef, and two glasses of wine, and I should be snoring. *But I'm not.* There's no way I could close my eyes.

I don't want to waste a moment of the time we have left here together.

And so I prop my head up on my elbow and watch Hayes from behind the mirrored lenses of my sunglasses. He's lying on the net, or trampoline as he referred to it, beside me. His eyes are closed, face shaded by the mainsail above us, and his hands are behind his head. I take the opportunity to look at him and memorize the line of his profile even though I already know it by heart.

"Are you staring at me again?" he asks, voice sleepy, smile spreading on his lips.

"Always."

"You used to do that all the time. We'd sit in that tree house with the fireflies around us and the stars above us and you'd always look at me instead of the sky."

I warm at the memory and how annoyed he used to get by it. "I was just preparing you for your future career."

"Funny," he mutters and turns his head to face me.

"I have my moments." He reaches out and swats at my leg and I scramble away.

"Be careful, Ships, or else I'll dangle you over the edge of the boat so your toes are in the water."

"No!" I giggle, my face a mask of mock horror. "I still can't believe that!" I shiver remembering that first nibble on my brightly painted toes from the tiny fish while snorkeling. We can only assume they must have thought they were food. It didn't hurt, but it sure as hell scared the shit out of me. And of course I surfaced with a yelp while Hayes treaded water laughing so hard he sunk below the waterline.

"See? I saved you from getting your fingers nibbled on too. Good thing I kidnapped you today and prevented you from endless hours of torture at the salon."

"My hero," I swoon with a roll of my eyes he can't see but know he knows I'm doing.

"Bet your ass I am. Haven't you seen me in tights?"

"Oh God. Please. The ego." I fall back on my elbows laughing and loving the sound of his laughter melding with mine. It's comforting. *It's us.*

The smile on his lips fades. "I didn't know, you know." His voice is suddenly serious.

"Didn't know what?" *He's lost me.*

172

"When I left, I didn't know I wasn't coming back."

I'm not sure how he expects me to react from his unexpected confession, but I can't deny that my breath catches. "It's in the past," I murmur, wanting to stick with the promise I made myself when I came here about forgiving him, and not wanting to waste the time we have left on things that can't be changed.

"I know it's in the past, Say, but it's important for you to understand. I left for a weekend trip to Hollywood, a cocky kid with stars in his eyes who sure as shit wasn't going to land a once-in-a-lifetime-dream role on his first audition."

"But you did," I whisper, remembering where I was the first time I noticed the hushed whispers of my friends who were averting their eyes every time I looked their way. How I finally confronted Ryder and found out Hayes had landed a huge role and wasn't coming home anytime soon. I screamed and yelled and begged to know why Ryder hadn't told me the truth. He admitted that I'd lost so much weight and was finally starting to smile again that he couldn't bear to tell me. He was too afraid it would renew the heartache and start the cycle all over again.

"I did." He nods subtly and even though his eyes are behind tinted lenses, I swear I can feel him searching mine to make sure I'm okay with the memories this conversation is evoking. "I walked in to the casting audition nervous as hell, wanting to say I tried my hardest and the dream wasn't for me, but walked out shell-shocked when I'd been cast in the part."

Silence falls between us as I fight the agonizing destitution I'd felt from clawing its way back. The grief. The loneliness. The heartbreak.

The silence.

"You left me a message."

"I left you a lot of messages." I can't help the rejected bite to my tone.

"You did. And I listened to every single one of them, Saylor. So many damn times. I was so homesick. And homesick meant missing you and Ryder and the normal everyday routine we had . . . but it mostly meant you. But there was one . . . fuck, there was one of your

173

messages that broke me, nearly made me pack my bags and come home. I'll never forget the sound of your voice. How you were trying to seem so strong but there was this slight waver in your voice that fucking killed me."

I know I left what felt like a million messages running the gamut from sad to angry to begging to crying to furious, but I know which one he's referring to. My final message. The one where I gave in and told him if he didn't want me anymore, he could at least have the guts to tell me.

I chew the inside of my cheek, surprised how talking about this is bringing back so much of the pain I swore I'd gotten over. "Why didn't you call?" I ask quietly, in an attempt to cover the hurt that still remains.

He shifts to a sitting position, his face downcast to watch his hands for a moment before looking back to me. "Because it was my only chance to get out of here. Away from my dad, his drinking, and quick fists and my mom and her acceptance of it. Everyone saw me as Dale Whitley's son. The kid who had no chance and wouldn't amount to anything—"

"I didn't."

"I know and that was part of it. I don't expect you to understand any of my reasoning or forgive me for what I did. Shit, looking back, I get what I did was fucked up. But you and Ryder and your parents were all the good I'd ever known. And God I was missing you. I was living in some shithole apartment, stuffing extra food from the craft service table into my pockets because I couldn't afford groceries, and knew no one . . . but I knew if I talked to you, heard your voice, listened to you cry over the line, I'd drop everything and come back. I missed you like crazy. I felt so horrible for not having the guts to tell you when I left for that weekend that I might not be coming back."

"I would have gone with you." God, how many nights did I have thoughts of packing up my shit and driving to Los Angeles to find him? My own naïveté not knowing how big a city it was and how hard it would be to find him.

"I know you would have. But to do what? Skip out on going to college? Stand by and watch me chase my dreams while giving up yours? I couldn't do that to you. You deserved the goddamn moon and stars, Say. *Still do.* I couldn't make you sit in that rundown apartment all day and worry about your safety, while I worked eighteen hour days. I would have hated myself for it and you would have resented me for it."

"So you just washed your hands of me and made it easy." My voice is quiet, reminiscent of how I felt for almost a year after he left. Then again, now that I think about it, maybe I never became that carefree girl I used to be.

"It was never easy. Not a goddamn single day." He fists his hands. Shakes his head. "If you only knew how I'd come home, collapse into bed from exhaustion, and miss every fucking thing about you."

His words cut open old wounds. Make me think of him all alone in a new town and feel sorry for him. But he needs to know what I went through too. "I walked around lost for over a year. We did everything together. You were my first love. My first everything. And you up and left and shut me out." I look out to the water beyond. To the snorkels sticking up out of the water in the distance. Hear the laughter of someone seeing the turtles, and I'm sure I sounded just as excited about it when I resurfaced. "I waited for you. I told you in that last message that I wouldn't, but I lied. I spent three years waiting. Three years adamant that every tabloid with pictures of you with some gorgeous actress on your arm was Photoshopped, or an innocent lunch date misconstrued. You tell me you missed me and yet, what I saw of your life? It looked like anything but missing me, Hayes."

"Saylor."

"No. It's okay. I know I told you in that last message that I wouldn't wait for you, but I did."

"You also told me you'd always love me."

I still do.

It's my immediate thought. One I hate and love. One I shove from my mind so I don't say it out loud, but regardless still leaves me reeling.

And I can sense the question on his tongue. The one asking me if my confession ten years ago still holds true. There's so much emotion clogging my throat, so much history thick in the air between us, that it's better if I just don't speak.

So the silence holds us hostage as we stare at each other from behind the protective lenses of our sunglasses. A part of me wants to see what his eyes are saying. The other part of me is scared to find out.

So, we hide.

"I came to your house." His confession shocks me. My lips fall lax and my heart constricts. "My mom finally left my dad. Said my leaving shocked her into reality so she kicked him out. I told myself I was coming home to help her get situated in her new place. And yeah, I did . . . but it was you I wanted to see."

"Why didn't you?" My still-hurt eighteen-year-old self knows that if he had, I would have been devastated all over again. Pain renewed. The fallout of seeing him, brutal.

"I did actually, but Ryder answered the door. Threw a punch before I could even say a word." He chuckles at the thought and rubs his jaw with the memory while my eyes widen in surprise. A part of me cheering for Ryder sticking up for me.

"*What?*"

"Yep. I don't think I'd ever seen him so pissed. He chewed my ass like I deserved. Told me you were finally starting to eat again. Just starting to be you again," he murmurs and his tone reflects how hard it was for him to hear how his leaving had affected me. The darkness I had lived in. Surrounded myself with and got lost in. "He told me he didn't think I loved you because how could I do that to you? But if I did in fact love you, I'd turn around and walk away and leave you be. He knew I'd become fascinated with the bright lights and big city and would just leave again when the weekend was over and then you'd be hurt all over again."

His confession weighs heavily in the space between us. My gut reaction is to be pissed at Ryder. For stealing a chance that was mine to decide if I wanted or not. But at the same time, he was trying to protect me and, at that time in my life, I needed protection. It's pretty rare to be a teenager and know the person you're dating is your soul mate like I did Hayes. And probably just as uncommon to have such an insightful older brother.

I take a sip of my water, while allowing the words to settle more, and the ones I hear more than anything are that he did truly love me. Showed it *when* he walked away the second time.

Something he said to me the other day echoes through my mind. *Never let someone steal your passion.* And I know he's right. I know that if he hadn't gone, hadn't left and walked away without my holding him back, I would have been responsible for stealing his passion. My selfishness would have robbed the world of knowing his incredible talent. It would have robbed him too.

"I'm glad you took the chance, Hayes." My voice is soft but resolute and I can see the visible startle in his body from my words.

"You don't have to say that, Saylor." His lips are tight. Head angled to the side as he looks at me.

"Yes, I do. Staying or me pulling you back . . . it would have stolen your chance to pursue your passion."

He nods his head a couple times. Contemplating something I'm unsure of. "The funny thing is, Say, the older I get, I'm learning it's okay to have more than one passion. One doesn't have to be more important than the other. They can complement each other."

The question is what does he mean by that?

And I think of Ryder. His ultimatum. How Hayes walked away.

He loved me. When I was hurting and swore he didn't care about me anymore, he had loved me.

I can't help but wonder when we part ways again, will it be under similar circumstances? That he loves me but will continue to pursue his passion, or he *loved* me, time's changed us, and there's no longer anything there?

The thought consumes me.

But he's here. Dropped everything in his crazy life to come here for me.

Doesn't that say something?

Twenty-One

Saylor

"RELAX." HAYES'S VOICE IS SOFT, THE HEAT OF HIS BREATH a comforting feeling against my ear as the wedding march begins. "You look beautiful. You are beautiful. And it's definitely his loss and my gain you're sitting here with me."

I take a deep breath and let myself lean into him for a bit more mental support. We're standing in the last row of seats, which is the only place I wanted to sit so I could avoid seeing Mitch before the ceremony. We're turned toward the aisle, waiting to see the bride.

When she appears, the guests suck in their breaths in reaction to how beautiful she looks while I do it out of surprise.

It shouldn't shock me, considering everything else about this whole situation, but when I see her wearing a dress so very similar to the one I had picked it could be *the same*, my mouth drops open. And when I add the dress to the color scheme and flower choices I previously selected, I can't help but selfishly feel like this whole event has been planned to rub my nose in what I could have had. Hence receiving a wedding invitation in the first place.

Is Mitch really that vindictive? He didn't even ask me to reconsider or tell me he still loved me. Not a single word of protest.

It all comes back to me. How when I looked Mitch in the eye and told him I was leaving, having already packed and taken some things to my brother's, he just stood there.

"I'm sorry, Mitch. I can't go through with this."

"With what?" There's annoyance in his voice. I must be interrupting the PGA highlights or something.

"Our wedding." And now I've got his attention. *His eyes narrow and lips pull tight in disbelief.*

"What the hell are you talking about?"

"Just what I said." *My voice is even, despite the riot of nerves I feel within.* "This isn't working anymore. Hasn't been for a long time. I won't be able to make you happy." And you don't know—or care—about what makes me happy in the slightest.

His chuckle fills the smothering silence of the room. "You're joking, right? Having cold toes or whatever it's called, are you?"

I lick my lips. Shift my feet that are anything but cold. Force myself to not avert my eyes. "No. I'm not. We're over."

The shock on his face is what I remember the most. Like he was appalled that I'd ever think of leaving him. And then it morphed into anger. Disgust. Impatience like I've wasted his time. "Not marrying me will be the biggest mistake you'll ever make. You know that, right?"

You're kidding me, *right? I bite back the smartass retort. Focus on keeping this as civil as possible.* "If that's what you want to think."

"No. It's what I know." *He takes a step back. Shakes his head. Looks back to me like I'm crazy—a pompous smirk on his lips.* "Leave your keys on the counter on the way out. Hope your cupcakes can keep you warm at night, but I doubt it."

And then he turned his back on me and walked away. Back to his Golf Digest or to polish his nine iron, or whatever it was that he cared so much about. Because it definitely wasn't me, and his reaction—or lack thereof—just proved it.

He didn't even seem angry. Or surprised. More than anything, he appeared put out. I had felt dismissed. *Not* missed.

So why did he send me the stupid invitation to this wedding if he didn't care about me then?

The guests in the rows in front of us block my view, so when people finally take a seat, I think I'm the last to do so because I can finally see clearly. Mitch, handsome and debonair as ever, looks nervous, but only in a way that someone who has known him for a long time can notice. It's the continued flex of his hands. The chuckle that sounds off. But then again, a lot of people are nervous when getting married.

And when she takes her place beneath the trellis and faces Mitch, her face falls perfectly into my line of sight.

The surprised murmur that Hayes softly emits says it all for me. Either Mitch definitely has a type—the blonde-haired, blue-eyed type—or it's a complete coincidence that Sarah Taylor could be my long-lost sister.

I sit on the edge of my chair, eyes blinking as if I don't believe what I'm seeing, but then again isn't it just par for the course? Hayes rubs a hand up and down my back, a tangible reminder to remain calm, while I watch the ceremony.

And I'm not sure how I feel. My insides are a hurricane of emotions, each one blowing through quickly to make room for the next one. My stomach churns watching the life I could have had be given to someone else. *Taken by someone else.* And she may very well be deserving of it. On the other hand, maybe this is the life and social status she's searched for, and if letting Mitch's mom plan the wedding is the price she has to pay, she's willing to give up the control to get what she wants. *Unlike me.*

I look to Mitch and his sure and steady movements. He's a bit calmer now, so I study his face, watch his hands, and wait for that gut-wrenching pang of regret to hit me. The one that knocks me upside the head and tells me I made the hugest mistake walking away from him. That I still love him.

But it doesn't come. *Not once.*

One of the two reasons I came here was to get this feeling and sense that I did the right thing. Sitting here, as a guest at the wedding I was invited to possibly to make a mockery of me, I can easily say I sure as hell did the right thing.

And I wonder how much the man beside me has helped to reinforce that feeling. How much hearing him validate some of my opinions, even though he didn't know he was, has helped me and this newfound sense of self. The carefree, spontaneous sense of self I lost so very long ago.

I also study her, knowing this will be the only time I can without people thinking I'm being rude. She is the bride, after all, and the center of everyone's attention right now.

Her hair is a similar shade to mine. Her makeup is flawless and her stature similar. She seems sure of herself. Happy. In love. Stunning. Classy. Timeless.

And so I watch the man I spent over six years of my life with marry a woman he met less than nine months ago.

Or maybe he met her before I left him? Maybe she was waiting in the wings and swooped in for the prize the minute she found out we had broken up? Or even worse, maybe they were sneaking around behind my back and that's why Mitch was so indifferent to my leaving? The errant thoughts grow crazier with each second that passes. But regardless how bizarre my imagination makes them, one thing remains the same.

When I look at Mitch, I feel nothing.

"You're awfully quiet." His arm drapes across the back of my chair so his hand can rest on my opposite arm. He gives a gentle nudge of his knee against mine. Little reminders to let me know he's beside me. But it's not like I could forget. Between the numerous guests staring at us to the camera phones snapping pictures on the sly, it seems that everyone knows Hayes Whitley is here. And a catty part of me wonders how many of the cameras left on the tabletops for guests to use to help document the reception are going to have pictures of Hayes on them. *With me.*

The irony is not lost on me. Nor is it on Hayes evidently by the way he was so generous with his time by taking pictures and giving autographs while we waited for the wedding party to finish their post-ceremony pictures.

The ones I'm most certain were taken down on the private beach beneath the palm trees I had chosen. I mean why not, right? Good thing for them this island has a pretty moderate temperature all year-round or God forbid with the change of seasons, Rebound Sarah might have had to make a decision on her own.

I'm not oblivious to the constant whispers that stop when I walk by and then start again or the sly glances of the women who all think they're better than me. But I do have to admit they sure as hell do a double take when they see Hayes's hand on my waist or how he pulls out my chair for me. I force myself to meet their eyes despite the unease rioting through me, knowing they are talking about and turning their noses down at me.

Confidence, Ships, a constant refrain off Hayes's tongue.

But I'm still on edge. Still waiting for security to show up and tell me I need to leave because I wasn't invited, and that's why I have the invitation tucked inside Hayes's suit jacket pocket. *Just in case.* And still in shock over seeing my meticulous preparations come to life before me and not actually be for me.

"I'm just thinking," I say quietly and look around once again at the centerpieces and linens and room setup.

"About?"

"About how Uptight Ursula sold this to Rebound Sarah. I mean, did she tell her the hotel offered a package deal where everything was already decided . . . and Sarah just went along with it?" *What sort of woman happily accepts a wedding completely organized for a different bride? By a different bride.* "Or was Sarah just so love-struck that she agreed to anything his mom wanted just to smooth over the waters because she can already tell what a controlling bitch she is?"

"Mmm." He nods his head before pressing a kiss to my temple. And I love the gesture, the feeling it gives me, but hate that I immediately wonder if it's for show or because he wants to do it. "I couldn't tell you."

"I mean as stupid as I now feel about allowing it to happen, I can stomach the similarities in our wedding dresses. Hell, even I had a weak moment and succumbed to Mrs. Layton's relentless ramblings about how very special it would be for me to wear a modern-day version of the dress she'd married Mitch's dad in. She had a designer bring in a couple of racks full of similar-looking dresses for me to choose from. And I did. And it was gorgeous. But that's where I drew the line in giving in to her demands."

Another murmur of acknowledgement from Hayes followed by a kiss to my temple.

And I love that he's letting me ramble on and get it all out. That he's giving me the *elbows in the batter* feeling I need and yet I'm nowhere near a kitchen or mixer.

The man really gets me.

I look his way to see his sudden interest in the room around us. "Something wrong?"

"Nah. There's just an all-round weird vibe here . . . but it's not our wedding, so who are we to judge?"

Not our wedding. I know he doesn't mean the words how I hear them, but it makes me pause for a moment. Ideas and images flicker through my mind of what our wedding would look like. Simplicity over grandeur. In the field under the tree house with shabby chic décor and mason jars with tea lights in them for mood.

"Ships?"

"Yeah. Sorry." My cheeks heat at getting caught thinking things I shouldn't be thinking. "The weird vibe? It's probably just because we're here."

"Nah. Don't look now, but I think it has to do with Mitch's mom over there shooting daggers at you while you're sitting over here with a drink in your hand and a smile on your face. I definitely don't think Mitch told her they invited you."

"But she had to have known. This is an all-inclusive resort. It's not like we've been hiding in the villa the whole time."

"Maybe she's just a bitch," he muses as he tips the bottle of beer to his mouth with a half-cocked smirk on his lips that tugs on places deep within me.

I snort in response. "Tell me something I don't know."

"*You're incredible.*" Two words. That's all they are. But the way he says them with a mixture of conviction, awe, and reverence, and with a completely serious look on his face as he holds my eyes captive, causes my heart to stutter a beat in my chest.

"And you're ridiculous." But I can't help my smile from growing to epic proportions. *You're incredible.* I try to laugh off my unease from the compliment but he won't have any of it.

"No, I'm serious." He leans in close, mouth skimming over my ear. His voice is low, just a whisper of a sound so that even surrounded by the hundred or so guests, only I can hear him. "Not many women would have the guts to show up here today. And if they did, not many people would know that it has absolutely zero to do with you. It has to do with your business. With not wanting to let Ryder down. I'm proud of you, Ships. Proud of you for walking in here with your head held high and a sincere smile on your face, when I know under your breath you're cursing at many of them."

I chuckle and lean the side of my head against his forehead. I hear the words he's saying and know the only reason I'm on the island, the only reason I was able to walk in here with such confidence, is because of the time we've spent together prior to this moment.

"I couldn't have done it without you. Thank you."

"I disagree. You've been doing it without me for a long time."

There's a pang of guilt attached to his words. A reminder of what it's like when he's not around. But this time there is no anger, no resentment over the past. He *came back* for me but then walked away when he knew he would just end up hurting me more.

Our eyes hold. The room buzzes around us and yet when he leans forward and presses his lips to mine, I zone everyone else out. The incomplete comments I heard walking to the restroom after the ceremony earlier, words like *disgrace* and *homewrecker* and *trash,* evaporate from my mind. It's just Hayes's lips on mine and the comfort, warmth, and calm they bring.

The kiss ends but so does the angst I was feeling. Once again,

Hayes has calmed me. And when I open my eyes and look over his shoulder, I freeze when I meet Mitch's gaze.

He's standing off to the far end of the banquet room, if you can call it that. The reception is being held in a round room with half the room enclosed like a normal hall while the other is an open-aired covered patio that overlooks the ocean beyond. He's standing where the open-air portion meets the walled portion, sneaking a peek at the reception before the DJ announces the wedding party.

The connection causes my breath to burn in my lungs and words to escape me, and yet I can't look away from Mitch. His gaze shows hurt. Reflects anger. But there's something else there . . . wounded pride or possibly *longing*?

I reject the thought immediately. Hate that I'd think so much of myself to believe Mitch just married Sarah—like minutes ago—and is standing there taking a glimpse of his reception while the camera woman is snapping shots of his new bride behind him . . . and is wishing it were me.

"He still loves you."

Hayes's murmur startles me and yet I don't move. Don't want to process the thought. Just want to pretend like I didn't just see it too.

I break my gaze from Mitch and look to Hayes with a forced smile on my face. My stomach churns over how horrible it would be to be Sarah if she just saw that exchange between us. Because while seeing him scrapes up the melancholy I should have felt over our break up, the affection he possibly feels for me isn't reciprocated.

Not like how I feel when I look at Hayes. My smile is always genuine and the emotion I feel is real. Not forced. "No, he doesn't." Something fleets through Hayes's eyes. I want to say disbelief or relief—either of them causes parts of me to stand to attention and wonder why they are there. But before I can ask, the DJ taps the mic to get everyone's attention.

And while the wedding party is introduced, while the cheers go up and the music pumps through the speakers, and as Mitch and Sarah immediately take to the dance floor for their first dance, I can't help but wonder exactly how I feel.

The moment I traveled all this way for is finally here, and yet everything I came here to prove doesn't seem to feel so relevant anymore. The meal unfolds, the typical wedding events transpire, and the whole time I'm preoccupied with the why behind this change of opinion. *My pride? My bakery?*

It all comes back to Hayes. He's the reason for all of this—the resolution of my past. The validation that Mitch wasn't the right choice for me as a husband. The overwhelming surge of emotions he's made me feel with his hands and his words when I didn't realize I could be made to feel that way to begin with. And more than anything the realization that it's okay to want more in all aspects of my life.

I feel like I'm starting a new chapter in my life. A different one where I have needs and wants and dreams and passion. While I may want to share that with someone in the future, I also know what makes me happy and that's just as important as making your partner happy.

Twenty-Two

Saylor

I WATCH MITCH AND SARAH TAKE THEIR SEAT AT THE HEAD TABLE. *Hear mutterings of my name followed by the word tramp.* I listen to their speeches professing their love to each other.

I have to stop myself from snickering at their lovey-dovey terms. The gentle nudges from Hayes tell me he feels the same way too. Wasn't it not too long ago that Mitch was professing the same love for me?

A murmur overheard at the table behind me about how I'm a gold digger. How I dumped Mitch and moved right on to Hayes just because he had more fame and fortune.

I eat the meal I had meticulously chosen to suit Mitch's preference of seafood and my like of steak.

Polite conversation with the members of our table. We're all the misfits who don't fit with any of the other guests. And yet their eyes narrow when I speak. Lips pull tight. Judging me through the rumors. And then of course they break out in a smile when Hayes turns his attention on them.

The clinking of forks against crystal to demand kisses of the newlyweds.

Sneers of disdain and the roll of eyes when I laugh out loud at one of the many things Hayes murmurs against my ear to bring me back to him. To calm me down. Because even though I was invited, in their eyes, I'm not allowed to enjoy myself.

And there's so much irony in the thought it's ridiculous. Do these people not realize that if I hadn't walked away, they wouldn't be here at all celebrating Mitch and Sarah's happy union? I walked. Mitch moved on and is happy. Sarah's happy. I think I'm missing something here. *Like how they need to move on too.*

Hayes and I are in a world of our own though. He knows no one although they all seem to feel like they know him and want to say hi. I know a lot of people and yet they want to act like they don't know me and make themselves suddenly seem busy whenever I catch their eye.

I feel like a pariah. The bits and pieces of comments I overhear confound me: *Whore. Homewrecker. It figures. It all makes sense now. How dare she?* But I ignore them. Have no choice but to. I knew people would be surprised I was here. I figured there'd be some unwelcome animosity—the charity case who rejected Mitch, and in turn them, and their more elite life status.

I hide the pang their comments cause me. I continue to smile despite the burn of tears in my throat. I accept the kisses to my temple with appreciation when Hayes offers them. I laugh out loud when he says something funny at our table of misfits to let those judging me know I'm no worse for wear when all I really want to do is head back to the villa to escape.

And I wonder why they came all this way to enjoy a wedding and are preoccupied with my presence instead.

I walked in here tonight expecting some vitriol, and yet what I didn't expect was how all of this was going to affect Hayes. How he bristles every time he catches a snippet from table ten when there is a lull in our conversation. How I can feel the tensing of his fingers on my thighs when he catches the two women with the god-awful dresses blatantly staring at me before laughing out loud to let me know I'm the topic of their discussion. The clench of his jaw at the heads being shaken back and forth as if I'm a sad sight to be had.

And despite this, his training is a godsend. His acting skills are perfectly timed when he smiles animatedly and waves a hello at the god-awful-dressed women letting them know he's heard them. Or how he declines an autograph for the daughter of table ten because *it's Mitch and Sarah's day and we're here to celebrate them.*

But we've had fun. We've been playing the "What's Next?" game where I guess what's going to happen next during the reception to see how much I remember of my own timeline.

And each time I'm right, we have to take a sip of our drinks. It's our way to relax. To make this event something different for us than it is for everyone else.

We're laughing over watching the servers begin to prepare for the cutting of the cake—which I accurately predicted would happen next—when I look away from Hayes and meet the eyes of Sarah and Mitch standing before us as they make the rounds to all the tables and guests.

"Saylor." Mitch is quiet. Serious. Sarah fidgets beside him with a smile plastered on her face, uncertain how to act when facing her husband's ex-fiancée. And I understand how she feels because I feel the same discord.

I know a million eyes are on us right now. The whole room waiting for a catfight from the ex-fiancée, so I do the exact opposite of what they expect.

I stand. "Hello, Mitch." Extend my hand to my replacement. "So lovely to meet you, Sarah. You look absolutely stunning. *That dress?* It's gorgeous. Thank you so much for inviting us."

Silence stretches for the shortest of moments. As if Sarah fears what taking my hand will say to the guests. But manners get the best of her and she reaches out and takes it. Her grip is soft. Timid.

"Thank you so much for coming. It was very important to me for you to be here."

"Oh." I think I do a good job of hiding my surprise. I glance over to Mitch and while his smile is there, the rest of his expression is the perfect picture of angst and irritation.

"You see," she says, lowering her voice and leaning in toward me, "you two broke it off rather suddenly. Lucky for me that happened because then he found me. But I think there are some unresolved issues between the two of you that need to be dealt with. And they need to be dealt with so when Mitch and I leave this reception tonight, he'll finally be over you. *Finished.* I love this man with all I have, and frankly, I'm sick of the ghost of you following us around."

I struggle to stutter out a response. My eyes are wide and my mind reels at how much I underestimated Sarah by thinking she was spineless and compliant. I guess it's only at her discretion. *Like when it comes to planning her own wedding.*

For some reason, I get the feeling Sarah is just as manipulative as Uptight Ursula.

"Oh." It seems to be my go-to response while I blink rapidly and look back and forth from Sarah to Mitch to see him just as unhappy with this situation as I am. Talk about being put on the spot. "Um." I shift my feet, lift my chin, and make sure my shoulders are squared. I want everyone watching to know I am not the least bit intimidated. "Couldn't we have done this at a different time other than your wedding? I don't want to take away—"

"I had planned on doing it at the rehearsal dinner. There was a reason you were invited to it, after all, but it seems you were . . ." she clears her throat, finds the words to continue, ". . . *otherwise occupied* last night." Her smile is tight and her eyes flicker over to Hayes to reinforce her implication. And I know it's just a lucky guess on her part what we were doing to miss the rehearsal dinner, but I'm sure I blush a little at the assumed accusation.

"Hayes Whitley. The one who otherwise occupied her." Hayes extends a hand to Sarah, and I love that he just put her in her place without the blink of his eyes or an inflection in his tone. "It was a lovely ceremony. Great choices all around on the wedding details. You must have had an incredible wedding planner."

I cough to cover my snort at his politely phrased insult.

The muscle in Mitch's jaw ticks. I'm not sure if it's because of what Hayes said about occupying me, or the fact that Hayes just called out his new wife to see if she's going to bite on taking credit for the planning . . . *she didn't do.*

She stares at Hayes. Ice-blue eyes gauging how to take the comment. As sincere or snide.

"It's about that time, ladies and gents. Will she or won't she? Will he or won't he? Yes. It's cake smashing . . . er . . . cutting time for Mrs. and Mr. Layton."

The room erupts into a nervous chatter of sorts, almost as if they're uncertain how this little talk between the four of us is going. When his mother starts clapping, the other guests follow suit to encourage Sarah and Mitch to move to the cake table.

And away from me.

Sarah's smile is forced, her gaze unwavering. "Please talk to him. For my sake," she urges quietly before she hooks her arm in Mitch's, smile now turning genuine, and heads to the cake table.

"Well, what do you know? Seems Golf Boy married his mother," Hayes murmurs under his breath. And this time I do snort aloud because he just hit the nail on the head.

And before I can process any of the last five minutes, Hayes casually laces his fingers with mine and tugs on my hand to follow suit with how he has now sat down.

"Can't say I blame her," he muses casually as one of our table members stops by to pick up their drink and head over to watch them cut the cake.

"Why?" I ask, even though I already know what he means. I'd want the same undivided attention from my spouse, but I'm not sure I'd go as far as she has to get it.

"*You're a hard one to get over, Saylor Rodgers.*"

Hayes's comment is on constant repeat in my head long after we eat cake. We're sitting politely at our table, waiting for the proper amount of time before we bail on the rest of the reception. If we leave too soon, guests will assume our exchange with Mitch and Sarah rattled me. And so we're kind of stuck, with comments becoming a little less obscure the longer the alcohol has flowed.

"C'mon," Hayes reaches his hand out to me, "if we're stuck at this damn party, we might as well have some fun."

I trudge behind him at first as he leads me toward the dance floor but then realize he's right. We are invited guests who have done nothing wrong. Why not enjoy ourselves instead of simply observing from our chairs? I gain more confidence with each step. Heads turn as we walk by. Drinks stop halfway to mouths. Elbows nudge the person beside them to take note of whatever it is we're doing.

Watch the bride and groom, people. They are way more interesting. And the reason you're here in the first place.

The music is slow and classical when we walk onto the sparsely occupied dance floor. I falter momentarily, unsure how to do anything other than bump and grind or the slow-dance-sway from back in high school. I mean, how many times in your adult life does one actually go dancing to learn otherwise?

"Take my lead," Hayes murmurs when he pulls me into him and begins to move. At first I think he's just doing his own thing, but soon realize there is a definite pattern to his steps. A defined rhythm and timing.

When I lean back to look in his eyes and question him, I catch the grin on his lips and my heart melts. Right there on the dance floor. With my ex-fiancé and his new wife off to one side of the dance area and a room full of judging eyes directed at us.

"Dylan Jax. Middleman's Move. I had to learn it for—"

"That one scene where you seduce your enemy's wife," I finish for him, remembering the movie quite clearly. Besides its complex plot and shocking twist, there were some pretty steamy scenes that may have had me rewind it once—or a hundred times.

His smile beams bright and eyes light up with pride. "See? You did watch my movies. I knew it."

I throw my head back and laugh. It's so easy to do with him. So natural to feel at ease. "Just that one," I lie.

"Yeah. Uh-huh." He spins me around before I can respond in any other way but laugh. The music changes to a more current song. It's sexy. Bluesy. Allows me to relax and not worry about messing up his carefully timed steps. Instead I just move with him. Against him.

He makes it seem effortless. All of this. How he turned on the charm in front of the jerks here. How he's helped me feel at ease in this awkward situation. How he makes me laugh and feel sexy and appreciated simultaneously.

Old feelings die hard.

But then again, I don't think mine for him ever really died.

Our bodies move against each other's. "You know what I keep thinking about?"

He asks it so casually that my response falls just as nonchalant. "Hmm?"

"I think you need to relax."

"Is that so? How do you propose I do that?" My voice is coy. My body already wanting what the suggestion in his tone implies.

Hayes leans in, mouth against my ear. "I need to get you out of this dress."

"Really?"

"Mm-hmm. While you look sexy as hell in it, I think it looks a bit stiff. Formal. Uncomfortable."

He twirls me out. Pulls me back into him. Chest to chest. Our feet move again.

"And how will being out of this dress relax me?" His thigh moves between mine and rubs against the apex of my thighs. A hint of what's to come.

"Because then I can taste you, Saylor. Run my tongue over your clit. Get you all worked up. Make you beg."

My chuckle? It's strained. Desperate. Fraudulent. "I won't beg."

He spins me around. I catch a glimpse of his challenging grin, and then I'm back against him.

"Oh, you'll beg." He presses a tender kiss to my lips that has my insides screaming when he ends it.

"Sound pretty sure of yourself."

"It's amazing the things a woman will say when her man is working his tongue in and out of her pussy."

My mouth goes dry. Between my thighs grows wet. The dark promise of his words seduces every part of me. He spins me out again, makes me more than aware of the audience of disapproving eyes watching us.

"Is that so?"

"Mm-hmm." He even makes *that* sound seem seductive.

"What exactly do women say?"

"Oh, yes. *Fuck me.* You last longer than I do. *Harder.* It's so big. *You're. A. God.*"

I can't help but laugh again at his breathless voice as he says the words. Know he's making fun of himself and love that he's confident enough in his more-than-adept sexual skills to do so. "Really?"

"Most definitely." He laughs. "But that's not how a man knows he's doing it right. *Words are cheap.* Actions prove everything."

"So how does he know he's doing it right?"

He spins me out and then back against him. In the few seconds apart, I'm already ready for the warmth of his body. His mouth is near my ear so the heat of his breath teases me. "A man knows he's doing the job right when a woman pushes him away, tells him to stop licking her, and begs for his cock."

That slow, sweet ache that has been simmering during this whole conversation—hell, who am I kidding, since he walked out of his room looking mouth-wateringly delicious in his suit and tie—has just been stoked brighter.

"*Oh.*"

He chuckles in my ear and I feel the rumble of it against my chest. Love the feel of his thigh rubbing between mine. "You still think you're not going to beg, Saylor?"

"Words are cheap, Whitley. Actions prove everything."

"*Hayes Whitley?* Seriously, Say? That's who you left me for?" Mitch's voice from behind me so bitter in tone, startles me, and yet I outwardly remain calm as can be.

So many responses flicker through my mind.

Married after only eight months?

Carbon-copy-of-Saylor-Sarah?
Still an asshole, huh?
I wish that were the truth.

I choose the higher road. Know even in the thirty seconds I've been in his presence that I made the right decision. I have absolutely zero love for him, and I can't believe I wasted six years of my life with him.

So I don't answer his question but rather decide to let him believe whatever he wants about Hayes being here with me and how that came to be. I'm not lying per se, rather just not giving any answers.

"You always did resent him, didn't you?" I murmur softly, figuring it to be my best plan of approach and more than aware of the sudden shift of attention over to us despite the music playing loudly.

I think back to the few times Mitch would see Hayes on television or a magazine cover and make some snide remark. Criticize him. For no other reason than because Hayes had me first. Caveman theory at its best, and Mitch's fragile ego at its worst.

"Seems I had every right to resent him, didn't I? I love Sarah. I really do. And yet all of her blabbing on about the ghost of you hanging around was driving me crazy so I'm here trying to give her what she's asked of me."

"My ghost?"

"Yeah. She says you're still everywhere even though you're not."

"That's because you moved on before the scent of my perfume even cleared the bedroom." There's a bite to my voice and I don't try to hide it.

"You're the one who left."

"Yes. I did." There is not an ounce of apology in my tone. *Why should there be when he was the one who made it clear he didn't care if I did? And is already married.*

Silence smothers the space between us. I take a sip of my wine and look toward the door to see if Hayes is back from the restroom yet. Shift in my chair.

"If you wanted to get rid of my ghost, then maybe you should have had your own wedding, instead of ours." I turn to look at him.

Raise my eyebrows. "A little originality makes a girl feel a whole lot more secure."

"It's complicated." He shuffles his feet, looks down at his beer, and then back up to me. "You know how my mom is."

"Yes, I do." He hasn't changed. He never will. Maybe I thought my leaving might help him realize that while he can love his mother and want to appease her, having a wife means you put her first, and not your mom. "Let me give you an opinion from someone who has in fact walked in Sarah's shoes. Your mom can't control your marriage, Mitch. You gave her a good start thinking she will by letting her orchestrate this entire wedding. The funny thing is, you were so busy being Golf Boy with your buddies and not caring about the details I was planning, that you have zero clue about how identical your wedding today is to the one I had planned. *For us.* Surely you realize the location and the invitations were the same, but did you notice everything else? The color scheme, the linens, the flowers? All my choices. And Sarah just happily accepted all of that?"

His features shift and evolve from disbelief to anger. And I know him well enough to know that as pissed as he is, he'll never confront his mom over it. God forbid, he ever stands up to her. Instead, he's about to take the brunt of his anger out on me.

I guess he's never heard the saying, *"Don't kill the messenger."*

"You don't get to have any opinion, Saylor. You don't get to criticize or judge or say anything other than *thank you for inviting me, Mitch.*"

Asshole. I bite my tongue. Make the conscious decision not to engage when I'd prefer to stand and shout and accuse and purge the lingering bitterness I feel toward him. Let everyone know the real reasons we're not together.

"Why'd you come anyway, Saylor? Why'd you show up? To rub my face in the fact that you're dating the big Hollywood star?"

And if I didn't know that bugged him, the disdain in his voice says it all. "Shouldn't I be asking you that, Mitch? Why'd you invite me? Because I know you say it was Sarah who did, but a little part deep down within you wanted me to show up here to see exactly what

I could have had. So you could rub *my* nose in it?"

I don't answer his question at all, but I don't care because it feels good to say some of what I think out loud. Words I've wanted to ask since I opened the envelope with the invitation.

He doesn't answer my question, either. And I'm okay with that and with the awkward silence that settles around us as we both figure our next step in dismantling a fence that will never stand again.

"It's always been him, hasn't it?" *Yes. It has.* I don't utter the words, just keep my eyes fixated on my fingers running up and down the stem of my wine glass when he continues speaking. "He's been the one you wanted even after he hurt you and walked away. I was the one who picked up the pieces after your parents died. Not him. But what? The whole time we were together, you were waiting for him, weren't you? Wanting him. Thinking I could take his place. And then obviously by the looks of the two of you, he came back and the wait was over. Dump me. Pick him. He wins . . ."

I don't think I ever looked at our relationship that way, or thought of Hayes in that regard. My subconscious was more consumed by the sting of hurt and weight of resentment Hayes left behind. And besides, by the time Mitch came into the picture it had been almost four years since he'd left. And yet hearing Mitch's words makes me realize that he just might be right when I never thought in a million years I was doing any of those things.

"It was the ghost of Hayes that ruined our relationship, Saylor. Just like Sarah wants me to confront you so that your ghost doesn't ruin my marriage. I thought what she was saying was just bullshit. Nervous bride crap. And yet, seeing you here with him . . . I know she's right."

Did he just admit that he still loves me?

Shit. Shit. Double shit.

I blow out an audible breath. His disdainful but honest words hit a little too close to home. I nod softly. Let him know I've heard him. I refuse to agree with him audibly because then I feel like he'll have control of this situation between us that feels so out of control as it is.

"What do you need from me to clear the ghosts, Mitch?" I try to sound reasonable. Attempt to give him what he needs so he can live happily ever after with Sarah and stay one hundred percent out of my life from here on out.

He clears his throat then looks me directly in the eyes. "I need to know if we ever had a chance or if we were doomed from the start because you were just waiting for Hayes to come back."

"Does it matter?" I shrug, hating the look in his eyes. The one that makes me wonder how deep his feelings still run for me when they should be one hundred percent consumed by the woman he just gave more than his last name to. And knowing that even when I tell him the truth, he's not going to believe it.

"Yes."

"It was never about Hayes, Mitch. I left because while I loved you, I don't think I could have continued loving you with the bitter resentment I continually felt toward you. You loved me but only the *me* you wanted me to be: sophisticated, non-working, non-baking, non-driven unless it was only to make you happy. You can't start a marriage loving only the end result of who you hope to turn your spouse into. You start a marriage by loving that person completely for who they are and with the knowledge you're going to grow and shift and change with each other. You never thought of me that way. You and your mom wanted me to be someone other than who I am to fit you and your circle's standards. It became more and more clear the closer we came to getting married. The subtle comments about how my job wasn't suitable for the Layton name. The hints left on hangers in my closet in the tune of thousands of dollars worth of clothes to show me how *you* wanted me to dress and look. The plans you fabricated, and the subsequent tantrums you pitched when you knew I had a big order to fill, so I'd feel like I was letting you down. So no, Mitch, my leaving you had nothing to do with Hayes and rather everything to do with me. My wants out of life, and everything that I am. Yes, I loved you, Mitch, *at one time*. But I think that love turned into bitterness and resentment."

His eyes are wide, body so tense that I can already see he disagrees with me. Know that he's ready to argue with me and I'm just done. With him and with this wedding. "*Loved*? As in past tense?"

I stare at him and realize he's not hearing me. He doesn't actually *want* to hear me. I shouldn't be surprised because it was the same when we were together.

And I know what I need to do. Know that it's not the truth but I need to be the bad guy here. Hurt him now to ensure Sarah has the best shot in a marriage with this emotionally stunted man who *she* loves.

"Yes. *Loved*. And I fell out of love with you a long time ago, Mitch." I shake my head, twist my lips, and my fingers twirl around a lock of hair. I give the best acting job I can give. Try to use the upset I feel over purposely lying to him to drive the emotion in my next words. "I lied. I'm sorry. Hayes came back a few months before our wedding. I accidentally ran into him and what I felt for him, Mitch, was so very different, so much more powerful, than what I'd felt for you. And so . . . I tried to get over it. Over him. Attempted to push him from my mind and focus on you and our wedding but I couldn't. The things you hated about me, he loved. The things you were trying to change in me, he praised. And I realized that even if Hayes and I never worked out, I couldn't marry someone who didn't appreciate those things about me."

There's hurt in his eyes. Wounded pride. And despite lying to him about the time frame, I realize everything else I've said is true.

"So it's all true then." He says the question as a statement, as if he doesn't want me to respond. His voice is resigned. Disbelieving.

"What's true?"

He shakes his head and chuckles beneath his breath like I should know what he's referring to.

"Let me ask you something." His voice lowers and eyes narrow. "What happens when you wake up one morning and Hayes is gone? Because *he will leave*, Saylor. He's left you once before. It's not like you don't know about him and his girlfriend, right? How he cheated and walked away. So what makes you think you're so special that he's going to stick around this time? Because sorry to break it to you, but you're not. You're nothing in comparison to that spotlight he lives his life in. The one he obviously needs because he picked it over you before and as sure as hell, he'll do it again. He's Hollywood and you're just . . . you. If you were devastated before, how do you think you're going to feel when he does it now, knowing everything you gave up for him?"

My throat burns from the emotion his words are conjuring up. They dig deep down into the recesses of my mind where I've been trying to play dumb and ignore the *what happens next* aspect of this weekend. But with Mitch in front of me and his words ringing in my ears, I can't avoid the fear they bring to me since the ghost of the previous devastation is still a shadow in my heart.

While I may feel unsettled, I know I sure as hell don't want him to see the emotions I'm most likely wearing on my sleeve either.

"Excuse me, I need to use the restroom," I say as I stand and clear my throat. "Best of luck to you and Sarah."

I stride confidently from the room.

And I was wrong before. This—*this walk*—is my best acting job.

Twenty-Three

Hayes

*B*ECAUSE IT'S *SAYLOR RODGERS.*

I remind myself again because I'm done playing the nice guy. Done standing here with a cheesy smile plastered to my face, taking picture after picture for the same people who've had no problem muttering shitty things under their breath all night long about the woman I love.

Another picture.

Love?

Flash burning my eyes. Smile a bit wider.

Seriously, Whitley? Love?

A shake of a hand.

Love.

A thank you for a compliment. Another autograph.

It's always been her in some way. Hasn't it?

Another photograph. Another hug I don't want to give.

Yes. Love.

Smile for Saylor's sake. To make them leave her the fuck alone.

Love. Hmpf. Who would have thought?

A forced smile. An apologetic excuse that I need to get back to my date.

Now what are you going to do about it?

A narrow escape from another hug by a woman smothered in strong perfume and a dodge of a lipstick smudge on my cheek.

Of course when I get into the main hall of the reception, Saylor's nowhere to be found. My mind's reeling from my realization and yet it shouldn't be. How did I not realize I still loved her the moment I saw her in her cupcake shop with blue flecks of frosting in her hair and that feistiness front and center?

She's not at the bar. Not at the table. Shit. I shouldn't have left her alone. Shouldn't have assumed she'd be fine despite her reassurances.

I see one of the others from our table. "Hey, do you know where Saylor went?"

"I saw her head outside a few minutes ago. Right before it started thundering."

"Thank you," I murmur and head that direction. The thunder rumbles the minute I head out onto the patio to look for her. It's dark now and the air smells like rain.

"She still loves me, you know." Mitch's voice comes out of the shadows behind me.

I pause. I truly hate the fucking clinch of my gut at his words but reject the idea immediately. There's no way she loves him. And yet didn't I ask myself if she still did before coming here? My mind flashes back to earlier. To his name she mumbled in her sleep the other night and to the look on her face when she saw him across the reception room earlier. Did I read her expression wrong? Was the disgust I thought I saw in it really something else?

Fuck him and his lies that are trying to make me doubt her.

"You always were a bullshitter, Layton." I turn around, take in the cigarette in one hand and the glass of brandy in the other.

And this *is what a* happily *married man does at his own wedding? Drinks and smokes . . . alone?*

I take a step toward him as I concentrate on how to play him and not let him know he's got to me with his statement.

"She left. Couldn't handle everything."

He takes a drag on his cigarette and I immediately know he said or did something to upset her. Every part of me wants to go find her, make sure she's okay, but I know she's tough. Besides, there's something I've wanted to do ever since Ryder told me over six years ago that Saylor was dating him. Let him know just what I think of him.

"Is it stressful being in the same room with the one woman you're supposed to love but don't wholeheartedly, and the one you *still* love who doesn't love you back? Is that why you've resorted to a smoke? A little nervous, are you, Mitchy-boy?"

I lean my hip against the rail beside me, refusing to back down when he steps closer. The pansy never intimidated me in high school, and this bullshit show right now from him sure as shit doesn't either.

"Fuck you." His voice is low. Angered. Full of spite.

"No thanks. I hear you're a selfish lay." A twist of my lips. A raise of my eyebrows.

"I bet that's all she is to you, too."

I don't take the bait although I'd love to step into him, cock a fist back and let it fly. Put him in his place for the prick he was way back when and the bigger one he is today. "Wouldn't you like to know, Layton?" My voice is aloof. My chuckle condescending. My eyes reflecting his own words, *fuck you*, back to him.

The flash of hurt in his eyes is brief but obvious and tells me what I already know. *He still loves her.* There's a quick pang in my gut as jealousy fires within because he doesn't deserve the privilege of loving her.

"You won't stay. You'll break her heart again just like you're doing to whatshername."

Whatshername? Saylor's comment from the other night ghosts through my mind. The truth I let her believe regarding Jenna and the rumors that are nowhere near true. How she's believed in me enough to let it go even though I never answered. And I'm sure a part of it is because it's been so easy to shut the outside world out while we've been here.

"I think you forget that you don't get to have a say in what Saylor does or doesn't do. What Saylor and I as a couple do or don't do . . . that's no longer any of your goddamn business. You gave up that right the moment you let her walk away without a fight. You sure as hell couldn't satisfy your fiancée, let's hope you can your new wife. But by the looks of things, you're spending more time worrying about your ex on your wedding night than you are your wife. Your future's not looking too bright."

And with that, I unclench my fists and stop wasting my breath on someone who doesn't deserve it.

I need to go find Saylor. It's become an urgency. And I hate that Mitch's first comment is stuck in my craw. Hate that for a man who's always sure of everything, I suddenly feel insecure when it comes to Saylor. And insecurity kills all that is beautiful.

And Saylor is my beautiful.

I use what I know to calm the unease over why she bailed from the reception. Remind myself that over the past few days I've tasted her kiss, felt her body react, and seen the unspoken depth in her eyes reflecting how she feels about me.

There's no way she still loves Mitch.

I hurry out of the reception area, hating the question I need to ask but knowing I have to. Just like she needs to ask me about what happened between Jenna and me and I need to tell her. Clear the air so we can both move forward with our pasts exposed.

I walk the grounds in a panic. Try to figure out where she might have gone and why she hasn't returned. The thunder rumbles overhead giving an ominous warning of what's to come.

The villa. That has to be the safe bet, but when I walk by a clearing that looks out to the ocean beyond—she's there. Her hands are braced on a railing in front of her while her dress flutters around her legs from the wind that's picking up.

And I swear to fucking God my chest constricts. I'd like to think it's because of my earlier revelation—that I do love her and have loved her for all these years—but seeing her magnifies that realization. Confirms it then unravels it from the tightly bound ball I'd kept it in.

But the other part of me wonders if that pang in my chest is from fear. What if she's out here because she talked to Mitch and realizes that six years is a long time to throw away with someone? And that even though he's married, maybe she still loves him like he loves her.

That's bullshit. I've known her longer. I've loved her harder. I've treated her better.

But you walked out, Whitley. You didn't fight for her either.

Lightning flashes off the coast.

"You love him still, don't you?" I don't mean for it to be the first words out of my mouth and yet I have to ask. Have to hear her say differently to get rid of the uncertainty.

The same uncertainty I made her live with day in and day out over whether I was coming back for her. Because I didn't call. Didn't respond. Made her wonder if I cared.

Her body startles at my question before she slowly turns and faces me, expression guarded in the darkness.

But you walked out.

"What?" Her voice is surprised. Or is that irritation?

The thunder growls around us.

"Do you still love him, Saylor?"

The first drop of rain lands on my cheek.

You walked out.

"No. I don't love him, Hayes."

Don't twirl your hair, Saylor. Don't show me you're lying. I watch her hands. Wait for them to move. To give her tell.

Rain echoes around us. Drops on plants. On sidewalks. On dirt. It's subtle but there.

It's washing off the dirt.

Her hands don't move.

"You don't?"

It's stripping away the past.

She laughs. Shakes her head. "You're being ridiculous, you know that?" There's a spark of temper. A flash of disbelief.

It's cleansing. A fresh start.

"Then what is it, Saylor?" I take a step toward her, need to know what's going on. "Why are you so upset?"

205

Thunder vibrates the rain and air. Electrifies it.

Our eyes hold. My lips open and close to push her for the answer, but I hold it back. Take another step closer and put my hand on her cheek. I feel the rain on her skin, smell it all around us.

"Because I don't want this to end."

"What to end?"

Thunder and lightning within seconds of each other. A perfect description of what I feel right now as I wait. Of how she makes me feel inside.

"*This.*" Quiet. Self-assured. Lashes fluttering from the drops of rain as she looks up to meet my eyes.

And I'm sucker-punched. The lightning and thunder collide.

"This?"

My thumb brushes over her lips as the rain falls harder.

"You. Me. This weekend." Each word is slow. Intentional. Fearful I'll disagree. She steps away from me, paces a few feet while shaking her head and then turns around to face me.

"Saylor." Thunder roars the same time I speak and drowns out my voice.

"Goddammit. I love you." Every emotion within me—hope, love, fear, acceptance, humility, want, need—surges and swells at her words. She throws her arms out, dress soaked and sticking to her body. "I've always loved you, Hayes Whitley. When I was ten years old with skinned knees and braces. And when I was fourteen, sitting in the tree house jealous of all the high school girls bragging about your kissing skills. Then we did kiss and I hated them all for knowing that, but you, you could do no wrong in my eyes. And even after you walked away . . . I still loved you." Her voice breaks. The emotion in her tone raw and real and tugging on every part of me she hasn't touched yet when I was sure as shit she'd touched everywhere over our lifetime.

I'm standing before her stunned. There's a veil of rain between us and yet a connection stronger than I've ever felt before. I start to speak, but she shakes her head, puts her hand up for me to stop.

Lightning flashes over the water and it lights up the wild in her eyes.

"No. I have to finish. I need to say everything I want to say. Mitch said you were the ghost between us. The reason we didn't work out. Always there. I told him that was bullshit. That he was lying. But you know what? He's right. You've always been there, Hayes. In my dreams. On my mind. In my hopes. Tattooed permanently on my heart."

Twenty-Four

Saylor

HAYES STARES AT ME WITH THE MUSCLE PULSING IN HIS JAW, his only show of emotion. His head tilts slightly like he's trying to make sure what I'm saying and what he thinks I'm saying are one in the same. I see relief. Hope. Desire. *Love*. His hair is plastered to his head, shirt soaked through, and eyes searching when he steps toward me. I've never thought him more handsome.

He places a hand on the side of my face, our connection rekindled. "Saylor." It's only one word said in that deep timbre of his and yet it's packed with so much emotion.

I came out here needing a breather. Mitch's words hit too close to home to the fears I had and to the doubts still milling inside. Then Hayes arrived and his face looked like a reflection of the turmoil I was feeling inside. Like exactly what he is to me: The storm that can bring me down.

Now's my chance to lay all my cards on the table because if I don't and he walks away, I'll always question, always wonder, if I fought hard enough to keep him.

"I've loved you, Hayes. Then. Now. I always have. And I'm scared to death of what's going to happen when we leave here. How, when we walk away to our separate flights, our separate worlds, that I'll never see you again."

He doesn't respond with words. His body is too tense. Emotion is strung too tight. And so he reacts the only way I think he can to express how he's feeling, to *show* how my confession makes him feel.

His lips are on mine as quick as the lightning flashing overhead. It's a bruising kiss. Hard. Fast. Desperate. Violent with desire.

And I don't hesitate. I'm all in. With lips and hands and heart. We're soaking wet, a tempest rages around us, and yet we finally find peace in our own storm.

"God yes, Ships." My name's a gasped word caught on the wind before he dives back in and takes what he wants from me. What I'm giving him. My body, because I've already handed over every part of me without even realizing it.

We move in desperation. Hunger and resolution fueling our actions. Our desires. Our want to connect. Our need to express the end of the turbulence that has kept us in the air over the past ten years.

We give no thought to where we are. To the rain drenching us or to the wind whipping around us. Because all we see is each other. All we feel is now. And with his mouth consuming mine—showing me how he feels, breathing life into me, before drowning me in his intensity—I don't want to come up for air.

But the crack of lightning shocks us apart. We stare at each other: chests heaving, eyes hungry, smiles shy but salacious, libidos begging for more.

"We need to get inside." His voice is strained. Posture a perfect picture of restraint holding on by a thread. The first few buttons of his dress shirt are undone. His erection straining his slacks.

"We do." I nod but step into him rather than head to the villa. I fist my hands in his soaked shirt and lean in to kiss him again. This time it's slow, seductive, taunting. I can't hear the groan in the back of his throat but can feel it vibrate against my hands and lips. And it only urges me to want to make him do it again.

His hands slide down my hips and cup my ass while mine move over his shoulders and loop around his neck. And almost as if on cue, he lifts me and I wrap my legs around his waist. Without a word, he starts to walk as we continue this long, drawn-out kiss. I take advantage of my positioning, of how our bodies fit together perfectly, and place kisses down his smooth jawline.

Sensations swamp me. The taste of salt and rain on my tongue. The scent of his cologne in my nose. His strained sigh in my ear. His hands gripping my ass tighter as I cinch my legs around him harder so that with every step down the path that leads to the villa, the bulge of his erection rubs firmly where I want it to.

It feels like it takes forever to get to the door and when we do, Hayes holds tight to me still wrapped around him while he fumbles in his pocket for the room key.

My body vibrates with the anticipation and the fierce desire burning within as I wait. But there is no key, no door unlocked, just a muttered, "I can't fucking wait any longer," before Hayes carries me down the private path that leads to the back of the villa.

My eyes are closed, and my lips are pressed against the base of his neck. I feel him step up some stairs, open the door to the screened-in porch with thick foliage on both sides, and then he leans over and lays me down on the double chaise longue.

And the minute he's free of carrying my weight, the control is snapped.

Gone.

Hayes grabs me by the ankles and pulls me down the chair so my dress rolls up beneath me, my legs fall off the end, and my torso is no longer sitting at an incline. I yelp out a laugh, loving this side of him. The *I want you and have to have you.*

And before I can even look up to meet his eyes, he dips down and licks a line over the thin lace of my panties. I cry out at the heady feeling of the muted sensation, already desperate for him to do it again. He moves his hands to my thighs, pushes them farther apart, and then he delivers. His tongue parts me through the fabric, licks down the seam of my sex and then back up to flick over my clit.

My head lolls back. My hands pull at his hair. A moan falls from my lips. And I buck my hips up, giving him access because the texture of the lace combined with the wet heat of his tongue evoke a different type of friction that makes rendering thought near impossible.

"You smell so fucking good, Say. So good," he murmurs against me, the heat of his breath a hint of what he's withholding from me. My body aches all over, burns from his praise, and from his words earlier tonight on the dance floor.

"Hayes." I tighten my grip in his hair and try to pull his head up to tell him I don't care about foreplay because our make-out session in the rain was more than enough for me. That and the fact that I just laid my heart on the line to him and he stepped into me instead of turning away.

I want him desperately.

Need him.

In me.

Right now.

Unwilling to give up the control, he shakes his head from my grip and in the action rubs the tip of his nose perfectly against my clit. I cry out as my body ignites.

"Not yet, Saylor. Don't worry. I'll fuck you, good and hard. I promise I'll earn every damn moan that you make. But not until I lick every damn inch between your thighs. Taste you. Feel you. Own you." His chuckle is low and rumbles in the space. His grin is full of sexual promise and I squirm beneath the touch of his finger where he's slowly running it up and down the line of my sex outside the fabric. Just enough to let me sink into the sensation before he pauses, waits for my muscles to relax, for my overstimulated nerves to calm, and then he starts the process all over again. "But since words are cheap, I guess it's time to prove it with actions. Hold tight, Ships. I'm not holding anything back."

My smile is quickly replaced by a moan. My declaration that I wouldn't beg falls to the wayside. My ability to form coherent thoughts obliterated when in a breath of time, Hayes has hooked my panties to the side with one hand and parted me with the fingers of his other.

Then there's his mouth. The heated skill of his tongue as he flicks it over my clit and works me into a frenzy. My hips writhe, my hands fist, and my teeth bite into my bottom lip. And just when my body begins to twist that coil of arousal so tight I know I'm going to reach the point of no return, he eases up and slides his tongue down to my wetness. Dips into me. Taunting. Teasing. Urging me to beg.

I'm so overwhelmed by the onslaught of sensations—the storm whirling around us and the need raging inside me—I don't think I could form words if I tried.

And between his fingers and tongue, the desire within me grows. My hands grip tighter, my gasps become harsher, and my resolve not to beg vanishes as the orgasm rips through me.

"Hayes. Hayes. Yes. No. Oh God. Stop." But contrary to my words, I hold his head between my thighs and lose myself in the soft slide of his tongue as he lets me ride out the ferocity of the climax he more than just earned.

I hear his chuckle. Feel its vibration against my hypersensitive nerves and squirm to shift away from him. But his hands on my thighs remain firm when he lifts his face so I can see the grin on his glistening lips.

"I'd like to gloat that you just begged."

He shifts back to his knees with my legs framing his body. His voice husky with the violent desire reflected in his eyes.

"And I will, Saylor."

He rips his shirt open causing buttons to pop onto the deck. I admire the sight of his firm biceps and lickable abs as he strips the sodden material from him.

"Oh, I will gloat."

His hands work his belt followed by the sound of a zipper. Then the unmistakable movement of his hand sliding over his cock.

"But fucking you is more important."

I wet my lips in anticipation. His eyes darken in ecstasy when he rubs the crest of his cock up and down my swollen sex. My moan is reflexive. My need unyielding.

The wind whips all around us but he stops to draw my eyes up to his. And when our gazes connect, he slowly pushes his way into me. I tense around him, my body and mind overwhelmed by the all-consuming pleasure the slide of his cock creates within me.

The groan he emits when he's fully sheathed is incredibly sexy. Everything about him is. The way his head falls back, how his lips part, and how his fingers tense on my thighs.

And then he moves. His first slide out and then forceful slam back in causes that sweet, painful burn to spread like wildfire to every single part of me. I know he's as consumed as I am. Lost in the moment. In the feeling of us connected. In every damn sensation between us.

Hayes sets a bruising pace from the get-go. There's no apology in his movements. Nothing uttered from his lips other than my name. No other focus than the end game.

Time occurs in flashes of lightning. Snapshots of time when his figure is lit up amidst the dark around us.

His shoulders taut. Hands firm. Hips thrusting. Mouth pulled tight. Eyes focused on our union.

It's erotic to watch him. Sexy. Empowering.

"Yes. God, yes, Say. Tell me yes," he groans out as his hips buck wildly against me. I'm transfixed watching the orgasm consume him. The expression on his face and the broken way he says my name will forever be burned into my memory.

Tell me yes.

Yes to what though? To him? To there being an us? To having a future together?

And all I can think as he slowly pulls out of me and gathers me in his arms is I hope that's what he was asking me to say yes to.

Because after everything that has happened between us, how could I say anything but yes? In this short span of time, he's made me feel validated, adored, accepted, and *loved*.

Everything Mitch didn't. Couldn't.

Emotionally, I'm spent. *Exhilarated. Revived.*

So many revelations on this day. So many mixed emotions. So many truths shared.

But this? Hayes asking, no, begging *me* to say yes?

Slayed.

Owned.

His.

Perhaps he's right though. Words can be cheap, but he's sure as hell proved it with actions.

So I give him the only answer I've ever had when it comes to him. "Yes."

Twenty-Five

Saylor

THE STORM HAS PASSED.

It's my first thought as my eyes flutter open and feel the sun warming my skin through the open blinds. We forgot to shut them last night when we finally collapsed into bed after a midnight snack. And another round of incredible sex.

The Captain definitely knows how to steer this ship of his to ecstasy.

I bite back the giggle over my ridiculously cheesy thought and snuggle deeper into the heat of Hayes's body behind me. I revel in the weight of his arm over my hip, the possessiveness of his hand resting on my abdomen, and the unmistakable morning hard-on pressing against my backside. Everything about him feels like my perfect heaven.

And then I remember what the morning brings: our last day. I sigh and close my eyes, trying to memorize this feeling, and enjoy it despite the sudden dread that shadows the few hours we have left together.

I run last night through my head. Mitch and Sarah get a fleeting thought. Their weird relationship and bizarre need to confront me at their wedding of all places. Then I move on to Hayes. To how he made me laugh and put me at ease despite the constant scrutiny and nastiness from the guests around us. Then *the dance*. Sigh. The dance where he lit the match just enough so I'd be left wanting but unable to have him. To my confessions in the thunderstorm and his long, slow, wet kisses that I swear could have lasted all night without any complaints from me.

Well, I lie. Because what happened next was pretty damn incredible.

So why am I the only one who did all the talking? All the soul-baring? I know he said words are cheap and action is everything, but I can't help wonder if stepping in to kiss me was his way of not having to figure his own feelings out. The thought triggers a flicker of panic. I shove it down along with the sudden unwelcome idea that maybe he doesn't feel the same as I do. *I told him I love him, had always loved him.*

Don't do this, Saylor. He showed you how he felt all night long. With tenderness and reverence and passion. I hold onto that thought along with the reminder that he was never very expressive about his feelings.

Cocooned in his security and warmth, I realize I need to accept what he was able to give me in the way he was able to show me.

Time passes. Seconds I soak up. I lose myself in the emotion. The acceptance. The hope for something more, something better than we could ever have imagined, and purposely try to ignore the particulars of how that might be able to happen.

The minute he wakes up I know it. I can feel the fleeting tension of his muscles and the break in his even breathing. And yet he doesn't speak.

So we lie in the silence of the morning, the storm having moved on, and the rain having washed away the grime from the past. The breeze blows in off the ocean and our hearts try to settle in their new places. A little fuller. And hopefully, a lot less permanently broken.

"I could buy us a house halfway between cities, you know."

It takes everything I have not to turn over and stare at him, mouth agape, because I'm shocked at his words. Surprised that his thinking is that far ahead when mine was merely afraid to even hope for something more than our *last day*.

I draw in a slow, steady breath in an attempt to calm the hope that just bubbled up before I respond.

"I couldn't ask you to do that." I say the words all the while thinking *YES. Please.* Anything to hedge our bets against the grim statistics of how many long distance relationships actually last. "You've told me yourself that there are some days you are on set for a ridiculous number of hours. I couldn't ask you to work that long of a day and then drive well over an hour—because let's face it, LA traffic is horrific, so we both know the commute home would be way longer than that."

"I would though, Saylor."

And I know he hasn't said the love word back to me, but that comment alone says it just the same.

"I know you would."

"It would be a compromise for both of us. It would allow us both to keep doing what we love to do as well as make *us* work. I know you love Sweet Cheeks but this would allow you to have some distance and a life separate from work . . . or as separate as you allow yourself to get." He chuckles against the back of my head. The heat of his breath causes goosebumps to chase over my scalp. "And for me, it would let me have a place where I could escape from the glitter of Hollywood and its endless bullshit. Give me the chance at living an everyday, normal life."

"You love the shiny lights and glitter though," I tease.

"Only if you're wearing the glitter."

"Such a charmer, Mr. Whitley."

We fall into silence and our breaths even out as we lose ourselves to our thoughts. To possibility. I think about the airport and wonder how we're going to bring ourselves to walk away when we've just found each other again. It's like someone loaning you a warm jacket when you've been freezing and just when you sink into it, believe its warmth is real, the person comes back and snatches it away.

"We'll figure it out, Ships," he murmurs, somehow knowing the direction of my thoughts. "It's not like this is a new relationship or anything. I mean you forget that I used to know you back when you used to pick your nose."

"Whatever." I roll my eyes and laugh but welcome his arms pulling me tighter against him and how his fingers automatically link with mine. And despite the humor in his comment, the worry returns. Because in his arms is one thing, but being apart is an entirely different situation.

"Talk to me. Tell me what's going on in that beautifully, complicated, stubborn, creative mind of yours."

"I'm just silently freaking out about what happens next," I whisper.

"Well, let's see. What happens next is I have a table read the day after tomorrow in New York. It's for the movie of that scene we were rehearsing. The director and the casting director will know from that table read whether or not they think I can play the part. As of right now they're not entirely convinced I can pull it off since it's so different from my norm. But to me, that's the whole point. So that's what I do next. I go there, kick some audition ass, and leave with the part. And you? You'll go back home and see if business will pick up now that the wedding is over. And if business doesn't pick up, then we'll brainstorm other ways to get customers in the door. The bakery is your dream so we'll do whatever it takes to make it work."

His continual use of the word *we* throws me. Triggers tears to burn in the back of my throat, and causes hope to slip on some wings and take flight.

"What?" he continues when I don't speak. I can't as I'm too overwhelmed from the emotion his words evoke. "You don't think a full-page colored print ad of me naked, holding a tray of your cupcakes in front of my dick won't help get the store some attention and sales?"

I can't help but snort as the image fills my mind. "Only if I get to strategically place the flour handprints on your body for added effect."

"You always were willing to take one for the team."

"It's a *hard* job, but somebody has to do it."

"Hmm. I wouldn't object. Your hands on me are always welcome." I wiggle my ass back into him, the feel of his hardened dick waking up all the parts of me still asleep.

"Mm-hmm," I murmur, mind veering to how it's even possible that I could still want him after the bouts of sex we had last night.

"So, see? We'll figure it out as we go. We'll talk and text every day. We'll be honest with each other when something's not working because we know damn well the alternative—not being together—isn't a fucking option. And we'll sleep at opposite places every weekend until we find out something permanent that works for us."

"How do you make it all sound so easy?"

"Easy? *Not by a long shot*, Saylor. You're not the only one on cloud nine right now, feeling like for the first time in ten years that someone gets you again. So don't think just because I'm the guy here that it's going to be easy for me to let you board that plane. You know me. I'm not good with words. Saying them or making sense with them. I never have been. So please believe me when I say this. I'm the one who walked away before, Saylor. I'm the one who fucked up and robbed both of us of this feeling every day over the last ten years. So, easy? Not hardly. But considering the alternative—not having you in my life—it's definitely worth it."

My heart struggles to beat as it's so overwhelmed with love for him. I shift to turn around, needing to face him.

"No. Don't turn around." Hayes arms hold me captive from doing so.

"Why?"

"Morning breath."

"Are you serious?" He's such a guy. Shifting from heartfelt, swoon-worthy confessions to thinking about morning breath.

"Dead serious. I desperately need to brush my teeth but you feel so damn good like this, ass up against me, that I'm not willing to move just yet."

"Like you have to worry about morning breath," I scoff.

"What's that supposed to mean?"

"Okay, Mr. I'm-A-Hollywood-God. The man who could have twenty-four seven halitosis and would still rake in the women. All you'd have to do is stand there shirtless in front of a female and she'd faint. And not from being bowled over by your morning breath."

"You're ridiculous." I start to squirm away from his fingers tickling my ribs.

"No, I'm not. You've never had a lack of confidence in your whole life."

His fingers fall lax on my ribcage and he rests his forehead against the back of my head. "Yes, I have."

"When?"

"Last night."

Once again his words not only surprise me, but prove to me how much he's matured and is trying to let me in. "Why?"

He laughs more to himself than to me and then falls silent. I give him time to answer. "I thought you left the reception because it was all too much for you. I thought you regretted calling it off. That you still loved Mitch." The fear he felt is transparent in his voice.

"Oh, Hayes. You're crazy."

"Maybe, but between that and you saying Mitch's name in your sleep the other night, that's what I thought."

"Mitch's name? What are you talking about?"

"You mumbled Mitch's name after the first time we had sex."

I wrack my brain to try and think of having had a dream about Mitch but can't remember for the life of me having any in recent memory. "I promise you, the only dreams I've had of Mitch are ones where I'm chewing him out." I shake my head and then really hear what he confessed to me. This time when I speak, my voice is full of wonderment. "How could you think I still loved him after everything that happened between us this weekend?"

"Because I know what it's like to see an old love and feel like you've just been sucker-punched. How it makes you regret all of the things you did to them and at the same time reaffirms everything you feel for them instantly. That was how I felt when I walked into Sweet Cheeks that first day." He pauses and a soft smile spreads on my lips because I felt the exact same. "Last night, I was freaked out and I couldn't find you. And then I saw you and you said what you said and it was like . . . like lightning striking."

"Oh, so apropos." I giggle, loving this side of Hayes Whitley who can express his thoughts so much better than the teenager could.

"Shush." The bed shifts and I'm lambasted with a soft down pillow to the head.

I struggle away. Giggling and laughing and finding purchase on a pillow of my own that I begin to swing with reckless abandon. We're both on our knees, face to face, duking it out with the pillows. For every thud of down to flesh, there's an equally loud sound of laughter and cursing and playful threats.

"Don't get too close," I squeal as he grabs my pillow and makes a sound of victory before gently tackling me to the mattress. His hands are on my wrists holding them to my sides and a smile is wide on his lips. "I thought I was supposed to steer clear of you, Mr. Morning Breath."

His eyes light up to match the smile on his lips. "You were." He shrugs. "But then you made fun of me."

"What are you going to do about it?" A lift of my eyebrows. A taunt of a smirk.

His gaze travels down my body, scrapes over every inch of my flesh. We were having so much fun I didn't think about the fact that we are both still naked from last night. Exactly how we collapsed into bed. When he looks back up, I can see the desire starting to darken in his eyes.

"I can think of a lot of things I can *do.*"

I'm more than ready to play this game with him. "No way. I'm gross and need to take a shower first." I attempt to squirm away from him.

His laugh is loud and amused. "It's only like day four and you're already telling me no to sex? That gives me zero hope for what our sex life will be like in ten years."

I hear his comment, his reference to our future, and while it makes my heart skip a beat, I don't argue with him. Desire is clouding my thoughts and spurring on my words. I flash a coy smile, bat my lashes and let my legs fall open so he can see the pink of my skin there. "Mmm . . . there are a few positions I can think of where your nasty breath isn't in my face."

"Really? Will the position help your crazy-ass hair because it just might distract my flow."

"Your flow, *Mister You're. A. God?*" I laugh out, repeating his words from last night. Loving his playful side.

"You'd know, considering you're the one who begged."

I swat at him with a pillow that's within reach. "I did not."

"Okay, Crazy Hair."

And I know the perfect way to win this battle. To shut him up and to get exactly what I want. *Him in me.* My lips spread into a slow smile. "Best cure for my crazy hair is to wrap it around your fist when you're—"

I yelp out, can't even finish the words as he flips me over onto my stomach in what feels like a nanosecond. His dick lays thick and heavy on the top of my ass. He fists a hand in my hair—just like I said—and takes control while running his tongue down the length of my spine.

"I like the way you think, Ships."

Twenty-Six

Saylor

I'M DRAGGING MY FEET, UNABLE TO COME TO TERMS WITH THE reality settling in that our time is ending here. Soon we'll have to get used to real life—a new normal—if we want to make this work.

I think of our morning. The cuddling. The sex in the shower. The cup of coffee shared on the patio. One last swim in the ocean off the villa. A walk on the beach hand in hand. How we soaked up every last moment with each other before resorting to having to pack.

"See? We were able to do it. To shut the world out and unplug for the whole weekend. As a reward, here's your phone, madam." I look up to see Hayes with my phone outstretched to me and realize he's perfectly right. I have been so consumed with him that my thoughts about DeeDee handling the bakery and any other trivial thing fell to the wayside without my phone.

I smile, just as I seem to do whenever I look at him. "You make it easy to shut the world out, Hayes." My fingertips brush over his hand when I take my phone.

"Don't be sad." He pulls me into his arms and squeezes me tight.

"We'll figure this out. We'll make it work. I promise."

Talk is cheap. I hate the words that ghost through my mind. The ones that cause doubt to wedge into my psyche and seize up my throat because I know we're never going to get this time back.

"I know. Do we have to turn them on?"

He runs his hands up and down my back. "*Unfortunately*. It takes a minute to connect to service or so I was told. At least we have that."

"I guess we should soak those minutes up then, huh?"

"Most definitely."

His lips meet mine in the most tender of kisses. The kind that makes your toes curl and body ache in the sweetest of ways. We sink into it, into each other, and the bittersweet emotions we're feeling.

Somewhere in the villa Hayes's cell phone rings. We both tense at the sound followed by his audible exhalation. "And so it begins." He chuckles against my lips before pressing one more kiss to them, tapping a finger on my nose, and heading off to find his phone.

I watch him leave and then lower myself to the edge of my bed, utterly enamored with him and completely depressed over having to leave this paradise without him.

But I'm so very thankful for this time where we were able to make amends, and unexpectedly strengthen the bond we've shared for years. And in doing so, I feel like he's helping me find the old, carefree Saylor from the past.

Begrudgingly I power up my cell and lie back on the bed. It doesn't surprise me that Hayes is already on the phone. Muffled bits and pieces of his conversation float down the hall. I can't quite catch enough to know what he's saying, but he sounds agitated, and I hate that within a few minutes of plugging back in reality is back in full effect.

I'm not ready for the real world to ruin our idyllic time in paradise.

And no sooner does the thought cross my mind, my cell begins to chirp like crazy, ding after ding after ding notifying me of texts. I squeeze my eyes shut, try to ignore them, but then start to worry when the alerts keep sounding.

Something has happened. There is text after text from DeeDee lighting up my screen and the few words displayed from each one confirms it. I'm freaked out.

DeeDee: I'm so sorry they did this to you. The oven's . . .

Unknown: An interview perhaps?

DeeDee: I don't want to bug you with everything that's going on, but . . .

Private Caller: I'd like to do a feature on you for the magazine . . .

Ryder: I'm going to kill him . . .

DeeDee: I'm baking from my house until Ryder can figure out pricing . . .

Ryder: I'm trying to get it handled . . .

DeeDee: The damn oven is on the fritz again, should I . . .

I'm on my feet instantly, number dialed, pacing the room as I wait for her to pick up. Unable to look at my texts while calling out, I try to make sense of the words I caught a glimpse of. Why is Ryder going to kill Mitch? Did the oven finally die? A feature? And interview? Maybe Ryder's and Hayes's theories were correct.

But that can't be. The wedding was just yesterday. The tide wouldn't be able to turn that quickly.

"Saylor?"

"Dee! I'm so sorry. I've had my phone off. What's going on?"

"I'm so sorry. I don't mean . . . I shouldn't have called with everything that's happening—"

"Tell me about the oven?" She sounds so flustered, and because I know she rambles I cut her off, needing to get to the heart of the matter. My mind shifts from paradise to reality and work in an instant. *My* norm.

"It's kaput. We had an order come in for a large birthday event and halfway through it started smoking and then there was a small fire and—"

"Fire?" My voice is shrill. Panic invoked.

"It's fine. Ryder helped me sort it out. I'm just cooking from my house at night and bringing them in the morning so the pastry cases remain stocked."

My head spins over how this can all happen in the short time I've been gone. "Dee . . ." I don't know what to say. My heart and my reason war against each other over the next step to take. I choose the tried and true, the one thing I know will be there regardless of what happens. "I feel like such an asshole. I'm here traipsing around paradise and you're dealing with all of this. I'm heading to the airport now to try and get an earlier flight out so I can . . . I don't know . . . not feel so helpless and like such a jerk leaving you like this."

"A couple of hours isn't going to change anything. Ryder's been great. He's helping with the oven and dealing with everyone out front waiting for you to get back."

"Everyone out front?" My feet falter. What the hell is she talking about?

"Don't worry about it. He's got it under control. You've got enough on your plate that we're glad to handle it and help out."

"Wait! Who's out front?"

"The reporters."

Reporters? "What reporters?"

"The ones that found out about you and Hayes."

Huh? Why do reporters care about Hayes and me? Then it dawns on me. While I may look at Hayes and see the boy who stole cookies from me after school, the rest of the world looks at him and sees him as a celebrity. One who flaunted his name around the resort this weekend on my behalf. And apart from the hotel guests approaching him for autographs or photographs, I was so consumed with him I hadn't given much consideration to the ramifications of being alongside him as a public figure.

How stupid was I to not think about this? About the outside world and the attention he brought us? Or how easily a photo can be uploaded to social media and shared thousands of times? All of it?

And by the sound of DeeDee's comments, someone here might have done just that. Instead, I was so focused on spending every damn moment with Hayes, working through our past, soaking him up, and then falling more head over heels in love with him than I ever thought possible.

But this is a stark reminder how love can blind me temporarily to life's reality.

"Okay . . . um . . . I'm trying to wrap my head around this. I just finished packing and I'm going to try and get an earlier flight and . . ." I stop, pinch the bridge of my nose and fight the sting of frustrated tears. "Hang tight. I'll be home as soon as possible."

We hang up and I force myself to take a deep breath. To not berate myself for having a weekend away from the bakery where I was able to not think about work, breaking ovens, or profit margins. And to remind myself that the R&R was deserved after how hard I've been working.

Plus, I closed the door on my life with Mitch and reopened another full of possibility with Hayes. How can I hate myself for that?

But reporters? Seriously? I guess I need to get used to this. The upside? Maybe I'll get some free publicity from it for Sweet Cheeks.

"I don't give a flying fuck, Benji. Are you fucking kidding me? You thought I'd be okay with this? Since when are you allowed to make these decisions without my input?"

Hayes's voice breaks through the silence. I jump when something slams on the counter. Uh-oh.

"Do you get what you did? What I've spent the last what feels like fucking forever trying to get back? No, I don't want to listen to the whys. Screw the money. Screw the NDA. Don't you get it? It doesn't matter. None of it does if you just fucked it all up . . . I just . . . I can't . . . You know what? I'm hanging up before I say something I'll regret . . . Yeah. I doubt it."

I wait inside my room and wonder what's happened to get him so upset. With my own thoughts frazzled over Sweet Cheeks, I hesitate whether to go out and ask if he's okay.

And the moment to approach him is lost when I hear him mutter again. "Pick up the fucking phone." I can hear his feet pacing on the wooden floors. Ten steps, then a pause, and then ten steps back.

His voice is muffled when he speaks next. I think he says a name but wherever he's paced to, I can't hear it clearly. And there's something deep, down inside of me that suddenly is dreading whatever is going on.

"Haven't you caused enough trouble?" His anger is palpable. The threat so apparent that I feel sorry for whoever is on the other end of the phone. His chuckle is a mixture of sarcasm and fury. "The charade's over. I'm not doing this anymore . . . No. That's bullshit and you know it . . . I was trying to be the nice guy. Trying to help you out. Help you save face at my expense . . . And you know what? I'm so done. So over your constant crap to feed your need for attention. I turn my phone off for a few days and when I don't respond, you pull this bullshit? Fuck the money. Fuck the movie . . . My image? I don't give a shit about *my image*. I wouldn't have agreed to this if I had. But you know what? I care about hers. And everything else about her . . . No. You used her. Just like you've used me. But you used her without asking. Without thinking about how your little *slip of the tongue* to save yourself from the heat was going to fuck her over. You threw her into the goddamn fire to save your selfish self."

His voice escalates in pitch, in anger, in exasperation, with each and every word he speaks and all I can do is stand against the wall where I've moved into the hall and wait. I hope Hayes hasn't missed something major to do with a movie or a premiere or whatever the hell actors worry about while being here.

And yet at the same time, intuition tells me this conversation has something to do with me. I'm not sure how that's even possible and yet I do.

"Well it backfired. *Big time* . . . You did it without permission. You leaked the comment. Let people assume what they wanted and you never once thought about anyone but you. Fucking typical, now isn't it? Must have not been getting enough attention and so you went and . . . NO!" His voice thunders into the house, echoing off the floors and down the hallway. "I loved you, Jenna. But this? This is why I'm over you. Why I'm done selling my soul to keep your secrets and fuck my life up in the process. Fuck the non-disclosure. Let them pull it. Let them sue me. See if I care . . ."

Hayes keeps speaking but I don't hear any of it because all I keep hearing is *I love you, Jenna.* Or was it *loved*? The phrase repeats over and over and over in my head. Those three words he didn't say to me.

I love you, Jenna.

But he did to her.

My feet move on their own. My heart so full it was ready to burst ten minutes ago now feeling like it will implode.

Twenty-Seven

Hayes

RAGE LIKE I'VE NEVER FELT BEFORE POUNDS THROUGH MY veins. Not since that night on the Schilling farm when I saw Danny Middleton forcing himself on Saylor have I been this livid.

It all comes back to Saylor, doesn't it?

Jenna drones on in my ear yet I don't hear her bullshit. Can't listen to another one of her endless self-serving lies. It's amazing how she used to mean something to me.

And now she means nothing. Nothing except the reason Saylor may walk the other way.

And to think I'm the dumb-shit who went along with this idea. Signed the damn NDA and got roped into her bullshit. But in the end, none of it fucking matters because she screwed me anyway.

"I had to do it. There was press snooping around and so I threw them a few hints to throw them off."

A few hints? More like *Here's Saylor. She's the homewrecker,* served on a goddamn platter.

"I loved you, Jenna. But this? This is why I'm over you. Why I'm

230

done selling my soul to keep your secrets and fuck my life up in the process."

"You can't mean that." Panic fills her voice. "What about my dad? What about the film? You signed a—"

"Fuck the non-disclosure. Let them pull it. Let them sue me. See if I care." I pace the room, free hand pulling down on the back of my neck as my mind reels an endless loop.

"NO! Please, I can't fix it but I'll make it up to you . . ."

When I turn to pace back toward the kitchen, I come face to face with Saylor. Her hair is piled on top of her head, her pink lips are parted, and her cheeks flushed.

But her eyes are swimming with an ocean of hurt.

Oh, fuck. She knows.

"Saylor." I throw my phone onto the counter without a thought to Jenna still spewing her bullshit excuses.

"*I love you, Jenna*?"

Fuck me. Of all the things I said, it's par for the course she heard that one the loudest. She's most likely already made it to be something other than how I meant it. And before I can even answer her unspoken question, her shoulders have squared. She's on the defensive.

And that means her temper isn't far behind.

"It's not what you think. Let me explain." I'm not sure which one I should say first so I say both as fast as possible, knowing I need to stop this before it starts.

"Not what I think?" She folds her arms across her chest. Shifts her feet. Clenches her jaw. "I'm trying to be calm here, Hayes, and not jump to conclusions but I'm having a hard time. Maybe you should explain why you're so upset. Why you're talking about image and doing something to someone which sure as hell sounds like you're referring to me . . . and why you told Jenna you love her when I'm *really* hoping you actually said you *loved* her."

"Jenna's a mess." I start the only place I can because the space between Saylor and me feels like the fucking arctic chill is freezing me out, and so I don't have time to waste. "She's been in and out of drug treatment centers for the better part of the last year and a half." Her eyes widen. Surprise fills them and thank fuck because it's a whole helluva lot better to see the surprise than the hurt that was there a few seconds ago.

"It's Hollywood's best-kept secret. Everyone knows but no one dares talk about Paul Dixon's daughter and her little nose candy problem. Shit, I didn't even know about it for the first six months of our relationship. We were working a ridiculous schedule on *The Grifter*, and I was either too tired or too preoccupied to notice the signs."

I think back to how it all started. The mornings she'd miss her call time. The endless excuses. The erratic mood swings.

"I tried to be patient with her. Thought I could help her. I don't know." I sigh. Run a hand through my hair. I'm restless. "I was in way over my head, but I liked her. Liked having someone who understood the pressure of the job. It didn't hurt we were on a remote location in Vancouver so we mostly had each other to pass the time."

"What does any of this have to do with right now? With what you said? I thought you guys broke up a few months ago."

I chuckle. It's a self-deprecating sound that reflects how stupid I feel now over agreeing to it. "To the outsider, we did, but in all honesty we were done way before that." Saylor shakes her head and tries to process shit I don't even understand. "We completed the film, and when we came back to Los Angeles she was out of control. She went off on the director, fired her agent, and publicly bad-mouthed both. She barged in on a movie her dad was filming, accused him of all kinds of unspeakable shit and embarrassed the hell out of him. Then in a horribly bad move, she pissed off the studio with an interview she gave where she criticized the film and the decisions being made surrounding it. Suddenly the film the studio had slated as their blockbuster of the summer was surrounded by bad press. There's no other word for the damage she'd done but fucking brutal. We had to stage an intervention that ended up with her checked into a rehab facility. Little did I know it had been her third or fourth time there in as many years."

"I remember the bad press about the film. But didn't realize any of this—"

"No one does. The studio was pissed. The backers and producers who gave huge sums of investment capital to the studios to fund their budget were pissed. Especially since this film's budget was one of their largest in the studio's history, they were willing to do whatever it took to make sure its success wasn't risked before it even released. But her interview got a lot of press. She was a loose cannon and the studio wasn't sure they wanted to risk losing the marketing budget for a movie when the lead actress seemed determined to undermine it. They talked about tabling it or sending straight to Netflix, but they knew they'd lose their ass. Some of the backers threatened to pull their money from the project if the studio didn't get Jenna's antics under control. And little did I know that some of the backers knew her history because they ran in the same circles as her dad. And that shared history led to them inserting an addendum in her contract that very few people knew about—me included." I shake my head in frustration. Remember how fucking furious I was when the caveat was revealed to me the day she entered rehab. "It stated that if she didn't stay sober, she agreed to forfeit her advance and all earnings from the film. And in turn, mine in a sense. To say I was a little blindsided is an understatement especially considering she hadn't stayed sober. Shit, the studio went into panic mode trying to figure out how to hide Jenna's breach of contract from the backers."

"Image is everything," Saylor murmurs, her eyes wide and interest piqued, as she sits on the top step of the stairs. At least I still have her attention.

"Yeah, well the money men thought so too. And the big thing was the studio wanted Jenna's little trip to rehab kept under wraps. They knew if the backers found out she'd broken the terms of her contract, they'd pull the remainder of the funds, which in turn meant less marketing, less everything . . . including us getting paid until after it's released and there's ticket sale money being generated."

"They can't do that."

My laugh is rich. I love her naïveté about the industry and wish I was just as oblivious most days. "I may be successful and a big-draw name, Say, but the money men . . . they have a lot more control in my world than people think. They give the money to the studios and since they're the ones shouldering all the risk, the actors must deliver on all aspects: acting, promoting, public relations. They hold all the cards. So the day after Jenna goes into rehab, I'm called into a meeting where I'm told the details of her contract, and the repercussions for both her *and* me if the backers find out she's using again. *Talk about a cluster fuck.* I freaked while my lawyers scrambled to find a loophole in my contract and demanded answers why I wasn't told this prior to filming. At the same time, Jenna's lawyers were in my face begging for me to stick it out to save the film. It was a nightmare I couldn't get out of without seriously damaging important business relationships and throwing a lot of hard work down the drain. During the chaos, they asked me and anyone who knew anything to sign a non-disclosure agreement. They didn't want word getting out and ruining the chances of the movie being released. They were banking on it to be the blockbuster that would boost their ever-waning profit margins in this constantly growing NetFlix, AppleTV, and online streaming world. They thought if we kept Jenna's rehab stint under lock and key and her image squeaky clean, we could pull it off. They released old pictures of us to the press or planted stories in *Page Six*. All kinds of stupid shit to hide she was in rehab. Anything to keep the perception alive that we were costars in love, on and off screen. Then after the movie releases next month, we could call off our fake relationship."

"Wait a minute. Your studio asked you to pretend to be a couple for *her* image's sake?" She sounds dumbfounded. Just like I am most days in this industry.

"Yes. But she didn't keep her nose clean. A few months ago she got into it again with her dad and he basically disowned her until she straightened her shit up. He knew the signs, knew she was using again, and wanted to show her some tough love, I guess. She came to my place crying hysterically and lost her mind when she saw Tessa was there." I think of the scene. Jenna's unpredictable actions and crazy temper. How she tried to hit Tessa and then me. Threw shit. Broke stuff. "That's when I realized that Jenna had an unhealthy attachment to me and that I needed to start distancing myself from her. It was as if she believed all of the bullshit stories being fed to the public about how we were still together. It kind of freaked me out, Say. I suddenly realized we—meaning the studio and how I went along with it—were so very wrong in how we handled the situation. And I'm not sure if it was the pressure of her father's ultimatums or realizing she and I were really all an act, but the night after I kicked her out, she attempted suicide."

"Hayes." And just like that, the sound of compassion in her voice tells me she just might not unravel when I tell her how she plays into all of this. Then again . . .

"Yeah. It was bad." I think back to that phone call. To the frantic feeling over whether she was going to be okay. From disbelief to guilt wondering if it was my fault. "And of course I immediately felt responsible for being the tipping point because I kicked her out of the house. Those first few days were horrible and for the life of me, I have no idea how her attempt had been kept out of the press. I can't imagine the number of greased palms and signed NDAs that her agent or manager or the damn studio for all I know, swooped in and used to keep everyone quiet. But they did. Until two days later when someone saw me heading into the hospital to check on her and started snooping around. I had no clue but somehow the studio found out. Their PR person, unbeknownst to me, decided to distract the snooper by diverting their attention to me."

"The cheating story." The way she says it, like she never believed it in the first place despite asking me, makes me feel a bit of relief.

Let's hope that feeling lasts. *Shit. Why the hell did I ever go along with this?*

"Yeah. The story about me cheating on her. When I woke up and saw the tabloids and found out what was going on, you can bet your ass I chewed out the studio. I threatened and raged but the story already had a mind of its own and there was no stopping it by then. What was I supposed to do? Cause a scene? Admit to the press and in turn the backers I was part of the studio's lies about Jenna's drug use and now suicide attempt? At that point I was just as complicit as she was."

"Which was just what the studio wanted."

"Bingo. I walked right into that one. But how were my agent and I to know Jenna was going to take a bottle of pills and try to off herself? I had a twenty-million-dollar contract riding on this and obviously an emotionally fragile ex-girlfriend. I was fucked in all the wrong kind of ways and it was no one's fault but my own." I look at Saylor and search for judgment in her eyes but find none. "So yeah, I let the PR company and the press paint her as the damsel in distress who had to take some time away from Hollywood after I cheated on and humiliated her. So I ignored the questions about what happened with us in interviews. Figured the less I said the better. It made me look like the asshole but it was better than telling more lies."

"And of course women can forgive assholes because they love the bad-boy vibe but they don't forgive other women. They vilify them."

"I never looked at it that way, but yeah, pretty much." I blow out a breath and hate she's about to find out firsthand just how bad the vilification can be.

"And so the *I love you* was more . . ."

She leads me into the statement, needing to hear me say what her eyes tell me she already infers. But I understand. If the situation were reversed, I'd probably feel the same way. Huh. Who am I kidding? I'd be pissed and demanding answers. Not standing there with admirable patience, listening to me make excuses for the woman who she has no idea just fucked up her world.

"She's a fragile head case, and I don't want to ruffle her feathers. That's why I said *I loved you.* Because I gotta admit, the longer this charade goes on, the more skeptical I am of her motives. I thought it was legitimate at first, but now? Now the special treatment and shitload of attention she's receiving makes me think she's feeding off all of this. That she couldn't handle fading from the spotlight so she pulled this stunt—the "attempted suicide"—to get more of it. Of course, I played right into her hands. Everyone's looking at her now, coddling her, paying attention to her. And it's becoming more and more evident that we've all been had."

"Why'd you agree to go along with it all?"

"Because I'm stupid?" My laugh sounds empty as I scrub a hand over my face and just shake my head at how ridiculous the situation is and how fucking gorgeous Say is. "Because at that point I was so deep into it I became just as guilty for covering it up as she was. Maybe because I felt sorry for her and the pressure she must always be under to live up to Paul Dixon and his shelf-full-of-Oscar's legacy. And maybe, selfishly, because it's a damn good movie. It's some of my best work to date and Jenna . . . off-screen she may be a mess, but on-screen? On-screen she's a goddamn genius, and I think this movie has the blockbuster potential the studio thinks it has and then some. So yeah, of course the twenty-million-dollar paycheck I have riding on it is definitely motivation to just ride it out. Let it release into theaters and then walk away and wash my hands of her."

"But how do they know the image they painted of you isn't going to hurt the release of the film?"

"They don't but the studio has already scheduled me into the ground for the next month so that I'm visible and smiling and showing I'm still the nice guy everyone thought I was. The one who still politely declines to speak about my very public break-up and any inaccuracies reported about it for the sake of *I'm a gentleman and that's a private matter.*"

"The company line."

"Yes."

"Unbelievable. You have every right to be angry. I'm still trying to wrap my head around how the studio has the power to make you . . . that she had the audacity . . . all of it." She purses her lips and looks at me with eyes full of disbelief. Dread fills me as I wait for her to ask the question written all over her face. The one I wish I didn't have to answer: "So what happened just now that made this escalate?"

Twenty-Eight

Saylor

O F COURSE I'M RELIEVED ABOUT THE *I LOVED YOU, JENNA* comment, but digesting everything he's told me isn't easy. How do people get away with all the lies and deceit? While I understand the studio's need to make the film a success, using Hayes and his reputation to ensure that feels dirty. And of course, good-guy Hayes lets them use him to take the pressure off Jenna in order to protect the hard work he's done and his future paycheck.

All of this I understand, so why do I feel like there's more to the story? I glance to the left of him at the granite countertop we made love on two days ago amidst a mess of sugar and flour. I'd felt euphoria then, but now? Now I just feel confused and uncertain. Like my world is about to quake beneath my feet when being with him this week stopped it trembling for the first time in months.

And the discord I feel is reinforced when I meet his eyes. It's in the expression written all over his face—a mixture of resigned regret and cautious trepidation—that tells me I'm not going to like the answer to the question I've just asked him. *I know this look.* He averts his eyes out the window and runs a hand up from his shoulder to his neck and back again.

I'm not the only one with a tell.

I used to see this when he would let down his guard and tell me little bits about the bruises he noticed on his mother's body or about the loud crashes against the wall in the night that would wake him up.

He's not coping well. Something's going on. What the hell is it?

"My agent thought it might be a good idea to use this trip as a way to get some good press in my favor."

Unease tickles the base of my spine. "What do you mean by *this trip*?" While I'm smart enough to infer, I'm trying really hard to control my emotions and to ask instead of immediately assume, which is a new thing for me. And that in itself tells me how much I care for Hayes and I want to make this work.

Patience has never been my strength and yet right now I'm trying like hell to hold on to it as tightly as I can.

Drawing in a deep breath, he takes a step toward where I'm seated and explains. "I mean as in, *Hayes Whitley really is that good guy you thought he was. Sorry, he can't make your premiere because he's out of the country, busy taking an old childhood friend to a wedding. That type of press.*"

I take in his explanation and let it settle while I try to figure out if I should be offended by this or just accept it. And regardless of whichever one I do choose, what does it have to do with what he's so upset about?

"Okay." I draw the word out. "So paint you as the good guy again. Try to get you away from the image of cheating boyfriend before the press junket begins, right?" I nod my head all the while trying to put the puzzle pieces into place and figure out what I'm missing.

"Something like that." His eyes hold mine. Search them. Make me suspicious.

"So did you offer to take me here with that agenda in mind or did you offer to come here and that became a side agenda once I said yes?" I hate that I have to ask. *Hate* thinking that maybe this whole thing was a hoax, and the selfless act was actually a selfish one.

"My offering to bring you here, Say, has everything to do with you and fucking zilch to do with my reputation. You need to know that, hear that, and believe that, okay?"

The sudden urgency in his voice confuses me. The tinge of desperation in it even more so.

I nod my head. Let him know I hear him, but the feeling of unease intensifies.

"What happened, Hayes?" It's my turn to have insistence in my voice.

"Believe me when I tell you I had no hand in this. No idea what was going on. My phone was off until just now and—"

"Just tell me." My heart pounds in my chest, an uneven staccato I suddenly hear pulsing in my ears.

"Jenna pulled one of her bullshit, self-serving stunts." He puts one hand on his neck and pulls down. His face a mask of regret.

"What did *she* do?" My voice is barely a whisper but eerily even despite the feeling I have that the dam is about to give way.

"Our first day here, she was calling me constantly then texting because she was pissed off that I wouldn't come visit her. Like I should be at her beck and call. I was so fed up with her that I turned off my phone."

"That's why you took my phone." I remember the look on his face. The determination for me to hand over my cell.

"Yeah. I didn't want any of her bullshit to ruin the time we had together. She has caused enough problems for me and I just wanted to be here—with you. I know you never get away from work and I didn't want her to distract me from what I wanted to get out of this weekend."

"And what did you want to get out of this weekend?" Curiosity has me asking.

"Originally I just wanted to make amends. Be friends. I told myself you were off limits because we live in two separate worlds and you'd just come out of a long-term relationship." He shrugs, a sheepish grin on his lips. "But I'm not that good of an actor, Ships. Even on my best day, I wouldn't be able to convince myself being friends would be enough."

The smile on my lips is automatic despite the tension of untold truths floating in the space between us. "I told myself we had to kiss each other and get it out of our system. That we could be friends after that."

"I don't think I'll ever get you out of my system, Saylor." His voice is resolute. Honest. But the concern in his eyes brings me back from romantic la-la land to the truth about what's going on.

"What happened, Hayes?" I implore.

"When I turned on my phone, I had a bazillion messages. The press knew I was here at this resort. Not a surprise since I've thrown my name around so that Mitch the Prick and his family knew I was your date."

"Okay." I nod my head. Try to think of worst-case scenarios. "So the press found out you were here. What are you not telling me?"

He inhales slowly. Averts his eyes before bringing them back to me. "They took pictures."

My mind flashes to our time here. To patrons in the bar or at the pool with their camera phones sneaking a picture of Hayes and inadvertently, me. The thought doesn't thrill me that I might be in some of those photos, but it's not the end of the world.

"Okay so pictures proving what? You went with an old friend to a wedding? That can't be all bad, right?"

"Saylor." He shoves a hand through his hair. Shifts the balance of his weight from one foot to another. The man who's always sure of himself is anything but.

"Hayes." My voice is a warning. A *just tell me.*

"Some of the pictures are of us around the resort. The others are us in the ocean the other night."

Thoughts connect. My spine straightens. "When we were skinny dipping?" I ask the question with apprehension in my voice. I'm already running the night through my mind, figuring out my state of undress in and out of the water.

He nods his head. His eyes are trained on mine gauging my reaction. "They're grainy at best and I know that you have your suit on in all of them . . . but it's hard to tell in the photos. They also have a few shots of our cupcake fight on the green. But those aren't what—"

"Oh my God. Last night. There are pictures of us last night on the back patio—"

"No. No. There are none that I know of." I sag in relief knowing pictures of us having sex won't be going viral. "And I don't think who-ever was snapping photos was willing to weather the storm to take pictures of something they never knew was going to happen."

"Hayes." His name again. A question. A statement. A placeholder for the rioting feelings I feel but can't express.

"If someone got pictures of last night, they'd already be sold and posted everywhere on the Internet and I'd currently be suing their asses, but there's nothing so I think we're good."

"Okay." I draw the word out again, needing more time to see what I'm missing in the big picture of things. My first thought is what's the big deal if there are a few pictures of Hayes and me out there. We're adults having way too much fun in paradise. Big deal. "Well, may-be there being pictures is a good thing. The studio wanted to restore your image, and now your fans will see you with the sweet, safe baker outside of Hollywood. You can't get any more down-home, salt of the earth than that, right?"

"They spun the story, Say."

"What do you mean, *spun the story*?" Dread drops like a lead weight into my stomach. Twists it.

"Jenna said that a reporter contacted her, fishing about why she'd been absent from her usual party circuits. Asked about the validity behind a rumor he'd heard stating she'd been in The Meadows facility and was asking what she had been admitted for. She said she freaked out and told him she'd only been visiting a friend there but he didn't believe her. So . . . she tried to shift his attention away from her."

"*What. Did. She. Do?*" I close my eyes, hang my head, and wait for the rest to be said. Scenarios run through my mind and none of them are positive. I fear what he's going to say next.

"She leaked information. Said I was off in paradise with the woman I cheated on her with while she played the victim card. She said she'd been admitted to the facility to battle the depression she'd suffered from our affair."

"*What*?" I laugh the word out like this has to be a joke. He can't be serious. Because I just went from thinking *so what, a few pictures of Hayes and me—childhood friends—having fun have been posted on the Internet* to realizing those same pictures—completely innocent in nature—have been twisted with the help of Jenna Dixon's little prompts to vilify me. I'm now the whore who broke up Hollywood's cutest couple. *Holy. Shit.* "What?"

"I'm sorry." And the way he says it—*the tone*—tells me all I need to know about how bad it really is.

I stare at Hayes but don't really see him. I blink my eyes repeatedly as if the action is going to help me comprehend all of this and then I notice the defeat in his posture and that tells me all I need to know. *It's way worse than I think.* The bottom drops out. Realization hits. And the bazillion images I've seen splashed all over the tabloids of every woman Hayes has been associated with since their public break-up flashes through my mind. I can only imagine what horrible things they've said about me. Hollywood's cruel and unrelenting cycle of drama.

And to think they even have real pictures to substantiate the rumors. Of us slinking around in the dark of night like we're having some secret rendezvous, when instead we were just living in the moment and skinny dipping. I can only imagine the headlines accompanying the pictures.

I know I should feel something. Rage and disbelief and confusion and vulnerability and every other gamut of the like. Yet as I sit here and stare at Hayes and comprehend what he's just told me, all I feel is numb. I just want to go back to the dream world I was in a few minutes ago where the only thing wrong was the broken oven. When I was still comprehending everything that was happening with Hayes was real, and all was going to be perfectly fine.

I was going to get my happily ever after with the only boy and man I've ever truly loved.

And yet right now, all I can imagine is the potential fallout. The damage. My name drug through the mud to help some petty, selfish starlet get the attention she needs to feed her ginormous ego.

I had thought the repercussions of leaving Mitch were bad. Hated being known as *the girl from the valley who left Perfect Mitch Layton.* But this is global. This time I'm the whore who violated Hollywood's picture-perfect power couple.

And in both instances I was innocent.

"Say something."

I can't. The only response I can give is to shake my head from side to side because I'm still trying to figure out how a woman can throw another woman to the wolves like Jenna has done to me.

Then comments from the reception last night come back to me. Mitch's. The other guests'.

Oh my God. Oh. My. God. They all knew.

They all knew and believed what was being said. And then there's my conversation with DeeDee earlier. Her mention of the people outside the bakery. Her apologies for interrupting me with everything that's going on. *I had no clue.*

And then there were Ryder's texts. He was talking about wanting to kill Hayes. *Not Mitch.*

How about the requests for interviews?

Here I was thinking someone was coming to do a feature on the bakery, when in reality they were waiting to twist any words I gave them to paint me as more of the home-wrecking whore they already believe me to be.

"I need to go home." It's all I say as I stand, turn my back to him, and head down the hall. This is not his fault. I know that. Way deep down in my heart of hearts, I know that and yet right now, I need to go take care of the one thing that has gotten me through everything else. Go to the one place where I feel safe.

Ryder. My baking. My salvation.

"Saylor." His footsteps are behind me. His voice a plea laced with concern. "Talk to me. Please?"

"I just need to get home." I start throwing whatever's left to pack into my bag: the swimsuit I took off that night on the beach, the little magnet with the turtle on it Hayes bought me after snorkeling, the cover-up I bought after he told me how pretty he thought it would look on me, his T-shirt—the one I slipped on when I got out of bed this morning because it still smelled like him.

I fight the urge to throw it in my suitcase. *I want him with me.* Instead I toss it at him where he stands in the doorway with puppy-dog eyes begging me to say something to him. *I don't want the reminder.* But I can't talk to him because I don't know what to say. I simply feel *violated.* He catches the shirt with my name on his lips again.

The tears burn, but the rage burns brighter. The anger I can't direct at anyone other than him. "So I came here to redeem myself in the eyes of the assholes affiliated with the Laytons—people I don't give a rat's ass about but wanted to try and give my business the best damn shot possible—and end up being sacrificed to *the masses* as a home-wrecking whore. *Talk about achieving life goals.*"

He sighs. Resigned. Defeated. His eyes truly reflect the pain of watching me suffer at the hands of *his* fucked-up world. "Yes. No. *Yes.*" He nods his head. Hating that he has to admit it. "I'm so sorry, Ships."

And for some reason, hearing that nickname proves to be my breaking point.

"Don't you *Ships* me!" I shout at the top of my lungs. "You used me. You knew all along and used me. You dropped the plane ticket off. Offered to take me. And all along, a part of you deep down invited me into your shitstorm without even warning me what was going on." My voice breaks. The weekend had already been a whirlwind of emotion to begin with. But this? "You are just as guilty for not telling me."

"You have to believe me when I tell you this was not supposed to happen. I expected an article here or there about me accompanying an old friend to a wedding in paradise. Anywhere I go, pictures are always taken. I never expected this, Say. How was I to know that turning off the phone and ignoring Jenna and her huge ego was going to cause her to lash out and try to hurt *you*? There's no way I could have known."

I swallow over the lump in my throat. Know what he's saying is true . . . and yet, anger reigns. "She threw me, my reputation, my business, and *my* name to the sharks. When I talked to DeeDee, I thought the reporters out front of Sweet Cheeks were having a slow news day and wanted some old dirt on you—innocent stuff about how you were as a kid or something. Cute stories. I thought the texts on my phone asking for an interview were to highlight the bakery and in turn get a glimpse of the woman in your life. I should have known how bad it was when I got Ryder's text saying he wanted to kill you. That should have told me everything I needed to know and yet I'm so damn stupid for looking at it through Hayes-jaded eyes."

"Don't do that, Saylor."

He takes a step forward and I take one back. I don't want to be touched right now. I don't want to be coddled. I just want to be left alone to try and figure out how I feel. I know he can sense me shutting him out but it's not intentional. It's just what I need to do to process everything when in reality I have absolutely no clue how bad the story is beyond these tropical walls.

"She sounds like a real class act." My voice is loaded with spite. Hurt. Accusation when it's not his to wear.

"Say, she prob—"

"Don't defend her." My voice is quiet steel issuing a warning.

"She's the last person I'd defend after this." His voice is grave. Eyes serious.

"How do you live in that world, Hayes?" My eyes fill with tears. My chest constricts as the realization hits me that this is the world I'd be stepping into if Hayes and I were to work out.

"It comes with the territory . . . but it's never mattered before like it does right now."

The sob catches in my throat as I turn back to my suitcase. To my everyday life that seems so very far away right now. How will my normal be affected by this? By the hints DeeDee dropped, I fear it's not going to be good.

Do I want to live in that life where pictures can be misconstrued and reputations are ruined over nothing but a rumor? A lie? A misconception?

"Will you stop packing for a second and look at me?"

"No. I need to get home." That's easier to focus on than the look of defeat in his eyes, and the riot of fear ricocheting through me. This morning I woke up sure about our future, and now I'm unsure if I can live in his world.

"Saylor." His hands are on my shoulders. I try to shrug out of them and he holds them still. "Don't pull away from me. We've been through too much for you to pull away from me."

He knows me well enough to assume what I'm thinking. The tinge of fear in his voice—the same one that is echoing in my heart—tells me this. So while he might think I'm strong, I don't think I'm strong enough for this.

"I'm not pulling away. I just need . . ." I hang my head and fight like hell to keep the frustrated tears from falling. "I just need to get home. I need time to think with a clear head, Hayes. Need to sort out the mess I fear my life now is."

"Turn around." And it's not like I have any choice when he turns my shoulders himself. His fingers are under my chin, forcing me to meet his eyes. "I know you're upset. Angry. You have every right to be. *I am too.* I'll do whatever I can to fix this. Whatever it takes, but I know as well as anyone that I can't control what people believe or don't believe. And so it only matters what we know. What we believe."

I nod subtly to let him know I hear him. The words he's spoken and the unspoken ones in his eyes that tell me he thinks I've been scared away. And a part of me has. I just don't know by how much.

"The oven died at the bakery. I need to get there to figure out what model will fit and its pricing and payment plans and . . . I just need to get back there." I let the lie fade off because I know what those answers are. But what I need is space to think. To breathe.

"I'm going home with you. I'll do an interview and explain our history. How we reconnected. Make it right again. Get the bastards to retract the stories." I know he means what he's saying, but I also know he can't undo what has been done because he'll be on the defensive. And the defensive is never a good place to be. *I traveled all this way here to avoid just that.*

"It's not going to matter. You know that. It's already in print therefore it's already believed."

"But it's better than doing nothing. I'll do however many interviews it takes to make them believe. We just need to figure out how to handle right now first."

I look at him through tear-filled eyes and try to sound certain in my words. "There is no handling to be done. What will happen is I'll go home to sort out the bakery, and you'll go to New York because you have a table read tomorrow. I wouldn't want you to lose the part because you missed it. I don't need to be coddled, Hayes. I've lived my adult life without you, so I don't need you holding my hand now." I hate the flash of fury in his eyes from my comment, but it's the truth. The sound of me closing the zipper on my suitcase in the quiet of the room reinforces my words. "I'm going to head to the airport now. Try and get an earlier flight back so I can get Sweet Cheeks back on track."

"I'm going with you."

"No." I laugh but there is no amusement in the sound. "I want to go by myself. If you rush back with me, they're going to think we're upset and trying to cover something up. Someone will comment that you missed your reading. Assumptions will be made as to why. The last thing we need right now is to give them more fodder for their lies."

"I don't give a fuck about their lies." His voice thunders into the room and echoes back to me. His rage is so raw, his emotion so real.

"I know you don't, Hayes. But please . . . you may be used to this . . . but *I'm not*. Not any of this. Just let me go on my own. Let me be a nobody in the shadows a little longer. I need time to process. To sort through it all. To get home and be in my own space and—"

"Why are you making this sound like a goodbye, Saylor?" His hands on my cheeks don't allow me to avert my gaze from his like I want to.

"It's not. But I don't know if I can survive in your world, Hayes."

He presses a kiss to my lips. It's tender and simple and yet loaded with so much feeling behind it that a single tear slips down my cheek. My heart aches. My mind is so confused. Every part of me is scared about walking away and never seeing Hayes again. Of never getting the feeling back that we had this weekend.

The love he feels for me is clear in his eyes. He rests his forehead against mine, our breaths mingling, our eyes closed, our hearts understanding they are about to break apart. "Please don't do this, Say."

A second tear slides down my cheek. *I love you, Ships.* My heart needs to hear him say the words. Give me something permanent to hold on to when I do what I need to do.

Walk away.

But he doesn't say them.

"I need some time to decide if I can. Goodbye, Hayes."

Twenty-Nine

Saylor

THE PLANE RIDE HOME WAS AN EXERCISE IN HOW TO CRY silently without anyone else on the plane knowing. The pictures and headlines of the tabloids littering the airport newsstands were horrible. The hurtful things they'd said replayed on a loop.

Image after image. Headline after headline. Lie after lie.

It was like the comments from the wedding reception on a loud speaker. On repeat. Each one worse than the last one.

And as much as I'd wanted to buy every single tabloid there—take them all so I could prevent others from seeing them, and read every single line to know what I'm up against, I didn't. I resorted to sitting in a quiet corner obscured by a trashcan with my face shadowed beneath a baseball cap so I could read them all via the shoddy airport Wi-Fi on my phone.

It was lovely (insert sarcasm here) to see Mrs. Layton weigh in with her opinions about me in one of the articles. The jilted ex-fiancé Mitch as well, because who knew the timing of Hayes's and my previous relationships and issues had both followed a similar timeline? So when Mitch said he suspected I was screwing around behind his back, he's not surprised it turned out to be true.

Therefore, I'm not someone who broke up only Hayes and Jenna's relationship, but *my* cheating ruined mine as well. *And of course there was nothing about Hayes in their articles. The pitchforks previously aimed at him are now directed at me.*

Fucking. Me.

And the stories, the headlines, just kept getting more creative, more slanderous from there. Painting me as a horrible person for breaking up the couple who the public had unceremoniously crowned Hollywood's It Couple.

Sitting in the airport I felt so incredibly alone and vulnerable. I would have given anything to call my mom and hear her soothing voice tell me everything would be all right in the end. To have her order me to throw the tabloids into the trashcan I was sitting beside and reassure me that no one in the airport was staring at me. To wrap her arms around me, murmur that everything happens for a reason, and that sometimes it takes time to know what that reason might be. And then to have Dad take the phone from her and tell me one of his god-awful Dad jokes to cheer me up. Remind me that all men are idiots and that's why God created women.

God, I missed them.

Instead I called Ryder. I listened to him fume over what they were printing when all I wanted to do was cover my ears and shut the noise out.

But nothing—not the tabloids, not feeling like I disappointed Ryder, not my fear of losing Sweet Cheeks because customers will boycott the store—compared to the look on Hayes's face when he walked me out to the waiting car to take me to the airport. Naturally, it was in the service bay due to the many photographers at the resort's entrance.

Not the images they printed of the clandestine lovers or the horrible, vile lies they printed without truth could compare to the wrenching of my heart when we shared the last bittersweet kiss. The kiss where my tears were constant and nothing could abate the empty feeling of saying goodbye.

I can still hear Hayes's whispered promise that he'd *make this right.* How he told me I was making a mistake walking away from him instead of weathering through it together. How I should just go to New York with him for a few days, do an interview together to show people what is really between us.

But I chose to walk away even though my chest hurts with every breath I take. I already miss him so much.

But missing him does nothing to ease how completely shaken I am by all of this.

I flew to the island a harmless ex-high school flame and, within a four-day span, fly home an adulterous whore hated by what feels like the whole world.

So I need this distance. Need my own bed. My own space. My own thoughts. Thoughts filled of him no less, but still my own. Without him crowding me and telling me *you get used to the lies* and *the attention over the lies* and *you learn to not let them affect you.* Because I don't want to live like that. I don't want to hear and see lies and be so cold to the world that I have to shut them out to live my day-to-day.

I know it's not Hayes's fault and yet I still need some distance so I don't lash out at him. Because knowing it's not his fault doesn't fix the humiliation over the horrendous things being printed and posted and tweeted and Snapchatted about me. It doesn't stop the cruel responses about how ugly I am compared to the flawless Jenna Dixon. It doesn't shut out the comments about how in the hell can Hayes Whitley ever pick me, a very ordinary baker, over the glamorous starlet. How I must be pregnant because that's the only justification as to why he'd stay with me when he could have her.

And it definitely doesn't ease the fear niggling in the back of my mind that keeps creeping in at random intervals. If image is everything in Hollywood, if studios have the pull to make actors appear to be with or not with other actors for precious images' sake, if the masses never accept me as Hayes's girlfriend because I've been branded as a homewrecker, then how will our relationship last?

Relationships are hard enough as it is. New ones especially. And to have all of this outside pressure on us from the get-go? To constantly worry about anything I do or say and how it will be mis-construed and posted in the press makes me panic. I don't want to be a liability for Hayes.

I don't want that added stress in my life.

Pressure can cause even the strongest person to crack, so I know it can break relationships too.

Let him be the judge of that, Saylor.

I know it's not fair to think all this without talking to Hayes about it, getting his input, and yet I can't bear to talk to him just yet. Reading his continuous texts is hard enough. I miss him. I love him. I just need to know I can walk into this relationship with open eyes and enough strength that when the shit hits the fan, I'm secure enough to be the person Hayes needs me to be in his crazy world.

I squeeze my eyes shut and pinch my nose as the taxicab exits the freeway. I'm overthinking all of this. In fact, it's all I've thought about between the bouts of tears and the constant doubt when all I want is the strength to *believe in us.*

When we turn down State Street, the usually quaint road is lined with cars. The parking lot of the strip mall just to the right of Sweet Cheeks is completely full.

There must be another high school event or craft show. Shrugging it off, I sigh with relief when I see the welcomed sight of the pink and white striped awning of Sweet Cheeks in front of us. Of DeeDee's red Ford Escape parked in the lot, and knowing my bed is upstairs.

Empty.

Without Hayes in it.

And I hate the thought immediately.

A new *No Trespassing* sign catches my eye as we pull into the parking lot but I'm so preoccupied swiping my credit card to pay for the ride that I'm completely oblivious to what's going on outside the cab. But when I open the taxi door I'm startled by the sight of a group of camera wielding men and their tidal wave of sound as they call my name.

I'm momentarily stunned. And I think I stand there blinking for several seconds as my emotionally spent mind tries to catch up with what's actually happening. But seconds feel like minutes in this alternate reality I've stepped into where the click of the shutter is a constant sound.

Click, click, click.

Saylor, this way. Is it true?

How does it feel stealing Hollywood's most eligible bachelor away from Jenna Dixon?

Click, click, click.

Are you moving the bakery to Hollywood now?

Is it true he's only with you because you're pregnant?

Click, click, click.

Why would you do that to Jenna?

Is he as good in the sack as rumors state?

Click, click, click.

Before I can blink, DeeDee is there in front of me grabbing my hand in hers. She takes control, gets my luggage from the driver, and steers me into the bakery—*my bakery*—and closes the door behind me.

I expect the noise to end. The shouts and clicks and the flashes so bright they feel like they are screaming at me to stop too. But they don't. They're muted now. Still a chorus of chaos outside, but not as loud.

When I look up, people are at the tables inside. With cups of coffee and empty cupcake wrappers and notepads. *Customers.*

"They may be paying for food, but don't trust them. They're one of *them*," Dee says with a lift of her chin to the photographers outside who are now directing their lenses toward the plate-glass storefront window where I stand. "Ryder says they may be assholes but we sure as hell will take their money."

I look at her. Shell-shocked. Overwhelmed. Wondering how they knew I'd be here when my original flight wasn't slated to land for another two hours.

And then it hits me.

It doesn't matter.

They've been waiting.

Wanting a piece of me.

Needing a new shot to sell so someone can create more lies about me.

Shit.

Welcome home to me.

Thirty

Hayes

"**I DON'T CARE. ISSUE THE STATEMENT. SET UP THE EXCLUSIVE.** Do whatever the fuck it takes to fix this or I'll break the NDA and take my chances . . . if I don't get paid, then you don't get paid." I look out the window to the city below, and chew the inside of my cheek as my comment hits my agent, Benji, where I want it to: right in the hefty mortgage he just acquired when he bought that house off Laurel Canyon.

"Hayes . . ."

I grit my teeth at his placating intonation and his *this will blow over* attitude. He didn't see her face or watch her hand fly up to cover her mouth as she stood in front of the damn magazine rack in the airport and read the bullshit headlines he had already warned me about. He didn't hide in the shadows and watch the woman he loves wipe the tears from her eyes as she touched the tabloids as if to see if they were actually real before skimming the fronts to read what they had printed about her.

Because, fuck yeah, I followed her to the airport. I would have followed her all the way home if I could have but her plane was full.

Not even bribery or my celebrity status was able to buy me a seat on the flight. My fight was subdued in comparison to how I felt inside. My need to not draw more attention to her by any lurking paparazzi readjusted my focus. No way in hell was I going to let her head to the airport and face a possible slew of photographers on her own without being there to step in if need be.

But it killed me to watch her hiding beside the trashcan, presumably reading the stories on her phone. Enraged me to know she gave an ounce of her attention to the lies.

Shit, while I watched her from behind my dark sunglasses and beanie, I had half a mind to walk right up to her and not give her a fucking choice in the matter whether I was going with her or not. Charter a damn plane myself if need be to get us out of there together because I'd lost her once and I wasn't taking the damn risk of losing her again.

Last time it had been right to walk away. I had justifiable reasons. This time? *Not a chance in hell.*

That look in her eyes. She was spooked. Freaked out by the fucked-up confines we Hollywood A-Listers live by. There's a helluva lot of privilege but also a ton of bullshit. And the only thing worse than watching her walk away—letting her go face this beast on her own—is losing her.

So I hung back on the other side of the tiny terminal. Wanting to be sitting beside her, talking her stubborn-ass through this, but instead I did the hardest thing for a man to do: I sat and watched the woman I love, knowing she was hurting and all I could do was sit there and fume.

Because fuck yes, *I love her.*

No doubt about it.

It was hard enough putting her in a car and kissing her goodbye. Biting back the words I feel but knew wouldn't mean a damn thing to her considering the circumstances. Saying I love you for a second-first time should be special, not because I'm afraid I'm going to lose her.

But I fucked up. *Big time.*

It was only after her plane took off that I realized my fuck-up. She heard me say the words to Jenna. But not to *her*. And there's no way to fix it except to earn the chance to tell her face to face.

But now I'm here.

In New York, my home away from Los Angeles, and way too damn far from her. So I'm depending on Benji to deliver because he's the goddamn reason I agreed to sign the damn NDA in the first place. His quiet urging. His commentary on how Jenna wouldn't dare fuck up again because she didn't manage her finances well and needed this big influx of cash the movie would bring. Trip after trip to a secluded, confidential rehab in Arizona, full of Zen gardens and yoga something or others with the best counselors money could buy, cost a pretty penny.

"Look, man. I've always respected your opinions. And I take full responsibility for the bullshit with Jenna, but I think you're missing the bigger picture. I. Don't. Fucking. Care." Each word sounds like another string to my control snapping. "About my image. About the film. About shit. This needs to get fixed and it needs to get fixed fucking yesterday."

There's silence on the line. My point has been made. He gets I'm not fucking around.

"I hear you, *loud and clear*, but no one's going to listen to you. You're too good of an actor, Whitley. You've had everyone believing you were with Jenna. And then with your silence, you had everyone falling for the broody, bastard boyfriend routine where the guys questioned how you could find better pussy then Jenna Dixon's. And the women, while hating that you might have cheated, were also pulling back their sheets and patting their Tempur-Pedics in invitation. You never broke character once. You didn't talk about it. You didn't—"

"Because I signed the fucking NDA on your advice," I grate through gritted teeth.

"Your balls were in a vice, man, with the studio acting as the henchman like I've never seen before. You had no choice. But you know as well as I do that painting the town red with interviews isn't going to do shit to change the public tide on Saylor."

And I fucking hate that. With a vengeance.

My hands fist in reflex. My teeth grind together. I feel the same fucking helplessness I had when she boarded the plane the other day and walked out of my sight.

"Get with Kathy. Figure out how to coordinate face time with Givens, Seacrest, and Cooper. The studio wants me to be their puppet boy? I'll do their dance, pimp the movie, and while I'm at it, I'll set the record straight about Jenna and me and where Saylor fits in the fucked-up equation. The studio wants a buzz leading into release day? I'll give them a buzz like they never expected."

"Watch it, Hayes. You've walked the line this far, make sure you don't step over it now." I can sense his frustration. Hear his sigh across the connection. Expect the heeded warning one more time. "I get you're frustrated. Know you want to shout on the rooftops the truth about Saylor, but I'm telling you your best plan of action is to sit and wait. This will blow over."

"You're right. *It might.* But *it will blow over* means a completely different thing to me than it does for Saylor. You know what it feels like the first time you open your car door and have a camera thrust in your face? Or hear the click of the shutter from somewhere in the bushes but don't know where until you catch the glare of the lens? It's fucking terrifying if you're not an attention junkie like we actors are. And she's the furthest thing from that."

"It will blow over, Hayes." There's sympathy in his voice this time, and it's still not enough.

I hang up without another word. Sit and look at the lights of the city beyond. Wonder how many people out there have read about Saylor today. Wonder if they immediately believed the lies. And then wonder why the fuck they even care about who I date in the first place.

I pick up the beer by the neck and down it. Exhaustion hits me, yet I can't sleep. I glance at my phone, my thumb instantly swiping to check my messages just in case I missed a text back from her.

But there's nothing.

Welcome to Hollywood, son, where dreams come true, and the one you want more than any of them won't fucking text you back be-cause she's scared of what those dreams entail.

Fuck me.

It'll blow over. Of course it will. Question is if it'll be a hurricane or a breeze when it does.

This is on you, fucker. Figure out how to fix it. All of it. You break her heart again, I'm going to throw more than just a punch the next time I see you. Ryder's voice rings loud and clear through my voicemail. His threat real . . . I wouldn't expect any less from him. And yet it brings a smile to my lips because it's the only message today that I fucking deserve.

The table read sucked. And not because I didn't know my lines or couldn't step into character, but because of that goddamn scene. The one I rehearsed with Saylor that had gotten me all hot and bothered and had rang too fucking true for the two of us. To our history.

The *I'd beg, borrow, and lie again right now to get the chance to see her again.* Just like the damn script reads.

So yeah, it was a fucked table read. In my own head anyway.

To everyone else participating in the read, I nailed it. The emotion. The feeling. Everything about it . . . because I *wasn't* acting.

Landing the part meant nothing though because I didn't have her to call and share the good news with.

And of course from there my day went to shit. Like catching the latest picture of Saylor on the scattered newspapers on the table in Starbucks while I waited in line. The one with her eyes wide and purse dangling from her hand as she got out of a taxi in front of Sweet Cheeks. To say the look of utter shock and fear on her face felt like a knife in the heart is an understatement.

But my texts remain unanswered. My messages unreturned. My frustration at an all-time high with my goddamn heart in a vise that squeezes tighter with each fricking hour I don't hear from her.

Next came the call from Tessa. Her tongue-lashing as to why I didn't take her somewhere and stage pictures to be taken so she could receive the attention Saylor was. *Because no press is bad press, right, Hayes?* And she could really use some more press and pictures taken with me to help her keep her visibility up. Talk about a fucked-up moral compass. She's dying for the attention—*heartless, conceited bitch*—and Say doesn't want any of it.

But I gotta admire her. Hollywood takes all kinds.

Then after that, yet another call from Benji and one from my publicist, Kathy. The promises that the interviews were being set up. That a location to hold them was being discussed. Followed by a gentle reminder of what was riding on this.

Yeah. *Saylor's riding on this.* The reason. The why. The fucking end game. Nothing else matters.

And of course Jenna's nowhere to be found. MIA. That little gem of information kills me. The irony that she can cause this tornado of bullshit by dropping malicious hints about Saylor and yet when I want to contact *her*, her phone goes unanswered. Her whereabouts unknown.

I'll find her and convince her to tell the press as much of the truth about us as she can. That we ended our relationship by mutual agreement, not because I cheated. And that Saylor wasn't even in the damn picture when it happened.

Or else I'll tell them. And with a dramatic flair, I'll throw in all the little extras that make stories like this juicy to the public. Like drug use and suicide attempts.

Simple.

If only.

What would be even better is if Saylor would pick up the goddamn phone when I call. But she hasn't and now I need to find another way to reach her. Break through to her.

Convince her that this world of mine isn't so bad when we face it together.

I just fucking miss her.

Need to be with her.

Hold her when she hurts.

And it's killing me that I'm not.

Thirty-One

Saylor

I'M LOST IN BATTER.

Sounds ridiculous but I am. It's in my hair, on my apron, and smeared on my cheek. My kitchen counter is a clutter of tins and ingredients and utensils. My apartment smells like the bakery should. The timer is beeping. My cell keeps vibrating on the table behind me with alerts I ignore.

And in this chaos, I can finally think. I can figure out which of the two ovens in the brochures on my couch I need and how I can make the monthly payments. I can avoid the looks by my brother downstairs who keeps shaking his head, asking me how I let this happen even though he knows I had no part in it. I can fight the humiliation over the newest round of insults printed. The ones about how I *supposedly* squirreled away Mitch's money—without him knowing—and opened the bakery of my dreams before dumping him at the altar.

Twisted lies. Mistruths believed by the masses.

I look to the vase of black roses on my table. My lovely gift from a Hayes admirer who threatened me for stealing him away from Jenna. They reflect the bazillion comments on social media this morning when I pulled on my big girl panties and decided to log on and brave the storm to see how bad it was. Cruel is an understatement. So I kept the flowers—despite Ryder begging me to throw them away—as a subtle reminder of the crazy I'm stepping into with Hayes. *If I step into it.*

So I woke this morning wearing the T-shirt he snuck in my suitcase—his welcome scent still lingering on it—before changing so I could bake to avoid my new unwanted reality. More importantly, to have the time to wallow in the empty ache in my heart that's been burning a hole there over the past twenty-four hours.

I marvel at how the trip to Turks and Caicos was a mere four days and yet they felt like a lifetime with Hayes. How the heart can remember what the mind chooses to erase. How Hayes and I reconnected and slid into being an *us* without either of us discussing it. Void of overthinking. And how it just felt right.

Was it because we've technically spent more than half our lives together so the transition was seamless? Or was it because our hearts recognized our first love deserved a second chance?

Out of everything owning my thoughts, my mind keeps coming back to that.

But then I hear the noise of reporters in the bakery float up the open stairwell. The door is ajar so I can take the cupcakes down to cool quicker in the refrigerated case before frosting them. And then start the process all over again from behind the scenes while DeeDee and Ryder take care of the customers. The customers that have since doubled now that I'm back in town from my *secret rendezvous* with Hayes.

So up here is where I choose to stay. Away from the prying eyes and crazy assumptions of the assholes and their cameras and the looky-loos suddenly having an urge to buy a cupcake when they've passed by every other day of their commute.

And I bake. For the increased demand. To lose myself in my thoughts. To combat missing Hayes. To forget that if I opt to be with him, the two-dozen reporters outside might be my everyday norm.

The day drags on. I shower after my twelfth batch of the morning, then force myself to put on makeup and look presentable just to prove to myself that I can function if Hayes isn't in the picture.

Yet I'm miserable. I hold his T-shirt to my nose and breathe in his scent. It makes me miss him more but also brings me a sense of calm.

And I wonder why I'm pulling the stubborn card and not talking to him. *Is it stubbornness or resilience?* If I talk to him, this craziness around us will disintegrate and I'll only see him. *Us.*

Maybe that's a good thing. Maybe that tells me he's all I need, and if I'm with him, then the outside noise doesn't matter.

But life can't be spent joined at the hip with your lover. What happens when he goes on location for weeks on end or is so busy filming we see each other only in passing? There would be no blinders then. There would be no Hayes to shield me from the mistruths being said. *The lies being spun about once a cheater always a cheater.* Can I handle that? The curious reporter wandering into Sweet Cheeks to try and get an inside scoop on Hayes Whitley? *On me?*

And hell, just because he was talking about ten years from now, that doesn't mean us being together is a given. So why am I worried about forever when I can't even give him today? Shouldn't I take one day at a time, and see from there?

"Oh my God," I groan with a shake of my head. I'm becoming one of those sappy, wishy-washy women I swore I'd never be. The one I'd roll my eyes at and tell to suck it up when she acts like it's a problem to have a man in love with her who wants to make it work regardless of the outside influences.

I'll give myself a few more days to see how long this kind of attention and chaos lasts. It's weird how I've lived so long without him but in this short span of time, not having him with me feels empty, sad, and lonely. I've been through this before and don't ever want to feel this way again.

This is more than missing him. This is knowing that without him I'm incomplete, as if half my soul is adrift.

"Saylor. You need to come down here," Ryder's voice calls up the stairs and every part of me bucks at the idea.

"What is it?"

"You need to get your ass down here to see for yourself."

With resignation but grateful that I actually look presentable, I trudge down the stairs, my posture defensive, my attitude sucky.

"Ry? What is it?" I ask as I swing around the corner and almost run smack dab into the backside of a burly guy in the back area between the stairs to my studio and the bakery's kitchen space. About the same time he mutters an apology, it dawns on me what he's moving.

"What is this?" I look over to Ryder standing on the other side of the brand new, shiny, stainless steel baker's dream of an oven that's being maneuvered into the space.

"It's a Baxter Rotating Rack Oven."

"I know what it is." I laugh feeling flustered as I stare mesmerized at the oven of my dreams. "I'm just trying to figure out how they're delivering it to the wrong place."

The guys moving it stop at my words and one of them pulls out paperwork from his back pocket. "Says right here: For one Ms. Saylor Rodgers, Sweet Cheeks CupCakery with a huge *paid in full* next to your name."

Startled, I look over to Ryder who just shrugs with a slight smirk playing the corner of his lips, eyes narrowed as if he's trying to figure out where it came from. A part of me knows the answer before I even ask to see the paperwork. And when I do, I know I'm right. That familiar signature I've known ever since he'd scribble on my homework to piss me off in high school. Then there's the handwritten note next to the name.

> **She'll argue or refuse to accept it. Don't listen to her!**
> **Hayes**

I want to strangle him.

Gritting my teeth, I huff out in frustration although the scowl on my lips is betraying me and beginning to turn up at the corners. I look at Ryder. "Did you know?"

"No clue but by the look on your face I can guess who it's from."

"The asshole." The comment is halfhearted and lacking any

conviction. How can it when Hayes just purchased the Ferrari of ovens for me?

"Hmm. Definite asshole," Ryder murmurs with a shake of his head and a half-cocked smile.

"Guess that's his way of getting me to call him, huh?"

Each ring of the phone feels like an eternity. I'm irritated, grateful, confused, and overwhelmed over how he could buy me something so extraordinary—something that costs as much as a car—when I've pushed him away.

"*Ships?*"

"It's too much. Thank you, but I can't accept it."

"Then I can't accept you saying you need time and being away from me."

His words warm so many parts of me. The parts that ache from missing him. The pieces that fear a love this strong. The unknown still swirling around us.

The want to know he thinks I'm worth fighting for.

My sigh must tell him how hard this is for me because he allows the silence for a moment. Knowing me like he does, he allows me time to process how far apart we feel right now, which makes me miss him even more.

"It's only been forty-eight hours, and I miss you." My statement is simple. The break in my voice reflects my struggle, the toll it's taken and how hard it is to admit.

"I know. Me too. I've bought a plane ticket home a hundred times in my head today."

"I can't accept the oven, Hayes. It's way too much."

"But you asked for time, and I'm trying to give it to you even though it's killing me not to be there with you," he says right over me, ignoring my refusal of the oven.

"Hayes, you're not listening to me."

"I'm listening. I'm choosing *not* to hear you."

My smile is instantaneous. The memories of how frustrated I used to feel when he used to use that defense with me when we were younger.

"I know you're smiling, Ships. I can hear it through the line."

"Maybe."

"And I bet you're rubbing your ear right now like you do when you have things you want to say but don't know how to say them."

His words make me lower my fingers immediately from their place on my ear. I hate and love that he knows me this well. Is it any wonder, despite the current chaos, I still love him?

"Perhaps."

"Ah, so that means I'm right because you always give one-word answers when you don't want to admit things."

"Possibly." He says the word the same time I do and we both laugh.

"See? I know you, Saylor Rodgers. Everything about you. And what I missed during those ten years without you, I want to spend time learning."

My eyes well with tears and I can't figure out how this conversation I wanted to have about how he can't buy me a shiny new oven turned into him showing exactly how much he knows about me.

"You there?"

"Yeah."

"You scrunching up that freckled nose of yours? Upset that the man you're so madly in love with and you *need space from* has already helped you forget all the bullshit of the last few days with a simple conversation?"

I close my eyes and slump against the wall. His words weave into those holes I've worried into my heart over the past few days—the ones I know I'm stupid for having because he's right. It's been a few minutes, and he's proven to me how, when I'm connected to him, I *can* handle everything else.

"Hayes." *I love you. I'm sorry. I miss you. You're right.*

But nothing comes out, because maybe I'm scared. Maybe what I feel is so damn strong, which explains why I'm hesitating even though every single part of me is telling me to go full steam ahead. Maybe that's why I can't tell him to get here as soon as he can.

"Agreed," he murmurs, followed by a chuckle that's both seductive and heartwarming. "I agree to everything you just thought but didn't say out loud. But, no. *Not yet.* You said you needed space. *Time.* Seconds. Minutes. Hours. So I'm going to give them to you, Saylor. Ten days to be exact. Two hundred forty hours where you can't talk to me." He pauses momentarily. "Fourteen thousand, four hundred minutes—yes, *don't laugh*, I just had to do that math on my calculator—of time where I'm going to prove to you why you can't live without me. Why the stories and tabloids don't mean shit. And how public opinion can be turned when you try hard enough."

"You don't have to—"

"Yes. *I do.* This is as much my fault as it is Jenna's. I've had a lot of time to think since a certain someone won't return my calls, and I've come to the conclusion that maybe I let it happen. Maybe I pushed Jenna's buttons to prove a point. *I* was too selfish thinking about how badly I wanted to shut her up and figure out how to seduce you, to know what it would feel like to sleep with you again, that I didn't give a thought about how she could retaliate. So, I'm sorry, Saylor. I fucked up. I played right into the studio's game and perfectly into Jenna's hand. So forgive me if I'm taking the reins when it comes to us, but I'm not taking a chance on this outcome. I'm giving you my A-game . . . I just hope you can handle it."

I feel like I haven't taken a breath during his entire speech. My chest burns and my heart hopes. My mind races with possibility while my cheeks hurt from smiling. *Hayes Whitley just told me he loves me.* I know he didn't say the three little words, but he said them nonetheless.

"What if I already know—?"

"Nope. Don't say it. Words are cheap. Action is everything. Ten days, Saylor. Ten days and then I'll listen to you all you want. Until then, once this conversation is over, mum's the word since day one starts now."

My laughter sounds like relief. My heart feels content, which is different from two days ago where I felt lost, confused, exposed, and betrayed. We had both needed this time to evaluate what was real and what was not, and I'm so incredibly thankful we both concluded the same thing. *That we wanted there to be an us.* And yet I can't resist . . .

"And what if your A-game is not strong enough to win me over?" I know he can hear the playfulness in my voice and that I'm throwing down a challenge.

"It's good enough, sweetheart. Just you wait and see."

"I'm a tough girl to please."

He laughs again. The kind that warms my soul and makes me feel a little steadier in this world of chaos swirling around us.

"Then we'll have to grudge-cupcake it out."

Thirty-Two

Hayes

EIGHT DAYS LEFT

TWITTER
@SweetChks Can anyone tell me how many people are in the world? #GrudgeCupcake #10Days #ShipsAhoy #WordsRCheap

"MR. DIXON."

"Hayes? What can I do for you, son?" The deep baritone of Jenna's father vibrates across the connection.

"Sorry to bug you, Paul."

"Is it Jenna?" There's concern and trepidation in his voice, and I hate that he immediately thinks of the last time I called him after I found out about Jenna and her suicide attempt.

"She's fine but she is the reason I'm calling."

"Yes?"

"Do you know where she's hiding? I've been trying to find her, and she's not returning my calls." I pause for a moment. Let the lie roll off my tongue. "It's about scheduling for *The Grifter*'s press junket."

"No need to lie, Hayes. She threw you to the wolves because she was jealous you found someone else. Probably hoped to scare that woman of yours away. Typical, selfish Jenna move. I'm sorry about that. Her actions are inexcusable and not something I'm proud of." His words shock me. Seems he's just as tired of her stunts as I am. "Last I heard she was at the place in Malibu."

"Thank you, Paul."

Thirty-Three

Saylor

EIGHT DAYS LEFT

*I*GNORE THEM.

Don't let them distract you.

I tell myself to focus on the new idea that woke me up out of a dead sleep last night and left me staring at the ceiling trying to conceptualize it.

A flash on the screen of my cell. Another glance up from the cupcake I'm designing to see yet another notification in and endless stream of them.

Quit distracting me.

I set down the piping tube and grab my cell. My will power is nonexistent when it comes to wanting to read the responses to Hayes's tweet from earlier this morning. I'm not quite sure why he's asking about the world's population or what it has to do with me but it helps to pass the day.

@MindiSocksLou

@SweetChks @HayesWhitOffcl Seven billion #ThanksGoogle What's a #GrudgeCupcake? I love you Hayes!

Focus, Saylor.

On the new idea. On what flavor combinations would complement the concept best. On how this little flash of creativity has gotten me down from the apartment where I've been hiding from prying eyes and back into the work area of the bakery.

And while I've relegated myself to the work area only, at least I'm there.

A notification flashes again.

The distraction works.

**@BookLoverJeniB
@SweetChks @HayesWhitOffcl A bazillion. Why are you asking? #GrudgeCupcake?**

I dirty my hands in the frosting, working on design after design trying to perfect my vision. I'm picky and particular and throw ten designs out for every one I keep, because *I have to get this right.*

Plus throwing myself into full-creative mode means I'm distracted. And distracted is so much easier than thinking about how much I miss Hayes and how frustrated I am with him and his damn ten-day rule.

So, creativity helps to pass the time slowly ticking away until I get to see him again.

My screen flashes.

This time I try to avoid getting frosting on it when I pick it up.

**@TBartley86
@HayesWhitOffcl Leave @SweetChks and marry me. I kiss better. #GrudgeCupcake – Answer: Population 7 billion**

The bell of the door alerting new customers is steady while I work. Curiosity is clearly still strong. Despite the sign that Ryder put on the door that says *No Cameras*, the photographers come in, buy a cupcake, and take a seat with the hopes that I'll step into the front where they can sneak a picture of me on their cell phones. The female fans stop in to buy a cupcake with stars in their eyes looking around in case Hayes shows up.

They're wasting their time. If they were true stalkers, they'd know about his ridiculous ten-day rule.

All the while the tweets continue to flash.

@Hollywood732
@HayesWhitOffcl @SweetChks 6.9 billion. Is this a trick question?

"You've been awfully quiet back here."

Ryder. I smile softly, knowing he's bailing on his regular workload during the days to help out (meaning keeping a big brother eye on me) and then going home and catching up on his own responsibilities.

"Just messing with an idea," I murmur as I step back and scrutinize my design.

"Hmm. So you being back in the kitchen . . . does that mean the new oven's too hard to resist or you've talked to Hayes and have figured stuff out?" He narrows his eyes as he waits for an answer.

"He's not giving me an option." I shrug. I don't fight the smile because I do feel better with the elephant's foot of pressure removed from my chest.

"He's not?" He raises his eyebrows and nods.

"Nope. And you didn't even have to clock him this time around to knock some sense into him."

"I was only trying to protect you." His expression is guarded, unsure if I'm going to be mad at him for interfering all those years ago.

"I know." I think of all the other things I could say to him: how I was a big girl and could make my own decisions. How he might have been the reason we never got back together. But I don't say any of them. Maybe we wouldn't have appreciated each other and the connection we rekindled if we hadn't had other experiences to compare them to.

"What's up with his tweet this morning?" It's my turn to show shock, surprised he noticed. "Hey, I check your social media following. Visibility is a good thing—means possible sales—and you gained several thousand new followers this morning."

Huh. Always looking out for me. *And* always business-savvy.

"I don't know. He's trying to win me over."

"I think he already has."

I start to say *maybe,* but stop when I see his head angle to the side as he notices the fondant tops in front of me.

Nerves jitter within as I step back and try to look at the cupcakes through his eyes. The first one looks like it has a needle sewing together the fondant with the words "*Oats to sow*" in cursive above it. The one beside it looks like shattered glass with the words "*One to throw*" in block letters across the top. The next pair is the same color scheme, just a darker tint. The first cupcake has no design and says "*One to smash*" with its partner saying "*He can kiss my ass*" and a pair of lips outlining the lettering.

"These are awesome. Who are these for?"

"Me."

"You?" He looks confused. "I thought things were getting better."

I laugh and nod. Then I proceed to tell him about Hayes and his grudge cupcakes. How cathartic it felt smashing them and the fun we had with it. And then how when Hayes told me the other day if he didn't win me over with his charm, his last resort was another grudge-cupcake match.

"So . . ." I shrug, ". . . he got me thinking about grudge cupcakes. And if people would actually buy them for their friends when they break up. So I make one to eat and one to smash; in a container it's a 50/50 split with cute slogans. It's the perfect therapy: *chocolate and aggression.*"

When he doesn't smile at my quip but rather just holds a finger against his pursed lips as he thinks it over, I suddenly feel ridiculous thinking this could work or have customer appeal.

"It was just an idea. It would probably never—"

"Would they be normal-sized? Smaller since you're smashing them? Give me specifics."

"You and your specifics," I mumble with a roll of my eyes but feel a little more at ease knowing he hasn't immediately rejected the idea. "I haven't gotten that far yet. I suppose we could make the ones to smash smaller but then we get into needing custom inserts for the boxes and the trade-off in cost. I haven't thought that far, Ryder. I'm working on the creative side for now. You know what? Never mind."

"I think it's brilliant, Saylor." *He does?*

"You do?"

"Completely."

I stare at him. Wide-eyed. Shocked. Feeling accomplished. "Wow."

"Now we need to figure how to go about marketing it so we can get the word out."

Our eyes hold and I've never been more thankful to have him as a brother than I am right now. He's always been protective of me but after our parents died, he stepped up to the plate more than I'd ever imagined he could. It was *us against the world*. He's stuck by my side and been my number-one supporter throughout all the ups and downs, sorrows and joys.

Sure I'd had Mitch to pull me from my grief, but it was Ryder who was my rock.

Still is.

A small part of me knows my parents are smiling down on us right now and that gives me hope that things might finally be turning around.

My screen lights up.

The distractions continue.

I'm so engrossed in perfecting little details on the cupcakes that it takes me a bit longer to check my phone. And when I do, I have to scrape a splatter of frosting from the glass to read the tweet.

And I finally have an answer.

@HayesWhitOffcl
The public has spoken. 7 billion people in the world. And I CHOOSE YOU @SweetChks ONLY YOU #GrudgeCupcakes #ActionsRLouder

Wow. Now there's a declaration in one hundred and forty characters or less if I've ever seen one. The man certainly knows how to get my attention.

Yes, Hayes, actions are louder.

Thirty-Four

Hayes

SIX DAYS LEFT

FACEBOOK
Hey @SweetChks . . . Just giving you back all of the things I stole from you over the years . . . Whatever could I mean? #GrudgeCupcakes #DayFour

"HAYES."

"You're a hard lady to track down." I don't hide the spite in my voice or the *fuck you* lilt in it. Jenna repositions herself on her lounge chair where she sits in the sun so her cleavage is more prominently on display. "I can see the recovery's been *rough* on you."

I catch her ghost of a smirk before her lips turn into a pout as she slips on her mask to embody the part of depressed victim.

"You have no idea, Hayes. It's so good to see you. Thanks for coming to check on me. Why don't you sit down?"

When she puts her hand in mine and tugs on it, I glare at her. A *do you really think I'm buying your bullshit right now* look on my face.

In the moment I question my judgment of character. How I ever looked at her and saw anything other than what she really is. An attention-hungry junkie willing to use anyone and every situation to her advantage.

"This isn't a social call, Jenna. This is me coming to you because you're too chickenshit to answer your phone and deal with the mess you created."

"Oh, Hayes." She chuckles that fake laugh of hers and it feels like nails on a chalkboard. "Relax. No one's talking about it anymore."

My fists clench as I try to restrain myself from picking up that tall glass of gin sitting next to her and smashing it to make sure I have her attention. But a part of me wants her to not take me too seriously. If she blows me off then she's had fair warning, and I'll gladly handle this on my own terms.

"Here's what's going to happen. Next Wednesday, you're going to get your ass in the car I'll have here to pick you up. It's going to take you to Saylor's bakery. You're going to walk in there and apologize to her, face to face. *And you will be nice.* Then you're going to walk out to the little café where I'll be holding the press junket interviews, sit down beside me, and explain how long ago and why we broke up. You'll explain that no one cheated and we were simply a case of two people not meant to be together. And then you're going to publicly apologize for letting the press think Saylor was the reason we had broken up and for not correcting them."

"You're being ridiculous. I can't do that. People would think that I lied and—"

"You DID LIE," I shout, fingers itching to pick up the glass again.

"I think I have a hair appointment that day."

Fucking unbelievable.

"Cancel it."

"No."

"Cancel it," I repeat as I squat down and take my sunglasses off so we are at eye level. There will be no mistaking my threat when I speak next. "Or I'll hold the interviews myself and explain how difficult the filming was because you're an addict and then casually mention your suicide attempt. How you did it as a publicity stunt because you're so goddamn in love with yourself and you didn't think you were getting enough attention. I'll explain why your daddy has disowned you, how the studio has threatened not to pay you, and why your career is hanging by the same thread your human decency is."

"You asshole." She grits the words out. My smirk in response is visual sarcasm. "You can't do that. What about the NDA? Our paychecks? You just can't—"

"Yes, actually I can. There are some things more important than money, Jenna. And Saylor is one of them."

"You wouldn't dare." Her hands tremble and voice wavers with a mixture of disbelief and anger.

"Try me, Jenna." I lift my eyebrows before putting my sunglasses back on. I stare at her a second, let her know I'm not fucking around, and then leave without saying another word.

Fuck, that felt good.

Thirty-Five

Saylor

SIX DAYS LEFT

> FACEBOOK
> **Hey @SweetChks . . . Just giving you back all of the things I stole from you over the years . . . Whatever could I mean? #GrudgeCupcakes #10Days**
> **1. Chocolate Chip Cookies**

I LOOK AT THE HUMUNGOUS BOX OF CHOCOLATE CHIP COOKIES recently delivered to the bakery. And not just any kind of chocolate chip cookies—*Chips Ahoy* to be exact. Between the play on his nickname for me and the memory of how he'd steal my cookies after school, the gift makes me smile. The thoughtfulness behind it warms every part of me.

And frustrates me considering he won't answer my call to say thank you. The only response? A text saying six more days. *Agh.*

Feeling more sure of myself today, I venture into the front of the bakery behind the counter. The talking ceases momentarily until the customers realize how noticeable it is and then start chatting loudly again as if that's not obvious either.

I talk over the week's astounding sales numbers with DeeDee as the photographers outside aim their lenses through the window. No doubt they're grateful they can actually see me after sitting out there for days bored to tears. I certainly have the advantage of living and working in the same building so there is no guaranteed drive to work like most other people they stalk.

I rearrange the display case, wanting to keep my hands busy as I try to get used to the feeling of being watched. It's almost as if they think I'm going to suddenly break down and confess to all of the horrible things their magazines say I did.

Hey @SweetChks . . . Just giving you back all of the things I stole from you over the years . . . Whatever could I mean? #GrudgeCupcakes #10Days
Chocolate Chip Cookies
Kisses

The delivery boy catches me off guard when he walks in the front door. At first I'm about to tell him to leave, mistaking him for a paparazzo acting as a delivery man just to get in the store somehow (silly, I know but I'm a bit paranoid with forty-plus pairs of eyes watching my every move), but then realize the package in his hand isn't a camera bag.

I watch as he leaves, how the paparazzi go crazy clicking pictures as if he's the secret messenger between Hayes and me. And when I open the package, I realize he is.

When I look inside the box, there is a cardboard partition that divides the box in half. One side is filled to the top with so many Hershey kisses I'm overwhelmed with the smell of chocolate. And the other side is empty save for a note taped to its bottom.

The box is half empty. I need the space because I plan on stealing a lot more in the future. -XO Hayes

My heart skips over a beat and a smile graces my lips as I do what any normal person would do. I pick one of them up, unwrap it, and eat it while I watch the photographers mill around outside. A thought forms but I shove it away. Disregard it.

But as I venture into the retail front and wipe down a few tables, see some of the tabloid magazines with my image on the cover left there, and overhear conversations about bragging rights over who got the most for each photo, I start to think my idea isn't a half bad one.

"Dee, I'm heading back into the kitchen for a bit."

And of course when I get to my workstation, there is another box. Another returned item from Hayes. And this time I know DeeDee or Ryder had to have helped him but I love that he went to this much trouble.

Hey @SweetChks . . . Just giving you back all of the things I stole from you over the years . . . Whatever could I mean? #GrudgeCupcakes #10 Days
Chocolate Chip Cookies
Kisses
Time

I open the box to find an hourglass inside. My fingers reach out to touch it. I'm overwhelmed by the effort he's put into these ten days so far.

I turn it over and watch the sand slide through the glass. Hypnotized by the sight, my thoughts drift. To how easily time passes. To Hayes. To not wanting to waste any more of it when it comes to being with him. Life is too short. When the sand runs out, the completed grudge cupcakes are visible through the curve of the empty glass.

Stop wasting time, Saylor.

I laugh out loud as pieces click into place for me. The paparazzi. They're using me to make money. To sell the image they want of me.

Why can't I use them for the exact same thing?

Inspired, I grab my set of perfectly decorated grudge cupcakes and I waltz out of the kitchen, through the front of the bakery, and out the glass front door for the first time since I came home from my trip.

The awaiting photographers scramble and stumble over each other when they see me striding out of the store like a woman on a mission.

"You want a statement?" I shout out as they fumble to slide their cameras over to video mode to record what I have to say. "I'll give you a statement. You want to know how I feel about everything that's going on? How it feels to be accused and vilified and lied about when no one has a clue what the truth is?"

I set the box of cupcakes down with a resounding thud on one of the tables I have out front for customers. I pause for dramatic effect to make sure I have their attention and give them time to get the best angle.

"I get angry. But I don't make up more lies and spread them around to make me feel better and to get more attention. I don't call reporters, lie to them about where to find more gossip, and drop hints that aren't true. No. Because if I did, you'd know I'm not the story here. Not in the least. But I have more class than that. More couth. Instead I bake. I eat chocolate. And I get out my anger by doing this."

I pick up a cupcake, flash the top—make sure the *One To Smash* is showing to the cameras—and then I smash it between my hands á la the grudge-match cupcake war I had with Hayes. The photographers startle as cupcake shrapnel flies everywhere.

The image of Hayes's bare chest covered in cupcake crumbs fills my mind and how I wanted to lick them off of him. And the thought is ten times more appealing than the slew of paparazzi in front of me but it makes seeing them that much more bearable.

"I make grudge cupcakes. Where there's one for me to get my chocolate fix." I hold up the one that says *Oats To Sow*. Take a small bite. Then hold up the *One To Throw* cupcake as shutters click. "And this one's to get my frustration and aggression out." And this time when I smash it, I earn a chuckle from them.

"So you see? Nothing important is going on here that you can take a picture of to sell, other than the ones you just took of me making grudge cupcakes and smashing them. But if you do sell the photos, make sure they're accompanied with some ridiculous headlines like, *'Saylor Rodgers goes crazy on a cupcake-smashing spree because Hayes Whitley has left her for Medusa's little sister.'* Because if you're going to lie, why not go all out, right? So print what you will. Say what you want. I know the truth. Hayes knows the truth. Jenna most definitely knows the truth. That's it. I'll just be in here making more cupcakes. I might even send a few out to compensate for your time since I'm not giving you any camera-worthy breakdown moments to sell. Everyone here like chocolate? Good. Sit tight."

With that, I lick a piece of frosting off my fingers, look to the box of remaining cupcakes, and decide to leave it on the table so they can take a closer look and maybe even take a picture or two. Perhaps that's why I make sure to strategically position the box so the pair of cupcakes I want to be seen are front and center for the camera lens: One cupcake says *YES, it's always been HIM* and its match says *NOT YOU, Golf Boy.*

Yeah. Those cupcakes are keeping me warm, now. Asshole.

And with a smug smile on my face because I know Mitch will see it and understand my message, I turn my back to them without another word.

When I open the door to the bakery, I feel the best I have since I woke up in Hayes's arms before the shit hit the fan.

And when I look up, Ryder is staring at me with wide eyes and a shocked smile, pride written all over his face. "*That* was brilliant, Say."

I shrug. "If you can't give them what *they* want, you might as well give them what *you* want."

"Free publicity is never a bad thing."

"Thanks, but I've had enough publicity for a lifetime the past few days."

I move to the back, wash my hands, and feel a little more sure of myself now that I know facing the beast wasn't as horrible as I thought. Of course I know the crowd outside is nothing compared to some of the other mob scenes I've seen surrounding Hayes when he leaves a club or a premiere or does anything, and yet it's still better than expected.

Baby steps. One after another, right back to Hayes's arms.

"For you." Ryder's voice startles me. I dry my hands on a towel and narrow my eyes at the package as he sets it down.

I carefully set down the box, but when I remove the top, *it is empty*.

All except for a red heart drawn on a piece of paper. The words written in the center bring tears to my eyes.

Sorry. I'm not giving this one back. Hayes.

Hey @SweetChks . . . Just giving you back all of the things I stole from you over the years . . . Whatever could I mean? #GrudgeCupcakes #10Days
Chocolate Chip Cookies
Kisses
Time
Your Heart

And if swooning were a real thing, a physical reaction, I'd be doing it right now. Because damn if something so simple doesn't mean more to me than the expensive oven.

I read the post again, my heart bursting, and then when I look down at the thousands of comments that have been made on his posts to me today, I notice a shift. They started out being crappy. Negative about me. But by the last one, the comments started becoming more positive. A *Get the girl, Hayes!* Or *If someone makes you this dedicated, you must love her.*

I switch over to my phone to text Hayes, like I have after every gift has arrived, and type: **You can keep it as long as I can keep yours. Thank you for my gifts.**

Thirty-Six

Hayes

FOUR DAYS LEFT

TWITTER
@HayesWhitOffcl
Get ready for my mad A-game @SweetChks. Do you have a Band-Aid? I scraped my knee falling for you. #10Days #GrudgeCupcake #Determined

I WATCH THE VIDEO ON TMZ OF SAYLOR AGAIN. OF HER WALKING out of Sweet Cheeks looking so composed and innocent with those brilliantly creative cupcakes, giving her little speech, and then smashing them in her hands. Shocking the hell out of the paps. The subtle dig to Mitch the Prick that will definitely be noticed. She comes off as playful, confident, and unaffected by the cameras being pointed at her. Like the unbelievably cruel things that have upended her world the last week don't matter at all.

She played *them* perfectly. And when she turns to head back inside, the angle of the video affords me a glimpse of the Saylor Rodgers smug smile that says she's figured this game out. Goddamn sassy, gorgeous, and without a doubt going to be mine.

God, I fucking miss her.

We went ten years without speaking so why is my self-imposed moratorium of not talking to her for ten days killing me?

Because this time I know it matters. This time I'm not willing to walk away from her again or let her walk away from me. I've chased my dreams. Followed my passion. Been successful. But what does it mean if I don't have her around at the end of every day?

To kiss hello.

To laugh with.

To dirty up a counter in flour with.

Scrubbing my hand through my hair, I review the agenda sent over for the interviews being held the day after tomorrow and check the list of things I need to do to pull off the surprises I've planned.

And then I hope like hell this has all been worth it. That not talking to her, not seeing her, not kissing her will only make her realize how damn lonely it is without me in her life.

Now back to researching cheesy pick-up lines to tweet.

If I'm making an ass out of myself, I damn well better be getting the girl in the end.

Thirty-Seven

Saylor

FOUR DAYS LEFT

> TWITTER
> @HayesWhitOffcl
> **You must be a banana @SweetChks because I find you a peeling. #10Days #GrudgeCupcake #Determined #MadA-Game**

I LAUGH WHEN I SEE HIS NEWEST TWEET. I CAN'T HELP IT. I'M standing with my hip against the butcher block, my hand to my mouth, and a smile on my lips. He's relentless. And adorable.

He has over one million followers, and he's posting cheesy pick-up lines and doesn't seem fazed in the least by what people are going to say about them. Maybe that's the point. Maybe he wants me to know he doesn't care and neither should I.

I skim through my own account, surprised to find more positive than negative this time around, and notice a lot of people commenting on my cupcake-smashing incident with more amusement than degradation.

"He's adorable, you know?" I look up to see DeeDee standing in the doorway voicing my thoughts out loud, tissue paper in her hand, and a smile on her face. And maybe it's because he's softened me with his humor, but I just stare at her for a moment and realize how lucky I am having her here to help me take this all in stride: making the bakery work and the chaos that comes with Hayes. "His tweets and his posts and everything . . . they're just adorable."

"I know. He's the closest thing I've seen to the guys in those romance novels of yours, Dee."

"Really? In all aspects?" Her eyebrows lift and a coy smile forms on her lips as I recall our conversation about romance heroes and guaranteed orgasms.

"Yes. *In all aspects.*"

"*Damn.*" It's all she says, and I love that my comment has rendered the always-talkative DeeDee momentarily speechless. "What were we talking about?"

I chuckle at the flush in her cheeks. "His adorable tweets and posts and . . . *everything.*"

"Not many men would put that much thought into trying to win a woman over."

"I know. He's being ridiculous."

"And you love every single second of it."

I nod. "Yeah. I just wish he'd pick up the phone and talk to me. He's already won me over."

"Isn't that the point though?"

"What do you mean?"

"Winning you over is one thing. But now, he's telling the world he chooses you. He's making a statement so you don't forget. And so they don't either."

The phone rings by the cash register and she hesitates for just a moment to make sure I heard what she said. And I did.

Loud and clear.

@SweetChks It's hard to breathe because you steal my breath every time I see you #10Days #GrudgeCupcake #Determined

There's *no way* I could have just heard that correctly. I stop moving ingredients to the butcher block and walk out to the front where DeeDee is in a conversation with a customer.

"Can I help you?"

Dee's eyes flash over to mine and silently thank me for coming out.

"Yes. One of the function organizers for The Club was saying she was looking for a bakery to supply morning tea on the third Thursday of the month. I am positive she would absolutely love your cupcakes. They're the perfect combination of taste and presentation."

"Did you say for The Club?" I swore I misheard her the first time from the back, know I heard her clearly the second time, but want to make sure one more time.

"Yes, dear. You know, The Club." She pats her hair and smiles. "And pardon me for asking, but aren't you related to one of the members?"

Once again, I'm left to look around for a hidden camera. This has to be a joke, right? But there is no camera. Just DeeDee's eyes widening and teeth biting into her bottom lip as she holds back a smile.

This woman thinks I'm related to Rebound Sarah.

"No, I'm not."

"Oh, because you could be the long-lost sister of the organizer's new daughter-in-law. You're the spitting image of her."

The irony.

I swallow over the sarcastic laugh threatening to bubble out and try to remain patient *and* professional with this obviously clueless-to-The-Club-drama customer. "No. I don't have a sister."

"Well, good thing," she whispers and leans over the counter and pats my hand. "The daughter-in-law is a tad . . . how do I put it politely? Pretentious? Conniving?"

"A bitch?" I provide the word for her since she's too polite to say it herself. Her cheeks flush instantly and the diminutive smile she grants me says all I need to know.

"Something like that, yes. The whole family is for that matter." She shakes her head indifferently and dismisses the matter. "Now where were we? Oh yes, cupcakes for The Club. It would be a great feather in your cap to get their business. The members have a lot of valuable connections you could benefit from. In fact, I'm so positive the organizer would love these, I'm going to go ahead and place an order for next week's meeting."

My smile widens to epic proportions as I lower my voice just like she did a moment ago. "While I'd love to provide them, you make sure to tell the organizer I am currently backlogged on orders for the foreseeable future. Besides," I shrug, trying to be cordial because she seems like a nice lady, which is a rarity for a member of The Club, "I think my cupcakes might be a bit too sweet for their tastes. Thank you, though."

"Well, I think they're delicious. It's a pity but I'll be sure to deliver the message."

"Yes, please do so," I say in my kindest voice as she nods to me in farewell before turning to leave the store. *With a box of cupcakes in her hands.*

I'd love to see the look on Uptight Ursula's face when she receives that message.

"Say, there's a phone call for you."

I murmur an acknowledgment, but keep my head down where

I'm working on some elaborate icing designs. The convention center's catering manager requested some samples so they could decide if we were worthy to make their preferred vendor list.

"And not from The Club."

"Ha. That's funny." And now she has my attention. "Can you take a message? I need to—"

"No. I think you need to take this."

I look up, her expression one of guarded excitement as she holds the phone out to me. Curiosity has me to standing to full height and taking the phone from her.

"Sweet Cheeks, this is Saylor. How may I help you?"

"Hi. Yes. My name is Sally Destin and I'm calling on behalf of the organization Divorce Support California."

"Hello." I narrow my eyes at DeeDee and am feeling slightly had here, but uncertain exactly how. "How may I help you?"

"Yes, I was just explaining to your assistant and she thought it would be best if I spoke with you. Is this the owner?"

"Yes, my name is Saylor. How can I help you, Sally?"

"I was wondering what your capacity and reach is for your delivery range. Are you just local or all of California?"

I grab a pen and pad to make notes. "Well, that depends on the quantity needed. If it's a couple of dozen, then just local, but if we're talking a larger volume we can deliver."

"Much larger." She chuckles and I glance back over to DeeDee whose smile is growing wider as she watches me. "We are a company who runs, manages, and coordinates California's largest network of divorce support groups. We have on average five different events a week in varying locations with an average attendance of a hundred or more members."

"That's a lot of members. So how can I help you?"

"We saw you on camera yesterday with those breakup cupcakes and would like to place regular orders."

My head starts swirling with specifics. Finding a reputable courier service. Volume packaging. Endless possibilities. I shake my head in hopeful disbelief, the excitement bounding off DeeDee starting to make sense.

"You mean the grudge cupcakes?"

"Yes, but we'd like to refer to them as *breakup cupcakes. Divorce cupcakes* or *fresh-start cupcakes.*" She chuckles at herself. "Sorry, I'm getting ahead of myself naming them. We can decide their name later once we schedule a standing order for them. Typically, I'm looking at about needing approximately five hundred a week. And once we establish those demands, I was thinking of creating some kind of partnership with you where when we unfortunately add a new member to the group, we send them a sampler as a welcome to the group type of thing."

Five hundred plus a week? Did I hear that correctly? Holy. Shit.

I think I blink a few times. Open my mouth and close it as I try to gain my composure. "Oh. Okay. I'd love to work with you and figure something out." My voice sounds calm but my trembling hands reflect my excitement. "I'd have to see the delivery range and work with you on what you'd like them to say . . . the details . . . and then I can come up with a proposal for you."

"That sounds great. I'm on your site right now so is that the email to use to send the info over?"

"Um. Yes. That's perfect."

"And you know, we do have someone from our main office typically go to each of the meetings, so if some of the events are out of your delivery range, maybe you can ship them to the main office and the counselor or staff member heading to the meeting location can bring them. Just a thought."

"That's perfect. Thank you, Sally. I look forward to getting the information."

"I hope it's not out of line to say this, but you've been put through the wringer this week. Someone needs to tell you that the way you handled yourself yesterday—smashing the cupcakes for the cameras—was inspiring. And the idea is brilliant. We've been looking for an idea like this for a while now. I'd love nothing more than to give the okay to issue a contract for your company. It's only a matter of time before other companies come knocking and I want to make sure we reserve our spot before you have to start turning orders away."

"Thank you. Truly. Thank you. And I look forward to making this work."

I hang up the phone and with eyes probably as wide as saucers look at DeeDee. We both give a little scream at the same time.

"Holy shit," I whisper.

@HayesWhitOffcl
You must be a keyboard @SweetChks because you're just my type. #10Days #GrudgeCupcake #Determined #MadA-Game

"You weren't joking, were you?" Ryder asks as he looks up from the email to meet my eyes.

"No. Can you believe it?"

"That's a huge amount of cupcakes." I can see him mentally calculating the profit and what it means to the store. "Like enormous."

"Yeah. I know. Do we have the capability to do it?" I ask, knowing it means I'd have to hold off on paying him back because I'd have to redirect those funds to buy the extra supplies needed to make this work. I bite my lip and wait for him to say no.

"If we don't, we'll make sure we do." Something about the way he looks at me right now causes my breath to catch. It's like looking at my dad. The expression on his face is identical to the one my dad would give me when he was proud of me. Every part of me preens from his unshakable support. "Breakup cupcakes. Who would've thought?"

"I know. We've received about ten orders for them today."

That catches his attention. I can all but see the cogs of his mind turning. "We need to update the website ASAP. We'll dedicate a whole page to this product and start looking into how to sell franchise opportunities to other stores to help with this increased demand. Internet sales are where it's at, and if we could get something going on that front then—"

"Whoa. Slow down, turbo." I laugh but feel the same excitement he does.

"There are divorce support groups like this all over America, Say. You could tap into this niche."

"One thing at a time." I roll my eyes at him but silently sigh in relief. This phone call might be just what the bakery needs to turn the tide toward success and not failure.

"I might not kill him after all," Ryder mutters as I walk out of the back room.

@HayesWhitOffcl
Are you a camera @SweetChks? Because every time I look at you I smile. #10Days #GrudgeCupcake #Determined #MadA-Game

Thirty-Eight

Hayes

TWO DAYS LEFT

"**D**UDE, DO YOU HAVE ANY COFFEE IN THIS JOINT?"

Fuck, I'm tired. And hyped. Dreading the long day ahead but loving that I get to see her today. I shuffle down the carpeted hall I used to practice my baseball slide on and into the kitchen. It's painted a different color now but that doesn't erase the memories it holds. Of where the jar used to sit on the counter full of the cookies I would steal from Saylor. Of the cupboard to the left of the refrigerator where Mrs. Rodgers used to hide a stash of candy we all would sneak from when we didn't think she was paying attention. Of sitting down for meals and there was always a place setting made up for me whether I asked to eat here or not.

Ryder sits in the same location as when we were kids, but at a different table and lifts his eyes to meet mine. He looks as worse for wear as I feel—and points his finger to the Kuerig on the counter.

"Thanks." I brew some coffee, doctor it, then sit across from him and think that this is where it all started for me. *My love for Saylor.*

We sit in comfortable silence. The kind two friends who have known each other forever can sit in without words and figure out how we feel about the turn of events.

"Do you think Jenna'll show?" He raises his eyebrows and pushes one of the tabloids to the side he was looking at to see if shit was dying down.

"If she knows what's good for her, she will."

"Hmm."

"Is my IOU paid off yet?" I chuckle. Thinking about back then—a few months after I'd left for Hollywood and was waiting for filming to start—how he helped my mom out, separating their mess of finances when my dad came after her in their divorce. How I had no money to pay him, but he called in favors anyway and got everything I needed to help get her taken care of. And despite his continued denials, I know he paid money out of his own pocket to get those favors done for me.

"Make her cry again, I'll still punch you. I don't care how famous your ugly ass is."

"So noted." I nod my head. Tuck my tongue in my cheek and prepare myself for the day ahead. "She have any clue about today?"

"Not a one."

Good.

I miss her.

It's sure as shit going to be hard to stick to my guns and *not* talk to her when I see her.

Thirty-Nine

TWO DAYS LEFT

TWITTER
@HayesWhitOffcl
@SweetChks Are you still in need of a cardboard cut-out holding a sign selling your wares? #10Days #MadA-Game #GrudgeCupcakes #Anticipation

@SweetChks
@HayesWhitOffcl Only if I get to place the flour handprints. In the right places. #IveGotGameToo #10Days #TalkIsCheap

@HayesWhitOffcl
@SweetChks Proud of you. Class act the other day. BTW, what's the most important thing in a kitchen to you? #GameOn #48Hours #ActionIsBetter

@SweetChks
@HayesWhitOffcl Granite slab on the island. With flour. And sugar.

#MmMmGood Can we skip the next #2880minutes?

@HayesWhitOffcl
@SweetChks I'm a man of my word. What are you going to do to try to break me of it? #Decisions #GameChanger #ILoveIcingInYourHair #CountersAndFlour

@SweetChks
@HayesWhitOffcl I've got my ways to make you talk. #MadSkillz #GameChanger

@HayesWhitOffcl
Better bring your A-Game @SweetChks Mine's stronger. #HayesFTW #ShipsSink

Forty

Saylor

TWO DAYS LEFT

T's hard to be in a bad mood when you wake up and have a Twitter flirt with Hayes. It's the first time he's responded and it's ridiculously silly that the small interaction put me on cloud nine. Yet it has.

Between the divorce organization proposal I spent all night working on that I sent to Ryder for his opinion, my little morning exchange with Hayes, and the knowledge I get to speak with (and hopefully see) him in forty-eight hours—after his asinine ten-day rule is up—today feels like it's going to be a good day.

I slowly enjoy sipping my coffee and spend a little extra time getting ready. I feel relief and contentment, which is welcome after a tumultuous couple of months.

"Say? You're going to want to come down and see this," DeeDee calls up the stairs, just as I finish getting ready. There's something in her voice that reminds me of the first time Hayes came to Sweet Cheeks.

I shut the door to my apartment and jog down the stairs to find the bakery abuzz. A camera has been set up in one corner. Men in dark clothes with headsets huddle in another. All of the tables and chairs have been pushed to the side of the room except for one set. A tray of my most lavishly decorated cupcakes has been set atop it.

What the hell is going on?

The slew of photographers outside has grown tenfold with their cameras held at the ready, all vying for shots of what's going on inside the store.

"What the—?" I'm about to lose my temper. Just because the letters on the logos of their jackets belong to one of the biggest entertainment networks—doesn't mean they can just waltz into my bakery and take over without asking.

It's then I catch the look on DeeDee's face—huge grin and excitement palpable—and then Ryder standing beside her looking just as excited but with guilt mixed in.

"What's going on?" My hands are on my hips and accusation is in my tone.

"The studio rented out the space for the day. They gave Hayes the okay to do a few interviews here for his upcoming movie." Ryder challenges me to argue with him but all I heard was *Hayes* and *here* and my heart leaps into my throat.

"He's coming here?"

"Do you not want him to?" The smirk on Ryder's lips is half-cocked.

"Yes. No, I mean, yes, he can come." I'm ridiculously flustered. A million questions and thoughts run through my mind, but the one that rings the loudest is *I get to see Hayes.*

I don't think of the crazy-ass press outside who I lied to when I said there was nothing exciting happening here. I don't worry about whether the Divorce Support proposal is good enough. I can't. Because my mind and body are focused on Hayes Whitley and getting to see him again.

Over the next hour, I watch the people in the bakery prepare for the interview. I rearrange the cupcakes on the staged table. I pepper my brother with what seems like a thousand questions as to how this happened, but of course, get very little out of him. I roll my eyes at DeeDee when she tells me she had no clue until this morning. Her answer seems suspect, considering her extra effort at cleaning up last night.

And my eyes keep flickering to the storefront, waiting, wanting, then waiting again to see Hayes. *It's been way too long. I miss him.*

The photographers scurry like mice when a black limo pulls into the parking lot, and the person who gets out of the car is the *last* person I ever expected to see here.

My hands stop fiddling with my hair. My feet stop shifting in anticipation. That simmering ache over getting to see him again burns cold. Every part of me freezes when Jenna Dixon emerges from the car.

The photographers become frenzied. Their cameras vie for the best shot. And she stands there, quite the picture in her skinny pants and low-cut top with her sleek hair—smooth and straight, and perfect lips turned up in a practiced smile. Completely soaking up the attention she needs almost as much as the air she breathes.

I dislike the bitch instantly.

"What is she doing here?" I sneer, saying it loud enough that the network camera crew inside chuckle out loud, telling me they are more than aware of the situation.

And within seconds the chaos from outside fills the bakery when she opens the door and steps inside. The door closes. The sound mutes.

But her eyes find mine. Hold. And every part of me wants to kick her out. Tell her to take her bullshit lies and get the hell out of my store, because *she's* not welcome here.

What in the world was Hayes thinking by setting up the press junket here when she's taking part? Is he crazy? He knows how quick my temper is. Surely he doesn't want me to give the tabloids any more fodder to print about.

The room falls silent and the tension stretches across the distance. I refuse to back down and look away first. I'm surprised when she walks up to me, the click of her heels on the floor the only sound I can hear.

"Is there somewhere we can speak in private?" Her voice is throaty. Reserved. Aloof.

Flustered but aware of the many pairs of eyes on us, I respond immediately. "Sure. Here. Right back here."

I usher her into the kitchen, then point to a stool if she'd like a seat and just stare at her as the unsettled feeling within me takes hold. Her lips purse as she plays with the strap of her purse. She all but looks at her nail polish so she doesn't have to look at me. It's not hard to infer she has zero desire to be here.

"I want to apologize for the things I said. I meant no harm by them and—"

I clear my throat at the blatant lie. She shifts her feet and looks around the room. The pained look on her face at having to rephrase her apology that's already hard enough for her to give is priceless.

But I'm not backing down.

While some good may have come out of the bullshit she handed me, it also caused me to question how I feel about being with Hayes. And because of that, let alone the myriad of other things she's put Hayes through, I find slight enjoyment in watching her squirm.

I have zero sympathy for her.

"If you're going to apologize, you might as well not lie in the midst of giving it."

There's a flash of anger in her gaze before she reins it in.

"I apologize for insinuating that you were the reason Hayes and I broke up." She spits the words out like a selfish child refusing to acknowledge she did wrong.

"And?" I prompt. And I'm not sure why I do because I couldn't care less what this woman says, and yet I'm curious how she will complete the phrase.

"And?"

My phone vibrates against the counter. The sound fills the room as I stare at her. "Yes. And?"

She emits a dramatic sigh and glares at me. "I'm sorry for any trouble I brought to either of you."

I twist my lips as I stare at her. Hollywood royalty in my tiny kitchen, and I'd *never* switch places with her for all the money in the world.

"Thank you."

That's all I choose to give her. Because while I'm not one to hold a grudge, I'm also not one to forgive blindly someone who has intentionally hurt those I love.

She turns with a flip of her shampoo-commercial-worthy hair and stalks out of the kitchen into the bakery. It's not until she's out of sight that I sag against the counter and let the nerves that quietly owned my body at what just happened take over. I blow out a fortifying breath, tell myself to get my shit together and be glad if I never have to see Jenna Dixon again.

However, I know how hard that must have been for her to do. Either that or Hayes threatened her with something . . . because I have a feeling apologies are not something she's used to giving.

My phone buzzing again reminds me I received a text during that uncomfortable exchange. When I pick it up, I'm greeted by a text message from Hayes.

I hope she's back there groveling for you to forgive her. It may not be sincere, but Jenna giving an apology is a miracle in itself. And yes—*surprise*—I am here today. Doing a few interviews. Setting the record straight on the things I can. But don't think I'm backing down from my promise. No talking. I said ten days, Saylor, and I meant ten days.

My breath catches in my throat when I realize that if Hayes knows Jenna was in the kitchen, then he's already here. And at the same time, I really hear the words of his text.

He's not going to talk to me? He's just going to sit there all day, be available to everyone else, cause a flurry of paparazzi with first Jenna and then him in my bakery, and yet he won't talk to me?

I snort. Yeah, right.

Needing to see for myself, I head toward the café up front. When I walk through the doorway and see him, every part of my body reacts. My heart. My breath. My nerves. My libido.

And then they shift into overdrive the second he looks up from the person he's speaking to and locks eyes with mine. I feel like the air has been sucked out of the room, but equally, I've been given air for the first time after being deprived of it. He grants me a half-cocked smirk, a raise of an eyebrow followed by an ever-so-subtle lift of his chin. My God, he is desire personified.

But damn him to hell because with his presence, my body comes alive. I want. And need. And crave everything about him. The emotional and the physical. His attention. His laughter. His next minute. *His forever.*

Time stands still in the seconds we're connected, so much so that the moment he's pulled away—a question asked to him by a guy wearing a headset—I wonder how I lived *without* this feeling. God yes, the current situation is a clusterfuck at best, and yet, it is worth it for this feeling right here. *He is worth it* and I marvel at how this connection between us can be so strong, so quickly.

But then again, hasn't it always been there?

Because love is like magic. You can question it—how it happens, when it will happen, why it bowls you over when it does happen, and how you existed before it happened—but you might never get the answer.

Sometimes you just have to believe in it and its process.

Forty-One

Saylor

WATCHING HIM IS TORTURE. HEARING HIS LAUGH AND catching his fleeting glances cast my way is comforting. That little zing of current when our eyes do connect before he returns his attention to the interviewer is empowering.

It's like my body is plugged into an electric current with him here. Every chuckle is a jolt to my libido. Every smile causes a tingle through my body. Each dart of his tongue to lick his lips results in a surge of want coursing through me.

So I opt to decorate cupcakes at the front counter today, unwilling to be separated from him when he's sitting here in my space. I feign indifference all the while paying attention. He's charming and courteous and funny during his interviews. He pays close attention to the questions, thinks before he answers, and is entertaining. He also takes the lead, not letting Jenna say too much but smiling politely when she does, except of course when the inevitable question comes up.

The "I'd not be doing my job if I had the two of you together and neglected to ask about the state of your relationship considering the tumultuous rumors over the past several weeks. Is there anything you'd like to clear up?"

"Thank you, but it's a private matter." If I wasn't already standing at full attention, I sure as hell am now with Jenna's response.

Irritation flickers over Hayes's face for the first time during the interview. I notice the break in his mask and hear the insincerity in his laugh. "It's a private matter that was made public, so I'll address it." He raises his eyebrows. Looks straight at the interviewer. "Jenna and I dated. We broke up quite some time ago, before it was public knowledge. The relationship had simply run its course. I did not cheat or sneak away to a tropical island to have a secret rendezvous with my mistress. However, in the months following our breakup, I did happen to run into my high school sweetheart whom I hadn't seen in almost ten years. She had recently split from her fiancé. We reconnected and feelings were still there between us. The rumor that I cheated on Jenna, or that my new girlfriend did anything unsavory, is a complete fabrication made up by someone to sell pictures to the highest bidder." Hayes breaks his gaze from the reporter and looks to Jenna. His jaw clenches as he waits for her to look his way. "Isn't that right, Jenna?"

She swallows over the contempt evident on her face. The look that says she wishes what he said wasn't true, but nods her head in agreement. "Yes, that is accurate."

"Thank you for being so candid, but I'd like to ask a few follow-up questions about the time frame—"

"Let's not," Hayes says with a flash of his smile before expertly redirecting the reporter back to discussing *The Grifter*. And a few questions into the redirect, Hayes glances over to me, and our eyes hold for a split second before shifting back to the interview. But I see the small show of a smile on his lips. Catch the *see, I said I'd make it right* in his gaze.

The day wears on. They get a small break between networks where Hayes chats with Ryder and Jenna busies herself with her phone, before they get a touch-up on their makeup and start again. The reporters change, but the questions remain the same.

I take phone orders. I make more cupcakes. All the while remaining present in case Hayes accidentally has a slip in his resolve and wants to talk to me. It's after about the fourth or fifth interview that my phone alerts with a text. **You can stare at me all day but I'm still not talking to you. 44 hours left.**

To which I reply, **Isn't this considered talking?**

The next interview takes place. Ends. The next set of texts are exchanged. **Not talking. Just letting you know how it's going to be.**

How it's going to be? A part of me likes this side of him. The other part hates it. I fire back a reply: **Fine. I'm not going to talk to you either then. 43 hours left.**

I watch Hayes take a seat for the next round, pick up his cell from the table, type something out, and then place it inside his suit jacket. Just when the reporter starts the opening question, my phone vibrates an incoming text. **Good to know, but I doubt it. I'll make you talk to me before the end of the day.**

When I look up to him, he has a hint of a smirk playing on his lips. Silently taunting me and I groan in frustration. *The cocky son of a bitch.*

You'd be surprised how much restraint I can show. I didn't punch Jenna, did I? See? Restraint.

For someone who says he's not talking to me, he sure is communicating. That tells me this silent treatment is just as torturous for him as it is for me.

I think of our Twitter exchange this morning. And smile.

He wants me to bring my A-game?

I'll bring it all right.

"I'm gonna head upstairs. I must have left the notes for the new recipe up there."

"Okay," DeeDee says, her perma-grin of the day still plastered to her face. She's a little star-struck and a lot fascinated with the exhausting press junket process that seems both monotonous and exhilarating. "I'll just be here. Watching. Swooning. Secretly hating you every time he gives you that *I want you* look of his."

I laugh at her comment on my way up the stairs. After a few moments, I find my notes, grab a bottle of water from the refrigerator, and when I shut its door, Hayes is standing on the other side of it.

His presence is undeniable. Eyes dark with desire and his fingers fidget at his sides like he's itching to touch me.

His cologne pervades my nose. The sight of him ignites every single nerve in my body. My nipples harden. My thighs tense while the delta between them aches. I open my mouth to speak—to say "*hi, I missed you, screw the forty-something hours we have left*"—but the ever-so-subtle curl of the side of his mouth stops me.

Reminds me.

Prevents me.

Tells me he wants to prove me wrong.

I bite my tongue. The amused curiosity in his eyes asks me if I remember my text swore I wouldn't speak.

A visual war wages between us while our bodies wave the white flag and want to surrender to one another. He lifts a brow. A non-verbal taunt. I respond with a lick of my bottom lip while I run a hand down the side of my neck and between my breasts.

He shifts his feet as his eyes fixate on my hand as it moves down my body. But it's my gaze that's caught now. On the bulge in his slacks. On the flex of his hands beside his hips. By the groan he emits deep in his throat that reflects everything I feel in this moment: want and frustration and desire and obstinacy and need.

Hope you brought your A-game, Whitley.

Forty-Two

Hayes

SHE WANTS TO PLAY THIS GAME? TEASE ME? TAUNT ME WITH AN *I'm not going to talk to you either?* How I wish it were my tongue running over her body instead of her hand.

You never mess with a man on a mission, and my mission is to have her. Everything about her. Every single way possible in my life.

Right now, included.

So that little text? It was like flicking a lighter and that first spark fizzling out. I plan on flicking it again though, and this time I'll get a goddamn wildfire. Just on my terms and in my own time.

She stares at me.

Don't do it, Hayes.

Eyes asking.

You've got ten minutes max before the next interview.

Lips pursed.

Flick the lighter, Whitley.

Nipples harden beneath her shirt. Teeth biting into her bottom lip.

But she texted. She taunted.

Body all but calling to me.
Light the flame.
Begging for me.
Said she won't talk.
Lips part. Chest heaves.
Yes, she will.

I clear my throat and know where this is going to go. How painful it's going to be for me, but love it all the same.

Her gaze shifts down and takes in my dick, desperately hard for her. Her tongue wets her lips. She draws in a breath and then looks back up to me.

I raise an eyebrow. An *I'm not talking, are you going to?*

She lifts her chin and just for a split second I'm reminded of double-dog dares in the field behind her house and her frequent defiance to prove a point. I thought it frustrating then. But now? Now with her standing before me—curves and sex and desire and lust in one fucking perfect package—I find her defiance irresistible.

Our eyes hold. Wage a war smothered in silence but loaded with desire.

And want.
And lust.
And need.

There's a split-second of hesitation where restraint is tested, taunted, and toyed with.

I take a step closer. *Flick the lighter.*

And then restraint's broken.

We crash together. Lips and teeth and hands and bodies. Her moan. My groan. Her fingernails scoring. My fingertips bruising.

Both wanting more. Nowhere near getting enough.

Her back hits the wall. I can't breathe. Can't think. It's her. All I want is more. All I think is *mine.*

And yet I say nothing. Neither does she. Somehow we're still playing the game, still waging the war.

Her fingers fumble with my belt. My hand palms her tit. She sighs as my mouth claims her neck. Jesus Christ. The woman tastes like heaven. Like a fucking addiction I don't want to quit.

My hands dip inside the waistband of her skirt. She pulls down my zipper. My fingertips touch her strip of tight curls, part her slit then slide down the line of her pussy.

Now *that*? That's heaven. The heat of her. How wet she is. I dive right in without warning. Fingers buried to the hilt.

She cries out. Not a name. Not a word. *Just a sound*.

And then she tightens around me. Grips my fingers as she drenches my hand.

There's no way in fucking hell I'm going to be able to stop myself. Fuck the plan. Screw the interview. Make them wait.

And when she wraps her entire hand around my cock and slides all the way down, I freeze. With my fingers still buried in her pussy, and her heat against my hand, I'm a fucking goner.

She works her hand back up, does a little twisting motion over my head, and assaults the nerves there in the best fucking way possible.

I close my eyes. Accept the pleasure. Groan in ecstasy.

And then I hear her chuckle. Know she's playing me at my game but fuck if I'm not enjoying how she just took the upper hand. *What can I say? This woman has her hand wrapped around my cock.* It's been eight days since I've been inside her.

Eight.

Whole.

Days.

Fuck.

I grit my teeth in restraint. Hold back—the *Fucking hell, Saylor*, I want to groan out, and try to process thoughts that she's slowly erasing with each stroke.

Move, Hayes.

A slide up. A roll of her wrist. A tightening of her fingers. A scrape of nails on the underside of my balls.

Don't let her make you talk.

My head falls back, but my fingers are inside of her. A reminder to her of what I plan on claiming. Taking. Using to my advantage.

My. God. She. Owns. Me.

It's only when she shifts, when my fingers slip from her pussy and a throaty laugh falls from her lips that I realize she's dropping to her knees.

To suck my cock. To wrap her lips around it. Use her tongue. And take what I give her.

She's winning the war.

I have to step back from the ledge. Do what's sacrilege: reject the blowjob that I know will rock my world. *And make me talk.* Because put a hot, wet mouth and a skillful tongue on a man's cock and there is no controlling what he says or how tight he'll fist your hair.

With a pained groan, I put my hand to her shoulder and push her against the wall to stop her descent. Her eyes—so fucking gorgeous beneath desire drugged lids—flash up and lock on mine. The smirk plays on her lips. Her determination to make me talk is written all over her face.

So I hold her there—with both my eyes and my hand to her shoulder—and slip my fingers back into her. I start to work her into a frenzy. With my fingers and thumb. In and out and over her clit. Slide and stroke and flick and rub. Then all over again.

All the while her gaze is on mine. Her lips part. Her hips buck harder into my hand. Her fingers dig deeper into my shoulder. Her breath becomes labored.

I pick up my pace when I feel her pussy start to tighten around me. It's now or never. So I work the spot within I know she likes. The one that makes her lose her mind.

"Oh. God," she pants into the room.

It's the sound of victory. The lighter caught flame.

And I stop all movement instantly.

I stand to full height as she stares at me—shoulders sagged against the wall, eyes wildly sexy, cheeks flushed, chest heaving—and smirk. Then casually glance down to my watch before focusing on tucking my rock-hard dick back into my slacks and zipping over it. *Carefully.*

"You bastard," she whispers—equal parts amusement, frustration, and disbelief.

And fuck if I don't feel the same way when I look up at her. I work my tongue in my cheek as we stare at each other. My need for her so strong it fucking hurts. And then with a nod of my head, I walk out, and shut the door behind me without ever saying a word.

I've only walked away from Saylor two times before. The first time was brutal because I never came back. This second time is just as brutal, but at least *I know* I'm coming back.

I take a minute at the top of her stairs to wait for my dick to calm down. I pull my phone from my pocket and with my fingers still wet from her, fire off a text.

While victory may be sweet, it's also reserved for those who are willing to pay a price.

And damn it to hell, I'm paying the price by walking away with her scent on my fingers and her taste on my lips.

Forty-Three

Saylor

Your A-Game? It's damn good, Ships. You almost had me. But mine's better. See I can show restraint too. Rematch in about 40 hours?

I stare at the text for the hundredth time, my body still strung taut from his touch and the smile still wide on my lips. I'm sexually frustrated but so damn content because he loves me. No man would go through this much trouble if he didn't.

You're a bastard.

I consider finishing myself off. Claim my orgasm he left unfinished but know half the fun is doing it with him. So instead I sit in the quiet of my room, with the paparazzi clamoring outside and the media filming downstairs. With a business proposal for a game-changing contract in the sent bin of my email, and a man I never thought I'd get back, owning my thoughts . . . and I wonder how all of a sudden this is my life.

And then he texts again.

Does it make you feel any better that I can still smell you on my fingers and it drove me crazy during that whole last interview?

No. It doesn't make me feel better at all. My turn:
Does it make you feel any better knowing I took care of what you didn't while you were in that last interview?

But that sure as hell does.

I watch the clock. Let three minutes pass while picturing him gritting his teeth as he imagines me up here getting off without him. And then I text him again.

Just kidding. See? A-Game.

Forty-Four

Saylor

ZERO DAYS LEFT - Finally

FACEBOOK
QUESTION:
**Where were you when you first knew you were in love
with your soul mate?**
#MovieRoleResearch #UnDeniable

I STARE AT THE POST FOR THE LONGEST TIME. WISHING I KNEW
more about *Undeniable's* movie plot to see where he's leading his
fans with the question. I'm sure it has a purpose. I just don't know
what it is.

I type several answers to the post but then delete them. Anything
I post is up for public fodder, and I want to keep our relationship as
private as possible.

So I read other peoples' comments instead. Try to waste time as
I wait for whatever it is I'm waiting for from Hayes. I skim my other
social media accounts, check my phone, but there's nothing written

from him to me. No countdown until I get to see him. No corny pick up lines.

No anything.

Just radio silence.

Two days full of it to be exact. He left the bakery to give one last interview with a prominent entertainment journalist over a late dinner. And of course the cocky bastard gave me nothing more than a nod of his head and a crooked smile on his lips when he closed the door behind him.

But there are reminders of him everywhere: In the crooked lamp-shade that was knocked askew in our little make-out session. In the bakery's furniture I decided to rearrange when we put it back after the interviews were over. And in the absence of paparazzi out front but in the presence of a line of people waiting to buy cupcakes today.

A line. That's a first.

So I'm baking like a mad woman. DeeDee's helping me too, along with a friend she brought in, so we can keep up with the demand. It's a good problem to have.

And yet, a part of me keeps looking around, keeps waiting for Hayes to show up and tell me the ten days are up so I can answer his question and tell him yes to all of the above, whatever that may be.

I tell myself it's no big deal. That he's done enough and the only thing I really want is him. But I'm frustrated. Hell, if he's still trying to prove his point, it's been proven. We can survive the paparazzi. We can handle the craziness. And even when we're surrounded by both, I still want him. Still need him. Still choose him.

Work overwhelms us. The sheer volume of customers today is ridiculous. Time passes quickly, but Hayes is always a constant on my mind. I look up every time the bell rings, grab my phone every time it alerts a text, and obsessively wonder when this ridiculous show or game or exercise in willpower will be over.

"Holy shit," DeeDee says as she plops in exhaustion onto one of the stools when we have our first lull of the day. "Today is incredible!"

I smile because I'm still amazed at it myself. Joining her on a stool, I drop my head in my hands, and close my eyes for a moment just to soak it all in. When I look up, DeeDee is reading something on her phone, and her smile just keeps getting wider and wider.

"What is it?" I ask, curious but exhausted and suddenly realizing that I still haven't heard from Hayes.

When she looks up at me, there are tears swimming in her eyes that contradict the ear-to-ear grin on her face. "Here." She thrusts her phone out to me.

When I look at the screen, it displays a new post on Hayes's Facebook page. And this one is meant for me.

ANSWER:
I knew I loved @SweetChks in this tree house. She thought I wanted to be with the cool senior girls when all I wanted was to look at the stars with her. Or maybe that was just my excuse to get closer to her. I knew it again, thirteen years later, when we came back here on the way home. I never told her the words though. Third time's a charm. I wonder if she knows where to find me so I can tell her this time?
#NotMovieRoleResearch   #RealLife   #RealLove
#ShipsAhoy #ImWaiting

My eyes flash up to DeeDee's, and I can't get out of the chair or grab my car keys quick enough.

It's dusk when I run down the path to the old tree house. I bypass the house and Ryder's car in the driveway. My mind is focused on one thing—getting to Hayes. And the closer I get, the wider my eyes grow. The structure has a fresh coat of paint and the slatted steps have been replaced.

The tree house my dad built us way back when has never looked better and I can't help but feel it's fitting that it's Hayes who has made it over. Almost as if by bringing me here, my father is somehow passing my hand from his to Hayes's and telling him he better take good care of me.

Overwhelmed, I stand beneath it and stare for a moment. That first time Hayes climbed in there with me comes back to me. It's funny how those butterflies are still in my stomach all this time later. And they grow stronger with each step up I take.

The door swings open before I can do it myself and there's Hayes with his hand outstretched to help me the last little bit. He pulls me up and the funny thing is, this time I love the small confines of the tree house because that means he's within arm's reach wherever he sits.

"Hi," I say and press my lips to his without preamble. And he reacts by kissing me back with that kind of soul-searing, toe-tingling, soft-but-demanding, desire-inducing, fingers in my hair, my hands sliding up his back, never-want-it-to-end kiss.

And when it does end, when I'm so soft and mushy with a firestorm of emotion that I just poured into the meeting of our mouths, Hayes leans back, brushes a lock of hair off my cheek, and smiles that shy smile of his that he reserves just for me.

"Hi, Ships."

My smile widens to epic proportions. "You're talking to me now?"

"I have a few things to say, yes." He shrugs and brushes another tender kiss to my lips. "Thanks for meeting me here."

"Thanks for asking me."

"I wasn't sure you were going to see the post."

It's my turn to laugh. "You kind of made me a social media junkie these past two weeks when I never was before. You see, there's been this boy I like . . . and he's been refusing to talk to me in person. But since he only talked to me online, I became one of those annoying people who look at their phone every five seconds."

"Is that so?" His voice is coy. His expression feigned innocence.

"Mm-hmm."

"You only just *like* him?"

I purse my lips. Scrunch my nose. Pretend that I have to think about it. "Hmm. More than like. Definitely love."

He grants me a quick flash of a grin. "There's frosting in your hair." He reaches out and touches it before his eyes find mine again.

"Sorry."

"I wouldn't have you any other way. Don't you know that yet?"

And those words.

Simple acceptance of who I am. It does funny things to my insides, or maybe it's the man who said them that does.

I smile softly at him, reach down, and link my fingers with his. "Thank you."

"No. You don't need to thank me, Saylor. You should never have to apologize for being you. Because you . . . you're beautiful and smart and sexy and defiant and creative and hot-headed and crazy-funny and spontaneous. I love every single one of those things about you, plus all the other things I forget until you do them and then that makes me remember them." He smiles again and squeezes my hand. My heart swells. "I walked away ten years ago thinking I could forget you. That I could chase my dreams and move on. That first loves could never be last loves. God, how I was wrong. There's something to be said for falling in love with someone you grew up with. I know all your flaws, Saylor. Your weaknesses. Your strengths. Your fears. Your mistakes. And I fucking love you for every single one of them. They make you, you. And in turn, they make us, us."

"Hayes." His name is a sigh of affection on my lips.

"No. Shh. I'm the actor, I get to hog the stage right now." I laugh as he does. Know he's joking and nod in agreement.

"What is it about actors and wanting attention?"

"Funny. Very funny," he teases before leaning in and kissing me again. This time though he slips his tongue between my lips and takes the kiss a little deeper. His hands tremble as they frame my face and that little action tells me everything I need to know. If he's nervous, then *this* matters to him, and I've been worth the trouble. "What I have with you, Saylor, I don't want with anyone else. You've marked me. Not just my heart with your love or my mind with your words, but more so my soul with everything you are. Everything you aspire to be. And everything you think we can be together."

He puts a finger to my lips when I start to speak. I try to tell him this is all too much, too kind, too overwhelming when for so long there was nothing but emptiness without him. But how can I say to stop when my heart feels so full, my soul so completed, when I can't remember it ever feeling this way before?

"I know it's been sudden, and that all of this has come out of nowhere. Knocked us on our asses in bright paparazzi camera flashes of light. But it's real, Saylor. *We're real.* The realest thing I've ever had in my life that I've built on making believe." He looks down at our fingers linked together before lifting his eyes to mine and smiling softly. "I can't promise you it will be easy because you've gotten a taste of my craziness, but I can promise you that we'll make us work. We'll figure out a way. Buy a house between our jobs. Or open a second bakery in Hollywood. Buy a damn chopper if need be so you can make your deliveries. Whatever it takes, I'll do it because I don't want to go another day without knowing you're mine. We've lost too much time already, and I don't want to miss any more. So what do you say, Ships? Want to try to make this thing work long-term for us?"

My whole body trembles from the truth in his words and the honesty in his eyes. Tears blur my vision but when I look at him, I remember the boy with gangly legs and a *Star Wars* obsession. I recall our first kiss and reminisce over the nerves we shared our first time together. Then I think of the few occasions he held me while I cried and the numerous times we've laughed so hard our sides hurt. And then I see the man he's turned into. The considerate, funny, handsome, intelligent, romantic man he is, and I know without a doubt we can make this work.

He's my soul mate.

There's only one love that matters more than your first love: *Your last love.* How damn lucky am I that both of mine are the same person?

With that thought on my mind, I lean forward and press the sweetest of kisses against his lips. Lean my forehead against his. Close my eyes. And feel at home.

"I know you say words are cheap but those words you just said? Those words were priceless, Hayes Whitley."

"So are you." He wraps his arms around me and pulls me tighter into him.

"And I think long-term suits me just fine."

"Good. Because I wasn't taking no for an answer. I brought my A-game again, and you know how good that is."

My laugh fills the space around us. So many things set right in our world. "About that A-game of yours . . . there seems to be some unfinished business it needs to take care of . . ."

And so by the light of the rising moon, in the place we shared our first kiss, we also share so much more with nothing more than love and possibility between us.

Epilogue

Saylor

ONE YEAR LATER

"WHERE ARE YOU TAKING ME?" I LAUGH OUT AS THE breeze blows against my cheeks and the ground beneath my feet becomes uneven.

"You'll see," Hayes murmurs, his hands covering my eyes over the scarf he's already secured to ensure I don't sneak a peek. "A little birthday surprise never hurt anyone."

We've been driving for what feels like forever. I'd like to say I'm good with direction and which way we went, but for all I know we've driven in circles for hours and he's just taken me back to the home we share nestled in the Hollywood Hills to mess with my head. I've tried to be patient. Tried to relax and wait for the surprise he has in store for me, and so I occupied myself thinking about the supplies I needed to order for the Brentwood store. And when I had that figured out, I moved on to the list DeeDee had sent over for the original State Street location she runs now.

Shut it down, Saylor. Enjoy the anticipation. Take in the moment.

Love your man. Appreciate that Hayes is still trying to be spontaneous and do a little something special for you. Still trying to put you first despite his hectic schedule and the ridiculous demands everyone puts on him.

"Are we going to get a puppy?" There's amusement in my voice over our long-running joke. How while a puppy is permanent, it's also the death of so many couples once they realize how hard it is mixing two different ideals to raise something together.

"I told you, we're not getting a puppy. I don't need a trial run with you, Ships. I know you're good for it whenever we decide to raise something together."

I laugh out loud as he holds me steady when I stumble. "You mean like a sea turtle?"

"If you want to learn how to lay an egg, then be my guest. We can do sea turtles but I was thinking something more along the lines of a blonde-haired, blue-eyed little girl someday."

"Oh. Okay." There he goes melting my heart and leaving me speechless. The man has a way of doing that on a continual basis.

And I'm definitely not complaining.

"A few more feet."

"Okay." I count ten steps and wonder how many more are his definition of few since the suspense of whatever he's up to is killing me. And as soon as I think it, he directs me to stop.

"Right here," he says softly, almost as if he's trying really hard to concentrate like he sometimes does when running lines. "You ready?"

I chuckle. Suddenly nervous. Was that *his* hands just shaking?

"Yes."

The heat of his body leaves mine. "You can look now."

I slowly pull off the black scarf and when I do, the sight before me takes my breath away. My mouth falls open, my eyes grow wide, and my head moves from side to side so I can take in my surroundings.

It's so perfect, so everything, that it takes me a few moments to breathe it all in.

We're at the base of the tree house, it's dusk, and Mason jars hang from the tree branches with votive candles lit inside them. Fairy lights twinkle within the tree's foliage, and are also lighting up the long wispy grass field beyond it. There are flowers too. My mother's favorite—hydrangeas in their various colors—overflowing from galvanized and patina canisters adorned with lace and burlap bows. *It's stunning.*

I'm overwhelmed and in awe and when I turn around again, I'm teary. Ryder, DeeDee, Hayes's mom, and other mutual friends from Santa Barbara and Los Angeles are here too.

It's like my brain is so overwhelmed by this breathtaking spectacle of perfection, that I can process the where and the what, but only after I take in the whole of the picture, can I finally process the why.

This isn't a surprise birthday party. Not in the least.

My hand flies to my mouth. My eyes widen and flood with tears as realization hits when I look back to Hayes in front of me. *How did he know this was my dream?*

Because he knows me inside and out.

Always has.

Now, he always will.

"What did you do, Hayes?" My words come out in a hushed whisper.

His smile widens. It has a hint of nerves to it but the look in his eyes suggests the nerves are the good kind. The *this matters* kind.

He glances to the unfamiliar woman off to my right and when she nods at him, the absolute adoration in his expression as he steps closer to me causes goosebumps to erupt across my skin. He reaches out and takes my hand.

"Surprise," he whispers as every single part of me falls head over heels in love with him all over again.

"Is this what I think . . .?" My voice fades off as I look around us again. Meet the eyes of Ryder who steps up beside Hayes and hands him something, smile so full of love and pride I know the answer to my question immediately.

"I have the stage, Ships. You know how we actors like to hog the spotlight."

My laugh is instantaneous. My hands tremble in disbelief, and my mind tries to wrap around what he pulled off.

"I tried to think of when I first fell in love with you, Saylor. I thought maybe it was that first day I knocked on your door, asking if Ryder was home, and you peered at me from behind your glasses with a princess crown on your head, a Teenage Mutant Ninja Turtle shell on your back, and your mom's high heels that were five sizes too big on your feet.

"But then I remembered that time in junior high when we ditched school and headed out to the lake. You were the only girl who would climb the tree with us and jump off the top branch into the lake without a second thought. The other guys thought it was so cool you'd do that, and I remember thinking how proud I was that you were with me.

"Or that time in high school when Nick Ramos kept bragging how a girl would never pitch well enough to strike him out. How you asked Ryd and me to teach you how to throw a knuckle ball so you could shut him up. How your dad let us stay out way past when the streetlight came on so we could practice. And how when Nick whiffed on that third strike—where you made that baseball dance to the plate—the entire bleachers roared as you put him in his place."

I stare at Hayes. The memories I forgot coming back to me. And I'm so overwhelmed that I can do nothing more than stand mesmerized and listen.

"You see as I tried to remember the moment I knew I first loved you, I realized there are too many of them to pick from. Because I fell, and fall, in love with something different about you every single day, Ships. You never cease to amaze me. And you're always making me see you in a new light.

"So I brought you here today because you're the one, Saylor. You've always been the one. And I don't want to wait another day to tell you that. I don't want to go through a year of details and planning to have a wedding. That's not us. We're spontaneous and unpretentious and only care what our family and friends think . . . and I don't want to ask you to marry me and then have to wait forever to make you officially mine. I wanted to do it in one fell swoop because why wait? The most important thing I've learned from your parents is this:

don't wait for the perfect time to take a chance on your dreams. And *you're* my *dream*, Saylor."

Speechless, swamped with love, and beyond amazed at him and this idea, I do the only thing I can. I step into him and plant a kiss on his lips. The guests hoot and holler as Hayes slides his hands around my waist and pulls me into him while our kiss lingers before pushing me away and chuckling. "Nice try, but I'm not finished yet."

He steps back, and with love in his eyes he clears his throat. "Saylor Rodgers, I promise to spend a lifetime loving you just like the first time I saw you—treat you like the princess you are, respect that you're a badass superhero who can take care of herself, and love that, as much as you are a lady, there's a little girl inside of you who still likes to play too."

My heart can't take any more. It's so full it might burst. Tears well and slide down my cheeks to meet the smile on my lips. A sob hitches in my chest as I stare at the incredible man in front of me. He squeezes my hand, and his eyes well with tears before he glances to the house up the hill from us. To where my mom or dad used to walk out to the patio and call to us in the tree house. Their way of making sure we knew they were watching in case we were doing things we shouldn't be doing but probably were. His smile softens when he meets my eyes again and I know he's remembering them too.

And it feels as though they are here with us right now.

"I want to make more memories with you. Like *kisses in a thunderstorm, frosting in your hair, sequins on Oscar night, pepperoni pizza with jalapeños, sitting on the floor watching movies with a dog asleep at our feet, and kids giggling in their bedrooms'* type of memories with you. You're it for me, Saylor. Always have been. Always will be.

"I know we don't need an official document or rings on our fingers to tell us we belong together, because we've always known it. Always will. But the part of me who looks at you every morning and is proud as hell to call you mine, wants everyone else to know it too. So I brought you here and spoke my heart to ask you a single question. Will you say I do?"

I blink several times as if I'm still trying to believe this is real . . .

and happening. But when I look down to find a ring I didn't even realize he had, being slipped on my finger, I know it is. The ring is sparkly with an inset diamond in the band and the fairy lights around us reflect in it. And even better, as I watch him slip it on, I realize he already has a wedding band on his finger.

I narrow my brow and look up to him. "I wasn't taking any chances."

"I can see that." Looking at him, there isn't a single doubt in my mind I want to spend the rest of my life with him. *Not. One.* I stare at our hands together. Our rings. Our fingers intertwined. Then back up to him. "Hayes Whitley, I. Do."

Our friends and family cheer wildly as I step into him and kiss him with every ounce of love I have within me. My arms are around his neck. His hands frame my face. Our hearts beat against each other's as one.

When he leans back, his chocolate eyes swim with the love he feels for me. "Saylor Rodgers, I do too."

We kiss again like we're each other's air. Until my laughter bubbles up and over and my lips spread into a smile against his.

So that's what forever tastes like.

"You really brought your A-game this time."

He throws his head back and laughs.

Away from the glitz and the glamour, and in a field where we once ran as kids. Under a tree house we shared our first kiss in, and on the property my parents once owned and filled with their unmistakable love. With a small circle of friends and family before us, and fairy lights twinkling around us. . .

I marry my best friend.

The boy who stole my chocolate chip cookies.

My kisses.

My time.

My love.

He's my once in a lifetime.

The man who forever holds my heart.

My happily ever after.

The End

You've already fallen in love with Saylor and Hayes, but many of you want to know more about Ryder? Check out his story in my upcoming novella, **Sweet Rivalry**:

Ryder Rodgers had a plan.

He was going to stride into the conference room, do the required song and dance over the next five days, and win the biggest contract of his career. But when he walked in and heard the voice of one of his competitors, all his plans were shot to hell.

Harper Denton. She was always on top. *In college.* First in their class. Always using every advantage to edge him out to win the coveted positions. The only one who could beat him. His academic rival. *More like a constant thorn in his side.* And his ego's.

When he heard her voice, he was brought back to years before. To the bitter taste of being second best. But the woman who meets his gaze is nothing like the drab wallflower he used to know. *Hell no.* She was all woman now: curves, confidence, and staggering sex appeal. And no doubt, *still brilliant.*

The fact that she's gorgeous *and* bright won't distract him. This time, Ryder's determined to be the one on top. *But not if Harper can help it.*

Sweet Rivalry releases February 28th, 2017 and is available for pre-order now at your favorite book retailer or visit www.kbromberg.com/sweet-rivalry for more information.

Acknowledgements

Thank you . . .

To the readers who have read since day one, thank you for letting me spread my wings and write something brand new. I hope you fell just as hopelessly in love with Saylor and Hayes as you have some of my other characters. Thank you for the continued support. You never cease to amaze me.

To the new readers, welcome and thank you for picking up Sweet Cheeks. I hope you enjoyed the story and hopefully you'll take a chance on some of my other characters, too.

To the bloggers and readers alike who help promote our books.

To my family for putting up with my chaotic, crazy world.

To you.

About the Author

New York Times Bestselling author K. Bromberg writes contemporary novels that contain a mixture of sweet, emotional, a whole lot of sexy and a little bit of real. She likes to write strong heroines and damaged heroes who we love to hate and hate to love.

She's a mixture of most of her female characters: sassy, intelligent, stubborn, reserved, outgoing, driven, emotional, strong, and wears her heart on her sleeve. All of which she displays daily with her husband and three children where they live in Southern California.

On a whim, K. Bromberg decided to try her hand at this writing thing. Since then she has written The Driven Series (*Driven, Fueled, Crashed, Raced, Aced*), the standalone Driven Novels (*Slow Burn, Sweet Ache, Hard Beat*, and *Down Shift*), and a short story titled *UnRaveled*. She is currently finishing up Sweet Cheeks a standalone novel out at the end of 2016.

Her plans for 2017 include a sports romance duet (The Player (#1) and The Catch (#2)) and the Everyday Heroes series (Cuffed (#1), Combust (#2), and Cockpit (#3)). She's also writing a novella for the

1,001 Dark Night series that will be out in February 2017. The novella will focus on Saylor's brother in *Sweet Cheeks*, Ryder Rodgers.

She loves to hear from her readers so make sure you check her out on social media.

CPSIA information can be obtained
at www.ICGtesting.com
Printed in the USA
LVHW081120151220
674233LV00036B/944